D1601587

SILVER VALLEY

ARABELLA ROSIER

Silver Valley
Book One

Find me at: arabellarosier.com
Instagram: @bookisharabella
Tik Tok: @rosierarabella

Printed in Australia.

First edition: April 2022

Paperback ISBN: 978-0-6453965-0-8
Hardback ISBN: 978-0-6453965-1-5
E-book ISBN: 978-0-6453965-2-2

Special thanks and acknowledgement to:
Editor - Chloe's Chapters,
Cover artist - Gab Nao Designs,
Formatter - Author Services Australia.

This book is written in British English.

To 14 year old Arabella—you actually did it.

This is for you.

PROLOGUE

"No, DON'T! Please, don't do this!"

Three royal guards, sheathed in their silver uniforms, haul a young girl into a cell made of metal and rust. Tears leak down her cheeks as one of them yanks her forward by her hair.

"Quiet, child! Or you'll die like your father," he tells her.

Her shoulders shake harder at his words.

The girl's arms are covered in scratches and her blue eyes swim with tears. She knows that it's over—her life and everything she's worked for.

Centuries ago, an alien species descended peacefully upon Terra, forming a well-concealed alliance with the government of the United Kingdom. Here in space, standing upon what used to be foreign terrain, the girl can't even begin to comprehend what Terra has become.

And yet, her life has been sacrificed for Terra.

She is going to die.

The cell door slams shut. She throws herself against it, dragging her nails between the bars. Her hair clings to her sweaty brow as she sobs.

She had been helping her father to unlock the mystery of the

Terran princess, who would ascend the throne and restore balance and peace to their planet. But it was treason.

She knew this.

She should have expected her life to end this way.

The guard now locking her cell had just killed her father. His blade is still covered in blood, drying at the edges.

"Let me out, I can help. Please, I know where she is! She's still a three-year-old girl, but I swear to god she can save Umbra one day."

The guards remain silent, withdrawing from the girl.

She pulls her hands back, shoulders bunched as she wraps her arms around them. They aren't listening to her. Nausea rolls in her stomach and she resists the urge to throw up her latest meal.

For years, her father had told her not to tell anyone what they knew. For years, they had snuck around the Silver Kingdom like rats and thieves. But they never thought they were doing anything less than what was required for their planet.

If they didn't do it, who would?

"Help me. Please, help me," the girl continues to beg.

But no courtier or Elder wants anything to do with Terra. Not even their guards.

Terra is so far away—situated in an entirely different corner of the universe, accessible only through a periodic black hole. But their ties to Terra run deep. This planet is, after all, known as Terra's shadow—a refined, superior replica.

Footsteps ring outside the cell, and the girl takes a step backwards into the dark.

The girl had a small blade on her moments before. A dainty little thing. But the guards took it from her, and when she instinctively reaches for it in her pocket, her hands grasp nothing.

The guards smirk at her.

Their visitor has come.

The girl takes a few steps back from the door, dirt kicking up around her feet as she eases into the darkness of her grimy prison cell. The face of an Elder emerges behind the bars in front of her. He looks young, but his cool blue eyes are ancient and calculating. The lights above him reflect against his blond hair, making him look like a fallen angel.

She wipes the tears from her face, letting the panels of light from behind him hit her eyes as she asks, "So… how will you kill me? Blade or Silver Magic?"

She tries to look him in the eye. But nothing can stop her from trembling.

The Elder smiles. "I hear you have some magic of your own, child."

She touches the silver stone hanging around her neck—the one her father had given her. Hearing him say it makes her heart sink. No one should know about her stone.

"I can only use the electricity of the planet. I'm not in tune with it. Does that matter?" she remarks angrily, forgetting all the defences she learnt from her father.

"Yes, I believe it matters very much."

He gestures to a guard to open the door and steps inside, his silver hair shining blue in the lights reflecting through the bars.

"There's a space shuttle taking some prisoners and civilians to the island. I can get you on it, take you to Terra, on my head be it. But I'll need you to use that stone of yours before embarking. Just one charm I'm sure you've heard of. Only then will I introduce you to my team. I believe you already know Liaison Stone?"

"I've met him," she says gingerly. "But why are you helping me?"

She sheds no more tears, leaning towards the man instead as her hands grasp the bars. She can hardly breathe.

"My dear, surely you agree the planet needs saving?"

"But you're one of them. Why would you ship me off to Terra? You're an Elder."

"And you're a Common. Surely, we can be more than our names. Or would you prefer your father die in vain?" he asks empathetically.

She glares at him. But when he offers her his hand, she takes it.

On his head be it.

PART ONE

THE FOREST

S ometimes I don't think there's such a thing as choice.

The café door shuts behind me and the chime sings throughout the small place.

I woke early this morning, watching the stars fade with the night to grab some peace. Space is vast and cold, unlike the claustrophobic heat in Sydney.

And it's not even 7am yet.

"Coffee, Savannah?" the red-headed waitress, Emily, asks. Her hand is poised over her small notepad.

"Double shot."

Amused, she shakes her head as she leans over her notepad.

I used to come to the *Coffee Corner* with Jasmine Spark, but she left Sydney what seems like decades ago in pursuit of a family business deal on a small island.

Today is the day I'm finally following her.

Again, not my choice.

Emily hands me my usual order, with an extra kick of caffeine. The cup burns my fingers as I take it to the bench at the side of the café.

Today is the last day I'll see her, but she doesn't know it yet.

I wait for my coffee to cool, but it still burns my fingers by the time she sits next to me. We spend every morning together. This is our routine.

"When does school go back again? I'm growing tired of the holiday season."

I take a long drag of my coffee. It scalds my throat.

"Not sure," I reply. "I'm not continuing year 12 in Sydney."

"Oh?" Her eyebrows rise.

We never talk about anything personal.

But today is different.

I rap my fingers against the bench under me.

Cars zip by outside, casting shadows over the café. Soon, I'll be among them. I can't say I'm miserable at the thought of seeing Jasmine again, but doing so feels awfully like running away.

"I'm leaving the city," I tell her. "And I probably won't be coming back."

She flicks her pen against her leg as she studies me.

I slouch against the wall, feeling the rough wood against my skin. I wish I got more sleep last night. The starlight woke me again, the constellations swimming beyond my window.

My mother used to point the stars out to me, trying to bond with me before leaving on some grand adventure. The memories are bitter. She told me tales of what it would be like to travel among the stars, always running, always in pursuit of adventure. As if it would help clarify why she left.

It never did.

And this time, I'm the one leaving. It feels wrong.

"When are you going?" Emily asks.

"In three hours."

The words sink like a stone in my stomach.

"That's… soon."

I lower my coffee onto the bench. My eyes dart around the café, landing on anything besides Emily's red hair and wide eyes.

But I feel her gaze on my face like a torch.

"It is."

We both don't know what else to say, so I take a large pull from my coffee.

I've never had many friends, but she might have been one.

I hold my breath before I turn to face her.

"Can I get some cookies for the drive?"

She nods. I watch her get up and weave around tables. The other staff members watch us. I know them all by name.

But I've never been the best at making friends.

My truest and only friend has always been, and probably always will be, Jasmine Spark. Her friendship was easy, because it was already decided for me before we were born. Our fathers worked at the same newspaper company. Then they had a daughter in the same year. The rest is history. We practically grew up together.

But they left the city a year ago, and now my father, the ever-faithful servant, follows in pursuit of them.

I wonder how much of that was his choice, too.

When Emily returns, her fingers clasped around a brown bag, I suddenly want to flee the café—a place that once felt like a sanctuary to me in this chaotic city. I abandon my half-drunk coffee on the bench as I stand.

"Well," I mumble, "I should probably go home. My dad should be packing the last of our boxes in the car by now."

I glance through the window at the commuters ghosting past the café with their heads lowered and coffees in their hands.

The sun has risen. The stars have fled the sky.

I smile at the waitress as she hands me the cookies.

"I'll miss you, Savannah," she declares.

I plant my palm against the cool glass door. I'll miss her too.

…I think.

My grey eyes blink back at me in the glass door's reflection as I push it open.

I can only hope Silver Valley has good coffee.

The forest opens for us, and I feel insubstantial.

I haven't breathed properly since I left the city, and each time our car hits a pothole, my breath hitches.

My father drives a small car, sleek and silver, made for navigating the city. Here in the forest, the trees gleam off the bright surface, mud splattering the clean underside of the car.

My 13-year-old brother, Mason, grabs the back of my seat and exhales. I turn to face him, but it isn't me his wide eyes are focused on.

"Can you see it?" he asks me. "In the distance?"

All I see are trees.

Brown trunks, their roots cracking through the gravel and making the car jolt. And lots of leaves. Leaves everywhere—on shrubs, fallen on moss, and arching into the sky.

They say Silver Valley is nothing but forest. They say the beaches are cold and fog hangs in the air. Your fingers always feel numb, even through your gloves.

And by 'they', I mean my best friend Jasmine.

My fingers shake against the phone in my hand. My ear is hot from having it pressed against my face for the last hour.

On the other end, my best friend is explaining what Silver Valley is like, oblivious that I haven't been listening.

"—Only two more hours. It feels so long. I really want to take you stand-up paddle boarding. Do you think you could stomach it in this cold? Oh, the waves down at the bay are so flat—"

"Dammit!" my father curses as the car strikes another pothole.

I gasp, head slamming into the window.

My brother falls back from my seat.

"For the love of…" I scramble for my fallen phone.

"Careful, Dad, pothole," Mason warns.

The car swerves around a bend, and my stomach lurches. I'm used to a world of concrete and metal and straight roads. This road is something else entirely.

I sink into my seat and stare at the sky. I rest my phone away from my ear, and on the other end, Jasmine is still chattering. It doesn't take much from me to keep the conversation going.

My father glances over sympathetically and I smile reassuringly.

But it isn't the pothole that's bothering him.

Moving homes hurts him. More than it hurts me. We're doing this without my mother—my selfish, abandoning mother, who probably never even loved him. I want to slap my father, tell him that leaving is a good thing. But slapping people isn't exactly how you console them.

Instead, I reach over the gearshift and brush my fingers against his arm.

He purses his lips when he looks at me.

I swallow and pull my arm back.

"—And you and I are so pale. Silver Valley is void of sun, but surely we can lather up in oils and *force* the sun to tan us… are you still there?"

I squish the phone against my face and turn back to the window.

"Yes. Sorry. I got attacked by a window."

She misses a beat before answering. "You what now?"

From the back of the car, Mason is snickering at me.

I keep my gaze locked out the window, at the cliff edge by the side of the road, flummoxed by the trees. A storm of white birds roams across the sky, chasing the sun in the distance. The clouds move above them, swirling, trying to scare them away.

The sombre weather scares me more than the birds.

Mason grabs the back of my headrest again.

And finally, I see what he is pointing at.

"There, look!"

He presses his small face up against the window, blue eyes gleaming the same colour as the blooming strip of water on the horizon.

"Jasmine, we're getting close to the ocean," I say into my phone.

Mason leans around the edge of my seat. "Jasmine, we're close!"

I yank the phone away from him.

In the distance, the ocean glimmers like a mirage. He keeps trying to point it out to me, as if I hadn't already seen it. As if Jasmine can.

I lock my gaze on it and try my best to pay attention.

"How long?" Jasmine pipes.

I can hear something tapping from the other end, as if her leg is bouncing in anticipation.

"Definitely less than two hours," I answer.

I swear I can hear her smiling on the other end.

I rearrange myself between the bags cluttered by my feet, pulling my legs up on my seat. My father pulls the car down the steep mountain and the ocean grows even grander before us.

My heart expands as it comes closer.

"I want to show you the town when you arrive. It's so adorably quaint, you'll love it," Jasmine says.

I can't imagine Jasmine living in a quaint town.

Jasmine Spark belonged in the city. The city bustle was frantic, and I found it best to keep my head low, whereas Jasmine pranced around like a wild stallion.

I've never seen her afraid of anything.

Except the day she left me. That day, fear flooded her eyes.

I smile into the phone. "I can't wait."

"I can't either."

At times, I wonder why Jasmine Spark ever left. She abandoned me like it was her mission. Like she knew, one day, I would follow.

For the life of me, I never understood.

Silver Valley is a reasonably self-sufficient town, and Jasmine's father resigned from his work at the press in the city to start the *Silver Gazette*, a newspaper on the island. It connected the people with the world, as well as basking its citizens in tales about their small island. It seems odd, as there isn't much money in starting a local rag on a small island, but our fathers were adamant to pursue it.

Ethan Spark founded the business, but he expanded the concept with my father every morning over coffee.

It shouldn't have been a surprise that my father would follow him to Silver Valley eventually.

And yet, it was.

But not for Jasmine. A part of me believes she had a hand in the planning all along.

"Okay, so, I have a proposition for you," she declares.

I gnaw on my lip. "Yes?"

"Eli's a friend of mine. He's in my classes. I know that you're home-schooling for your final year but hear me out—wouldn't it be nice to meet some new people? Eli is throwing a party tonight as a start of term celebration. His father owns all the real estate in the valley, and he practically lives in a manor house. Please, please tell me you'll come with me."

The line falls flat as she holds her breath.

I haven't been to a party since Jasmine left last summer.

"I don't know, Jasmine…"

"It'll be fun!"

I slouch in my seat. Outside, the road begins to decline, pulling me towards my fate in the valley. No one can say no to Jasmine.

Especially not me.

"I'll think about it."

She exhales. "Better than nothing."

I roll my eyes. My friendship with Jasmine feeds us both—my blood sings for her adventurous spirit and wild ideas, whereas my practicality keeps her grounded. That's the beauty of moving to Silver Valley—being near Jasmine makes me feel alive. The yearning for her daring lifestyle sets my soul on fire.

"Let's explore the valley first. I'll show you all my favourite nooks, and then we can go from there," she continues.

She doesn't phrase it as a question. Jasmine Spark doesn't ask for permission, she just makes the decision herself and sometimes gives you the benefit of leeway.

I try not to laugh at the familiarity.

"I gather you have drinks lined up and an outfit prepared for me already?"

"Yup. All you need to do is get dressed. Easy-peasy."

Heat roars in my veins. Without my friend, I'd felt half asleep.

I smile against the phone. "Miss Jasmine Spark, everyone. Always prepared."

"Does this mean you'll come?"

I shake my head and try not to laugh. My father sees me sitting low in the chair and glances over for too long. Through the window, I hear the calls of seagulls.

"You already know my answer."

"Hallelujah. Oh my, I'm so excited. I have so much planned before the rain season starts again. I hope Mark realises I'm going to have you booked out for the next few weeks." I hear the smile in her voice. I can almost picture her, sprawled across her bed with her phone pressed up against her round face, blue eyes wide with joy.

"I'm pretty sure he figured that out before you did," I say.

Her laugher is short and sweet.

I rise in my seat and glance through the window. The trees make way for the water, and beyond lies infinite ocean.

Somewhere out there, we will find Silver Valley.

The car's engine quiets, and I utter a quick goodbye into my phone.

Jasmine sighs. "Okay, but message me when you're nearly here. I'm so bored. I've been sitting here waiting for you since daybreak."

"Glad to know I'm just someone to talk to when you're bored," I laugh. "See you soon."

I hang up before she has the chance to complain.

Mason jiggles his leg up and down and pushes on the back of my seat as my father leaves the car, wandering towards the docks ahead of us. Dad lowers his glasses and glances at my brother.

"Stay," he tells him. "I won't be long."

Mason reaches over the console and watches him walk away under the cloak of clouds. The water glistens around the large dock, waiting for a ferry to sail towards us, and my brother stares at it longingly.

"I wonder how the beaches look. Don't you wonder, Savannah? And the forest, did you know most of it was left alone for preservation? How cool is that! The forest will be so much better than what we saw just then on the road. Our house is right near the forest and the beach—it's all walking distance. Aren't you excited?"

I pick at a frayed piece of fabric on my shirt.

"I guess so."

"What if mum comes to visit us here? Do you think she would like it?"

I watch the water lap at the dock, slapping against the rocks. In moments like these where my brother's innocent optimism cracks through his features, I forget that he's no longer a child. I gnaw on my lip; the memories of cooking my baby brother dinner and singing him to sleep batter against my skull, just like the waves before me.

My eyes drift up along the water, stroking the area where the sky meets the sea. It's hard to imagine such a place exists.

It's exactly the type of place my mother would have run off to.

Remote. Surrounded by sky. Far from the city.

"I think she would like it very much," I tell him.

But she won't come.

There is no way in hell I would let her.

"Look at this." He shows me his phone, zooming in on a map with his fingers.

Silver Valley is a small town situated in a dip between two small mountains on the island. The island is small, and apart from the town and surrounding farms, it's entirely uninhabited.

Mason points to the beach on his map.

"They have cafes and restaurants all along the bay. It's like a small promenade, but it doesn't look as coastal as most beach towns," Mason tells me. His eyes grow hazy with contemplation. "Imagine having my birthday party down there. You can help me plan it?"

I try to ignore the feeling of my gut dropping at the hopeful look on his face. He abandoned all his friends in the city weeks before his birthday. Who's to say he'll make any friends to celebrate with him in time?

I run my fingers through his dark hair, pushing his head back into his seat. "Of course I will. But these townspeople need to visit a real beach one day. One with lots of sun and ice cream."

Mason snorts.

I vow to be there for him on his birthday.

I will make it special, even if no one else can.

Not my mother. Nor the friends we left behind. *Me.*

That's the way it has always been and always will be. It wouldn't surprise me if my father ends up spending all his time at work on the island—struggling to pay our bills just like he had in Sydney. Just like he always will

Mason smiles to himself, oblivious to the turmoil in my mind. He takes after my mother in that sense, eyes always on the future, not the past. Always desperate for the next grand adventure.

Out on the dock, my father wanders back towards the car. Mason darts upright in his seat again and watches him.

Dad's grinning at us, tickets in his hands. Pretending to be happy. But there is no mistaking it. Even *he* is a little excited.

Mason's hope is infectious.

This change is good for my father.

He will see his friend again, oversee his own newspaper business, and create a new life without the pain my mother brought him.

And maybe a small part of him is starting to recover from that.

Mason leans over the console again, grasping for the tickets that my father passes over to me. I bat him away and hold them in a stack against the dashboard.

The top one glows under a small ray of sun parting through the clouds.

February 6th, Silver Valley, one-way, admits one adult.

Suddenly, my chest constricts and flutters.

"You guys ready?" I ask them, bouncing my knees against my seat. They turn to look at me.

"Yes," Mason exclaims, eyes sparkling.

"You have no idea." My father beams, his eyes brighter than I've ever seen them.

This time, I don't stop the smile from surfacing on my face.

Maybe there is such a thing as choice after all.

J asmine Spark is an enthusiastic person.

I take off my seatbelt as we leave the main road, leaning forwards to spot my friend. The moment my father pulls the car up the driveway, she is running across the lawn towards us.

Her hand finds the passenger door, and she yanks it open while the car is still moving up the driveway.

"Woah, stop—"

"Finally!" she exclaims.

I clatter onto the pavement and into her arms.

She clasps her dainty hands on my shoulders, blue eyes sparkling.

Through a break in the clouds, the sun illuminates the blonde mane of her curls, making her look like an angel.

"You're insane!"

Never in my life have I fallen out of a moving car—it's incredibly awkward.

Trying not to gasp, I rub my knees, easing the burning sensation where they scraped the driveway. But before I ease any of the pain, she yanks me up again, pulling me into a tight embrace and leaving me with a sense of whiplash.

"Not insane," she answers, "just socially deprived." The pinkness in her round face and her quick breaths insinuates that she ran here not too long ago.

Despite the frantic pounding in my chest, I smile.

She brushes a stray piece of dark hair off my cheek, eyes caught on something behind me. I turn around, spotting Mason pushing open the backdoor. He stands under the carport, watching us as though he's unsure what to do. The carport is covered in an entanglement of vines and throws a patchwork of shadowed bruises across my brother's pale skin.

Jasmine releases me. "Mason!"

He takes a step back as she skips up the driveway. Her blonde curls bounce around her shoulders, fluttering like a golden banner.

Shaking my head, I make my way up to my new home.

It's almost like a small cottage, but something about it feels timeless. The wooden weatherboards are an earthy, faded brown that bleeds into the trees, except for some white detailing hanging off the lip on the roof and windows. The trees all hang around the house. I can feel the forest perpetually hugging me, standing off just a short distance from our cottage home.

It has a cosy yet frosty sensation about it. The trees are all coated in a lacquer of dew and fog begins to spill down from the mountains above us.

My breath gets lost in my throat again and I shiver.

It's nothing like the houses in the city. It feels like I've stepped foot into an enchanted forest.

Mason crawls out from the carport, his head low and wary. "Want a cookie?"

Jasmine throws her pale arms around him.

"I said a cookie, not a hug."

Jasmine releases him. "Nice to see you, too."

He throws the cookie bag back into the car and stalks towards me. "I don't know if I've missed her or not."

Jasmine grins. "Oh, you've definitely missed me."

He shakes his head at her.

Along the front of our house where I stand is a garden bed filled with rose bushes. Only one lone rose is in bloom.

Mason walks straight across the garden, ignoring the path between them.

"Mason, careful…"

But he's too distracted by the house to pay me any mind. I touch the rose petals lightly with my fingers to apologise before I wander back to the car to help with the bags.

"It's a nice place, isn't it?" my father asks me.

He frowns, wide eyes darting between me and the house. I try to ignore his fingers tapping against my duffel bag.

I smile and take it from him. "It's wonderful, Dad."

"Do you think you'll like it here?"

"It isn't me you have to worry about," I say.

He chuckles at me.

Jasmine pulls the bag out of my hands and steps between my father and me.

"Wait until you've seen the inside of the house, and the view you get of the forest," she exclaims.

She moves to place the bag back on the ground, but I grab it and sling it around my shoulders before she has the chance.

Jasmine's saying, "The houses along the street are pretty separated, so you probably won't see your neighbours unless you're nosy."

"So, you've met them all?" I say.

"Yeah, I'm nosy."

I roll my eyes.

"The people two houses down have a labrador, and it's the cutest thing I've ever seen." Her blue eyes squint through the sun as she turns and points. "I'm trying to convince Dad to get us one."

My father opens the boot of the car. "Ethan and Ella have always considered getting a dog. It's just hard in the city."

"You and I think the same, Mark," Jasmine winks at him.

He smiles and throws a bag at her feet.

But she's already spinning towards the house after Mason, and I lift what she's abandoned.

The walk up to the house is short, but walking through wet grass is a sluggish procedure. Jasmine skips ahead and holds the door open for me.

"Mason has already claimed the room with the road view."

I frown. "How can you tell?"

She waves her hand at me dismissively. "He asked for pictures of the house weeks ago."

"Pictures?"

"From when I toured it."

"How come I didn't get pictures? I've been trying to find some online."

She grins and feigns a look of innocence. "He asked me, and you didn't."

I shove her shoulder with mine and push my way into the house.

"The one facing the forest is better anyway," Jasmine whispers into my ear.

She tilts her shoulder, almost guiltily.

I smile at her. "It's okay, I like the forest."

I think.

She bites on her lip, unsure how to reply.

But despite reassurances, I discover the view in my new room to be breathtaking. The trees sway in a gentle breeze, fog spilling out across the grass between our house and the edge of the forest. It's beautiful. Like looking into the soul of the island.

I toss the bags onto the floor, picking up a fine blanket of dust.

Jasmine waves the smell of dust out of her face.

"It looks neglected," I point out.

She tries not to cough.

But I almost don't mind the dust—not when I push open the window to the forest outside, and the smell of nature replaces the scent of abandonment. I stare out into the trees, letting the smell of pine make a home in my soul. I blink against the fog and my heart skips a beat—something black dashes under the trees. It looked like a person. I blink, shaking my head.

Just an animal.

There must be so much life out there.

How could you possibly live in neglect when you have a whole forest watching?

Jasmine lies down on the new bedframe, her head tilted in my direction. I join her and together we take in the view of the forest.

Suddenly the room doesn't feel neglected at all.

～

"Can we go now?"

"My answer hasn't changed since the last ten times you've asked," I tell my friend.

Sighing, she collapses onto the couch I've just arranged in our living room.

I'd feel bad leaving my father to unpack by himself. Jasmine can wait, even if she's terrible at it.

To pass the time, she has been telling me stories about the valley. Upon my refusal to leave, she lapses into yet another one.

"The person next door doesn't like rhubarb pie. I was eating some one day when I went to introduce myself. I accidentally brought mud into her house from the rain, so I offered rhubarb crumble pie as a peace offering, but she almost hacked my head off."

I bite my tongue as Mason finishes setting up the TV and decides the best course of action is to plant himself directly in front of it.

"I don't think that was the pie," I tell Jasmine, deciding to ignore my brother.

She shrugs.

"My favourite people on this street are the young labrador couple. Did you know they almost got a black lab instead of a white one? Her name is Sadie—the dog, I mean."

"Didn't know," I call out, pulling another packing box aside.

My father has most of the furniture organised in the main rooms, and he collapses onto the couch, a cup of tea in his hands.

"Should be enough for today, pumpkin," he says upon seeing me.

Jasmine hears this and her face lights up. She bounds towards me. "Can we finally go?"

"The sun will set soon."

"And? Let's get you a coffee in the village. I need a break. All this hard work is exhausting."

"You haven't done anything."

"I've been watching you, and watching you is exhausting. Let's get coffee."

I just have time to grab a jacket from my room before she hauls me out of the house.

My father nestles himself on the couch next to Mason, trying not to laugh at my reaction to my friend. He turns to fish a copy of the *Silver Gazette* off the table next to him, his eyes glazing over. Once he's opened the first page, I know we've lost him. He dials a number into his phone as Jasmine pulls me through the door. "Hey Ethan, we just settled in, do you think we could go over ideas for—"

Jasmine slams the door.

The cold hits me hard the moment we step outside. The sun hasn't set, but the fog is already spilling around the trees lining the street, coming in and out of view in gusts.

"We're not taking a car," she says. "I want to walk you through the village so you can see everything."

Jasmine skips down the road in nothing but a summer dress.

I wrap my arms over my chest, shivering at the sight of her.

She dances back to me, pulling me forwards, and lapses into yet more stories about Silver Valley. She explains how the town only has eight streets, all connecting to one long lane that travels through the valley and down to the beach. Beyond the roads, peppered within forests, are multiple farms.

We wander past several fences, the fields and crops all beautifully concealed by the forest. Chickens, cows and lambs trot under a canopy of trees. I don't spot the black animal from my window again, but my eyes strain the trees for it anyway, pondering…

The forest here looks rather European; an Australian rainforest coated in pines and mossy undergrowth, with an extra enchantment that feels like it shouldn't belong on this continent. I feel the pressure of it pressing up against me with every step, baffled by how close it is to civilisation.

Slowly, the main village begins to pepper out around us.

Jasmine points out stores she's familiar with—the baker, the ice cream parlour, a small nook that sells trinkets.

Silver Valley feels timeless—a frozen segment of history—and all the storefronts are old and weathered. Some are made of stone whereas others are made of weatherboard, casting us backwards in time to a colonial era where horses and carriages were dominant.

Jasmine hums as she leads me into a small café, utterly placated. "Cappuccino?" she asks.

I nod and take the coffee once it's ready.

I'm not used to cafes having such short lines. There is only one other customer besides us. He tips his hat at Jasmine when she exits.

Most people are wandering the village on foot, I realise.

I hesitate as we cross the street, expecting an onslaught of cars, but the roads are filled with pedestrians.

Jasmine grabs me to hurry along faster, the setting sun a timer against us.

A young child waves at her from outside the ice cream store, and an older woman wishes her a good afternoon. I watch them come and go. They seem to disperse into the village like the smoke pluming from the baker's chimney.

We pause as we near the end of the village. The wafting smell of meat from the butchery whirls out of the store behind us.

My face stares back at me in the reflection of the butcher's window. My grey eyes are peeled open like wide coins, brows furrowed. I've never seen a village like this before.

Jasmine watches me, teasing out the frizz in her hair with her fingers.

"Let's go to the beach?" Jasmine asks.

I turn away from the butcher's window.

We pass a wishing well that indicates the end of the town, asking people for coins in exchange of good travel, and then we're submerged in a canopy of trees all the way until we reach the beach.

The sensation that the forest is watching us makes me shiver. My eyes track across the trees, searching for eyes, wondering if it was the black figure I saw outside of my window. The lure to both go inside and to run away battles inside me.

I expect Jasmine has some sort of adventure planned with the forest—be that hiking or swimming in a secret river somewhere—and the concept makes me shaky with anticipation, so I ask her:

"Is there anything else on the island?"

"Nope, just the village, farms, beach, and forest."

"Have you been into the forest yet?" I wonder, brushing my fingers against some leaves besides us in wonder.

The forest makes my blood sing, as if by magic.

But Jasmine gives me a strained look.

"You haven't?" I frown.

She spins a blonde curl around her finger, eyes on the sky.

I shrug a shoulder, ready to brush off the question until I notice the tension in her face. I brush my fingers on her arm, but she doesn't respond. Instead she jerks back from me, gasping sharply, bunching her mouth into a firm line as she turns to glance at the forest.

"Jasmine, did something happen in the forest?" my words puff out in a cloud before me and I shiver. "You know you can tell me anything."

She swallows before answering, rubbing her arms as she utters quietly, "It's easy to get lost. Don't get any ideas, okay?"

I kick a stone off the path with the tip of my shoe. It darts into the treeline and Jasmine's wide eyes follow it anxiously.

"Wasn't planning on it."

The bitterness in my words comes out unintentionally, and she chews on her lip. I shiver under her searching eyes.

I look around. The mist hangs over the trees now like a veil, as if it's hiding a foreboding entity.

The feeling of being watched doesn't help.

The Jasmine Spark I remember lives for the thrill of the unknown. To prohibit us from exploring the forest seems like a twist to the gut.

My fingers rap against the coffee cup as we walk the perimeter of the trees.

This isn't the Jasmine I know—the girl who would lean out the car window, hands outstretched towards the city lights; the Jasmine who would convince me to go skydiving with her, only to end up doing it herself before I could free up my weekend; the Jasmine who would ditch school with me to visit museums and the botanical gardens.

She purses her lips, watching me with a slight tremor touching her lips.

"You don't trust me," Jasmine whispers.

She wraps her arms around herself so tightly that her knuckles turn white, wide eyes glazed and unseeing ahead of her. She walks beside me on autopilot. I've never seen her look so still. She's usually like a hummingbird, always moving, but now she doesn't even blink.

Could there be something inside the forest?

Something dangerous?

I shudder, rubbing my fingers over my arms. The coffee in my other hand is nearly cold and does nothing to ward off the chill.

"Trust you? With my life, Jasmine." I cover my frown with a shake of my head. "I'm just… confused."

"Silver Valley isn't like the city you remember, the society you're familiar with," Jasmine advises, her fingers beginning to shake.

"I can see that… Silver Valley is a different world."

"You'll find that people live differently here, *think* differently," she explains. "It's cold here for most of the year, but does that stop people from using the beach? No. We're cut off from the mainland, grow our own produce. But does that bother people? No. And most importantly, we *share* the island with the forest. Do we intrude upon nature and cut down trees we don't even need in the name of trade and business? No. We don't."

"That has nothing to do with entering the forest," I snap. Her words crawl over my skin like insects.

Cutting down trees isn't the problem—it's the way the forest watches us and the way her body starts to shake at my words. I scan my eyes across the trees for that black animal, wondering if—impossibly—there's a herd of them watching us from the trees.

"Savannah, the forest is wild. It's untouched and it isn't safe." She stops walking to face me, and her eyes blister my face when she speaks. "Whatever you do, *do not* go into the forest."

Her wide eyes search my own frantically, her hands shaking lightly.

All the thrill I had at seeing my friend again evaporates. "Sure."

Whatever you do, don't leave this bloody apartment. Don't you dare follow me down these stairs.

My mother's words ping in my brain. Haunting me. Mocking me.

She left me with my child brother, left me to become the mother figure in his life as my father struggled every day to make ends meet for us.

On the days she abandoned us, I always followed her out of the apartment block. Eventually, she started locking the door after her.

Don't you dare follow me down these stairs.

I shake the memory away, grinding my teeth.

This is Jasmine, not my mother. This is my friend, not a haunting piece of my past. *Pull it together.*

Jasmine pulls her eyes from me and strides towards the beach.

I clench my coffee cup and follow her.

She doesn't say anything for the rest of the walk, and I follow her lead, keeping quiet, head spinning.

I try to pay extra attention to the world around me, taking everything in.

By the time we reach the ocean the sun is kissing the water. The ocean is flat—so flat, the waves never seem to peak, just rolling and rippling gently towards the beach. The cove is sheltered, locked in on either side by the forest.

I rub my hands against my arms as the sun goes down.

The promenade beside us looks cold under the grey sky; planks of rough wood looking weather-worn and sinister.

Jasmine barely turns her head towards me as she stops in the sand.

"So, you're not going to make me swim today, are you?" I ask.

"Not unless you're up for it," she says absently, rubbing her hands down her arms.

Her eyes are glassy. She isn't thinking about the beach. Sporadically, her head dips towards the forest.

I reach for her shoulder, but she pulls away, wincing.

I swallow a deep sigh. And kicking my shoes off into the sand, I sit down. The crust is still slightly warm from the sun, but below that the sand is cold as ice.

She sits, but she doesn't speak. She's never usually this quiet, and I wonder what unspoken words mill within her mind.

"Jasmine, what's wrong?"

She smiles, but her face is empty.

"Nothing in particular."

I give up and lean into the sand, letting my dark hair cascade across the small white grains.

This finally gets her attention, and she lies down beside me.

"You're going to get sand in your hair," she says.

"So are you."

Her lips twitch.

Her eyes stay locked on the sky while I keep mine pinned on hers. Eventually, she turns and faces me, but it isn't for long.

"You know, I don't think I've ever felt as close to anyone as I am to you. Ever. Weird how that's happened…"

I roll my eyes. "Because all your other millions of friends get sick of you after a while."

I expect her to mock me, but instead she just shrugs as if that wasn't what she meant. I glance over at my friend and suddenly she looks older than the skin she wears, ancient and cold. But I blink, and the feeling is gone.

She turns her head and smiles at me, letting love fill her eyes.

"Home has never been a place for me, Savannah. Home is wherever you are. But now and then I remember it's all built on a lie, and I hate it. I never feel like myself, because I'm always running away from something. And I hate it. I really hate it."

My veins turn to ice as she turns to face me.

And I don't know what to say.

Because nothing, absolutely nothing she just said makes sense.

"The city?" I try.

She ran away from the city. Abruptly. It was like she stole a part of my soul when she left, and now that I'm reunited with her that piece she stole feels like the only part of my old life that I have left. It's as though I'm starting my life again, only… at the beginning of the end.

Maybe she feels the same.

But she shakes her head.

"The city never felt like my home."

I wave a hand around me, indicating it all, eyebrows raised. My hand drops when it meets the forest at the bay's end. It still feels like it's watching us, the haunting feeling of eyes raking my back pressing me.

"Not Silver Valley either, I've realised," she responds.

She sucks in her lips. There's pain in her eyes. Something about the forest… it's like a trigger for Jasmine.

"If this is still about the forest, I promise I won't go into it," I say, the words tasting bitter in my mouth.

She laughs softly. I feel like I've missed the point.

"Thank you, Savannah."

I squeeze her shoulder. Immediately, my heart feels heavy with shame.

The moment the words left my lips, I knew the promise was a lie.

Don't you dare follow me down these stairs.

My soul urges to run my fingers down the leaves. To see what's watching me. To discover *what* is so dangerous in there. Usually, Jasmine is the person I can turn towards to make any reckless fantasies happen.

But I push the thoughts, the desire, away. For now. For my friend.

"Silver Valley is a strange place, Savannah. Just promise to stick with me, yeah?"

Her gaze is desperate. As though, by asking this, everything is resolved.

"Of course, that's what you and I do, we stick together."

She snorts.

"You ran away from the city, and I followed you all the way here, for crying out loud."

Jasmine stares at the sand, the corner of her lips tilting, as if she never expected anything less.

"Yeah… I suppose you did."

She pushes her hair back from her face and casts her eyes back on the sky. "I may run away from things a lot," she admits, "but I promise I won't ever run away from you."

"I don't think you could even if you tried." I nudge her softly.

But she doesn't catch the humour. Instead, she grabs my hand and pulls me to my feet, grinning. All she needed was validation.

Sometimes I wish it were that simple for me. I gasp as I stand, the cold evening air biting into my skin.

"Now come *on*," she grins, pulling me forwards as the solemn shadow lifts from her face, bringing back the sunshine I remember well. "I showed you the town, and now we have a party to go to. Last stop of the tour: the Spark residence."

She spins on her heels and prances up the beach.

The last rays of the setting sun catch her curls as she twirls away from me.

And as always, I follow my friend.

Silver Valley is a strange place, Savannah.

I shake the thought away.

We race against the falling sun back to Jasmine's house, the fear of running in the dark catching up to us. My heart lightens with each step, but the nerves never cease.

With the darkness, the forest seems to loom over us.

And I can't help but stare back at the eyes watching me from inside.

The hairs on my arms stand on end, and with a shudder I realise I will not be able to let this go. My once confident, brave friend is more spooked than I've ever seen her.

And I intend to find out why.

4

"I'm not sure how fond I am of pre-drinks."

My stomach rolls as we turn down Eli's driveway.

Jasmine's room is on the top floor of her house, and I sat in her window from dusk and well into the evening before Jasmine started offering me drinks.

One tequila shot and two cans of cider later and I was finally prepared to be adorned in various outfits until Jasmine found something she liked on me. "*The burgundy in my mesh top sets off the chocolate tones in your hair,*" she had said.

"Speak for yourself," Jasmine responds to my statement about the drinking.

She hasn't had anything to drink yet.

Exactly as I'd hoped.

If Jasmine drove us to the party in her father's jeep, I knew she'd be sober enough to watch my introductions at the party. However, I have no intention of participating.

"Steady, Jas, we're nearly there."

The bending driveway rolls up towards a large house, teeming with people and cars. I keep my eyes on the forest. Beyond the trees, the stars glow like a canopy.

I ditch my third cider back into the carton. It's nestled between stacks of papers her father had forgotten to take out of the car.

I lift the first one up from the stack.

THE BEST WAYS TO RUN YOUR FARM–FACT VS FICTION

"How many old newspapers does your father have?" I ask her.

"Too many to count."

Jasmine turns the car off and reaches between my feet for a drink. I move my legs out of the way.

Part of me wants to advise her to take it slow. Like I usually do.

I drop the paper back on the stack. "Interesting."

Another car pulls in behind us, its headlights sending light beaming off the sequins of her top. I squint against the light. Jasmine opens her door and waves at whoever was driving.

In the back of the car, we've packed a camping mattress with an array of toiletries. In the city, we could take a bus or train home, but on the island, we have to be more inventive.

It was Jasmine's idea.

I toss my jacket off and throw it into the back.

"Savannah, meet Stacey," Jasmine hollers from outside.

The girl has orange flames for hair, knotted into a crown of braids above her head. She waves at me from her car, but I don't reach her in time to say hello.

The poor girl is already too drunk to stand.

I watch her clamber up to the two-storey house with a cluster of friends. Jasmine follows behind.

"Hold this." Jasmine hands me a new can of cider.

Feeling tipsy already, I decide to test my luck on Jasmine.

"The forest is close here," I tell her, waiting for a response.

She makes a grand point of ignoring me as we dash up the stairs to the house, and my heart droops as I turn my back on the forest.

The door is open and Jasmine sails through like the house belongs to her. Cars litter the driveway outside, and a few people mingle, but no one gives us much notice. The party is inside, and everyone slowly drifts towards the music.

I tip half of my new can into a pot plant by the entrance.

The first floor is extremely large, but homey. In the distance, a drunken group mix their drinks in the kitchen, giggling like children. But Jasmine doesn't bother explore the first storey of the house.

She bounces up a grand staircase towards the party upstairs, her shoes clinking against the wood. The staircase leads to a sitting area, lush couches and bookshelves adorning the space, then leads to a few doorways I assume to be bedrooms and a large arching entrance at the far back where the party is held.

"I'm going to hide our tequila so no one else can steal it," she tells me once she reaches the top of the stairs. There's a bookcase there, and she takes a swig before placing the bottle on the top shelf. She winks at me and the glitter on her eyelids dances in the light.

This is, without a doubt, where Jasmine belongs.

She spins like a dancer, twirling around into the thick of the party. The set of double doors have already been cast wide open. The upstairs room resembles a large ballroom, with skylights and marble floors, the walls panelled with more windows. Through the foggy glass I can see the forest and the edge of the island where the trees meet the sand.

"My god," I mumble.

Clouds slowly begin to wash over the sky above us, blanketing the stars. I stop in the entrance for too long, mind drifting with the clouds, when Jasmine suddenly yanks me forwards.

"Beer-pong!" she declares.

The room is thick with bodies—dancing, talking, lounging—and off to the side, a long table is scattered with beer and cups. I follow Jasmine like a lost pup.

A tall boy stands by one end of the table, his slim fingers twisting a ping-pong ball. The light falls on his dark skin as he leans across the table to wave at someone, laughter breaking across his face simultaneously, his straight white teeth dazzling.

He's still laughing by the time we arrive, the deep bass reflecting off the glass walls behind him, and I let the sound of pure joy envelop me. "How much do you bet Henry will make a move on her tonight?"

"I'll bet the rest of my can here," Jasmine declares.

He turns to face us. "That's weak, Jasmine!"

Another boy stands at the other end of the table. His deep blush matches the red in his shirt.

The boy with the dark skin grins and twists away, mischievous delight twinkling in his eyes as he yells, "Hey, Stacey! Wanna play with us?"

I hardly pay attention as Stacey appears from the crowd, her thumbs up, to stand next to Henry, who looks to be a shade of purple. Stacey looks over at him, having the decency to look flustered at the sorry sight.

Jasmine snorts and hands the dark-skinned boy the rest of her can.

He laughs, downing it, the light reflecting off his eyes.

"Eli, this is Savannah." Jasmine pushes me towards the table.

Eli hands me his ping-pong ball, another wicked grin lining his face. "Want to be a team?"

I blink.

Jasmine pats me on the back and winks. "Good luck."

"But, I've never—"

Jasmine spins off to join the group Stacey came from. One girl hands her a plastic cup, and I'm all but forgotten. I gape after her, my stomach churning.

"Never played?" Eli asks quietly.

I hold the ball firmly in my hand and turn to face him. "Maybe..."

He stands aside to give me the space to shoot, running a hand through his wavy brown hair as if he's nervous.

I've seen people play this many times before, always spectating. Throw the ball into the opponent's cup. How hard can that be? I square my shoulders.

If I don't win, I'll be too drunk to navigate the forest.

"Prepare to lose," I shout.

From beside me, Eli's grin widens.

ᔆ

Eli tips our last cup into his mouth. Game over.

The others scream victorious, and the sight makes me want to laugh.

Why? I don't know why. But it's so damn funny to me that we lost.

I grab the edge of the table and smile as the world spins. I never drink, and the alcohol hits me hard after consuming several cups so fast.

"Son of a—" Eli doesn't finish his declaration.

At the other end of the table, Henry reaches for Stacey as she flails in excitement. I turn away as he leans towards her; she's still smiling as their lips meet. His hands cup her cheeks, her eyes wide with delight.

I plant my gaze firmly on the table, making a point to tear my gaze away.

From a distance, I see lights flashing, feel music pounding.

Something reverberates into my skull with equal pain and woozy delight. I take our losing ball from Eli's cup and place it in a clean cup for the next game, somewhat aware that groupings of spectators look eager to begin another round.

My mind spins as I fumble around with the ball.

Dammit. I need to sober up.

"You did great," Eli whispers over my shoulder.

I jump.

"I, ah… no." I rub the spot where his breath lingers on my cheek. "I made us lose," I say.

He shrugs. "Well, it *was* your first time."

My first time? My brain spins.

Oh.

I take a steady breath and plaster on a smile. His dazzling eyes are so close. Too close. I suck on my teeth and stumble backwards.

"I'm going to do something else," I announce.

I spin on my heel, stumbling as I do so, and I hear a faint bemused chuckle following me.

I don't really want him to follow, but I'm too intent on finding Jasmine to say anything.

I push my way through the heat of bodies, trying to weave a web so I can lose him. Unfortunately for me, Eli's just as good at navigating these crowds as Jasmine and remains plastered to my back with ease.

I find her sitting on a leather couch—one of many around a cluster of tables—playing another drinking game. She looks up when I arrive, spotting Eli behind me, and frowns at the distance between us. She lowers her cards onto the table. I can almost hear her thoughts: *You guys haven't hooked up yet?*

I reach for her hand to pull her up. It's rather clammy.

She slips and stumbles around the bodies encasing her.

"Woah, careful…"

She giggles and knocks three people's cups over, spilling the contents all over the wooden floor. "Oopsie, sorry."

Her friends splutter curses at her back as I yank her into the shadows. Her cheeks are flushed when she glances up at me.

"Why do you want me to hook up with the host of the party?"

"He's cute, he's rich, and he likes brunettes." She laughs at my sour face. "Come on! It was funny!"

I brush some hair out of her face.

Jasmine stares at me, eyes glazed. Her focus latches onto Eli a foot away from me, leaning against a wall with that goddamn smile on his face.

I sigh, taking a step back from her and rolling my eyes, lip twitching.

"See, it *is* funny."

"I'm laughing at *you*, you dickhead. Come on, I think you need to take a walk."

She tilts her head at me. "To the bookshelf?"

I wince when I say, "Yeah, okay."

She claps. "Oh, goodie!"

Is it really that awful to let her make a bad choice if she will make that choice anyway, despite what I say?

Outside the ballroom, the foyer and staircase is packed with people and we have to push our through. I spot Stacey and Henry looking very intimate by the pot plant downstairs.

I pour Jasmine her drink as she observes the slightly raunchy sight.

She blinks, then her eyes wander to the people clustered by the entryway on the ground floor. I begin to twist the lid back onto the tequila just as she reaches for the banister.

"Savannah, let's slide!"

"Oh, no you don't."

I grab for my friend, and she falls into me, moments away from leaning over the banister, my arms twisting around her shoulders. She hardly notices my fear, and her fingers find the cup of tequila. Easily distracted. Or trying to, for my sake.

"I think we should dance," she declares, spinning around in my grip. And just like that, she dashes back to the dance floor. I reach for her, but she's already gone. I have no choice but to follow.

Jasmine is impulsive, often doing things without a second thought.

When I make rash decisions, it tends to be with purpose…

My mind snatches back to the forest as curiosity gets the better of me. Is there someone watching me from the forest? Or was it an animal outside my window? Are the trees… sentient?

Chills dance up my spine and I wrap my arms around my chest, cursing the fogginess in my head. "You know what, I think that's an excellent idea," I mumble to myself, despite my gut churning incessantly.

I yank my fingers through the thick falls of my hair—limp from sweat and alcohol—and return to the lion's den.

My heart almost shudders with relief when Eli drops his hand onto my shoulder.

Stumbling backwards as I face him, my back presses hard into the doorway, unaware of the thrum ahead of me as he lowers his head to my cheek.

"You look like you could use some fresh air."

Yes please.

"I'm not particularly fond of wandering off with sweet-tongued strangers," I say instead.

He blinks, and I wonder if he even heard me.

I sink against the door, and he presses closer to let someone past behind him. The heat from his body feels like an inferno this close to all the drunken dancers, and I place a tentative hand on his chest to keep him back.

"Let's stay here then." He says it almost like a question, but I don't respond.

Instead, I slowly drift my eyes to Jasmine, grinning at me from the dance floor.

The dancers knot around her, bodies pulsing with the heat and music, swirling around the blonde-haired girl like weeds blowing in the grass. She lifts the bottle of tequila I didn't realise she had swiped from the bookshelf to her lips in a silent salute.

It's as if she can read my mind, seeing the swirling trees and the green depths luring me and making a home in my head. I want to trace my fingers along those green leaves, feel the dew on my fingers, welcome the cold blast of air. And she knows it.

I debate telling Jasmine that I need to use the bathroom, but that would only buy me a few minutes, and until she is plastered out of her mind...

I snap my gaze back to Eli. In the light from the stairway, he is all soft angles. He hasn't once taken his eyes off me, looking at me not like I'm a sweating mess, but a girl out of her comfort zone severely needing attention.

The hand on his chest works of its own accord, not waiting for my mind to catch up, and shifts slowly towards his face, the tips of my fingers brushing the soft material of his shirt.

I can feel the poor boy's heart pounding, his golden eyes drifting closed as I graze those fingers through his hair. My hand rests on the back of his neck, and I have full control as his face reaches down to me, claiming my lips.

He tastes like summer—sweet like the last drink he had—and hot with unleashed excitement as his hands slam against my waist and push me deeper into the wood behind me.

I gasp as he eases his tongue into my mouth, and my eyes slowly open and lock once more onto my friend.

She laughs boundlessly and reaches for the closest boy to her right, twirling in complete ecstasy around him on the dance floor, the sequins in her shirt reflecting light like a disco ball.

My shirt sticks to my skin with sweat, and I knot one leg around Eli's as he works his mouth around mine. In the glowing lights, the wet sheen on my pale skin makes my hand look like a ghost.

I pull my fingers from his hair and grip his chin, stopping his lips an inch from my own until I can feel the warm summer breeze of his breath caressing my skin.

"Water," I whisper.

His lips twitch, and he gnaws gently on his bottom lip. Feeling like a mess, I push him away from me, and it takes all my control to not gasp in contentment at the small waft of air that separates our bodies.

His large hand encases mine and pulls me to the stairs, and my eyes barely snag on Jasmine as I depart, who seems to have forgotten my existence for the moment. Good.

My heart erupts into a deep crescendo at the thought and my fingers slip from Eli's as we reach the bottom of the landing. Cold air swirls into the foyer from the door constantly being opened and closed, but no one notices except me, the alcohol dousing everyone's senses.

Tearing my gaze from it, I step up to Eli and place my fingers on his cheek. They look wrong there. Too pale, too ghostly. "I need a moment," I whisper.

He doesn't question me as I pull my fingers away and walk to the front door in deathly silence, the ghost of his lips still clinging to mine. I turn and whisper, "I'm very sorry," and plunge into the sanctuary of the night.

I grit my teeth as I step past the threshold, the night air smacking right into me.

"Sweet hell."

I pause for a moment in the entrance of the doorway, bracing myself against the cold, Eli's shadow behind me.

Just off to the side of the house is the forest. It punches me with feeling, warming me from the insides. Taking a deep breath to steady myself, I make a dash for it, disappearing into the night.

I don't allow myself to question the decision as the sound of the party reverberates down the driveway.

But everyone stays far away from the forest, as if they all know something I don't, which gives me the perfect chance to dash around them unnoticed. The cars are all parked up by the house and people mingle around them, acting like the drunken fools they are. Some-one jumps on top of a car and hollers, and soon everyone's attention is on him.

Others slowly clamber onto the car. They're singing along to the music inside, voices breaking in perfect harmony.

I slip around the car. No one notices me as I dive into the trees.

"The beach is north," I whisper to myself. "Which means I want to go south."

I wander towards a tall pine and glance up into the sky.

"Where is south again?"

The crowd behind me scream so loudly to the music it breaks my thoughts. I attempt to navigate the clouds but it's incredibly futile.

After several moments, I decide to just start walking.

"Just keep straight," I assure myself.

Surely I know how to keep to one direction?

I curl my arms around my chest, trying to block out the cold. My breath hovers in a fog before me, disappearing in wisps.

I pause again by a cluster of trees, panting. From cold. From fear. From Eli. *Everything.* It takes me a few beats to calm myself. Slowly, I lower my arms and steel myself.

The canopy presses down on me as I navigate my way farther in. My footfalls are quiet, muffled by the heavily packed dirt, save for the occasional crunch of leaves underfoot. I focus intensely on my feet, trying to make sure I don't fall.

The ground is even, but I don't trust myself in the dark.

Branches snag at my sleeves, trailing their fingers across my skin, and I reach out to push them aside to no avail.

Eventually, the ground begins to slope upwards slightly, and I trace my eyes across the darkness to figure out what it could mean.

I don't see the tree until I crash right into it.

My hands scrape bark and I feel my brain shake in my skull; my reaction dulled by the alcohol. I rub my forehead, brushing away the feeling. "Ouch."

It's some sort of pine—not old, but not a sapling either.

I place both hands on the tree in front of me as I walk around it, but the bark feels uncomfortable against my fingers, drawing tiny scratches into my palms. I quickly release it.

But as soon as I'm past the tree, I realise I'm not walking a straight line anymore.

I slow my footfalls, and the dirt muffles and catches them.

The trees appear to soak up all the light. The house glows from behind me, a beating pulse of sound and life, but the forest is a black pit of nothingness. I pat my pockets for my phone to use as a light and sigh.

I left my phone in the car.

Grasping the branch of the next tree, I curse myself.

I'm sober enough to navigate a forest, but not when it's this dark. Not tonight.

What on earth was I even thinking? It's just a damn forest.

There's nothing magical about it.

There's nothing watching me.

I stand completely still and strain my eyes, hoping they will adjust. Waiting. Hoping.

They don't.

People shout and laugh in the distance. I think about Jasmine and consider how poor this plan was.

Of course it would be dark here. It's not like the city, which is covered in lights at night. In nature, the only thing that helps us navigate the dark are the stars, and I've forgotten most of the constellations, not that I can see any hiding behind the overcast sky.

The freaking clouds have sucked away all hope, all light, all sense of depth and direction from my little world.

The farther I wander, the more lost I'll become, and I growl at the thought.

I lean against the blasted tree behind me and rub my knuckles into my eyes.

The nightlife whispers a lullaby around me, animals humming and cooing along to the sound of thrashing waves in the distance, and I focus on that instead of the party.

Squeezing my eyes shut, I debate heading back, but the thought tears at me. In the forest, the world is dark and cool and peaceful. I can just… lose myself.

And I would like nothing less than to submit myself to that sticky ballroom, with the chilly forest so close and so promising, no matter how dangerous it is. No matter what is waiting for me in its depths.

I lean my head back against the tree.

And freeze.

My heart bolts immediately from its calmed state back into a panic.

I can hear footsteps.

Human footsteps.

They pause when I do, several metres in front of me, lost in the dark.

They aren't coming from the house. They're coming from the forest.

My heart erupts in my chest, and I stand as still as the trees.

I strain my eyes against the darkness.

I can't bloody see.

Slowly, I trace my fingers across the bark behind me, searching for something I can snap and use as a weapon. But the tree is large and impossible, the first few branches beginning metres above my head. My fingers twitch futilely against the trunk.

"Hello?" I try.

But of course, nothing talks back.

I'm tipsy, paranoid, and I'm blind.

No sane person would go into the forest. Everyone keeps a safe distance from it.

I inhale deeply. It's probably just an animal.

My feet slip against the loose soil as I shuffle, grabbing onto the tree to stop myself from falling.

But the thing doesn't startle from my movements like an animal would.

I strain my ears to see if I can still hear the footsteps, but all is quiet.

Maybe it's just plain paranoia.

No one would be coming out of the forest. That's ridiculous.

I take a few steps back, keeping my eyes forward. I lift each foot slowly, heart pounding in my chest.

With each step, I quicken my pace, feet stumbling over roots and branches. My fear ebbs into uncertainty when the footsteps don't follow.

"Careful. You're about to smack into another tree."

The male voice comes from the darkness.

I turn around and run.

When I find my way back to the house, Jasmine's puking in the bushes.

"Jasmine?"

She wipes her mouth and squints at me.

This time, I go in search of water and rush back to the bushes by the porch to hold her hair back. Both Eli and the boy she danced with are nowhere to be seen, and I assume that Jasmine made a frantic dash from the party when she realised she was going to vomit.

"Feeling better?"

She doesn't respond. Just wipes her hand across her face.

I pull my friend from the ground, spying the tears raking her cheeks.

At least not many people have seen.

I help her stand and ease her towards the car, coaxing her with promises of sleep and warmth. The walk back to the vehicle keeps me on edge, and I frequently glance not so subtly into the foliage beside us. The house drops away behind mist seeping out from the trees onto the driveway, and we disappear into near darkness with nothing but the distant throb of house lights to guide us back to the car.

The gravel crackles beneath our feet. Jasmine sways against me.

Before long we huddle into the car, both feeling too overtired to sleep.

Jasmine's body rocks from side to side against mine, her gaze searching for the light of the stars hidden behind clouds, like she's trying to steady her mind. She still smells faintly of puke, so I make her brush her teeth and change her top.

I can't turn off the pounding in my ears or stop my fingers from tapping against the blanket. The man's voice replays over and over in my mind. I try my best not to glance out of the rear window where the canopy of trees meets the sky. Eventually, the drag of sleep erases the nagging thoughts.

"Sorry for puking," Jasmine says by way of goodnight.

"Sorry for leaving when you had to puke," I answer.

And we both go to sleep.

$$\backsim$$

I'm still shivering when we wake the next day. The blanket rolled off me overnight and a streak of sunlight cuts into my eyes like a knife. I sit upright and glance at the forest through the back window. It looks harmless in the daylight.

I should've listened to Jasmine yesterday. I never should have gone in.

I begin to shake, gripping my arms around my chest, expecting the man to be watching us even now.

Maybe he is.

"You okay?"

I jump slightly at the sound of Jasmine's voice, then turn around to give her a weak smile.

"Just cold."

Her lips thin, but she doesn't pry.

I shake away my reverie, and slowly, we crawl into the front seats of the car to go home. The driveway is already hauntingly empty compared to last night.

"Let's just go," I say.

Jasmine punches on the car engine and the sound splits through the trees.

I don't have any plans for the rest of the day, and I'm glad of it. I'm both too haunted and too tired to do much of anything.

And I'm not the only one.

Jasmine drops me off at home and I gather my minimal possessions from the car. She nods at me when I leave, and I nod back.

She looks like she's about to be sick again.

Hangovers have never been our strong suit.

I avoid Mason when I walk inside, heading directly to my bedroom. The house looks as empty as Eli's driveway.

"You look weird," Mason says from the kitchen, head lifting from a small plate and startling me.

"Tired," I reply, easing through my bedroom door. "Goodnight."

He waves at me, one side of his lip tilted. Spinning around on the bar stool, he continues to eat his sandwich.

I quickly shower, letting the water run down the scrapes across my arms from last night. I'm greeted by a patchwork of small red lines when I step out of the shower, a web cut into my skin from the trees.

When I go to grab an apple and a glass of water from the kitchen, Mason is gone.

Head pounding, I trudge back to my room.

I wish I had some curtains set up so I could ignore the view of the forest. It watches me as I fall asleep to the sound of birds.

The empty walls in my room make me feel like I'm stuck in a cell.

↶

I wake up shivering again, but not from the cold.

It's night outside. I hadn't realised how exhausted I was from the move and slept through an entire day. Despite the dark, the thought of sleeping more makes my muscles itch.

I rub my arms.

The creeping fog outside my window makes my skin crawl and I stare at how it breaks apart around the trees, concealing everything beneath the foliage. What if he's watching me right now?

Shaking the thought away, I clamber out of bed and join my family for dinner. My father made us a roast chicken lathered in butter, and a steamy loaf of bread wafts from the centre of the table.

I pull back my chair and reach for the knife to slice the bread.

My father leans back to look at me, eyes sweeping across the pale sheen on my face. "So, I take it the party wasn't good?"

I shrug. "It was fine."

Mason mumbles, mouth stuffed with chicken. "Why do girls always say that when something is bad?"

"Calm down, sunshine," I chuckle. "The party *was* fine."

Mason mumbles something around the food in his mouth, shrugging.

My empty plate smiles back at me when I lower the heavy knife, but I don't reach for any food.

"The food here is great, though," my father continues. "Fresh bread! And this chicken was just killed this morning."

Mason lowers his drumstick.

"Please don't talk about how our food was alive this morning, Dad. Please," I utter, gaze on my plate.

Mason watches our father with a stuffed mouth, frozen in place.

Dad reaches for some bread when he says, "There's only one

butcher in town, did you know? Said our chicken was named Sally, one of the farmer's girls give them all names—"

"DAD!"

Mason pushes his plate away. "I think I'll just eat bread."

"What? It's sweet. The butcher said she calls all the chickens Sally, and the males are called Richard. I think it was Richard... or maybe it was Bernard."

I throw my hands up in the air and Mason takes the chicken off his plate.

"Well, I don't think Mason will ever have an appetite for Sally anymore." I glance over at him stuffing bread in his mouth, as if to make a point.

My father looks over apologetically. "Sorry, it's the reporter in me, I can't help—"

"But throw out buckets of facts without regarding the consequences."

"Yeah." He eats his chicken in solitude. "That."

I laugh at the sour expression on his face and reach for some chicken—despite the roiling in my stomach—to show Mason it's okay to eat. Sally may be dead, but she was killed humanely, and that's all any of us can hope for in the end.

But Mason doesn't eat any chicken and utterly disregards my efforts.

"I say give him a week. He can't hold off eating protein for that long. He's a bit of a sucker," I tell my father as we tidy the table.

He glances at Mason putting dishes away.

"Don't talk about your brother like that." My father sighs, but he's trying to keep the laugher from his expression. My brother *can* be a bit of a sucker, but we love him for it.

I shrug. "Says the guy who gave our roast chicken a loving name."

He does nothing but shake his head at me.

I clean the crumbs off the table and bring the empty breadboard into the kitchen, the round dish of chicken balanced spectacularly on my other arm.

Across the kitchen, the windows facing the forest sing with crickets and the trees occasionally rustle throughout their slumber. Maybe it's my imagination, but I can really feel the forest watching us now—as if the person I heard in there last night still lingers.

When my family gradually head to bed, I make a start on the homework set for my home-schooling, too numb to sleep. With my desk still not set up from the move there isn't any place to do it except the kitchen counter, but the talk of Sally has killed the mood there, so I return once more to my bed.

Moving in year 12 is hard but continuing with the same school through a distance education program is even harder. My mind grows hazy as I work. Eventually, I throw my pen onto the floor and stare at the windows.

The windows stare back.

I pick my way across the room, gingerly weaving around boxes. The glass feels like ice before me, and I place a hand upon it, eyes wandering into the trees. My breath catches on the glass, fogging it up the way the mist does around the house.

When I can't see the forest anymore through the fogged-up panes, I raise my voice with false bravado.

"You weren't someone at the party, were you? You came from inside the forest."

Silence greets me.

"Are you from the Valley?"

The alternative seems too unlikely. But the forest feels otherworldly. Already, my heart begins to race, and I lean forwards, desperate to explore.

But instead of leaving, I wait for an answer.

Of course, the forest doesn't give one.

I pull back from the glass, staring through my window so intensely that my eyes strain. I can feel a presence staring back.

Needing to do something physical to deal with the adrenaline pumping through me, I start to unpack my room.

I've nearly finished by around midnight, and my memories stare back at me from my bed—a picture of Jasmine with her arms around me, a candid snap of Mason and me in front of the opera house, and photos of the night sky from my old house peppering the wall above my head, among others.

I go to sleep with these memories racing through my head.

The next morning, a gentle breeze wakes me.

I roll over the blankets, disgruntled at the cold once more. The morning sun dances over my sheets, turning them various shades of gold, and I wipe the brightness from my eyes. It takes me several moments to realise why my bedroom feels like a freezer.

My windows are cracked open. But I don't remember doing it.

I slide out of bed, mind whirring.

Something silver blinds me and I lift the winking object from the windowsill.

It's a silver necklace, adorned with a simple round pendant. My hands start to shake holding it.

This isn't mine.

It wasn't here last night, and I hadn't opened the window.

The pendant swings from the chain between my fingers, swaying in the cold wind. The chain is thin but strong, and the pendant dances off it, twisting around in the breeze. It looks like a smooth coin.

I glance out the window.

The forest has eyes again, and I feel like I've stolen all its attention.

The hairs on my arms rise. Shivers unrelated to the cold trace patterns across my back.

I toss the necklace out the window and fall onto my bed. Pulling my knees up to my chest, I try to not stare out the window. The breeze plays tricks across my bare skin.

He was here.

Is he watching me?

I take a deep breath, steadying the knots swarming in my stomach.

Inhale. Exhale. Inhale. Exhale.

I push my shoulders back and flex my fingers, easing the shakes away. Rolling across the bed, I snag a jumper dress and some stockings hanging on the railing of my bed and swipe my phone off the bedside table. When I change, I duck down beside the bed so the forest can't see me.

With the necklace gone and the window firmly latched shut, I feel myself calming.

My heartbeat slows as I locate Jasmine's number on my phone.

Savannah: Café in the valley? My shout.

Jasmine: I'll meet you at the one next to the post office. Ten minutes?

Savannah: Perfect.

I leave my room and don't look back.

My father hardly notices me when I leave the house, and Mason is nowhere to be seen. I wonder if he's made friends already. I haven't asked.

It only takes me three minutes to drive to the café Jasmine described. It's the same place we got coffees during my tour of the village.

The cloudy sky gives way to a gentle rain, and I stand plastered against the café window, waiting. Jasmine arrives shortly after and pulls me inside so we don't get wet.

"Have you had breakfast yet?" she asks.

"No, haven't had the chance."

I shake off thoughts of the forest and submerge myself into the familiar atmosphere of a café, basking in the routine.

It's small and not very grand—more of a takeaway place than anything else—but the bustle reminds me of the *Coffee Corner*.

We find a free table near the window and Jasmine orders us muffins and coffee. She only eats the tops off her muffins, so I practically eat a muffin and a half.

We spend most of the day there, huddled in the café, and some of the tension eases from my shoulders

I miss this.

I miss wasting hours with Jasmine in a random nook in town.

"I tried to dye my hair white once," Jasmine suddenly recollects.

I furrow my brow, tearing my eyes from the rain-soaked windows.

"I feared one day my hair would grow darker, so I got some cheap bleach and tried to dye it. I ruined it. Everyone with light hair was so beautiful, and I envied it. But in the end my dad had to cut all my hair off because of the dye. I looked like a boy for months, and everyone noticed my hair then, maybe even for the first time. I made it worse for myself."

"I don't remember that," I claim.

"Because you weren't there."

I gnaw on my lip. "I've known you since we were kids, I'm sure I would've seen you with a boy cut."

"Yes, but you weren't there for this." Jasmine drops her smile. "I'm telling you because I don't want you to ever dye your hair. Your dark hair is what makes you unique. It's powerful."

"Thanks… I guess."

She smiles softly, and I don't think much else of it.

We leave the café shortly after.

༄

Throughout the week, Jasmine's demeanour shifts back into the mould of her bubbly self.

I spend every day I'm with her searching for answers, but she's too light-hearted and flippant and I get nothing else out of her unless I pry… which I don't do out of courtesy.

It isn't until next Sunday that I discover an alternative.

Sitting by the rose bush out the front of my house, we stretch our toes across the grass; she brought a speaker, and music drifts down our street.

At one point, my neighbours wander by with Sadie the labrador.

Jasmine bounds up from the sprawl of pillows on the lawn to go and say hello. I almost follow, but by the time I rise, the dog and the man have resumed their trot down the street.

Just as I stand, Ethan Spark pulls his car into our driveway.

"I should probably go," Jasmine says, casting her eyes upon his car. "I spend way too much time here, I think my mum is getting jealous."

"You sure you're not just saying that because your dad is here?"

She grins. "Maybe."

She helps me take the pillows and blankets back into the house. Ethan leaves the front door open for us and I find my father in the lounge room, chatting amiably.

"—Pretty quiet now, I told the staff you might come by this afternoon," Ethan is saying to him.

"Sorry about this morning… yes, I could swing by now."

Ethan lowers a stack of papers onto the coffee counter. The lip of one has a familiar stain on it—cider.

"Mind if I use your bin?" he asks.

My father leads him towards the kitchen.

I turn to Jasmine. "You said your dad has lots of old papers?"

She shrugs, tossing a cushion back onto the couch. "Yeah."

I try to keep the smirk off my face as I turn to follow them to the kitchen, but Jasmine grabs my arm.

"If they're going to the warehouse, I'm going to walk home, want to come with me?"

I brush her hand gently away and lower my eyes to the floor. "I have schoolwork to finish this afternoon, maybe see you tomorrow?"

"Sure."

As soon as she makes it to the street, I rush back into the kitchen.

"I brought Mason to the post office this morning—he still insists on sending his mother post cards, and I have to pretend to know her address. It was pretty last minute," my father admits to Ethan, still intent on making excuses.

He reaches for my father, eyes apologetic when he says, "Ella should take him out for ice cream tomorrow, she's free."

"Isn't it too cold for ice cream?"

"Not for Ella and Mason, you know how they are."

I smile. Jasmine's mother replaces our own when I'm not around.

My father lifts one shoulder half-heartedly. His eyes flicker towards me and I try and make myself look busy, but his gaze pins on me.

Tapping my fingers on the kitchen bench, I squirm under his stare, recalling the words he had said once, years ago.

"I see your mother in you, Savannah. You both have eyes of silver steel."

I swallow.

"It's not too late to swing past *Gazette*?" my father asks Ethan, rubbing his eyes under his square glasses.

It's difficult to see much of myself in him. He has the same constellation of freckles across his face, the same dark hair, but otherwise he looks more like Mason—with their lean faces and wide eyes. They both have hair that curls in the rain and skin that darkens quickly in the sun.

My breathing quickens. I'm my mother's child and Mason is my father's.

Ethan pulls his keys from his pocket.

I blink back into focus and furrow my brow at the stack of papers in the bin. Stories. Articles about the forest.

I shadow my dad and Ethan to the front door.

"Can I come?" I ask.

"Come?" My father turns.

"Yeah, I want to read up on Silver Valley, look at some old papers."

He cocks his eyebrows at me. I've never shown interest in his work before.

Ethan looks delighted. "I have an entire storage cupboard full of old prints that have been collecting dust. I wanted to empty it out next week and use the space for filing. Take as many as you want."

I grin.

Ethan opens the door for me, and I don't bother concealing my excitement.

Because today I'm getting answers.

I don't speak during the trip in the car.

Mark and Ethan chat about business, and I drift in and out of thought, my mind still on the forest.

We dart past all the streets I'm familiar with walking on foot, and from the window of the car, I can spot more farms dotting the land where the trees have been swept clean.

The bare nakedness of the terrain feels wrong.

When Silver Valley was founded, the first settlers must've swept away sections of forest to make space for farms.

Once upon a time, our civilisation wandered through the trees. They roamed from boats packed with their families to make a new settlement, exploring the forest for the best place to live. Then they chose this cove on the northern part of the island to make their nest.

They must have traversed the entire island.

But now, it's forbidden for me to even try.

How rude.

"Savannah, look."

I turn to face an area I haven't yet seen, sucking in my lips.

"I didn't realise the warehouse was that small?"

The car rolls to a stop. I wonder how I haven't yet been to the *Silver Gazette*. It's only a short walk out of town.

"Well, it's a small island," my father responds.

It's much newer and shinier than the weathered buildings closer to the village, with a sign in black paint titled *Silver Gazette* in glimmering font.

I clamber out of the car and follow them inside, where Ethan drops my father off at his office. It's small and smells of newspapers, with a single window opening behind his long desk, allowing the ocean breeze to wash through the room.

I don't stay long. Ethan quickly leads me down the corridor to a storage cupboard, where I begin to pile the old papers into the car.

We don't stay long after that, and I smile during the drive home, the smell of papers lingering in my nose. I watch the rain race down the window of the car, hypnotised by the translucent droplets, heart soaring at the prospect of being one step closer to finding answers.

By the time we get back to my house, the rain eases to a drizzle, but I leave the papers in the car out of fear they'd get wet. My father pops an umbrella for himself and Ethan behind me, but I dash across the lawn with nothing but my hands covering my head.

When my feet hit the front porch, I hear the familiar sounds of Jasmine Spark laughing from inside the house, and all thoughts of tackling the papers leave my mind. I brush the rain out of my hair, sighing, and an exasperated groan involuntarily escapes my throat as I shove the door open.

"Savannah?" Jasmine enquires.

"Wonderful timing."

My father and Ethan are still chatting about the newspaper when they follow me into the house, drifting slowly towards

Ella Spark, who's unloading take-away food from plastic bags in the kitchen. I wipe my damp hands on my pants and wander to the couch.

Jasmine is holding Mason hostage by the TV.

She still has her jacket on, and small beads of water slide down her arms. She's claimed whatever Mason was fiddling with, flicking it back to him.

"Go away," he groans.

I hold in a sigh. Before my brother is a tower of playing cards, his schoolwork abandoned on the corner of the coffee table.

Jasmine just laughs at him.

"You know, it's taken me ten minutes to get it this high," he tells her.

She flicks another card at his face.

"Hey," I warn.

Jasmine pulls her arm back slightly. I grab her wrist, not trusting her.

She turns to me, eyes wide, lashes batting against her cheeks. She lowers her hand, hiding the card in the folds of her dress.

"Oh, hi, Savannah," she says. "Mum and I thought Dad would be here a while talking about work, so we brought dinner over."

I never would've thought that seeing this much of my friend all the time would be so annoying.

Reluctantly, I sit next to her.

"And why, exactly, are you harassing my brother?"

Mason looks at me with gratitude, but something playful flickers behind his eyes. He tries not to smile at Jasmine.

"He told me he's doing schoolwork." She points to his stack of books. "I'm merely explaining to him that stacking cards isn't schoolwork."

"Hey," he protests, "it's nearly dinner time, and Dad says I can be done then."

"Dinner isn't ready yet, dimwit." She laughs, taking the card from her dress and flicking it at him.

"Oi," I chuckle, lunging for her.

She puts her hands in the air in defeat.

"Don't worry, Savannah," Mason sighs. "She's ruined it already." Begrudgingly, he wipes his hand across the table, destroying the stack of cards. He stands, departing for the kitchen while mumbling about privacy invasion.

I knee Jasmine in the back lightly.

"You'd make a horrible sister."

"Nah, he loves me."

The aroma of dinner drifts from the kitchen and I wrap my hands over my stomach to stifle its grumbling. Jasmine's wide eyes are suddenly pinned on me. She leans towards me, wrapping her legs underneath her.

"So," she says, looking at me.

"So?"

"Have you checked the date on your phone? It's Valentine's Day today," she tells me.

I blink. I hadn't even noticed. "Wow, that means it's been over a week since I've come to the valley." It feels like I've only just arrived.

Jasmine rolls her eyes. "That's not my point."

"What's your point, then? It's not like I've done anything deserving of romance lately, so it doesn't matter."

My gut churns at the memory of Eli.

She glares at me as if reading my thoughts and exclaims, "*Come on,* Savannah. Eli is a nice guy."

I nudge her with my shoulder, refusing to encourage this conversation.

Her eyes pin mine, piercing my soul.

"I guess I just want a reason for you to be a part of my life, my friends. Maybe it'll stop your eyes from always wandering to the forest." She raises her eyebrows.

My stomach drops.

Oh.

I sink deeper into the couch, trying not to look guilty. Does she know?

She nudges my shoulder with hers and rises from the cushions, head turned towards our fathers. A small tree right near our house starts to sway outside in a gust of wind, and a couple raindrops leak down the glass.

I don't bother following their boring chit-chat about the papers, but something has caught Jasmine's attention, and she pounces like a cat.

"Mark said you went to the warehouse…?"

I bat my lashes.

Jasmine raises her eyebrows at me.

Behind us, our fathers are talking about the storage cupboard and how they'll be discarding the rest of the papers tomorrow morning.

I slouch into the couch.

"Yeah, I did."

"Why?"

Jasmine has her eyes on me, blue and wide.

"I was curious."

She leans in. "Curious about what?"

Her intensity scares me. "Just curious about where our dads work, I guess," I tell her.

She watches me, something behind her eyes burning. And then she shifts and reclines against the couch, fixing her gaze on the TV. But her eyes don't follow the movements on screen.

"M'kay," she murmurs.

She doesn't look satisfied, but she shakes her shoulders and jumps up from the couch towards the kitchen as Mason comes back with a plate of food.

"Ooh, dinner."

Shaking my head, I follow her.

ᔑ

The rain doesn't subside for a week. Instead, it worsens.

I hardly bat an eye at Jasmine's oncoming calls.

Rain makes her grumpy, and the clouds hang in the sky like a thick blanket of depression. But it gives me plenty of time to research and even more time to be annoyed about the lack of findings.

There's only so much pointless prattle I can endure, and I must have thrown the paper about landscaping across the room at least three times.

Jasmine is at school, and everyone's upset about the last days of summer in Silver Valley. Apparently, studying in your final year of adolescence is worse when the weather is bad.

Home-schooling isn't what I expected—you get set coursework for the week, and your parents are responsible for checking on your progress. I finish most of my work hours before the day's end, and my father is notoriously absent, which gives me plenty of time to myself.

When Jasmine isn't at school, she comes to my place or I go to hers and watch movies and play board games until darkness blankets the sky and I return home to continue my research.

I'm just about to throw one of the papers out the window in anger when my phone rapidly chimes from my bed.

Jasmine: I gave Eli your number.

Eli: Hey, Savannah! It's Eli. Jasmine gave me your number.

Eli: How have you been? School sucks. We should hang out soon.

Jasmine: I want to hang with Eli soon. He's a right pain in my butt, won't shut up about you.

Eli: Jasmine said you would be keen to do something soon? Let me know.

I roll off my bed and groan.

I purposely ignore Jasmine's messages and sit staring at Eli's for a while before deciding to ignore them, too.

By the time Jasmine finally comes over, my head is pounding.

I massage my temple as restlessness quickly settles in.

The newspapers amounted to nothing, and I doubt Jasmine will give me many answers about the forest if I ask.

I realise there's only one thing left to do if I want to figure anything out at all. I need to go deeper into the forest.

꙼

The next morning, I message Jasmine that I'm feeling sick with a headache.

She isn't happy, but she acknowledges my excuse enough to not track me down.

I sigh and stash my phone in my pocket, annoyed at her and everything else.

It's still very cloudy, but I'll have no trouble navigating the forest during the day. The rain decides to hold itself at bay for now.

I find Mason in the kitchen trying to make pancakes. Something about baked goods always puts him in a good mood.

The only problem is Mason can't cook very well.

"Whoa, whoa, don't put that much milk in the batter, otherwise they'll get too runny," I say, grabbing the carton off him while he's still pouring. Milk splashes the kitchen surface.

"Thanks," he murmurs.

I hand him the flour to thicken it up a bit. "Do you need help to make them?" I ask him.

"No."

"You sure?"

"I can make pancakes by myself," he tells me.

Feeling shut down, and suddenly very antsy, I grab an apple from the kitchen and walk towards the window near the lounge room.

I'm not certain, but I think my father is at the warehouse, and Mason should be busy for the next half an hour if he doesn't burn anything or set himself on fire.

I stare out the window, gnawing on the apple so fast I could choke.

It's now or never.

I take a deep breath and stride purposefully to the door.

"Where are you going?" Mason asks.

"Just a walk." I throw the half-eaten apple in the bin and walk towards the coat rack by the door. "I'll be back in time to have some pancakes."

"Who said I'd share them?"

I close the door behind me, pulling my jacket tightly around my shoulders.

The street is quiet due to the weather. The last remaining rose in our garden has died and wilted to the ground, and the driveway is covered in debris. Branches and leaves scrape down the road, skittering in an uncanny way. I walk around the back of the house, leaving the sombre street behind me.

Sticking close to the building, I try to locate a game trail in the forest, but the weather has been so wild, the foliage is strewn across the ground. Giving up on any notion of easy passage, I locate a small gap above a pile of leaves and dip through some branches.

The spindly wooden claws snag at my skin, but within moments, I'm inside the forest.

The trees wrap and bend around me, the wind making them dance and sing hauntingly. Most of the trees stand tall and proud of their history and survival, but others near the ground continue to pull at my skin.

I feel young and unworthy underneath the canopy.

The farther I walk, the more minuscule I feel, and the village behind me feels smaller than ever. Silver Valley is just a speck, a small pocket hidden on the edge of the island.

I pick my way carefully through the bushes—wispy little things that bend in the wind and persist in making my journey difficult. Now and then I grab a branch to steady myself as I twist around a spiked plant or a pile of fallen branches.

Walking here is nothing like it had been the night of the party. My chest feels warm, the comforting feel of moss and cracking branches underfoot singing in my veins. The only similarity is the feeling of being watched. It doesn't leave me. It never has.

I try to walk in a straight line again to keep some sort of bearing, but even a fool would know the forest isn't that simple.

Eventually, the ground begins to incline, which doesn't surprise me this time. The village is in a valley between two mountains. But I slow my pace, because it means I'm breaching the borders of the valley.

I debate with myself if it'd be worth it to leave the valley entirely—walk up over the hills and see what's beyond.

But I recall Mason's pancakes and stop walking.

"Baby steps, Savannah."

I lean against a large tree next to me.

It seems as if I've wandered into a small clearing. It isn't very far from my house, considering that my street is near the back of the village, but it appears to be another world entirely.

I sweep my eyes across the quaint spot. Surprisingly, the ground is relatively untouched by large debris. A few metres around me, soft grass coats my sneakers, and a couple of large orange leaves sail down from a slanted tree, giving the small clearing a speckled appearance. The grassy clearing is the size of our bathroom back at the house, but it feels massive, as it's the only open spot I've found.

I sink onto the grass, stretching my legs out over the leaves. The wind is only a gentle breeze here and peacefulness settles over me.

Surrounded by stillness, I hear the forest in higher detail. There are the usual sounds—fleeting birds, trees moving in the wind, the bubbling of a stream somewhere—and then footsteps. They grow louder with each moment, and then suddenly stop altogether.

Metres away from me.

I scramble up from the grass and walk back to the edge of the clearing so that my back is against the largest tree.

"Why are you following me?"

Silence.

I itch to run back the way I came. The only problem is, I don't know where the person is. I could run right into him.

"What do you want?" I call, voice reverberating until it's silenced by the forest.

My heart pounds in my ears for a few beats. And then…

"I'm returning this."

My palms sweat.

I recognise his voice from the night of the party.

"Returning what?" My voice sounds surprisingly steady.

Something small hits the ground in the clearing, and I stiffen. But I relax as soon as I see it.

It's a small package wrapped in newspaper, a shining silver chain peeking out from inside. It's as if the man was trying to wrap the necklace by stuffing it inside the paper.

He didn't do a very good job.

I tilt my eyes up from the package, following the line where it was thrown from, and realise the man must be standing directly ahead of me. A thick tree stands ahead, and as I squint, I can just glimpse a corner of a black jumper peeking out from the side of the tree.

"Why? It's not mine, is it yours?" I ask.

"It's not mine," the voice says. "It's rubbish, useless, but it might be able to give you some answers. Find who the chain belonged to. It won't be hard."

I'm about to ask why on earth I would do such a thing, but just as I'm about to, I see the man move. I freeze, not daring to speak.

And I watch as he races away into the forest.

My breath catches. I don't dare take my eyes off him for a single second. From behind I see a black hoodie, black jeans and shoes—he looks like a dark phantom.

And then...

Gone.

Disappearing into the forest as if I had imagined the whole thing.

Shaking, I move slowly into the clearing towards the package. I swipe it up and dash back to my tree.

The newspaper is crumpled and worn, old indents indicating where it'd been folded and re-folded again branding the paper. The texture feels fragile and soft, nothing like the papers from the *Silver Gazette*. I unwrap it gently.

The necklace falls into my palm, cold and heavy. I run the pendant between my thumb and forefinger and find a harsh indent on one side.

I hadn't noticed that before.

A small circular dip is on the coin-like surface, like a stone or disc had been moulded into the pendant.

I place it gently in my pocket.

I'm just about to leave the clearing when I notice something peculiar about the newspaper.

It hadn't just been crumpled from folding, it had also been torn. Straight along the top and bottom, as if it had been carefully ripped into long, horizontal pieces. The start and the end of the article are missing, and on one side of the paper there's a photo, so worn I can't decipher the exact image.

Maybe it's because I've grown attached to newspapers lately, or because my curiosity gets the better of me, but I smooth the paper out and read it.

...An exact week. That's how long we have until she comes into creation.

Through the great influence of Lythia May, daughter of the seventh Elder, a wish upon the stars was cast, renewing hope in the hearts of our people and revealing a girl with the power to reshape our old home. Many attempts have been cast to speculate the root of this...

My heart begins to beat faster.

This isn't a clipping from the *Silver Gazette*. It's something else entirely. But it's impossible to tell where—or even when—it's from.

"This is a clue."

With shaking hands, I place the newspaper into my pocket along with the necklace and slowly pick my way out of the clearing, my mind buzzing.

Did the hooded man intend for me to find out about Lythia May? If so, why did Jasmine want to hide this from me?

Taking a deep breath, I smile at the weight of the clue in my pocket.

Finally, I have somewhere to start.

"   *A wish upon the stars*," I mumble to myself moments
before falling asleep that night.

• • •   Those stupid words haunt me like a plague.

My mind drifts to my mother. She had always been fond of the
stars.

She told me once: *"You were made for the future, Savannah—for
glory and history's pages. We both are. It's festering inside us, kid. Like
a disease."*

I never believed her. Maybe I should've. It always felt like the
most genuine piece of advice she's ever given me, if you could even
call it that.

I dream of one very specific memory. It was 5am, I was only a
few years old. It was a rare night my mother had been home. Only,
she didn't care for me, didn't shop or clean like the other moth-
ers, and my father was always working. It was one of those nights

where I learnt to fend for myself, become independent, and curse the ghost in my father's bed every step of the way.

I had woken in the middle of the night to grab a glass of water, and she had paused to sit with me in the kitchen before she left.

It was dark. I could hardly see her as she approached me.

My silhouette was a smear against our foggy window as I glanced down at the lights in the city. We propped candles on the windowsill, our eyes cast on the sky. The stars hung like banners that night.

Below our apartment, the city slept, but the sky was theatrically alive. She told me how each star, each galaxy, offers chances and dreams so exquisitely different from ours.

"How do you navigate?" my mother had asked me. She always asked me this.

I started reciting constellations, pointing at the sky.

"Good. And the others?"

The ones without names, the ones she told stories about.

The constellations that didn't exist.

"The one shaped like a heart points north, and the one shaped like a hat points south."

My mother had patted my head. *"I'm following the heart tonight."*

How can you follow a fake constellation?

When our gazes dropped, she blew out the candles. She stood up and left without another word, swirling in the aromatic smoke.

I had continued to watch the sky—searching and searching for constellations that simply weren't there. Trying to fathom where she was going and why.

After Mason was born, I started to forget those memories. I forced them away. My mother came home less and less. And when she did, she hardly spoke to us.

I became a mother for my brother.

I forgot the names of her constellations.

Mason pined for her. I hated her. And eventually, I learnt not to care. I didn't need her, just as she didn't need us.

Her home was never with us because her home was in the sky.

ᔕ

I wake up gasping. I don't know why.

The memories of my mother mean nothing to me now. The last thing I would wish upon the stars would be for her return. In fact, I'd rather she never existed at all.

The moonlight brushes against my window through the clouds. The sky has cleared a little overnight, as if the stars themselves have given me the memories of my mother.

Finding a sock on the ground, I cover the newspaper article on my bedside with it, hiding the words.

It's early. My digital clock ticks over to 03:08am.

I pull the thick blanket over my head and block out the moonlight drifting through the small window. Above me, the stars still sparkle.

I ignore them.

ᔕ

The next morning, it's the sun that wakes me. The clouds roll away, finally letting us breathe.

I spend the next few hours until the rest of the family wakes reading the newspaper over and over and munching on some toast. When my father finally lumbers from his room for breakfast, he brings shocking news.

"Have you read the paper today?"

I slide my mug of tea over the worn paper clipping on the table, so he can't see.

"No, why?"

"Day off today. The school, I mean. They got the announcement yesterday, but it was only printed today." My father shrugs.

"Apparently the school's covered in debris and a classroom had a leak—it flooded through a few rooms. They're saying they're utilising the warm weather to be more cost effective in clean-up hours."

I almost laugh. Jasmine should be in a good mood today.

"Sounds like Silver Valley's equivalent to a snow day, except in good weather."

"That's *exactly* what it's like."

Laughing, my father turns to make himself some toast for breakfast.

I leap from my chair and head for my bedroom, forgetting my breakfast. Hurriedly, I put the paper clipping and the necklace back under the sock in my bedroom and decide to call Jasmine.

She isn't an early riser, and I'm just about to hang up when she greets me.

"For heaven's sake, are you crazy? It's only 9am."

"Morning to you, too. You know, most people get up at this time of day," I claim, watching my father move around the kitchen from my bedroom door.

"Yeah, well, goodnight. I'm going back to bed."

She hangs up.

I sit on my bed and call her again. She picks up on the second ring this time.

"Jasmine, I think I'm being stalked by someone," I rush out before she has a chance to chastise me again.

Silence plays out on her side, and then I hear the faint shuffling of her quilt. She's getting up.

"How do you know?" she asks, deadly serious.

"Look, why don't I come over to your place? It's sunny today; maybe we can get some ice cream and walk down to the promenade. I've heard the school is closed?"

"Okay, I'll be ready in five minutes," she says.

"It'll take me ten to walk over. Don't stress, Jasmine."

She repeats, "Five minutes," and then hangs up.

Sighing even deeper this time, I grab a thin cardigan and shoes, and wonder to myself if telling her is such a good idea after all.

It ends up taking me almost thirteen minutes to get to Jasmine's place. She isn't too happy about it.

I'm halfway up her driveway, avoiding yet more debris, only to find her racing across the lawn.

Her house is larger than mine and looks a lot more modern. It's double storey and all the bedrooms are upstairs. Jasmine's bedroom is on the corner of the house, so she has a view of both the forest and the street, whereas her parents' bedroom overlooks the forest. It wouldn't surprise me if she convinced her parents to give her the master bedroom.

She meets me by the small camphor laurel tree out the front of her house. The leaves brush half a metre above our heads, casting us in shade.

"Who's stalking you?" she demands.

She looks unhappy. I may have ruined any hope of the sunny weather putting her in a good mood.

"Have you had breakfast yet? Maybe we should get you a muffin or something before we tackle the ice cream," I say, grabbing her arm softly and walking her in the direction of the beach. She follows reluctantly.

"Are you actually being stalked, or is this just an evil way to get me out of bed?"

"I was serious, but I also believe you're a bit too worked up to have this conversation right now," I admit.

"That's bull. Just tell me."

I glance at her sideways, and then pull her onto the road so she doesn't stumble over a tree branch.

"Jasmine, calm down. You look terrified."

She looks at me, puzzled. "And you aren't?"

I shrug. "I'm just confused."

She continues staring at me like she's seeing an alien.

"I'm getting stalked, not murdered."

"What's the difference, really?"

My stalker seems to want to tell me something, not kill me. He doesn't feel dangerous. A little creepy, maybe. But not dangerous.

"Savannah," she warns softly.

I turn away from her.

We reach the end of her road, coming into the village. Everyone seems to be out today, enjoying the lapse in wild weather. We walk past the bakery and the smell of bread and melted chocolate coaxes us as we pass. A couple of children dance around us to get inside, and a little brown-haired boy hits the debris out of the way for the girls with a large stick. I smile at him, and then realise he's throwing it in the direction of the girls. They squeal in response.

I watch the girls and the boy, but Jasmine has eyes only for me.

"Savannah, please," she urges.

I turn to face her as the kids enter the bakery.

She speaks quietly, so only I can hear. "I'm scared for you. Let me help."

Her seriousness shakes me for a moment. I can usually count on Jasmine to shrug off serious matters. Maybe a part of me hoped she'd dismiss it and joke about it—reassure me and convince me it's nothing.

This is only making it worse.

"Look, it's not a big deal." My mind battles with how much I should tell her and whether I should admit that I went into the forest. "I've just noticed someone has been following me. At least, I think so. And I want to get my mind off it."

She reaches for my arm and grips on tight.

A man on a bicycle zooms past us. Two women near the takeaway café wave at him and smile.

People pack the streets more than usual. It's still so early, but the sunshine drew them all outside.

Jasmine and I head down to the beach. It's hard to tell who's leading who. I nudge Jasmine towards the promenade, and she steers me away from all the people, protecting me.

She holds onto me as if I'm about to lift off the earth and fly.

The beach is a lot less packed, but the promenade is still bustling with life.

It's too cold for swimming, but the odd surfer here and there has decided to tackle the waves. It's quite amusing to watch, given Silver Valley isn't a surfing town. The waves are gentle, and the surfers can hardly stand on their boards. But Silver Valley is a place for innovation and imagination.

"Have you ever considered taking up surfing?" I ask Jasmine.

She doesn't say the valley is too cold, or that the waves are too small, instead she says, "I'm more a stand-up paddle boarding type of girl."

We walk along the promenade, searching for a breakfast joint. Unlike most boulevards I've visited, this one is mostly made of wood decking, lined with shops and restaurants. It isn't long, but it's spacious. People have propped little red umbrellas outside their shops, overlooking the beach, and the stores and cafes practically spill out around us. Jasmine ends up steering me to a café close to the end of the promenade, near both the beach and forest, and we lounge at a small wooden table under an umbrella.

Jasmine orders us muesli and coffees. I let her take control when I notice she knows the waitress by name.

Her familiarity reminds me of *The Coffee Corner* more than the takeaway place had, and I realise I don't even miss my old haunt. I thought I would.

Once she's ordered, we're left alone in a thick silence despite the people buzzing around us. It doesn't take long before Jasmine can't help herself anymore and she blurts, "Can you tell me more? I know you don't want to, but it seems only fair since you've sprung this on me."

My mind whirs, shifting between Jasmine and my phantom stalker.

I never really kept anything from Jasmine before, but I feel oddly reluctant to share this with her. I don't know why.

Perhaps because Jasmine's also holding back about the forest, and it feels like it's a path we both must take alone.

But her piercing gaze gets the better of me.

"It's the forest," I say quietly. "He's always watching from the forest."

She sucks in a breath. "Always?"

"I saw him at Eli's party, and again yesterday. But I think he's always been watching. Or most of the time, anyway."

"What does he look like?" she asks me.

For some reason, this question bothers me.

"I don't… I don't know."

"You've seen him, though?" she presses.

"He hides from me," I admit.

We both hold our breath and Jasmine glances in the direction of the forest. From this end of the promenade, we can hear the trees brushing in the wind.

"I don't like this," she whispers.

I lean towards her.

"Jasmine… you know something about this," I tread carefully. "I can tell."

She turns to face me suddenly.

She's about to reply when our waitress arrives. Jasmine clamps her mouth shut. We both watch our food and coffees being placed on the table with sudden tension. When the waitress leaves, Jasmine lifts her coffee up with shaking hands and drinks to avoid talking.

"Please," I press. "Jasmine, please tell me."

She takes another sip.

Why are we keeping secrets from each other? Why can't we just talk freely, like we used to when we were younger? We've always worked better as a team.

I chew on my lip.

Jasmine started it.

But that's such a childish excuse.

And besides... *I encouraged it.*

"Please be honest with me before I do something stupid," I tell her.

She considers this, and I watch her think it through. She knows I'm right. She lowers her coffee.

"All I can say is that the forest is full of danger for you, and I want to keep you away from them before you get taken advantage of and..." She shakes her head, biting her lip. Her words sound strained, and I can see she's been holding this in for a while.

"Them?" I ask. "Who's *them*?"

She glances up from her coffee, and I'm surprised to see her eyes are glossed with tears.

"People who will use you, *kill you*—people who might not realise how innocent you truly are."

A tear rolls slowly down her cheek.

"Kill...?" I mutter. I bunch my hands into fists on the table to stop them from trembling. "What does that mean?"

She reaches over and takes my hands, smoothing them out.

My heart starts to pound erratically in my chest.

"Savannah, I know you can see there's more to this." Her eyes hold me hostage, glistening with fear. "But have faith in this. Have faith in me. And whatever you do, stay out of the forest."

I sit like a statue.

I don't understand, but I nod, I smile, and I eat my muesli.

The weight of her words hangs over us, and I'm aware of the threat of the forest nearby. Jasmine doesn't cry, save for that one rogue tear, but an obvious sadness radiates from her. She's like a girl who's lived a thousand lives, lived a thousand secrets, and is getting crushed from the weight of it all.

I don't understand it.

I don't recognise this side to Jasmine.

The forest's opened something between us, and I'm not exactly sure what it is.

How well do I even know my best friend?

The promenade grows busier as the day progresses. And even more oddly, the weather grows hot and wet. The heat clings to my skin like a heavy weight, almost like the weather is holding its breath.

Once we've finished our food, I pull Jasmine from her chair and across the promenade. We wind through bodies and more displays until eventually our feet touch sand. I toe off my shoes.

"Want to go for a swim?" I ask her.

She scrunches her eyebrows. "It's freezing."

"And it's also extremely humid. I know you want to—you've wanted to since I've arrived," I say. I give her a pointed look. "I'm only offering once."

A smile lights up her face.

"I hope you wore nice underwear," she smirks. "I have no intention of buying more swimmers just for this."

I hesitate at that but push through my insecurities and smile.

"Underwear it is."

I work at unbuttoning my shorts. They brush the sand, and the moment they land, I hear a deep chuckle reverberate across the beach. Jasmine and I turn at the same time, only to see Eli and two friends grinning at us like the idiots they are.

"Care to join?" Jasmine sneers.

The boys make their way towards us, parting with the bustle of the promenade. Eli's gaze meets my own, his dark eyes dancing.

I flush as they watch us like we're the most amusing things they've seen all day.

We probably are.

As they come closer, I realise I know them all by face. Eli, Henry, and the boy Jasmine danced with at the party.

"I can't see why not," Eli replies.

Henry makes a face, and I'm sure he could list a hundred reasons why.

But Eli has his shirt off already, smiling like a fool. Jasmine raises her eyebrows at him.

"You do realise the water will be cold, right?" the boy Jasmine danced with asks. He runs his hand through his dark hair, looking unsure.

"You do realise that's half the fun, right?" she rebuts.

He smiles at her, but it doesn't quite reach his eyes.

Henry sits on the sand with his legs out before him. I almost wish to join him.

"You guys go ahead," he says. "I'll mock you from afar."

Jasmine's tall, dark-haired boy seems to have made his decision also, and begins to undress.

I pretend not to notice, taking a deep breath.

Confidence is key, Savannah.

In one quick movement, I pull off my blouse. I turn towards the waves before it even has the chance to touch the sand.

"Oh, goodie!" Jasmine skips up behind me, looking delighted with herself.

"Save your breath for the ocean," I advise her.

Ignoring me completely, Eli shouts: "Beat you to the water!"

He shoulders past us, nearly knocking me from my feet. Jasmine cries after him. "No way!"

She lunges like a spiral of sunlight, her legs as pale as the beach as her feet pick up a storm of sand and shells.

Eli's laughter slows him down. They match pace perfectly.

The tall boy catches up with me and sighs.

"I wonder who's more the fool, the ones dashing to their deaths or the two idiots blindly following them?"

I shrug. "My money is on the fools. At least the idiots know how to sense danger."

"Do they?" he asks.

I suck in my lips at his answer, my mind once again returning to the blasted forest.

Do I know how to sense danger? Am I really that wise at all when it comes down to it? My breath skitters with each footfall taking us closer to the waves. My heart rate speeds up, and suddenly I wish I was as carefree as Jasmine Spark.

"I don't know," I admit.

I suppose it's better to not overthink things. So, I give the boy a small smile and dash towards the waves.

"Idiot," he shouts after me.

I don't really care. Maybe it's better that way.

The waves slam into my feet and I try not to cringe. The cold is like whiplash, stealing my breath. But I carry on.

The tall boy sounds like he's laughing at me from behind, and I use that as motivation to continue faster, to prove I'm just as carefree as the others.

This *was* my idea after all. Not Jasmine's.

My feet struggle for purchase on the hard sand but the waves slide them around and compromise any foothold. I arch up onto the balls of my feet as I walk, my body inching away from the water.

The current is soft, the waves kind, but the cold bites hard.

Ahead, Jasmine is once more squealing, water beating up against her chest. Eli's trying to drag her underwater.

I don't understand how it feels so cold. It's supposed to be summer in Australia. But no, Silver Valley is a different world, far out to sea in a climate of its own.

As if some higher power is trying to control the island.

My skin itches at the sinking thought

The cold water licks over me, coating me in salt and sea. I've nearly reached Jasmine and Eli. Both are still half dry and trying to force each other into the water. I glance up at the sun, at the waves, at the world around me, and dive into the ocean.

The cold hits me immediately, but I remain underwater. My toes brush against the sand and the waves push my hair back into a sail. I dart under the waves like I'm flying. We never really visited the ocean when we lived in the city.

Turns out I quite like it.

Is it possible to miss something you've never had?

I spin around underwater, noticing Jasmine's feet near me, and I swim towards her and pinch her ankles. Her feet kick up a storm, dancing in a cyclone of sand, and I emerge from the water gasping for breath.

"Devil!" she shouts upon seeing me.

I open my mouth but can't find the words to defend myself. The sun settles on my shoulders and coaxes warmth back into me, pulling me away from the present. And, as it turns out, I don't have to say anything at all.

Eli uses my distraction to lift her up and drop her into the next wave.

She comes out of the water coughing and laughing all at once.

The other boy is kind enough to lend her a hand.

"T-t-thank you," she chatters.

We don't last long in the water. The waves are soft and roll towards the shore—there's hardly any whitewash, and we float back to the beach along with them.

"Do you guys *ever* get summer here?"

"Yes, of course," Eli says. "Our summers are cooler than yours but can be warmer than this."

"Can be?" I catch on, hesitant.

"Oh, it will be, after this rain. Take my word."

"I mean, it's pretty hot out there today," the tall boy points out, eyes on the promenade.

"Yeah, the ocean feels like a steaming sauna," Jasmine jokes.

Eli pushes her into the next wave.

I try not to laugh and instead help my gasping friend.

"Can we leave now?" the tall boy pleads.

Jasmine squeals and dashes away from Eli. "With pleasure!"

We're nearly back to the shore. Once free of the waves, the warmth hits us again, and it doesn't take long for our teeth to stop chattering.

We stroll towards Henry, who's lounging under the sun and looking very pleased with his choice to stay on the sand.

I lean my head onto Jasmine's shoulder. Her hair is sticky with salt.

"It's a shame not to have you around at school," Eli says to me, taking a seat with us.

I lean against Jasmine.

"Can't say I miss it," I shrug.

Eli reaches his hand out next to mine. It's only then that I realise how close he is.

"Did you receive my texts? I was worried they weren't going through."

I open my mouth and pause, then close it again, embarrassed.

It's true, my phone has been going off, but I haven't been answering it. Mostly, I receive grouchy messages from Jasmine and pleas to hang out from Eli. It became a habit to regard my beeping phone as background noise.

"I—I'm sorry." I wince. "I've been busy."

Jasmine frowns at me. "What have you been doing?"

I clench my hands in the sand, careful not to touch Eli's splayed fingers beside me.

"Schoolwork." My reply is instant. "I don't *go* to school, but I do *have* school."

"Why don't you transfer to Silver Valley High?" Eli asks me.

"I finished grade eleven in the city, and the thought of transferring in my final year seemed pretty rough—my school offers distance education programs and so my younger brother and I decided to follow that. But when I graduate, Mason will probably continue school with the rest of you lot. Makes it easier on my dad that way."

Eli smiles. He's always smiling.

"Well," he says. "I hope you at least have weekends off. Maybe we can get a coffee next Saturday?"

I train my eyes on the horizon, enchanted by the effect the sun has on the water, making it dance like a silver pendant.

I'm hesitant to say yes, but there's no way to turn his offer down without being rude, so I say, "Maybe. I'll let you know."

Jasmine lurches upright. "Hey, we should make it a thing! Cole and I can come, and we can double date."

The other boy smiles, a blush spreading over his cheeks. Cole. It suits him.

I rip my hands out of the sand and pull my knees up towards me.

Eli doesn't look pleased with this idea, but no one is less happy with it than I am. For more reasons than one.

First, I don't want to lead Eli on.

Secondly, Jasmine isn't going to leave me alone anymore, all because I told her about that man in the forest.

"Next Saturday?" Eli asks.

"Next Saturday it is," Jasmine agrees. "You keen, Cole?"

He practically beams at her.

"Thanks for the invite, guys," Henry interjects.

"No problem," Jasmine laughs. "You're invited if Stacy's free."

Henry shrugs. "Sure. Where do you want to meet?"

I resist the urge to groan. Instead, I stand up and make way to leave.

"I'm going to head home," I say. Eli shifts his gaze from Jasmine.

"Want me to walk you back?" he asks. His sweetness makes me feel even guiltier for acting the way I have. But I can't help it.

"No, I got it," I say. "Thanks."

Jasmine leaps up. "Savannah, wait, I'm coming."

I tug on my clothing and grip my arms around me. When Jasmine moves beside me, I try to smile. It feels fake. I feel claustrophobic.

"Next Saturday?" Eli calls after me.

I extend my smile to him. "I'll let you know."

Jasmine grabs my hand, yanking my arms apart. Her eyes settle on me, trapping me in the ocean of her gaze.

"I don't need you to come with me," I tell her. "Have fun with them." I nod back to the beach.

She ignores me and laughs. "You can't get rid of me that easy, Savannah Shaw."

J asmine Spark is the human embodiment of a hawk.

She watches me closer than the forest does. Which is truly saying something as I still don't have curtains.

I spent the whole evening being shadowed in my own home, my best friend plastered to my side like sticky tape. What does she expect? The hooded man in the forest to leap out from under my bed, guns blazing?

As I wander over to bed, yawning, she rummages through my pyjama drawer to get something for herself. By the time I brush my teeth, she has already nestled under my covers.

I wake up with the sunrise. Thank heavens Jasmine sleeps like the dead. My clock ticks away steadily: 08:02.

She usually sets her alarm at 08:45 for school.

The familiar scent of coffee wafts through our halls, my own personal alarm clock. I pad into the kitchen.

"Morning, Dad."

He lifts his head up from the bench, eyes glazed from ruffling through old newspapers. I recognise one from June 23rd, 2015; the headline is about forest preservation.

"Hello, pumpkin. The kettle is still hot if you want coffee."

"Perfect, thank you."

He doesn't lift his eyes from the table. "Any plans for today?"

"Don't know yet. I don't have long until Jasmine wakes up for school, so I might do some work this morning as well."

"She didn't tell you?" my father asks.

"Tell me what?" I wonder.

"She doesn't start school until midday. They're still cleaning, and most first period classes are taken in the flooded sections. They had a lot of reshuffling to do today. Some people get a later start for that reason. Ethan said she didn't shut up about it yesterday."

Add that to the list of things Jasmine doesn't tell me.

"How do you know so much about the school?" I pry. I lean against the counter and sip from my coffee. It scalds my tongue.

He jabs a finger down at the papers in front of him.

I chuckle. "Right. Well, in that case, I might go for a walk before Jasmine wakes up."

I place the coffee on the bench and head for my room. It's too hot to drink yet, and I don't want to waste time.

My father hardly notices me leaving, but he mumbles, "Have fun, pumpkin."

I clasp my fingers around the metal necklace on my bedside table, and quietly latch it around my neck, then retrieve the newspaper from its pathetic hiding spot so Jasmine won't find it when she wakes.

I tread quietly, stepping gingerly upon the floor as I depart. But Jasmine doesn't stir.

The front door quietly hisses shut in my wake, and the cold morning air stings my skin.

I keep my jacket firmly wrapped around me.

It's hard to keep my thoughts at bay—Jasmine, Eli, the man in the forest. My mind is a nightmare, a constant swirling of thoughts.

I promised Jasmine not to go back in the forest. But it's the only place I can find solitude.

I glance back towards the house, take a deep, steadying breath, and sink quietly into the trees. My pace is slow, and I press my lips together, fighting against the uneasiness churning in my chest.

So many secrets.

The trees knot a familiar path ahead of me, and I glance at each one with increased trepidation, a mingling fear of getting lost or getting caught.

It isn't long until my feet remember the vague rhythm of navigating the forest, and I follow my previous path to the clearing.

The day is bright but cold as the sun peers from behind a thin curtain of clouds onto the canopy, not quite touching the fog that travels down the mountains.

I pretend that I'm farther from the house than I actually am. I'm up in the mountains. I'm by myself. No one can find me here.

It works.

I cock my head towards every bird, every rustle of branches. A slow smile builds on my lips. It isn't long until I find my clearing, but it feels like I've been strolling the forest for centuries.

The tree closest to me hangs over the clearing, its leaves making a cavern above me, half hiding the sky.

I take a seat against the trunk, unconcerned with my legs touching the mud. This was the one the man hid behind last time. I draw my knees up to my chest and gaze into the low canopy.

I wonder if he's here.

I check the time on my phone. Its 08:47. I have no new messages.

I put my phone in my pocket and raise my hands to the necklace looped around my neck. My skin has warmed the pendant and the weight of it is oddly soothing.

The quiet brings most of my thoughts to the surface.

I swallow sharply and trace my eyes across the perimeter of trees, wondering if the man in the forest is close.

I want to talk to him. To gain answers. The forest is quiet, and I can't tell if he's here or not.

My phone beeps in my pocket, startling me, and I jump.

"Don't tell me Jasmine's awake."

She isn't. It's my father.

Had to head to the warehouse early, should be back soon. If Mason isn't awake before I get back, remind him he has an online schooling class this morning. Thanks. Dad.

I exhale a shaky breath and put my phone away. I continue to fiddle with the necklace, my shoulders stiff and hunched.

I will never escape the role of being a mother for my brother. The truth that she won't ever come back for Mason hurts. But I don't have long to think about it.

My whole body suddenly goes rigid.

Footsteps.

Coming towards me, from behind the tree. Suddenly, my mind has forgotten all its woes except one.

I'm so close to him. *Too close.*

I don't dare breathe.

The footsteps travel at a gentle pace, as if he's scared to frighten me. I know I should run away, hide in bed with Jasmine, but I don't. I can't shake the feeling that he isn't dangerous.

His presence is noticeable behind the tree. I can feel it wash over me like a cloud, looming ever closer.

I press my back into the bark, determined to keep myself concealed—protected, even though I know he could easily wield a weapon against me in this position. All he'd have to do is reach around the tree.

"Do you follow me because you want to hurt me?" I ask him.

The overwhelming presence of him on the other side of the

tree consumes me. My heartbeat accelerates. I swallow sharply and count my breaths.

"No."

His voice is smooth, but something about his tone sounds off, as if I've offended him.

I'm suddenly aware of nothing else but his heavy presence, the crunch of his feet on the grass, the faint brush of skin on bark.

He moves so quietly it's alarming.

"Can you sit with me?" I ask.

He pauses, as if he knows I'm listening for any sound he makes, and for the shortest moment all I can hear is my own heartbeat thrumming in my ears.

The rustle of clothing breaks the silence. Bark scraping as he leans his back against the other side of the tree. Sitting. Right on the other side.

Silence fills the clearing once more. Neither of us speaks.

We sit here, back-to-back, with nothing but a tree between us.

I have so many questions to ask him, but right now the only sound I hear is the blood pumping through my ears.

Waiting for my heart to calm, I count each beat.

One, two, three, four, five…

Distantly, I pick up on the brush of his arm as he moves. Slowly, like a hunter. The sound of moving grass… fingers running through it.

Six, seven, eight, nine, ten…

I tilt my head down to my lap, expecting a weapon against my head at any moment. But it never comes.

Eleven, twelve, thirteen, fourteen, fifteen…

My heart rate slows when I don't hear him move anymore.

His hands have knotted themselves in the grass on either side of him, his fingers wound around the blades of grass, as if he needs to place them there to steady himself.

I grab a broken branch by my feet and hold it steady. If he moves those hands, this stick is going right through them.

Maybe he's just waiting for the right time to kill me.

I take a deep breath, hoping he doesn't hear the fear in it.

"This…. pendant," I start softly, cautiously. "Something was inside it once?"

He doesn't move his hands from the grass when I speak. I make sure of it.

My hands shake against my will as I wait for his answer, and suddenly breathing becomes difficult again. Confronting my stalker isn't as easy as I'd thought.

"Yes," he answers.

"Do you know what it was?"

"Yes," he says again.

"Can you tell me?" I speak more confidently with each answer I get.

"No."

"Why?"

"I want you to figure it out from the owner."

I memorise each word he says. The way it sounds. The way he speaks. There's a slight accent underneath his words. British? European? I can't tell, it's too subtle. I tighten my hold on the stick, and suddenly my hands aren't shaking anymore.

"I'm figuring it out now," I tell him.

There's a beat. A bird sings in the tree above us. The sun goes behind a cloud.

"Wrong person, princess," he says.

I'm gripping the stick so hard I'm scared it will break.

Maybe I should run. Maybe Jasmine was right.

I pull my knees up to my chest and release the air from my lungs.

"How old are you?" I pry.

The urge to go around the tree and see his face is overwhelming.

I wonder what he looks like. What if I've seen him in the village, but didn't know it?

What if he's Eli, or Cole, or Henry?

But I'm sure I would've recognised his voice. Right?

"Nineteen," he scoffs. No, he's laughing, but trying not to.

At least he's not any of the boys I know. They're all the same age as me. Unless he's lying, but I don't see a reason why he would lie about his age.

I tilt my head back against the tree again and glance up at the leaves. The sunlight comes out from behind a cloud and illuminates them, turning them semi-translucent in yellows and bright greens. I run my eyes over the veins in each leaf, watching the sunlight shift through them.

"I'm seventeen," I answer quietly, feeling it's only fair.

"I know," he replies. He says it softly, and then stammers, "I don't mean... that I know everything about you. In fact, I hardly know anything at all."

Maybe he's catching on to the idea that I consider him a stalker.

My phone chimes, disrupting the quiet of the forest. I knock my head back against the tree in shock.

"Good heavens."

The boy pulls his hands from the ground, and I hear him stand. It must have startled him as well.

It's Jasmine.

Where are you?

My heart speeds up. I've dropped my stick.

The hooded man is standing, and I'm defenceless.

"I have to go," I tell the boy, as if that's an excuse to play fair.

I can't hear him over the sound of blood in my ears.

I stand up cautiously, eyes darting around the trees. Not expecting a reply from the man, I jump when he speaks.

"If you walk to your left, you'll make it out right behind the village bakery. Bring something home from town and no one would guess you were with me."

My heart thumps and my feet are suddenly locked on the ground.

Did the mysterious man notice my fear? Is he *helping me*?

I gauge whether I should listen to him. Could it be a trap?

My phone beeps again and I leap out of my skin.

The sound weakens my resolve and I listen to the man starting to walk out to the right. I don't have any other choices.

But I stop before leaving the clearing.

Should I thank him?

I shake my head. No one thanks a stalker.

But his presence behind me feels oddly suggestive.

My phone continues to beep. I yank it out of my pocket with sweaty hands and finally message Jasmine back.

I'll be back soon.

I raise my head and take a deep breath.

Out of courtesy, I don't turn around to face the man, but I'm acutely aware that he's standing near the perimeter of the clearing.

"So… you're not a threat." It isn't a question.

"No."

I should leave. Now.

"Then stay with me," I say instead.

The man sounds farther away now, but I don't fail to hear his answer.

"Like a shadow."

I smile as I dash towards the bakery.

"Where in *god's* name were you?"

My front door slams from the wind.

Jasmine's blue eyes pierce my soul, and I shiver and head into the lounge room where my father had put a heater on. At least the café by the bakery had a fireplace.

"Coffee?" I ask, giving her one of the lattes in my hands.

She snatches it from me.

"You're covered in mud."

I shrug.

She fixes her attention on the coffee, only mildly irritated. She collapses onto the couch next to my brother and sips it lazily.

I walk over to Mason and hand him his drink.

"Ew?" His eyebrows perch higher up his forehead.

"It's hot chocolate."

He grins and takes it from me.

"Yeah, you're welcome, Savannah. Thanks, Savannah," I mock, rolling my eyes.

He's too busy to listen.

I kick off one of my muddy sneakers and drop it to the floor, dirt crumbling off it. I ignore the mess and work the other one off my foot, determined to get any trace of the forest off me. But it isn't just on my feet.

Mud has smeared on my palms and rubbed onto my jeans from where I was sitting on the forest floor. Brown hair tickles my face as I turn, exasperated.

"Savannah, you're getting mud on the carpet," my father tells me, walking out of the bathroom.

I step off the carpet just as Jasmine turns and faces me. I open my mouth to defend myself, but Mason beats me to it.

"Jasmine, why aren't you in school? I swear you're never in school, or even around it when I'm there."

"Morning off." She puts her cup down on the counter. "And *yes*, I have school. You never see me around the grounds because I've perfected the talent of being the first out of class."

I lean against the window, gritting my teeth.

"You've hung out at school?" I ask my brother.

He shrugs. "Yeah. I'll be going there next year."

"And he hopes he can go this year too," my father calls from the kitchen. "I have half a mind to let him, he's always there with his new friends, anyway."

It irritates me that I don't know any of this.

I've been so caught up in my own problems since arriving here that I've hardly spoken with my father and brother. And compared to Mason, who sends Mum letters every second week, I'm downright awful.

"Who're your new friends?" I ask him.

He speaks between sips of his drink. "Axel and Alexis. They're twins."

"They have flaming red hair," Jasmine says to me, circling her hands around her head, trying to describe their features. "Girl and boy. Their dad owns the post office."

That would explain how Mason met them. His letters.

My father walks out of the kitchen and regards me with distaste. "Savannah, I'd really appreciate it if you didn't get mud all over the furniture," he tells me.

I roll my eyes and pick up my shoes.

Jasmine buries herself beneath a worn blanket she's thrown over hers and Mason's legs. It's our mother's. Tattered and old as it may be, and despite how many times I've thrown it out, it keeps reappearing.

Mason tries to tug it back from Jasmine, his eyes wide. He holds it like it's more precious than gold.

My eyes sting.

He doesn't remember my mother well before the divorce, so he's concocted this idea of an angel figure in his life.

I remember another night in the city when I'd sat by that window where my mother and I watched constellations from, a book about fairies pressed to my face. The sound of my mother's heels had echoed out the door, and Mason had trotted behind her, just a babe.

"Mama, Mama," he had said, dark curls mussed from sleep as he dashed down the corridor in the dark.

I wasn't supposed to be awake that late, so I had slouched against the dark window, my back pressed against the glass. It was hard and cold as ice, and I'd raised my book before me like it could conceal me.

I was only nine.

"What're you doing out of bed? Go away, Mason," my mother had snapped. Her eyes were always clear and sharp as ice, and her voice wasn't much kinder.

I've wondered many times what my sweet father saw in her.

"Can I come on an adventure, Mama?"

My mother had shaken him off and spun on her heel. Her hair was almost silver, but she dyed it dark to match her husband's. Her roots were growing out, and it made her pale forehead look larger in the dark.

"Not this time," she had said. And she had closed the door with a soft click.

As soon as I knew she was gone I had scrambled out of my hiding spot and guided my brother back to bed. There were no tears in his eyes. I thought that peculiar at the time, but now I know why. He thought his mother had given him a promise.

Not this time.

And to this day, he still believes that one day she will take him on one of her adventures.

Not yet. But one day.

I wish Mason would realise it wasn't a promise, but a dismissal.

I gather myself from the lounge room and head towards the bathroom, my stomach churning. Mason hardly notices me leave but I can feel Jasmine watching me from the corner of her eye.

"When do you go to school?" my brother asks her.

She shrugs. "Couple hours."

This gives me an idea.

"Hey, wait for me to finish showering," I tell my brother, knowing he tends to vanish on his own adventures sometimes. "Then we can go and get some brunch down at the promenade before dropping Jasmine off at school? I'd love to meet your friends there."

My father doesn't hear this. He probably wouldn't approve as Mason has an online class this morning. Granted, attendance is optional if the designated coursework for the week is completed. But Mason gets too distracted with his schooling without the weekly check-ups.

High school is hard, he claims.

Jasmine narrows her eyes at me, and I feel insulted that she's not immediately on my side.

She must hate the idea of leaving me alone all day. But I won't be alone, I'll be with my brother.

Mason smiles at me, his face lighting up. "Okay."

I rush into the bathroom. The floor is still wet and slippery from my father, and a cloud of steam fogs up the mirror. I close the door and shimmy out of my dirty clothes so fast that I almost slip.

It doesn't take me long to finish. I rush out the bathroom with a towel around me to discover Jasmine and Mason still arguing over who has more of the blanket. I throw on some tights and a baggy jumper and dash out the room with goosebumps on my arms.

"Hey, Savannah." My father stops me from the kitchen. "Ethan told me he has some more papers to get rid of and was wondering if you'd like to take them off him?"

I divert my attention to my father. His head is tilted towards me, brows scrunched. He pushes his glasses higher up his nose and I smile at him.

"No, thanks," I say. "I don't need any more."

My thoughts flick to the large pile under my bed. All worthless. I've been looking in the wrong places. The man in the forest has answers, and apparently the right newspapers. The necklace sitting warm against my chest also holds more secrets.

"Oh." My father blinks. "Okay."

I make my way to move past him, but he grabs my arm.

"Savannah," he says seriously. "I know you. You're rifling through the papers because you want to find something. Can I ask what?"

I resist the urge to pull away.

"I thought... I thought I'd read up on Silver Valley." He blinks at me as I say it. "I can't say I found any of it too exciting though."

He drops my arm.

"Okay," he mumbles. "That's okay."

He steps away, leaning against the wall as if he doesn't know what to do with himself. It takes him a few moments to recover and then he bustles back to the other end of the house.

"I'll be in my office," he says.

In other words, *please look after your brother while I'm busy.*

Mason snaps some foul words at Jasmine and wins their argument over the blanket. He bundles the rough material into a ball in his lap and shoots her piercing looks. Jasmine smiles, places her hands softly in her lap, and glances at me like nothing has happened while I was gone.

"Ready to go?" I ask them both.

Mason grumbles.

"Of course," Jasmine says. She looks at me warmly and glides off the couch. "I think I might take a day off today. The weather is quite nice."

I glance out the window. I wouldn't say the weather is *nice*. In fact, it's begun to sprinkle with rain while I've been showering, like a soft cascade of mist. The sun blinks at us for the moment, but clouds threaten to stifle it at any moment.

"Jasmine—" I begin.

She holds up a finger as she walks past me. "Don't start. School can deal just fine without me."

"But can you deal just fine without school?" I wonder, following her.

She shrugs. "Basic maths and English essays? Please. The schooling system in Australia could do with an upgrade."

It's true. Jasmine has always received brilliant grades in school. I've always been a little better than her, but that's because I study. She floats by.

I shoulder my complaints and set my jaw.

Whatever.

Mason waits for us in the passenger seat, and Jasmine trots happily to the back. He looks very pleased with himself by the time I start the car.

"Do you think the rain will hold?" I ask Jasmine.

"Nuh-uh," Mason answers instead, pointing at the clouds over our heads. A large, blackened cloud swells in the distance.

"Wonderful."

The rain begins to pick up as I start to roll the car out of the driveway. For once, Jasmine and Mason don't bicker, and everything is silent but the sound of tires over wet gravel and the wipers beating across the windscreen. Jasmine reaches from the back seat and fiddles with the switches on the radio, the speakers blearing to life as I drive down our street.

Mason puts his feet up on the dashboard.

Houses whisper past us. The neighbours with Sadie the labrador have just come back from a morning walk, and the happy pup skips merrily ahead of his owner with a long stick in his mouth. His owner shields his eyes against the rain, wincing.

He's just seen the dark clouds looming overhead.

The news blares on with a report. "Another rainy week is on its way. Tonight should be a wild one, with heavy winds and high swells. I'd recommend everyone stay indoors and wrap up in a toasty blanket. Stay warm, folks!"

Jasmine scrunches her face up at the words.

"Do you think the promenade will even be open?" Mason asks us.

No one responds.

I tighten my hands around the steering wheel as we go through the village. The road is slick and covered in leaves and twigs swept out from the wind, and I keep my eyes ahead of me, doing my best to ignore Jasmine, who keeps sighing from the backseat.

Along the town centre, villagers mill in and out of the coffee shop, carrying brown packages with bread and meat from neighbouring stores, their arms padded in jackets, beanies on their heads and faces ducked from the wind. Most wear gumboots, but only a few carry umbrellas. The weather feels enchantingly cosy, but the constant wailing of the wind and the biting chill still makes me quite averse to it in comparison to the villagers.

"Maybe you should just go to school, Jasmine," I utter. I can feel myself frowning at her, but she pretends not to notice.

My words settle in the air.

She remains silent, bunching her hands into fists in her lap, but as a song comes onto the radio, she retreats into the back of the car and bobs her head along to the music, studiously ignoring me.

We pass the village and begin ascending the hill leading to the beach. With the rain, the forest feels even more dense and overwhelming around us. I grip the wheel harder and lean back in my seat.

"WATCH OUT, STOP!" my brother yells.

My body jolts forwards, foot slamming on the brake.

The car skids.

I shouldn't have braked. The ground is too wet, and the car sails along the road, thankfully not catching the dirt on the edge of the asphalt.

Jasmine cries out and my breath locks in my lungs.

The car stops. Parallel across the road.

The air clatters out of my lungs and my fingers shake on the steering wheel.

"What on *earth*, Mason?" I snap.

Rain cascades over the car, the windscreen wipers pumping and radio screaming. My brother exhales and points at the road in front of us.

A figure stands right by the car, blocking the road.

He wears all black and his gaze pierces into mine.

My hands shake hard. Leaning forwards, I try to make out his features, but he's nothing but a smear behind the rain.

He shakes his head at me and runs back into the forest.

My nerves are on fire now.

"Who's that?" Jasmine asks me. "What happened?"

I'm shaking too much to speak. But Mason isn't.

"Someone jumped out in front of the car."

My hooded man.

"So, are we going to the promenade now or what?" Mason asks. I'm still shivering from the incident, and it takes me a moment to collect myself. *Why did he jump in front of our car?* I bite down on the words, gritting my teeth.

"We're going home," I answer sharply, earning a furrowed brow from Jasmine in response. She shoves her blonde hair behind her ear and glares at me.

My hands grip the wheel tightly, knuckles popping white under my pale fingers. I'm still shaking too much to drive, but I bury my nerves and do it anyway. Thrusting the car into reverse, I straighten up and do a U-turn towards the village.

My brother leans against the dashboard, scanning the trees.

"He went into the forest?" Mason asks. "Why would he do that? It's raining."

Is he following my car? I ask myself instead. Hell, I'm driving slowly. But not slow enough for someone to *follow me*. The hairs on my arms stand on end, just as my hands begin to shake.

"Yeah." Jasmine's tone is accusing. "*Why* would he do that, Savannah?"

I take a deep breath, leaning over the steering wheel. I don't answer.

The green leaves of the trees bordering the forest droop as a cascade of water slides down them. The rain falls onto the canopy and gushes into the dirt below the trees. I try to find the man there, failing to spot him.

Of course he can't follow a car.

I can still feel him watching us as I pull away.

But not for long. As I drive slowly through the village, I feel his presence fading.

He looked so unnatural on the road, blurred behind the rain on our windscreen—dressed all in black, his clothes slick with rain and the hood shadowing his face. I didn't see his eyes, but I can still feel his gaze, piercing me with the force of a thousand swords. He didn't look like any normal villager.

I already know that, but Mason and Jasmine don't.

Their eyes burn holes in my skin, speculating my bizarre response to the man.

Finally, Mason is irritated enough to speak out.

"Can't we at least go *look* at the promenade?" he whines.

"I don't think that's a good idea," I say.

The rain picks up even more. It's battering now.

He frowns at me, his pink lip jutting out as he whips his gaze back to the window.

"Why?" Jasmine butts in.

She knows a lot more than Mason does, probably putting two and two together.

I don't blame her for not trusting the mystery man.

She hasn't met him.

I ignore them both and push the car down our road. The clouds overhead look deadly now, an angry whiplash of dark grey, spinning up a gale around our car.

"I wanted to get food, see the twins and actually *do something* today," Mason continues to complain.

"You can still see the twins after school," I reassure him. "Borrow my phone, it's in the cup holder."

He begrudgingly claims my phone and swipes up. Years ago, I added his face recognition into my phone in case of emergencies.

"So... what are you planning to do now?" Jasmine asks as we pull into the driveway.

"I suppose convincing you to go to school is out of the question?"

"Yup," she agrees.

"Then just have a day at home. Maybe some board games, movies?" I rattle absentmindedly.

Jasmine smirks, leaning back with a glint to her eyes. Of course, she's glad that she'll have me locked up all day.

"Sounds fun," she encourages.

There isn't any doubt in her words.

"Sounds boring," Mason retaliates.

He throws my phone back into the cup holder, grumbling about school. His friends are probably already in their classes.

He waits until the car stops and then quietly slips out, walking up the pavement with his head down against the wind and rain.

I take a deep breath and follow my brother.

I catch him seconds before he reaches the front door. He tries to dodge me, but his energy isn't in it.

"Hey," I say, tugging on him, "You do know I'm not doing this to annoy you, right?"

He grumbles, scrunched eyes darting towards the house.

"I didn't think it was safe, Mason."

"Why?" he snaps. "Because that weird forest person and you have a secret code or something?"

I shake my head. I don't know how to explain.

"I just have a gut feeling," I remark.

"Well, your gut is stupid," he retorts, pulling his arm out of my grip. He yanks the front door open and storms inside.

"Your gut isn't stupid," Jasmine says, coming up behind me. "The fact that you listen to your stalker is stupid."

I clench my jaw and sigh heavily, not for the first time. "I'm not sure he's my stalker, exactly."

Jasmine shrugs. "Your words, not mine."

I should never have told Jasmine about him. I shut the front door, closing us off from the rain. The wind starts to whip like a tornado outside, collecting bits of debris off the ground. My dark hair is dampened by rain, and I use the sleeve of my jumper to dry myself. But it's just as wet as anything else.

I wonder if the hooded man has made it to my house yet.

My teeth start to chatter, the hairs on my arms sticking up more. It's difficult to tell if it's the forest or the man that makes my breath quicken, but my gut drops into my stomach all the same.

He's around me all the time, pressing in, choking me.

I wander to the lounge room window and watch the grey, thunderous clouds pass above the forest.

Of course, Jasmine follows me. She leans against the window frame with her arms crossed, examining my face. I try to school my features, but I don't know exactly what I'm trying to hide.

I search the trees, sweeping over the leaves and the entry I have been taking, overrun with foliage. The wind is sinister, raking through every tree, sending them almost sideways. I remain still, listening for the claps of thunder that never come.

"You're back already," my father announces. He wanders out of his bedroom, a laptop in one hand and a phone in the other. "I wanted to use the car to go back to the warehouse."

He brushes his hand on my forehead, wiping droplets of water off my skin, and smiles as he turns for the door.

I take a step towards him, but Jasmine grabs me.

"Dad, there's a storm coming," I warn him. But he's too lost in thought to listen.

Jasmine snorts and pulls me back. "He'll be okay. At least they have coffee at the *Gazette*."

I shrug her off. "We have coffee here too."

"Calm down, Savannah," she snorts, her lips twitching.

I spin and glare at her, fingers shaking. I work at picking a loose strand out of my clothing to give them something to do and take a deep breath.

My family's safety is *not* a joking matter.

But I swallow the trepidation in my throat and turn away from her.

I wonder where Mason has gone. To do his online class, I hope. My father would be happy with that.

But instead of following up with Mason, like I know my father would expect, I lean against the window beside Jasmine and try not to squirm under her gaze.

"Have you ever been fascinated with the rest of the world and what lies beyond the valley?" I ask her, staring into the depths of the trees.

My question catches Jasmine off guard.

"Have we moved onto the gaming portion of today— twenty questions?"

I ignore her sarcasm. "Everyone's so concerned about the life they know, the people they know, but what of the world beyond that—what of those people?"

Jasmine freezes beside me. "Savannah, you're starting to scare me," she whispers.

I turn and face her. "Why are you so scared of the trees? And why do you never answer me?" I press. "You speak like you know what's there, *who's* there. But you never tell me."

"Savannah…"

"You told me the forest is full of danger and harmful people. You can't possibly mean the terrain is dangerous and the people are from the village."

She shakes her head, shoulders sinking with my every word.

"Why can't you see that I'm trying to protect you?" Jasmine's voice is shallow.

"Protect me?" I hiss through my teeth. "Jasmine, all you're doing is keeping the truth from me. That man in the forest, *he's* protecting me."

"You can't know that," she says.

"Based on recent actions, I can make a damn good guess."

Her hands shake as she traces the window, fingers chipping away at the wood absentmindedly. Her eyes flutter from the trees and back to me. There's history beneath those blue eyes, I can tell. She has all the answers.

"Why do you keep trying to live a different life, when this one is perfectly okay?" she wonders.

Blood roars in my ears as heat climbs my throat. The chills raking across my arms vanish, my skin suddenly feeling hot.

"Dammit, Jasmine." My fingers curl into fists. They clench and unclench as I try and ease the tension out of them. "I never said anything about changing my life. I just want the truth!"

Her watery eyes meet mine. "The truth can kill you."

I should be scared.

I should stop asking.

But this is ridiculous. It's just a bloody forest.

"Curiosity kills the cat, huh?" I say. I hate the sharp edge of my tone, but I can't help it.

My face feels hot as I flatten my hands out in front of me. The last thing I want is to hit my friend.

She arches a blonde eyebrow at me.

Her lies are feeding my curiosity. She's almost encouraging my need to know, instead of squelching it.

"Close enough," she replies in a hushed tone.

She sucks on her lips, her wide mouth disappearing into a thin line.

I look at my friend then—a petite girl with angelic blonde hair and large, fearful eyes. She's a walking newspaper, with pages and pages of information, but she's also just a girl. She's Jasmine Spark.

A slam of thunder rocks our house, piercing our ears. Jasmine screams and covers hers, and suddenly all our lights pop out. Silence follows, then darkness. We stand there panting, refusing to touch each other.

"Savannah, the power's gone!" Mason calls from his room. "This means I have to do my freaking homework."

I should've known he wasn't doing his online class.

He probably hasn't finished any coursework.

"Mason, don't swear," I say. But my voice is quiet. He doesn't hear me.

Jasmine turns to the window, her lips trembling. She gasps, her fingers fidgeting around her throat, and I turn to see what she's looking at.

It's the man. He watches from the perimeter of the trees, dripping with water, like he swam across the ocean fully clothed. I lean closer to the window, wishing I could see his features.

Jasmine grabs me. "Don't," she warns.

My skin pinpricks against the chill once more, sending my body shivering.

I pull my arm back from her. "Jasmine, you're going to tell me what you know, or I *will* get answers myself."

The man hovers at the edge of my vision, as if he's beckoning me. I shove my shaking fingers against my chest, crossing my arms.

Jasmine shakes her head breathlessly, her mouth opening and closing. "You don't know, Savannah… That's such a mistake."

I whip around to her. "Of course I don't know! Dammit, just speak to me, please."

Lightning flares outside, flashing white across my vision before plunging us back into darkness. I wonder if my father is safe inside the warehouse.

I lean against the window as tears start to fall down Jasmine's cheek. She trembles before me, her whole boding shaking. Her raw emotion shakes me.

She's breaking… I'm tearing my friend apart.

I take a step back, my breathing hitching faster and indecision grasping every strand of my mind.

My gaze flicks between her and the man outside. He grips onto a tree to stop from blowing over in the wind. Watching him out in the torrential weather, I almost fear for his life.

Habitually, I reach for the necklace he gave me. It rests warmly on my chest under my jumper. Jasmine's eyes follow my movement.

The hooded man also sees.

I feel every stare pinned onto my person, as if the world is tilting in slow motion as I slowly free the pendant. I pull it from my chest and wave it at the man tauntingly, resisting the urge to roll my eyes at the stupid little challenge he set for me, but the moment it's freed from my jumper, Jasmine gasps in shock, and the man is forgotten.

Her eyes are pinned to the silver chain. The world stops around me. All I can focus on is my friend.

Her blue eyes grow even wider.

Her pink mouth pops open and all at once her tears stop.

"Where'd you find that?"

I turn to face her and find recognition on her features. Incredulous, I frown at my friend.

"You know who it belongs to?"

Fear. Complete and utter fear swims on her face. "Yes," she exhales.

Her word hangs in the darkness.

"Who?" I press.

I can't take my eyes off her, for fear I might miss some of the truth.

Her shoulders shake and she wraps her arms around herself.

"Jasmine, who?"

I touch her shoulders lightly and she recoils.

Tightness swims in my chest, and my head begins to pound as

the blood rushes back into my ears. Voice deepening in frustration, I grab her shoulders again. "Who, Jasmine? Tell me!"

She shakes her head, tears splattering down her cheeks and onto the floor, each drop falling soundlessly in rapid succession.

When will I stop making my friend cry?

"No," she breathes. "No, no."

I lower my hands. Her eyes are pinned on the necklace.

"I blame the boy," she mumbles. "And I blame the whole universe above. Savannah, please don't leave me. I changed my mind."

I wish I understood what she was asking.

I snap the necklace off my neck and hand it to her. She grasps it like its poison.

Another loud clap sounds outside, accompanied by blinding light. All the breath escapes my lungs and I stumble, fingers grasping for the window in support.

Jasmine grabs her ears.

The whole world goes white, and when the light clears, the absence of thunder continues to ring in my ears, leaving me spinning.

I almost don't hear the crunching sound from the forest until Jasmine grabs my arm.

Outside, a tall tree snaps.

Falling.

Towards us.

My body stiffens. Mason. Jasmine. Will it hit them?

I grab Jasmine and yank her away from the window. My leg slams into the couch as she squeals. The tree pounds into the earth, its leaves scraping the window.

I exhale, but my heart continues to race. The tree missed us by mere inches, crunching onto the ground right outside our house.

Right where the man was standing.

"Is he safe?" I gasp at Jasmine, my fingers scrambling for the window. "Did you see?"

My heart beats chaotically in my chest as I scan the terrain outside of the window.

She shakes her head soundlessly, too shocked to speak.

I pull away from her and race to open the front door. Slowly, she registers what I'm doing. It takes her a moment before she picks up her feet, gingerly walking behind me.

"Where are you going?" she demands.

"We have to save him," I say, forcing a shoe onto my foot.

My fingers shake, making it difficult to tie the laces. I almost fall over in my haste.

She grabs my arm, nails biting into my skin. "Are you mad?"

I tug free and glower at her.

The wind pummels us through the entryway, the rain slicing over my exposed flesh. My hair's still wet from earlier, so I ignore the sheet of rain sweeping in.

"I have to go."

"Don't." She reaches for me, breathless.

I plunge into the rain, her fingers barely brushing my jumper.

She follows me for a moment but stops on the steps as my feet sink into the wet grass. I look back at her. A broken girl, a house covered in debris, a rose garden stripped and dead in the rain.

She rakes her fingers through her bushy hair, her round cheeks splotchy and red, fresh tears mingling with the rain battering her face. She holds her pale hand against it; short nails curled like claws as panic flashes through her ocean eyes. I can spot a world of knowledge behind her eyes, but only because I know her well. To anyone else, she would look nothing but broken.

It's enough to make me pause.

"I have to save him." *Please understand that.*

"Your stalker!" she hisses.

I watch her claws tremble and curl into small fists, but her anger only fuels mine. "No," I snap. "My protector."

"No stranger would protect you. Only those who care about you can do that."

I clench and unclench my fingers, my breaths coming short and fast. All my pent-up frustration lashes like a cracking dam.

All these secrets.

All these lies.

I'm *done*.

"But you really don't care about me *that* much, do you, Jasmine?"

She opens her mouth to reply, but her eyes are rimmed red with pain, and she sinks onto the porch, unable to defend herself. She averts her eyes, slumping against the steps, her pink face turning ashen in the rain.

"No best friend lies as much as you do."

She grips her chest, the necklace still wound through her fingers.

I turn away from her. "*Don't* follow me."

For the first time, Jasmine Spark listens. I don't know if it's my anger or her sadness, but she doesn't muster the strength to rise from the ground.

My ears are still ringing from the thunder when she calls after me, saying my name, over and over.

"Savannah. Savannah! Come back, please."

Ever so faintly, I hear her next words.

"Sav… the necklace is mine."

But I don't turn back. I step into the forest, and I leave my best friend crying on the steps.

PART TWO

THE NEW WORLD

T he storm roars around me like hellfire.

But I only have one goal in mind. Save the man.

My fingers work through the foliage, pulling apart branches from the fallen tree in order to enter the forest. They scrape my skin as I work my way through, and I break into the forest with scratches on my arms. The tree flattened a lot of the terrain around it, but it's hard to tell the tree from the surrounding debris.

"Savannah!"

I take a deep, calming breath.

Her voice is barely audible over the storm. She must still be on the stairs out the front of the house, blonde hair plastered to her skin. A pale angel drowning in the rain.

But her confession isn't enough to make me return. She said what she did solely out of desperation—I will not delude myself into believing she's finally willing to offer answers.

"Please, Savannah!"

Gritting my teeth, I head towards where the hooded man had been standing.

The fallen tree is massive—one of the larger pines—and I can't see where the man would've stood from this side of it. I debate walking around the tree but that could take too long, so instead I grab onto some branches and pull myself over the trunk, hands shaking in the cold.

The rain makes it hard to scale. I place one foot between the network of branches and locate my next handhold, my fingers wet and dirty. Heart pounding, I yank myself up. The wind suddenly shifts and slams into me, and I lose my balance, rain gushing into my face.

My hands slip off the trunk.

I scramble for grip.

But my foot loses traction and I'm too slow.

My ankle twists to the side at the sudden movement and a burning lance makes my foot throb as it impacts the earth. I scream, but the sound is lost in the wind.

Collapsing into the mud and grass, I sit still for a moment, pained and confused. My fingers flutter over the tender spot, shaking against the cold. I rotate my foot and the movement catches the sore point, darting up my leg. The ankle moves stiffly, throbbing at the action.

A sprain, I'd wager, but I force myself to ignore it and push on. At least I've made it over the tree. I trace my hand along the trunk, using it as a guide into the forest. The rain pools around my feet, causing small landslides in the mud. But I hold steadily onto the trunk, knuckles turning white.

My eyes rake the ground, searching for a lump of familiar black clothing.

The tree fell on him, right?

He was here. He was standing right here.

I continue faster now, my feet slapping the mud, the sore ankle screaming in protest. I find the place where the tree snapped, and I keep walking, favouring my good foot. Onwards. Towards the only other place he might be.

A wild urge to scream chokes me, but I don't make a sound. The forest is loud anyway and would block it all out.

There's no way Jasmine could find me now.

Somewhere above, a large branch snaps. I gasp and dart aside, and it topples beside me, leaves whipping in the gust. I hug my chest and continue on the vaguely familiar path.

My jumper is sodden, chilling me to the bone.

My teeth chatter uncontrollably, skin turning to ice as the rain soaks through my clothes. But it's my ankle that distracts me the most—it feels unsteady on the ground, the sharp bite of pain travelling up my leg with every step.

I grit my teeth and push onwards.

Maybe he made it out alive. I need to believe that. Otherwise, this would be futile.

I grip onto a tree branch to bat it out of the way and water cascades down on me. It hardly makes a difference. My clothes are plastered to my skin, and I wish I wore more layers. Or better yet, a rain jacket.

Rain jackets are severely underrated.

I scale some more fallen branches. The wet bark rubs off the old trunks and sticks all over my skin, but the rain washes the debris off me instantly.

My sprained ankle yells with every step as I slip in the mud, but the other is firm, carrying me on. I set one foot after the other with purpose, hands grabbing and pulling at trees.

I'm close to the clearing. Even in the storm, I can't mistake it.

"Hello?" I call out.

My voice is hoarse and unsure.

The clearing parts for me and I slow down, feet pressing the once lush grass into a brown, matted blanket. No one is here. *He's not here.*

I'm utterly, perilously, alone.

I fall backwards against the tree, gripping my skull.

The clearing is empty and hazardous. The wind shrieks through the canopy like a snapping flag.

Everything's grey and angry.

No matter what path I chose in life, I always end up alone and in pain. My heart cracks at the still-vivid memory of my mother abandoning me, and a sudden sob rips from my chest. I try my best to forget her, but sometimes it's difficult.

Jasmine, my mother, my stalker… they all leave me in the end.

I cannot rely on anyone but myself. And it's so lonely.

I wrap my arms around my chest, trying to control the shivers rattling up and down my body. I'm a foreign entity out here; I don't belong.

The wind presses the trees into me—the once magical and enchanting place now threatening to suffocate me like a cage. I slide down the tree trunk, ripping my clothes, and curl into a ball at the base of the tree.

I grip myself so tightly, my muscles strain and the shivers slow. I try to hold the cold away from me, steeling myself. Eventually, the shaking stops until I'm still and solid on the ground, surrounded by a raging forest.

Maybe, just maybe, Jasmine was right, and I am stupid. This is so stupid. Curiosity killed the cat.

But just as I begin to think this, I hear him.

My whole body loosens. The shivering returns. And even over the wind, the rain, the clapping thunder, I can hear the splash of his footfalls in the mud.

"Sav… Savannah?"

Slowly, I look up.

Curiosity killed the cat, but satisfaction brought it back.

He stands by the edge of the clearing.

Only… it isn't him.

Instead, I see a ghost.

Or at least, what looks like a ghost. A girl stands entirely still in the downpour, light-brown hair plastered to her face, pale white against the stark forest. She's dressed like a medieval warrior, wearing what looks like a simple, old-fashioned white dress held tightly to her waist by a thick brown belt and one glove that runs up to her elbow, the fingers cut off. Her dress clings to her body, the water running down the fabric, pattering against her leather boots.

My blood runs cold at the sight of her. The moment our eyes make contact, I'm filled with a choking sense of otherness. I focus on my breathing, mind spinning at how the sight of her fits in so perfectly with the magical feel of the forest. Whatever dangers reside within the trees, she is one with it.

I don't know her, nor do I think I want to.

I feel the blood draining from my face. My arms shake as I pull them out from my body, searching for a branch to protect myself. My fingers land on a sharp piece of wood and I level it at the girl before me.

She holds her hand on her chest as she watches me, mouth slightly parted, her perfect brows furrowed.

I don't shift a muscle, watching for her next move. Tentatively, she places a foot in the clearing.

"Don't," I warn.

She does anyway. The petite girl wanders across the grass and kneels before me. I balance the sharp end of my branch at her chest.

She looks young and old at the same time. Her skin is perfect, smoother and more unblemished than anything I've ever seen. But it's her eyes that strike me as the most peculiar.

They're bright silver.

Not grey, like mine. But as clear and startling as molten metal.

She doesn't look… human.

She reaches out, placing a gentle palm over the hand latched to my stick, raising her voice over the wind. "Savannah Shaw?"

My breath heaves in and out. Her hand feels hot on mine, and it's enough to make me hesitate, soaking up her warmth. I tilt my head towards her and stare deeply into her terrifying eyes.

I yank my arm back sharply, making her drop her grip.

"What're you doing in my clearing?" I demand.

She stares at me, her small mouth a thin line.

The wind slams into her, but it doesn't jostle her form at all. She rocks back on her heels and a smile quirks the corner of her mouth—such a knowing look on such a tiny girl.

I sweep my eyes around the clearing, and finally, *finally*, my eyes land on the person I've been searching for.

My hooded man.

The girl was never alone.

He looks the same as he did when standing by the edge of the forest, except for the confidence. He walks up to me with conviction. For the first time, he doesn't hide his face, doesn't care if I see him.

From up close, I notice his black jacket is actually a dark blue.

It's almost enough to make me smile.

Until he glares at me.

He doesn't kneel with the girl, but stands behind her, guarding her. I notice his hand slip next to his belt. A silver flash. A knife.

He thinks *I'm* the threat?

"You were supposed to keep a better eye on her," she tells him without turning her head. Her voice is stronger than the wind.

"I was. It's not my fault she's an idiot," the man says.

I grip my branch in both hands and squint at his knife. There's no telling how many more weapons he has. This piece of wood is hardly appropriate. And yet, I spin it around my fingers menacingly.

The man watches it slide around my pale fingers with an unreadable expression. I wait for him to make a move, but he doesn't.

"I'm not the one who nearly died," I retaliate, voice steady despite my chattering teeth.

His dark eyes pierce my soul, and I tremble slightly. Every nerve in my body burns with awareness, but instead of glaring back, I loosen my features and smile.

He cocks a dark eyebrow at me. They slash low above his eyes, stark against his white skin, which looks as flawless and unblemished as the girl beside him, save for the faint stumble at his jaw. He's beautiful, in a terrifying sort of way—all sharp angles and angry features. He clenches his hand around the knife, and I swallow at the way his muscles move.

This isn't a man I could beat in combat.

But I raise my brow back at him, putting on the act that I *could* if I wanted to.

They both watch me quizzically.

I must be a vision, splattered in mud and sprawled across the grass, trying to threaten *them* with my pathetic excuse of a weapon. But they don't call me out on it. Rather, the girl watches me with a slight air of approval.

The hooded man slides his blade into a hidden pocket inside his clothing. "And yet," he says, "you're the one who looks like death."

I set my jaw.

To prove him wrong, I unlock my arms and stand. He tilts his head at me, brown hair dripping with fat drops of water. His stance should have me worried—I can already tell he's some sort of mercenary—but I don't falter. My stiff muscles refuse to unlock, and my ankle throbs under the sudden weight as I lift myself up. But I keep my gaze high, my face blank.

"Thanks for that clarification."

The man glares at me. I make sure my entire body is focused on his stance, his deft hands, and the way he angles himself towards me. But he doesn't even twitch under my analysis.

"We should go," the girl interrupts, "before someone *does* die."

I blink. Go? With them?

I take a step back. My sprained ankle hits the mud and slides a fraction across the grass, and I wince. Quickly, I even out my expression.

Don't let them see your weakness.

But the girl's silver eyes dart to my feet, and she waits for an explanation. I take a deep breath and set my shoulders.

Don't let them know your ankle is affecting you.

"The tree that almost squashed my dear stalker here," I explain flippantly. "…I twisted my ankle a little."

"How heroic," the man says.

The girl shoots him a glare. "Jesse, quiet."

Jesse.

The air rushes from my lungs.

His eyes shift towards me, and this time I spot a flicker of curiosity cross his face.

What a besotting notion.

I finger the naked flesh of my neck where the chain once sat, fingers tracing my collar, watching his eyes follow me. My heart begins to thrum when I realise how close I am and how much I don't have to risk anymore, just to ask the right people one very simple question.

"Answers," I demand. "Can you give me answers?"

"Is that why you ran away?" Jesse jests.

"I didn't run away," I snap. "I tried to save you."

The girl holds a hand out to him, causing him to still. I think I see him twisting the blade in his palm again.

"I'm Melanie Beckett," the girl intervenes, "and this is Jesse Hayes. We met on a voyage to the island many years ago."

I furrow my brows, mind stumbling over the words. Another non-answer. She sighs when she sees the stiffness of my shoulders.

The wind starts to subside, and I can hear her words better as she says, "Okay, here's the truth."

My breath hitches at that, but it doesn't matter. I can hardly breathe anyway. My chest feels so tight.

"The truth is, our society is decaying, both on the island and… interstellar." She licks her lips, shaking her head. "It was never my intention to hurt you, Savannah, and now that I've found you, I simply cannot leave and allow you to walk blindly into danger. I believe many other people are about to discover your identity, as I have done. So, please, let us get you out of this rain."

"Interstellar?" I press, grasping at her words as they vanish in the wind.

I gaze into the canopy above me, remembering my mother. I pull my mind past the rolling thunder, the dark clouds, and imagine the stars beyond, the constellations hidden behind them. The memory is a stain on the back of my eyelids.

"Will you follow us?" Jesse asks.

They know what Jasmine knows—maybe even more than that. Hidden within the words she said, there are clues.

Something rings loudly inside me. I squeeze my eyes shut and breathe deeply.

If I leave, Mason will think I got lost in the storm. But I can't ignore this.

So against my better judgement, I open my eyes, nod my head at him and say, "Like a shadow."

And for the first time, Jesse Hayes smiles at me.

I've never been this far into the forest.

Maybe it's my imagination, but it feels wilder out here. Deadlier. With each step I take away from the village, I stumble closer to danger. I have no control here, not anymore.

"Careful on that decline," Melanie advises.

I shuffle downwards, feeling my feet slide on the loose terrain. Melanie's fingers brush my shoulder to steady me.

We've been walking for hours, cresting the summit above the valley, and then clambering back down the other side. The rain has drenched every crevice of the forest, making every leaf look like it's crying. But at least the downpour has stopped. The clouds continue to rumble above, but they're more fractured, producing glints of sunlight behind them.

"I got it," I tell Melanie, brushing her off.

She takes a step back, raising her hands in surrender, one hand exposed and the other gloved.

The forest floor flattens, but the surface is ridged, and the terrain is bumpy under our feet. Through the canopy, I can spot another large summit ahead and my twisted ankle groans at the thought.

It's occurred to me that hiking on a swollen ankle is *not* something you should do—especially after a storm.

So, I avoid looking at the looming hill.

Each time my foot hits the ground, a blaze of fire lashes up my leg, searing my muscles. I use most of my focus on how to place my sore ankle on the ground to minimise the pain as much as possible.

Melanie keeps glancing at it, but I never catch her blatantly staring. She seems to have perfected the act of hidden observation. Perhaps everyone on the opposite side of the island has. It sends shivers down my spine, knowing I'm being watched, but having no clear evidence of it.

Now and then I sense Jesse wanting to offer me a hand, his palms fluttering by my side, but I never accept his help. Eventually he stops offering, and I wonder if he ever intended to offer me a hand at all, or if I imagined it.

Walking through the forest has never been so unpleasant. We continuously climb over debris, kick it aside or pull sopping tangles of it out of our way. When we do, the mud and water threaten to trip us. My legs buckle, bend, and slide all over the place. A steady burn had begun working up my body moments after beginning the climb on the first hill, and now it's utterly aching. I inhale sharply with each breath. *Come on, Savannah. It's just walking a mountain. You can do this.*

"How much farther?" I ask Melanie, since she appears to be the one leading us.

Jesse answers me sharply. "Just shut up and walk."

Melanie tries to keep a smile off her face.

We met on a voyage to the island many years ago.

I'm betting they're lifelong friends. When Melanie moves, Jesse moves, echoing each other's thoughts and intentions with perfect accuracy.

It's almost like watching how I used to be with Jasmine. That is… until we came to Silver Valley.

The beginning of the end.

I pull myself up with a branch, and soon our feet begin to hit the incline of the next mountain. Melanie keeps us to the side of the crest, as if she's slowly working us towards the western beaches on the island, and not to the summit.

I trace Melanie's profile out of the corner of my eyes. Raindrops scatter down her soft honey-coloured hair, pattering onto her shoulder. The rain has passed over the forest, but Melanie's hair continues to rain. Drip after drip.

While I walk, I secure images of snowy glaciers in my head, and tell myself I'm lucky. This is only a small mountain.

I take steadying breaths. *Just fifteen more steps… now ten more… five more… now fifteen again…*

"Farther right," Jesse whispers from behind me, words meant for Melanie.

I shiver as his breath strokes my back, and Melanie lures us towards the right.

Ten more steps… five more… now fifteen again…

Despite the cold, I'm sweating.

Isn't that how hypothermia starts? I stroke my arms, easing some warmth into my skin. I haven't brought anything with me from home except for the clothes on my body and my worn, white sneakers that squelch with every step.

My eyes dart around the trees, stroking the patterns in the leaves, finding safe handholds to pull myself forward with.

Ten more steps… ten more…

Now five… five more…

My feet find an area upon a rock with a smooth surface. I take a deep breath.

There, you've made it. Come on now, another fifteen steps…

Sweet hell, I really hate hiking.

"You okay, Savannah?" Melanie asks.

"Superb."

I step around a mud puddle and latch my eyes onto the top of the mountain. It's closer than I thought.

The musky smell of the forest returns in greater strength with the end of the storm, and the surrounding animals begin to scuttle out of their hiding holes, basking in the small streaks of sunlight. I let my mind drift with the buzz of birds and tilt my head up to the sky. My feet continue to pound, but the promise of nearing the top of the mountain makes it significantly easier to ignore the blaring pain in my ankle.

I risk a peek backwards and notice I can almost see the promenade from here.

I feel Jesse and Melanie slow down around me, and I do the same. Leaning to see the village, I almost don't realise where we are.

We've made it to the top.

I've done it.

Pride rushes through me and I almost forget the pain in my ankle.

Knees trembling, I turn around and take in the view. Silver Valley is hidden, lost in the wilderness. It's easy to pretend it isn't even there. The only thing still visible is the small cove—the sand bright and stark against the sea and treeline. The promenade peeks out behind the hilly landscape; just a small lip of wood slashed across the sand.

Jesse tugs on my arm impatiently and I sigh deeply, following them downhill. The decline feels like a blessing. I savour the speed at which I race down the earth, my ankle singing with each footfall.

The rest of the forest coils out like a lush green blanket ahead of me.

It's so beautiful.

But I hardly have time to take it in before the forest takes the view from sight.

I continue to focus on my footfalls, but realise the decline makes our footing sharper and harder with the velocity, and my ankle becomes distressed at the growing speed of our gait.

I try to distract myself again.

"Jesse." I whisper his name, almost in question.

I don't hear his reaction or see it, but I can feel his hesitation behind me. The quiet hangs in the air, and his name echoes in my head. *Jesse, Jesse, Jesse.* "Did you intend for me to get that newspaper?"

The thump of our feet and the soft patter of water falling from leaves fill the momentary silence.

"Obviously," he finally says, voice low and hesitant.

"Can I have the rest of it?"

Melanie looks at me as we speak but remains silent.

"Whatever you want, princess." His tone is heavy with sarcasm.

"Jasmine might find the piece you gave me," I say, ignoring the malice. I left them in my muddy clothes from this morning.

"That doesn't matter," Melanie intercepts, expecting a rude remark from her friend. He inhales deeply, shrugging it off.

Tightness swells in my chest and I release a strained breath. I want to slap the answers from him.

"Can you tell me why you did it?" I press.

He doesn't answer. Maybe he feels uncomfortable being so directly addressed after weeks of hiding in the dark.

Or maybe he simply never cared for me at all.

Melanie gives him a side-long look.

"You wanted answers, didn't you?" he says half-heartedly. "I assumed if you discovered answers to questions yourself, you'd be more likely to accept them, instead of having answers thrown at you all at once."

I digest this for a moment and realise he's right. I'm reminded of my mother. The harsh reality of the days she left would always knock the breath out of me, causing me to sink in denial.

But had I discovered the truth earlier, I might have paid more attention to the smaller things—the day she began keeping her clothes in a suitcase, or the way my father would always glance at her with tears in his eyes. Perhaps I might have picked up on how she spoke about the stars, lusting for adventure more than the security of home. In those instances, the impact of the truth might have been less significant.

Instead, the truth crept up on me slowly.

In a way, anyone might've guessed the truth all along.

"How did you know the necklace was Jasmine's?" I ask him.

He picks up his speed to walk beside me, muscles tight and his hand on his belt. The sensation is uncanny. My hooded man, who once hid in the shadows, now walks beside me.

"I didn't. I'm the beauty, not the brains."

Melanie rolls her eyes. "I did some digging, then one day I found the necklace and traced it to Jasmine, which then led us to you. That's how I found you. Jasmine possibly used this necklace—or specifically, what was in it—on you. I have several guesses as to what it was used for, but it's about as much a mystery to you as it is to us."

I shiver, clutching my arms over my chest.

She used the necklace… on me?

"Do you know what was inside the necklace? Or do you have any guesses?"

She shrugs, the question obviously troubling her, and picks up her speed a little.

"A stone not from Terra—Earth. They're quite… rare. You need to find someone to power the stone, for instance. There's only one person to date who had the ability to do so, and she's dead."

Not from Earth.

Interstellar.

"I'm sorry, what?" I blanch. "Are you guys… astronauts?"

Jesse chokes next to me, trying to cover a laugh with a cough.

I flash him a glare.

"We stem from an alien race," Melanie elaborates. "But it's a long story."

Aliens.

I track my fingers across my arm, rubbing the puckered skin under my jumper. It would explain their pale, ageless complexion—like a grown person fresh from their mother's womb. Is that an alien thing?

I blink rapidly, staring at them with a shake of my head.

"But lucky for you, Silver Magic doesn't work on Terra, so we are exceptionally ordinary," Jesse winks.

Magic?

I scratch a spot on my arm, nausea churning in my gut. These people… this forest… is filled with magical aliens?

And Jasmine has gone off this planet to obtain one of their magical stones, or gotten it from one of the aliens in the forest?

My body trembles.

Surely, she hasn't.

She's *Jasmine*.

Jesse watches me, his gaze deep and piercing. A hint of amusement dances across his face. "I suppose I was correct in assuming too many answers at once would blow up your little human brain."

Human. Alien.

Jasmine.

I bite my lip. Of course, it's silly to assume that humans are the only species in this universe, but the fact that aliens might really exist coats my tongue with acid. I haven't eaten anything today except a coffee, and nausea rolls in my stomach, threatening to choke me.

I stare openly at the people—aliens—before me and take a shaky breath.

"Oh, leave her alone, Jesse," Mel says from ahead of us. She lifts a branch out of the way and releases it into his face.

I jump at the sound, inching away from them.

Slapping the wet leaves out of his eyes, Jesse snidely remarks, "I'm being nothing if not a gracious host."

Brain a spinning mess, I enquire cautiously, "The person who powered her stone... who is she?"

Jesse wipes water from his face, fuming, and Melanie jumps in again before he opens his mouth, not turning around to face me when she speaks.

"Lythia May."

I remove my arms from my chest, catching a branch before me as I miss a step on the bumpy forest floor.

Good gracious. "Lythia May and the seventh Elder."

I step around the particularly large branch, holding it away from me.

"Holy stars, she remembers," Jesse comments.

I let the branch go, hitting him clean in the gut.

He chokes back a gasp and blinks at me. I glance at him, trying not to smile as I trot ahead.

"*Daughter* of the seventh Elder," Melanie corrects, her eyes twitching as if she wants to comment on my behaviour... until realising she did the exact same thing moments before. Granted, she only threw leaves into his face. But still. I try to keep my satisfied smile from widening as she continues. "She was quite remarkable, or so I've heard. But she didn't have kids. No direct descendants."

"Bummer," Jesse says wistfully, rubbing his stomach clean from the branch. "I heard she was a pretty girl."

"Pretty *woman*, Jesse," Melanie retorts. "She was a woman, and I doubt she would've been interested in you."

"Ouch, Mel. You underestimate me."

She rolls her eyes.

I don't particularly care for their banter, focusing instead on the sounds of the ocean rumbling in the distance. I hold another branch aside for Jesse, eyes on the horizon, and he has the nerve to shoot me his middle finger before taking the other route around the tree.

Whatever. I snap the branch back and continue.

Melanie scales a pile of debris ahead and reaches back to offer me a hand. Foot already on the edge of the pile, I ignore her, and she quickly withdraws her arm. Jesse watches me stumble across the loose leaves with raised eyebrows. It takes all my attention to focus on my footfalls and arranging my screaming ankle in a precise manner. Jesse's intense stare only makes it harder to concentrate.

By the time I make it to the other side, I almost feel like applauding myself.

Melanie takes the lead again, weaving down towards what appears to be the western edge of the island. My ankle continues to slow our pace, but no one says anything. We just glide through the forest in silence.

The valley feels so far behind me.

I doubt I'd ever be able to find my way back alone.

I bound down another small hill, enjoying how the leaves and mud slip under my heavy footfalls, and try not to think about it. No matter how difficult the terrain is to traverse, I don't stop, mostly out of fear that I wouldn't be able to keep going if I did.

"We're not actually flying to space today, are we?" I ask them sarcastically, not quite believing it to be a possibility. But the moment the words leave my mouth, my breath starts to quicken at the thought.

Melanie glances back at me, her eyes scrunched. *Trying not to laugh.*

"Oh, stars, no. We're taking you to the village over." She holds aside another branch for me, and I slip under it.

Jesse walks around the tree instead.

The village over.

"I wasn't aware there was another village." A swarm of murderous people—aliens?—lurking in the forest, maybe. But not a *village.*

A whole *horde* of them.

"Good," Jesse mumbles, as if that secrecy is the whole point.

"It's been concealed for too long," Melanie continues. "It's under threat of being cut off completely."

I shake my head, resisting the urge to rub at the headache forming at my temples. I lick my lips. "I don't understand."

"The history will be easier to explain once we arrive, but if you don't want to stay after that, I'll take you back home," Melanie tells me. "You have my word."

I swallow, trying to get moisture back into my mouth before I ask, "But why? What's it to you, my mindless curiosity?"

"It's everything to me," she says. "And it's hardly mindless curiosity. You would've ended up here eventually, I have no doubt about it. No one could've hidden this from you forever."

Jasmine did.

Or tried to.

I grit my teeth, trying not to gnaw on the inside of my mouth. My palms are sweaty, fear a constant trickle down my spine. I make the decision to stop talking, not even sure at this point if I can bring myself to speak anymore. Words churn like butter in my brain.

The slope downhill begins to even out once more, and soon we're walking on flat terrain. I wonder how far we've walked—if the screaming tendrils of pain in my ankle are any indication, it's been quite a while.

The ocean whistles loudly ahead of us. I doubt we've covered the entire island; it's just a matter of how far we've travelled down the perimeter of it. Silver Valley was north and I have no idea what's south. We are west.

"Everyone will be none the wiser should you choose to leave, we can assure that," Melanie continues. "And I don't mind what you choose. Sure, I have preferences, but it's your choice after all. It's better to make a choice knowing the truth than not knowing anything at all."

"You're too freaking nice, Mel. Ease up," Jesse remarks.

"I don't believe being too kind is a thing."

He snorts. "Yeah, you do."

Something reflects on Melanie's face—a memory—and she laughs. Jesse remains impossible to read.

I can't tell if he was joking, and I don't know whether to be scared or not.

The sound of the ocean encircles me, and the dirt beneath our feet grows speckled with sand. We walk out of the forest to where the trees meet the beach.

The sand's wet surface has hardened into a crust, and it crunches beneath my feet as we walk. The waves near the village are usually gentle, but here the tides are rough from the storm. I hesitate as I walk onto the beach. Melanie and Jesse lead the way, undaunted.

I cross my arms, placing my hands on my shoulders.

"I think I left it here somewhere," Melanie's saying to Jesse.

She wanders along the sand, eyes scanning the tree line. Jesse follows, his face hard.

"If you've hurt her, I swear on the stars I'll—"

"Calm down, she's fine."

Melanie continues to eye the trees, searching for whoever is hiding here. I keep my eyes on Jesse's hands, making sure they stay well away from his knives.

I limp hopelessly after them. My heart's pounding, sending jolts shooting down to my ankle and up again. My body seems to be giving up on me slowly. I truly hope we're close to their village.

We're so far away from home.

I bite my lip at the thought of Mason doing schoolwork in his room, waiting out the rain. He would've loved to explore the rest of the forest with me, always up for an adventure, our mum's faraway look constantly reflected behind his wide eyes. He's a dreamer, and I feel like I'm living in his dreams.

I didn't even say goodbye to him.

My hands start trembling again.

I wonder what Jasmine would tell him about me? What sane

person launches into a storm, headfirst into a forest of falling trees? How will Jasmine clarify that?

And then there's…

"My dad," I whisper, not realising I've spoken out loud until the words escape my mouth.

"He made it to the warehouse," Jesse says quietly in front of me. The nicest thing he's said to me.

I exhale deeply.

It's now up to Jasmine to look after them until I return.

"You stopped me from going to the beach," I say to Jesse. "Because you knew it was dangerous to be by the water during the storm."

"Obviously," he says.

It wasn't really a question.

He keeps his eyes ahead, watching Melanie. I'm practically forced to run to keep up with them. My ankle blazes with every step.

"Thank you," I reply softly. I mean it.

I may have still been safe on the beach, but with the weather picking up as it had, it would've been safer to be home. The fact he didn't want to take the risk says more about what he thinks of me than words do.

I grit my teeth against a smile as we move closer to the trees again, where the sand isn't as firm beneath my footfalls.

I feel his eyes on me before I turn.

He's stopped walking, dark blue eyes locked on my ankle. It occurs to me that this man has been watching me for quite a while now. He's used to it—it's how he tries to understand me.

I hate it.

Pain lashes me, but I walk faster and faster, gritting my teeth with every step until I'm right beside Melanie.

These people are strangers, and Jesse has a belt of knives.

I can't let them see any weakness.

Melanie suddenly stops before me, her eyes bright, lips tilted.

She brushes her wet hair out of her face and waves her hands out towards the trees, as if declaring something. Her hair begins to dry around her face, and it lightens to a soft brown—almost a dark blonde.

I'm so busy watching Melanie that I don't notice Jesse dashing past me. Excitedly, he pulls something out of the trees.

Not a person, a vehicle. I take a step back.

It's like a small terrain rover except... it floats. It doesn't even have wheels.

Jesse eases it out from behind the trees, pulling it through the air. It remains a metre above ground, shifting as the earth dips up and down, like a magnet holds it rigidly in place.

I chew on my lip, wondering why Jesse's gazing at it like it's the most beautiful machine on earth. It's rather ugly.

It's the same colour as the sand at our feet. The pattern on it even looks like sand. Camouflage, perhaps? The thing is small and boxy, unequipped to travel at speed. It almost appears as if it's a first draft, the first one of its kind created and pocketed with impracticalities— no seat for the driver, a deep square box in the centre of the machine as if the creator only vaguely thought about passengers, and most obviously, a large net around the machine, securing all sorts of items.

It's like Jesse lives in this thing. I can see old food packets, a toothbrush, weaponry, old machinery, a rope, a tarp, clothing, and countless other items knotted around the rear frame of the vehicle.

I wonder what makes it float. It looks heavy.

Jesse thumps a hand against the side of the machine like it's the best thing in the world and then walks over to me and scoops me up in one effortless pile in his arms.

The wind gets knocked out of me.

I gasp as he thumps me into the square hole in the back of the vehicle. The sides reach up to my neck.

I have a feeling he uses this compartment to store things—a place for loot. I trace my fingers over the scratched metal surface.

I'm the loot.

He places his foot on a hidden step and pulls himself up into the machine. Without uttering a single word to me, he toggles some gadgets and activates some sort of screen in front of him.

"See to her ankle, would you?" Jesse absently murmurs to Melanie.

I sink my shoulders deeper in shame.

Melanie joins me and pulls a bumpy brown bag out of the net, eyes flickering over my sunken form.

"I'm no doctor," she tells me, "but my mother was. She tried to teach me some stuff. I'm going to try my best."

That's wonderfully reassuring.

Jesse presses something with his foot and we zip forwards unexpectedly. I gasp. My body slides across the floor in the square compartment, slamming me harder against the wall. I wince, keeping myself frozen in a crumpled form amid Melanie's legs.

She seems oblivious to the speed of travel.

Who knew this ugly box could go so fast?

He pulls us closer to the trees, turning a ridiculously fast corner. Melanie's pills go flying out of her hands.

"*Stars*, Jesse, try not to drive so fast."

He chuckles, but the wind takes away the sound. "I am, sweetheart."

Gingerly, she gathers the small pills from across the loot box. They roll towards me, gathering up along the wall.

They all look the same to me. Like various shades of blue pebbles.

Melanie thrusts one towards me, sitting in the hollow of her palm.

"Swallow it," she instructs.

I pluck it from her hand.

Trying to not watch the dizzying stream of trees and sky flitting past, I tilt my head back and coax the pill down my dry throat.

She watches as I do it.

"I suppose this should be interesting," she mumbles.

My hands begin to shake, and I pull back, retreating into the corner.

I rake my eyes along the planes of Jesse's body. Crouched as I am, everything below his hips is obscured, so I can't see what he's pressing with his feet to make the machine move. His body covers the control panel out front. He angles himself from side to side, and each time he does the machine follows the direction he leans.

My eyes glaze over from watching him.

"Melanie, I feel… numb."

She closes the small ceramic pot that holds the pills and lifts her head.

My tongue trails my lips, but I hardly feel myself doing it. The trees speed by frantically above me, dissolving not into blurring streaks of movement, but into a frenzied sort of spiral. I squeeze my eyes shut to block away the sensation.

"Oh, stars," Melanie mumbles.

I open my mouth to ask her what's wrong, but my head rolls sideways.

And all at once, the world disappears.

I ram my hand into something soft, a scream bursting from my throat.

The first thing I see is Jesse Hayes.

"Rise and shine, princess."

I struggle to pull myself upright, but the world seems slow and indistinct, and I can't support my weight.

I don't regain full consciousness immediately. I drift in and out of two hazy worlds until my eyes are pierced with something shiny. I don't want to see it, but I open my eyes anyway, only to be greeted by slashes of blinding silver stabbing my skull. Metal walls.

Rolling to my side, I notice something warm and scratchy around my head. I'm not in the loot box anymore.

The loot box wasn't this soft. This warm.

I'm in a bed.

I twist my ankle under the covers and notice all the pain from my sprain is gone. Huh. I move my feet under the blanket.

I'm wearing socks, but no bandage.

With a frown, I take a deep breath and lunge for Jesse.

He grabs my wrists and knocks me backwards, snarling. His weight pins me to the bed, restraining me, and I hold myself completely still.

I feel his breath, heady and warm, puffing against my neck, and for a moment we both stay there staring at each other. I throw as much hate as I can into my gaze and watch as the dark sapphire in his eyes pools into molten liquid.

He snaps his teeth together and withdraws, reaching towards the guard behind him for something too dainty and pretty to exist in this metallic room.

The sound of clinking china clatters against the bedside table.

I wince at the sound.

"Drink."

The buff guard behind him is holding a silver, dangerous-looking weapon, and my heart quickens. I watch as his fingers trail down the sharp metal, a stone-cold expression on his face.

Releasing the air from my lungs, I try to breathe evenly.

But that blasted blade keeps distracting me.

I wait for my brain to catch up with my body, but it feels like I'm witnessing the world through a veil of water. Jesse's face swims before me, shooting displeasure towards me.

God knows why.

I fist the blankets under me, trying not to writhe as my heart pedals. I don't have a weapon.

As if reading my mind, Jesse wanders out of view. I lift my head up after him.

"You—"

And he slams the door shut behind him.

The guard left with him, but I doubt they went far.

With a shudder, I trace my fingers over the blankets. The bed feels small, and my feet brush the end. I'm not a particularly tall person; I've always thought my height was average at best, so the bed must be small.

The quilt is frilly and white and looks like it belongs in a Jane Austen film. The poor attempt at making the room appear cosy makes me want to blanch.

The small room I'm in has reinforced walls, with neutral, white décor to soften the feeling of being inside a prison cell. The bedside table is also white, but hard like metal—a futile effort to make the room less harsh. I trace my finger over it, and it leaves a chill on my skin.

On top of it sits a floral cup of tea.

I yank the frilly blankets off me and trail my fingers over the ankle that was sprained, brows furrowing.

Their medicine must be stupidly complex if it were to heal a sprain that quickly… unless I was asleep for weeks.

With a shake of my head, I blink the sleep out of my eyes.

Before me, a white gauzy curtain brushes in the breeze from the cracked window, and behind it a village unravels. I can't fathom the shapes of the houses through the pounding in my head, but all the angles look sharp and modern. *Too modern.*

I stumble out of bed, ignoring the steaming drink, and rush to the door. It's nothing more than smooth metal—no handle—and it's locked from the outside. I thump my fist against it, hoping against hope that it'll sway open with a push. It doesn't.

It has a small peephole, like a grate in prison doors. I press my eyes against it, squinting into the dark hallway. Jesse's gone, but two guards stand outside my door, covered head to toe in silver. One rests his hand on his belt, covering a weapon, but I can't make out any more than that from this angle.

Fear swells in my chest.

I'm trapped.

The realisation sinks in my stomach. *They trapped me.*

I take a step back and my mind starts to clear. Whatever Melanie drugged me with seems to be leaving my system, as the fatigue is slowly wearing off. I take in the room, searching for something I can use as a tool to escape. Apart from the bed, the white bedside tables, and the cup of tea, the room is barren.

The walls feel like they're pressing on me, straining my breath.

I can't believe they did this.

I run my sweaty palms through my knotted hair and curse. Jesse isn't outside my door, but probably isn't far.

The cold seeps from the floor into my feet. Someone had taken my shoes. And my clothes. I'm in a scratchy grey dress, but thankfully my undergarments are the same.

I try to steady my breathing as I stand, heading towards the only other possible escape.

The window. The whole wall slants to the side, as if the building is on an angle.

I could escape through the window and climb down if the wall continues at this inclination.

But I really, *really* don't want that to be my only choice.

I hesitate.

Voices drift from outside the door as I cross the room. Laughter. I freeze and plaster my back against the wall, breath hitching. I don't move until the voices drift past my door and leave.

"Wonder how long it will be until they realise the drug is lethal—"

My pulse quickens.

The laugher is swallowed up down the hallway and I tremble against the metal door, processing those words.

Were they talking about me?

Someone else?

Good god, does the distinction even matter? I need to get out of here.

This place must be some sort of facility, for if it were a prison, it wouldn't have any windows.

I drift closer to the doors, straining my ears to hear something else.

The guards posted outside of my door appear to have moved elsewhere.

Jesse left me while I was in still in bed. Hopefully, due to my frazzled state, he'd give me a chance to wake up. I use this knowledge to buy myself some time.

Placing my hands onto the cool glass, I glance out at the world sprawling beyond it.

I wouldn't call it a village, as Melanie had. It looks like a futuristic city or war camp. Tall buildings of metal and glass spiral skywards in place of the trees, forming a new canopy separate to the forest. Compacted dirt covers the ground, tracked with roads. There isn't a soul in sight from this angle, except for the occasional vehicle—which are all like Jesse's, but smoother and more aerodynamic, and generally prettier to look at. I hold my breath, watching the vehicles disappear into tunnels under the surface of the ground.

I squint my eyes, making out the occasional network of greenery among the city—trees and fields for agriculture and animals, with robotic mechanisms roaming throughout it all, farming it. These aliens don't need to farm their own food like we do in Silver Valley. Why would you when you can create machines to do it for you?

Chills dart up my spine.

Far past the canopy of buildings—spires and deadly looking things that reflect the sunlight—I can vaguely make out a rectangular building bordering the perimeter of the beach from this vantage. I can't see the sand, but out at sea I spot round metal disks that look like landing pads.

I chew on my lip, unsure why they are out there.

Unless they go under the ocean?

I rub my temple, brain still sluggish.

They're large—large enough to be doorways for aircrafts.

Aliens.

Spaceships.

This must be a space centre, or a military base at best.

My palms start to sweat as I notice something opalescent rising from behind the buildings and arching up into the sky.

A dome.

A glimmering, perfect dome.

I scan the edges up and down and across, my heartbeat accelerating.

It shines in the daylight, iridescent, seeming to ripple with movement despite being near invisible.

It makes me feel sick. Trapped.

But I don't have much time to recover from the feeling. Voices mumble from outside the door and I hear a lock chime.

School indifference, I tell myself, and turn to face my visitor.

It's Jesse again. I can see him more sharply now. The reality of the world before me has sucked the haziness out of my brain.

"Do you not understand the concept of drinking tea?" he asks.

I cross the room, keeping my eyes trained on him. The top of my head reaches his jaw, and I have to tilt my head up.

"A *village*?" I gesture towards the window. "Are you bloody mad?"

He doesn't smile. Doesn't say anything. He just picks up the tea and thrusts it into my hands. It burns where it touches my skin, but I don't shy away from it.

"Drink up, buttercup."

I grip it steadily, but I don't drink.

"How long have I been asleep for?" I demand.

"How am I supposed to know?" he shrugs.

"You and Melanie drugged me," I reply.

"I can't exactly recall when you fell asleep."

Asleep?

The bastards drugged me. I didn't *sleep*. I keep my face blank. Control the heat bubbling heat inside of me.

"Liar."

He doesn't seem shaken. "I was driving, in case you forgot."

I haven't forgotten. He *trapped* me here.

I vaguely remember Melanie's promise. *"If you don't want to stay... I'll take you back home."*

If she was lying to me, then it's only fair that I lie back to them. I need them to believe I trust them. It's the only way to escape.

With shaking fingers, I lift the teacup to my lips. It brushes against my tongue. One sip.

"How many people live here?" I ask.

"A lot."

"How big is it?"

"Big."

"Is this the only village like it?"

"No."

I sigh. "Jesse."

He pulls something from a pocket in his jacket. "Welcome to Dome City," he says, eyes flashing, lip twitching.

I'm trapped in a room built under a dome.

I take a deep breath. *Indifference, Savannah.*

He's had time to change out of the wet black clothing. His new jacket is well-worn leather, dark brown but bright against the bland colours of the room. His trousers and shirt are dark. I memorise every detail, his light skin, his blank features. I brand him to memory. Just in case he's an enemy.

I lower the china and try my hardest not to flinch when he holds his hand out to me. It's a newspaper. Nothing threatening.

I take it from him quickly, careful to not let our skin brush, and my breath gets caught in my throat.

The paper is torn in two, but the rips don't align.

"Familiar?" he asks.

I flatten it out clumsily, my hands shaking so hard the letters blur.

He spins on his heel and leaves me alone. "Drink it all," he instructs before departing.

I put the cup down to read the paper, not bothering to watch him leave.

Thursday, December 24th, 2009

AN ANSWER

On Wednesday, the idolised Lythia May, daughter of the seventh Elder, regrettably passed in the riots that had been driven from fear of the Argenti. It is a sad day for the people of Umbra and Lythia May will be sorely missed among all.

Among the riots, the after-effects of the Moon Blitz continue to ravage our planet, and despite many attempts to restore our once mighty home, all efforts have so far been futile. But even in death our great prophet leaves us with hope. As revealed by the government Elders, we now reveal Lythia May's final prophecy:

"The chocolate-haired princess will sail from Terra to take over the throne and neutralise the destruction of our planet. An exact week. That's how long we have until she comes into creation."

Through the great influence of Lythia May, daughter of the seventh Elder, a wish upon the stars was cast, renewing hope in the hearts of our people and revealing a girl with the power to reshape our old home. Many attempts have been cast to speculate the root of this chocolate-haired princess's heritage, yet neither Commons, Argenti, or Elder has any lead yet to confirm the prophesied princess' identity.

The Elders advise all to take this time for solitude and mourning, and to remain vigilant yet passive in these times until more information regarding Lythia May's death has been identified. By the favour of miracles, we have been given hope.

We can only pray that this is our answer.

I lower the clippings onto my bed.

My shoulders droop and I stare at the ceiling.

What could this all mean? My head begins to pound.

No. *No.*

My teeth begin to chatter at the thought. *Surely* not.

I pluck up the paper again and scan the words, trying to convince myself otherwise.

It was published December 24th, 2009.

An entire week. That's how long we have until...

Until I was born, a week later, on the 31st.

Chocolate-haired.

Jasmine had praised my dark hair that day in the café shortly after telling me the story of when she'd bleached her own.

Sail from Terra.

Interstellar. Aliens. The stars, and the many nights my mother had taught me to navigate them.

I crunch the paper in my fists. What do they expect? Me to hijack a spaceship?

Take over the throne.

I throw the paper across the room. No, no, no. It can't be me.

Neutralise the destruction of our planet.

"Are you for *real*?"

I jump off the bed, the breaths coming shorter in my chest. I hold the bed frame as I wander around it, sucking in the suffocating air around me as my head spins. My heart pounds incessantly in my ears and I can't *think.*

I stumble over my feet as I move towards the window and grip my fingers against the ledge, trying to school the dizziness overwhelming me. It doesn't look like I'm too high and the metal building slants down in a curve. If I'm careful enough, I can slip down the wall like a slide.

The window isn't thick. I can break through it.

I grab a blanket off the bed and press it into the gap under the door to muffle the noise. Everything in the room is reinforced to the floor or the ground. Everything except the tea Jesse brought me.

I take a deep breath, pluck the tea off the table, and launch the cup at the window.

The glass shatters in one loud break.

I don't move a muscle.

I listen for the sounds of footsteps or voices, but nothing makes a sound.

Releasing a heavy breath, I take a step back.

The window is marked in a broken web, with a fist-sized hole gaping in the centre. The cup is lost somewhere below.

The socks on my feet are thick, so I use the heel of my foot to shatter a wider gap, the fabric protecting my skin.

Panting with adrenaline, I peer down the building.

There's another window below me, then the wall almost entirely flattens. There's a joint facility attached to the building I'm in, looking to be a storey tall, if I were to wager. The sloping wall from my building blends down into the roof of the second building, creating a long metal slide.

I take a step back and drag my fingers through my hair. They get caught halfway through, and I untwist them from my chocolate locks, shaking uncontrollably.

I have pillows, blankets… I can use them to my advantage.

I run a finger across the sharp glass. The edge will cut me if I try to get through. But I can use the pillow to smash out the remaining shards.

So I dash to the bed and grab the last blanket to drape over the hole in the window, smashing and covering the glass. Satisfied with the mediocre exit, I race one last time back to my bed.

Something in the tea has cleared my mind. My head rattles off ideas in a clear manner.

I should've drunk more, as Jesse had advised. But that doesn't matter now.

To hell with their pill bottles and anomalous teas.

I shove a pillow under my armpit. It's hard to climb through the window with it slung under my arms, but I do my best.

Allowing one last glance back at the door, I throw my leg out the window.

The thin windowpane beneath the blanket is extremely unsteady at this angle. I slide my hand outside, feeling the wall. The window merges directly onto the metal panelling outside and the window on the storey below is closed, so I could easily slide over it. From there, the surface becomes nearly horizontal, the roof ahead long enough to decrease my speed.

It's pure luck that I'm not in a cell higher in the building; otherwise I wouldn't be able to escape without dying. But this low down, it'll just be a bit of a joy ride.

I place a pillow under my first leg and swing my second out of the window, so I have the pillow beneath me. Gripping it so tightly that my skin strains, I shove myself out of the window.

And I fall.

The pillow snags on a piece of glass as I leave the window, but I grip it tight in my white knuckles and yank it along with me, forcing it around my buttocks like it's my salvation.

The wind pushes me into the side of the building, tangling my hair.

I slide down the long slide, over the window below, eyes on the edge of the roof in the distance.

But I don't scream, holding my breath as I slide.

Time slows around me, my breath hitching in my throat.

It feels like sliding down one of those massive slides at a carnival. My eyes strain, tears lining my face against the slap of the wind.

My scream is jammed in my throat, like a bulging knot I can't free.

It takes seconds. Only seconds.

My blood pounds in my ears as I slide across the horizontal

roof of the facility below, my eyes locked on the impending edge of the building ahead of me. It's a long surface, but it still ends at some point.

Instincts have my feet grazing across the hot metal roof, trying to slow me down.

I feel my socks burning, gaining me no traction, the heat of the roof blistering through the material. It's this that finally makes me scream, the panic overwhelming me as I scramble my feet back onto the pillow.

I choke in a sob, my heartbeat threatening to explode out of my chest.

My speed slows, but the edge of the roof lurks ever closer.

I hold my breath and roll sideways off the pillow, my shoulder slamming into the metal. My pillow spins off somewhere, body rolling across the roof. The metal feels hot and angry against my skin, searing my flesh.

I keep rolling, over and over.

Until finally, I stop.

My entire body stills. I'm sprawled, panting, several metres away from the edge of the roof.

Bloody hell.

I sit upright and stare at the way I've come. And then I laugh until I'm overcome with hysteria. What a sight that must have been.

I collapse onto the roof, controlling my giddiness.

"It's a shame no one saw that."

14

Once the adrenaline begins to ebb from my system, the pain threatens to choke me.

Body shaking, I tilt my torso to look at the damage. Instinctively, I had balled my arms over my face as I'd rolled, so my shoulders are now gleaming and raw. My body trembles from the burning agony, tears glistening as I take in the liquid oozing across the open grazes. It feels as if I've been dragged through hot gravel, the skin seared and screaming.

Luckily, the slide was short, and the roof was long enough to slow my speed enough to roll off. It could have been much worse, but that doesn't make the throbbing across my skin any easier to bear.

The sun blinks down through the clouds, promising a day without rain. It's high in the sky—maybe just after 1pm? That must mean I've missed a whole day sleeping—if I'd wager their advanced medicine to be the cause for fixing my sprain, and not time I spent sleeping.

It also means the metal had some time to get hot in the sun.

I wince, gritting my teeth against the pain.

But instead of catching my breath, I shimmy towards the roof edge. My body feels giddy with adrenaline and pain, but I move hastily enough.

I need to get out of sight before Jesse notices the window.

The metal under me is smooth and flat, save for a couple of cracks where they placed the panelling together, so it's easy to navigate. Behind me, a trail of pillow stuffing lingers on parts of the roof. I feel sorry for the person charged with cleaning my room.

I reach the end of the surface, the roof dropping down onto the road below me.

Swinging my legs over the edge, I take a deep breath. There isn't a lip, so I thump my ankle against it, and it vibrates from the sudden pressure. Glass. The building I'm on must have floor-to-ceiling windows.

Hands shaking, I grip the edge and lower myself down.

The ground below is solid dirt, stamped flat and whispering with swirling motes of dust from a gentle wind. It's one of the roads intersecting the village compound, but it's a small, insignificant one, hidden amongst the magnitude of the building behind me.

My knuckles turn white against my skin, the trembling slowing.

One more storey. I can do this.

I let go, and the wind temporarily tugs at me, gravity rushing past my fingertips as I thump onto the ground. My knees buckle and my arms catch my fall. Some dirt gets into the peeled skin at my shoulder, and I clamp my teeth against the sudden pain.

But I've made it.

Breathing rapidly, I pull myself to my feet.

And without hesitation, I dash off to the side of the road, my feet slapping the dirt.

I keep the wall to my back and stare at the glass window I just jumped past. It's some sort of medical research facility. Scientists stare at me, donned in white, confusion dawning on their faces. The dusty road has tracked up onto the glass, staining it brown, but I can see them clear as day, surrounded by machinery and vials of colourful liquid. Three or so watch me, all pausing what they're doing.

I lift a sheepish hand and wave at them. "Good afternoon."

One of them waves back in a stupor.

Sucking in a deep breath, I race down the street at top speed. I can feel their eyes following me.

Abandoning my room was a rash decision, but I'm suddenly overwhelmed with a heady sense of affirmation that I did the right thing. They convinced me to come here, drugged me, and locked me up. Where's the trust in that?

Maybe it was all planned.

I take a sharp corner. Vehicles like Jesse's sit idly around the next wall, not floating, but fastened down by thin arms of metal. It's like a parking strip. I debate stealing one, but I wouldn't know how to unlock them from their clasps. Instead, I wander down one of the aisles of machines and study them.

They're all so beautiful. Slick and deadly, and remarkably futuristic.

None of them have a loot box and look ten times deadlier than Jesse's.

I peer up at all the buildings where anyone can see me, and I run away from the vehicles and down the next street.

This place isn't like any city I know. It's eerie.

I try to draw on what I remembered seeing up in the cell and map out the compound in my head. I wasn't high enough in the building to see everything, but I saw enough to go by.

Where I had come from appears to be a research and development zone—largely facilities of different sorts. The structures closer to the ocean resemble apartment buildings; speckled with windows and balconies on each. Right near the beach is that long, imposing building adorning the sand, and then the landing pads out at sea.

That's where I need to go.

The space centre, cargo bay, and launch zones would be the perfect place to find answers.

I hug the walls to keep my back covered. A soft bubble of voices chime around me as I make it to a zone with lower buildings. Hands still shaking, I hold my breath in order to still myself.

An intersection lies ahead, and flashes of people appear from behind another parking strip. They all seem to be mingling outside a pub of sorts. I turn to my left and see more restaurants and bar joints, as well as a convenience store. They seem relatively empty. Most of the people head into the pub directly in front of me.

The dust kicks up around their feet, like little storms around their ankles. Everyone has dark hair and dark clothes; I could've fit in if I weren't so winded and wandering the streets in nothing more than a grey slip of clothing.

My skin throbs where the metal sheared a layer off. I try to ignore it as best as I can, but the pain continues to ring down my arm in a steady throb.

I count my breaths as I walk, matching it to the pace of my feet.

The pub before me is made of wood and sandstone, with accents of metal intersecting it. The design makes it appear as though it's been caught within a metal tree, the branches winding around the colonial building. This part of the compound looks significantly less reflective and metallic, appearing more ancient in architecture. It's as if I'm snatching glances of how the compound looked centuries ago, back when it was first founded.

A tall man nearly knocks into me as I slip into the gathering crowd, but I narrowly avoid him. The fabric of his jacket breezes across my grazed skin and I hiss.

He pulls back from me and blinks. "Why the nightgown?" he enquires, then takes in my grazed skin. "Are you a fighter?"

His eyes are dark and lined, and I shiver under their gaze.

"Yes?" I respond softly, heart hammering.

He raises an eyebrow and I quickly duck towards the pub before he has time to answer.

Playing the game seems safer than questioning it.

Even if I have no idea what he meant.

I migrate with those gathered in the pub, deciding it's probably best to buy some time. Melanie and Jesse would expect me to head straight to the space centre or to leave the dome, but never to go inside a pub.

It takes all my willpower to not look behind me every few seconds to see if I'm being followed, my hammering heart sounding like a loud signal to anyone around me. Eyes wide and flicking to every face, I keep my head held high and merge into the shadows of the pub's doorway, not for one second convinced I'm blending in. Above a boxy entrance, a metal sign hangs stiffly. The Nook.

It isn't as crowded inside as I thought it would be, but voices and exhilarated shouts echo from somewhere within. I linger in the entrance, a two-metre tunnel bathed in a light wash of orange flickering from old lamps that lines my way towards the cavernous space.

Farther inside it's warm and cosy. The walls are made of wood and stone, and the bar is cradled under a nook by the back of the room. Bottles of all colours line shelves in an ornate display among glasses and prettily arranged decorations—old pool balls, tattered books, dried flowers, a few blunt darts and an old dart board—like a bird has collected bits and pieces from the pub across the decades and left them on the shelves nostalgically.

There's only one bar staff, but the atmosphere's quiet, so that doesn't seem to be a problem. Two men sit on bar stools and chat with him. Several more people adorn green leather chairs scattered across the room in casual groupings, and another small group occupy the pool table that's sheltered in the corner under a dipping roof.

I don't hesitate too long in the entrance.

My instinct is to order a drink, but I'm underage and have no means to pay for it. So I pick my way to one of the green lounges. Taking a seat, I pluck a cocktail menu off the table. I hardly have time to read it before I overhear two men by the bar.

Their voices drop, and one man shuffles closer to the other when the bartender wanders over to the other end of the counter.

I lean forwards in my seat, as much in awareness to not touch my throbbing shoulders against the fabric as it is in curiosity.

"Did you hear the news?"

The first speaker is younger, with heavy dark hair that he continuously brushes out of his eyes.

They both appear to have just come off work. Their shoulders slouch, heavy over the bar. Both wear thick shirts and pants and very heavy boots. Bits of grease line the hands of the one with the greying hair.

"Nah, been working with that little intern all day. He doesn't speak."

"I've been told there's more news about her. We know she's out there now… people are scouring the village across the island for her. Would be a pretty thing if she was actually found, don't you think?"

"You know I don't believe she exists, Mike." He downs the remaining ember liquid in his glass. He seems indifferent, but his eyes hold the younger boy's. He pretends to be careless, but I can tell he wants to know what's going on. "That would be too much of a precious thing."

"I almost hope so for her sake. The girl may die before she even knows her role in this. You'd never know if the person who finds her is supportive of her or loyal to the Elders." Mike clutches his beer and condensation pools against his skin.

"So you're one of those people that believe May was right, then?"

"It would be weird if she wasn't. I doubt she was making it all up just to inspire hope. And now, something is happening, Fred. If she's out there, she'll be found soon." His eyes turn away from the other man. If possible, his slouch deepens further.

"So this thing could actually happen, then?" Fred almost sounds afraid.

"She's out there. Miss May was never wrong."

"I hope you're right. But I also hope you're not."

I drop the menu.

I don't remember leaving the room or which path I took to slip out of the light. I plunge into the shadows all the same, hands grasping a cool sandstone wall, my breaths heavy and fast.

Jesse and Melanie must be wrong about me.

I can't possibly be the girl everyone's searching for.

As I drag my fingernails down the cool stone, I lean my head upon it. The cold clears my head, and I turn around.

I've reached a tunnel ending in a heavy wooden doorway. The voices I heard earlier sound louder and sharper from beyond it.

I peel my back off the stone, eyebrows perked, just as someone new enters the pub—someone with a heavy, angry laugh. A small woman with short, spiked hair follows him. They plunge directly towards me, and the woman glares at me as they pass, as if I shouldn't be here. The man pushes open the door and the couple disappear into the loud crowd on the other side. I follow them without hesitating, using their arrival to approach the enclave unseen.

The room is hot. I gasp and inhale the dank stench of sweat and dust. Everyone is jeering and cawing like birds. I try to figure out what for but can't see past the cluster of bodies. It seems as if I've missed some sort of event. The crowd presses and moves like a wave, bending around each other in synchrony.

I bounce between them, holding my breath, and then I tuck my shoulders and plunge forwards.

"Confidence," I whisper to myself. "You belong here, Savannah. Act like you belong here and no one will bother you."

The people I followed into the room disappeared in a blink. I try my best to mimic how they vanished into the crowd.

I push people aside gently until I reach the centre. A large portion of the dusty floor has been cleared and raised like a step. People move around it like it's a throne, too afraid to approach it but respectful and adoring. Spotlights stand around the stage, one in each corner. There's nothing else in the room except for a chalkboard with the words *Train against Terra's greatest, here, today.* Other than that, the stage is the focus.

"What on earth…"

My voice gets whisked away in the crowd.

This doesn't really feel like a training room.

It feels like a cult.

A bald man in nothing more than loose pants sits on the floor upon the stage, blood shining wet and bright across his pale skin.

He looks almost as beat up as I am.

Another man towers over him, grinning, eyes flashing bright in the light. They reflect almost like Melanie's but are muddy around the edges and dulled in the light.

"The blood of the Argenti flows through my veins, my friend," the brute says sweetly to the man bleeding on the ground. Something about his tone makes me want to hit him.

"No, you're just a man." The man on the ground winces as he speaks. A heavy rock sits firmly in his palm, coated in his own blood. A weapon.

The other just laughs and leaps off the stage, embraced by arms and hands. He shouts, "He just doesn't shut up, does he? I've already proved him wrong."

He laughs to himself, and the others laugh with him.

I linger by the edge of the crowd, my body turned so I might appear to be a part of a group near me but hidden well enough by everyone else to avoid notice.

"So," the bloody man points to the chalkboard. "You never specified your prize."

And for the first time I notice lists of goods lining the bottom of the board. Prizes, with people's names written under them. Each name has been scratched out except for one in each section. It's like some sort of gambling system. The fighters line up to win an array of what I presume to be stolen goods.

Training against 'Terra's greatest' is probably just a ruse—a cover-up for the real action. And it doesn't exactly take a genius to see it.

"My prize?" the winner laughs. There are no unclaimed items on the leader board. This fight was out of pure spite. "Beating you is my prize."

The loser grunts, and then pulls himself off the stage. I suppose he must be glad. It could've been worse.

"What a weakling," a girl mumbles beside me. She twirls her tacky white hair. Bleached in all the wrong ways.

The loser stands close to me now, his breath shaky. I watch in terror as his fingers tighten around the rock before he hurls it at the girl's feet in anger. She squeaks and leaps away, pushing into the crowd.

The people around her turn and glare at him, immediately congregating in a pack.

Realising his mistake, the man's eyes widen. He stumbles, his shoulder hitting mine.

"Run," I whisper to him.

He turns and looks me dead in the face.

"Quick," I hiss, resisting the urge to push him.

His wide eyes flash before he clambers out of the room so fast that I lose sight of him immediately. The girl next to us laughs. But no one laughs with her.

"All this for a simple little knife," the winner of the fight growls.

I take my eyes off the bloodied man.

The knife *is* simple. The wooden handle is so small it's engulfed in his grip—hardly a weapon large enough to fight with let alone risk your life for.

"Mahogany is *rare*," another person snaps, his eyes honed on the small blade, tongue flicking across his lips. "It's a Terran substance."

"We *are* on Terra, dickhead," the woman snarls.

The winner of the blade twists it in his palm. He doesn't seem concerned by the hungry stares, but lifts it higher so he can warrant more attention.

"Anyone else want to try?" He raises his eyebrows and makes a point of looking into the eyes of every hungry gaze pinned on him. "It's so easy to steal. I would know, I got it from a little girl around fourteen years ago on the shuttle. Couldn't fathom what such a young girl was doing with a blade. She had such a soft face, must've only been a few years old. She didn't want it anymore. Seemed very sure of that, so I took it. Now who else wants to try to take it? Come on, it'll be easy."

The way he tells the story sounds like he's recited it many times before, spoken like a storyteller desperate for attention. But the crowd pauses at his words. They watch as he pulls the blade out of the sheath, the silver reflecting in the harsh light, almost as breath-taking as the gold in the hilt.

"It isn't common for children to come to Terra," his friend says, as if trying to understand how someone could be so lucky.

The brute grins at him. His whole face seems to glow in the spotlight, greed licking up every second of attention he's given. It's this that makes him slip, giving me enough precious details. I thank the stars for the greed of others, lingering on every word.

"I remember her so fondly, because of how rare it is to see a child. Her hair bounced like golden honey. Her eyes wide and pretty." His own eyes dance with devilish hunger, and I shiver involuntarily. "She said her name was Jasmine, that she didn't have parents. Poor little Jasmine."

He doesn't look sorry for her.

"How dull. You stole a weapon from a child," the woman rolls her eyes, turning away.

My fingers turn to fists beside me.

Jasmine, owning a rare switchblade.

Jasmine, on a shuttle bound for Terra when she was only a child.

It couldn't possibly be *my* Jasmine, could it?

My heart thumps in my chest and, dizzy, I suddenly struggle to breathe. The world starts to spin.

It can't be Jasmine Spark. I've known her my whole life.

And yet…

The small gathering before me begins to talk of something else, but my mind's still on that blade, and the brute holding it seems to have noticed me staring.

I take a step back, my breaths whisked away from me as I freeze.

"You alright there, sugar?"

He smirks at me, and I suddenly can't breathe at all.

I shouldn't have continued to stare once the attention dripped away from him. I should've stayed at the back of the room, where he wouldn't see me.

Well, too late now.

Calmly, I loosen my fists and push back my shoulders. He smiles at that.

Forcing myself to breathe, I try to smooth the fear from my face, stomach flipping with nerves.

He takes a step towards me, and I take a tentative step back.

He cocks his head at that. If possible, his delight increases.

I have two options: run or fight. He has a weapon, I don't. He's spent years of training, I haven't. He's the size of the hulk, and I'm not.

The smart choice would be to run.

But lately, my choices haven't exactly been smart. And besides, *I need that switchblade if it's Jasmine's.*

I take a step towards the man.

"Aren't you too scrawny to be a fighter, love?" He whispers the words like a caress, as if the sight of me staring him down is a sweet, precious thing.

I ignore his question. "I want your blade."

That gets the attention of everyone in the room. The man laughs. Each echo sends shivers down my spine.

"They all say that before they run away wet and bloody."

"I'm not running," I say suggestively.

This is a horrible idea.

But if that blade is Jasmine's, I need it. It doesn't belong in the clutches of this vile man. For a moment I completely forget any anger I still hold against my friend. All I can think about is how I need to save this part of her past.

No one makes a fool of my family. Sure, she may have thrown the switchblade away first, but I highly doubt she'd want this crowd to make a mockery of that choice.

The brute cocks his head, the bright light dancing over his face as he grins down at me. "You win, you get my blade. I win, and I get to keep *you* as my little pet. Sound alright, love?"

My gut wrenches.

Everything in me is screaming to *run*, but instead I reach out slowly and clasp his hand.

"Deal."

I'm standing on the stage, all eyes on me.

Lights cast over my pale skin, highlighting the blood and scratches. My muscles are tense, and I feel my heart fluttering like the wings of a tiny bird.

The brute stands over me, switchblade spinning through his fingers. He's tall. Extremely tall. I should have noticed it before I accepted this ridiculous fight.

How on earth can I beat this man?

Is it worth it for a small blade that might not even be Jasmine's?

His hair is wispy and yellow, and like the girl with the bleached hair, it speaks of a poor dye job. Sweat and blood plaster it to his face, the memories of previous victories clinging to his very pores.

If I were Jesse Hayes, I could probably beat this man.

But I'm not Jesse.

I *despise* Jesse.

Yet my mind runs over the memory of him, highlighting the moments I watched his body move, the way he held his shoulders, and the powerful stance he maintained with every footfall.

If I want to win, I need to move like Jesse—need to move like a fighter.

I roll my shoulders back and shift my feet into what I think is a fighting stance. Every placement of muscle feels wrong. Unbalanced.

The brute strokes his thick fingers along the sharp end of the switchblade lovingly, each caress sending a sickening jolt through me.

I try not to think shrink in his presence and bend my thoughts around the blade and how I can snatch it from him.

"When you came to Terra, did your shuttle land on the island?" I ask him. My voice is quiet and barely audible above the din of the crowd, but the stage is small, and he's close enough to hear me.

He pauses; idle and curious, standing across the stage like a predator admiring his prey.

"Yep. They never give us a choice…. the island, the mountains, or the desert. Can't say I didn't hope for the desert."

He licks lips his at me as I tilt my head.

Stall, Savannah. Think.

"Why did you come?" I ask him.

The light bounces off the metal, patterns dancing on the silver roof.

"I resigned as a guard."

Damn.

I scan my eyes over his hungry posture. Years of scars layer his skin. Too many scars. Once he maintained order, but this is his new sport—a fight without rules, where he can pick on weaker people under the yellow lights on this stage.

Unregulated training.

"And the girl whose blade you own?"

His face flickers with bemusement, as if my questions are both confusing and flattering. Oh, how he craves attention. If I put on a show, perhaps he will delay in killing me.

I raise my brows. And, of course, he obliges an answer, but doesn't seem overly interested in the questions I'm asking anymore.

He shrugs. "Never asked. Looked like a runaway."

That fits. Jasmine's the sort to have run away.

The word thrums though my head, almost as loud as the buzzing crowd. I'm quite sure Jasmine hinted to it once, what seems like months ago, the first day I came to the island.

I may run away from things a lot… she had said, *but I promise I won't ever run away from you.*

She had run away from the city, leaving me behind.

But this…

I clench and unclench my hands under the yellow light.

I can't possibly imagine what Jasmine Spark was doing on a shuttle to Terra at the age of three—especially with a rare switchblade. And where were Ethan and Ella, her parents?

The girl I'm fighting for might not even be my Jasmine, but the story fits with her lies and everything she seems to know about this island.

I suck in a breath and sink deeper into my fighting stance.

I mustn't think of this now. First, I need to find a way to survive this madman and retrieve Jasmine's blade.

If it's really hers, I have to try.

Frantically, I search for an advantage while he tosses the blade in his hand tauntingly. It doesn't aggravate me like he obviously intends. Instead, it gives me a few moments to think.

I raise my chin. "I don't have a weapon. This isn't a fair fight."

He laughs. "Oh honey, this isn't meant to be *fair*."

My gut hits the floor. But I keep my chin high.

"No weapons," I reply firmly.

"Should've included that in our bargain."

His grin stretches oh so happily, chin rising higher so the crowd can have a clear view of him.

How do you trap a man who craves attention?

Lure him in with the promise of the spotlight.

The crowd quietens around us. I throw my arm out towards them, banishing my fear to replace it with a false smile of confidence.

"Wouldn't this be *more* entertaining if I'm not beaten immediately? Let's give these people a show."

The crowd starts to chant.

The bleached blonde girl raises her hands skyward. Some of them begin to pound their feet against the ground. I grin, stepping backwards to ensure most of the attention is on the man.

He frowns slightly, but hunger dances in his eyes, and just like I predicted, he tucks the blade into the pocket of his jacket.

"Whatever you say, little fighter," he purrs.

I smirk at him, eyes flashing with resolve.

The lights on the stage blind me, silhouetting him.

I shouldn't have been so distracted by the small win. I'm not ready when he comes at me.

He throws his weight against me and I'm still smiling when I'm pounded into the floor. His fist collides with the side of my face, and the world spins as I roll out of his clutch, eyes blurring with the sudden movement. He pulls back and I ask myself again, what would Jesse Hayes do?

Rashly, I dive towards the side of the stage, trying to gain a breath of space, my mouth tasting of battery acid from my rebelling stomach.

He predicts my movement, clipping my cheek with such force I'm knocked into the light-pole. It creaks at the sudden onslaught of weight, dipping towards the ground, hanging on by nothing but a thin lip of metal. It casts an even lower circle of yellow light onto the stage.

I cling to it, panting, trying to ignore the blossoming pain biting through my skin and bone. My brain feels shaken, aching relentlessly as it rolls in my skull, and I can hear nothing but a loud ringing. The cheers of the crowd seem distant.

I want to puke. I've never wanted to do anything more in my life. I clutch my stomach, feeling everything in my body moan as my stomach threatens to spill across the stage.

The world around me feels unstable as I push myself away from the light-pole, my head sluggish. The brute before me is cackling, and I study him before he moves. I notice it instinctively—the slight shift of his weight, leaning towards me before he steps. I duck desperately. His fist misses me, sailing across the stale air above my head.

Jesse tries to stay ahead of the game, like when he anticipated me to run outside in the storm at the sight of a tree almost crushing him.

Maybe that's what I need to do.

After dodging the brute, I scurry towards the other end of the stage, struggling to think past the splitting pain in my head. But he's still in fighting form, and he follows hastily.

I slow, trying to map out a way to get behind him, rubbing my eyes against my blurry vision, head spinning as I try to come up with an offensive plan.

But I hardly make it to the edge of the stage before my head is dragged back and I fall to the ground. I land on my side, and he yanks my hair up, pulling me into a sitting position.

My skull roars in violent protest, and I yell along with it.

My scream is lost in the crowd. They cheer and gasp in perfect harmony, and I think I hear the brute's blonde female friend laughing gleefully.

"Stand up," he snarls at me. He pulls my hair harder until I'm on my knees, whimpering, hazardously dragging my legs under me so that I can stand and face him. The moment I'm on my feet he releases me. He grins with delight, swinging a fist.

I crumple onto the ground at the impact. He struck me right on my shoulder—on the exposed flesh still burning from the roof.

I bite back my scream, the taste of blood churning in my mouth.

No more.

I'm done.

My hands are shaking, my whole body heaving with pain. I want nothing more than to curl into a ball and cry, but that won't help me at all.

So I try to steady my breathing, to push through the ringing in my ears and my faded vision. And I stand. A hiss escapes my lips, sounding more like a gasp as I spit at him, "I need that switchblade."

He erupts into laughter.

I wasn't sure if he would hear me. I try to take that as a victory as I turn and face the crowd. They don't know why he's laughing, but some of his friends join in, anyway. Others continue to cheer and stomp, lost in a world of twisted delight, watching a young girl getting pounded to near-death.

The brute's eyes are focused on the crowd, scanning the tops of their heads.

Not on me for once.

With a strength I thought was drained out of me, I swing my leg out across the backs of his knees. He stumbles, catching his footing.

I duck, rolling across the ground until my back is resting flat on the stage. I kick my leg upwards, my foot planting itself solidly into his groin, desperation and adrenaline sending a forceful current behind the blow.

The man screams in shock, instinctively curling over to protect that region, face pinching in pain.

Thinking his pain is surely nothing compared to mine makes me want to laugh. But I don't. Instead, I scramble upwards and plant a kick into his shins, hitting any place I know that hurts.

The cheers and laughter of the crowd morph into confused

shouts, and then increase once more into newfound delight. The tempo changes, and I convince myself that's a good thing.

But I don't know how many more hits I can get in.

I throw my leg back to kick him again, but he grabs my ankle before I can strike. The force of my kick shudders through him and he stumbles, but he isn't daunted, and he yanks my leg up.

When he drops me, my head pounds onto the stage first.

Splitting pain.

Ringing in my ears.

Blood blooms more rapidly in my mouth. I must have caught my cheek between my teeth when I fell.

Stupid. So stupid.

The man places his boot on my neck and presses down. I choke in the ripe sweetness of the room, catching any air I can muster into my lungs. He presses harder, my airways closing off beneath his boot.

"I'm not so sure if I like you anymore," he hisses through clenched teeth.

My hands grasp onto his ankle, and I tear my fingernails across his skin. Ready to try anything to get free.

I must cripple him.

I can't…

Black spots scatter across my vision, blood pounding in my brain. All I can see is him snarling down at me. The light of the teetering pole tears across his features, making his angry face look even wilder.

My throat sears as I strain to open my lungs. The crowd is so quiet, either because I can't hear them over the ringing or because they're not used to seeing murders happen onstage.

He shifts his weight so that his breath scatters across my face. It smells of blood and alcohol.

His jacket brushes my sides.

His jacket.

I reluctantly release my hands from his ankle, fighting instinct. Blood drips down his boot, feeble gashes and puckered skin where I dug in my nails. His attention is on my face, so he doesn't notice when I slip my hands into the pocket of his jacket.

I'm shaking so hard. It's a relief like nothing I've ever experienced when my bruised fingers brush the mahogany handle.

I take it out slowly, switching it open.

The blackness is taking over, but vaguely, I register his eyes following my movement.

The switchblade lodges into his ankle, seconds after his eyes drift from my face. He screams and scrambles off me.

I clamber across the stage, blinking the spots out of my eyes. Gasping. Sucking down air.

I don't have time to faint. Not yet.

Ignoring the protests of my body, I pull myself onto my feet.

The brute yanks the blade out of his ankle and snarls at me.

Blood gushes from the wound, leaving a bright red trail across the stage as he lumbers towards me, murder dancing in his eyes. The light reflects off the metal in his hand. He angles the blade, intent blazing across his face as he aims the weapon at me.

With the last of my strength, I reach to the side and push on the pole.

I intend it to land on him. It doesn't.

The pole crashes onto the stage, the sound drowning out the crowd. The light inside pops, sending sparks showering around him.

He nearly drops the switchblade in surprise.

The sound seems to echo down the tunnel back to the pub, as if signalling everyone to where we are. But I don't expect backup.

Stepping away from him, I stumble to the edge of the stage. The drop isn't far, but it seems like miles. Much higher than the building I sailed down earlier.

I crumple onto the ground. The crowd parts for me, their eyes flickering between my predator and me. He looms over me; hate billowing in his dull eyes. They're no longer bright but a muddy grey. The sight of them on me makes me gag.

He angles the blade towards me, but I'm too weak to move.

The blade soars down towards my face, but he pauses, the weapon hanging mid-air, reflective in his hand.

Suddenly, like a popping radio, the crowd goes deathly silent.

I turn my head towards them, straining to see. No one watches us anymore. They face the entrance of the room, some looking irritated, others scared.

"I think it's finally time I intervened," a clear voice rings out. The crowd parts for the man as he makes his way towards me.

I try to focus on him around the blinking black spots in my eyes. His stride is purposeful, his eyes deep and thoughtful. A light wash of hair covers his neck in a smooth tangle, bound by a leather tie. He holds himself like he's seen many years, but he looks barely older than twenty. His skin is smooth, unwrinkled, unblemished. Like a child with an older man's face.

Six guards follow closely behind the man, sheathed in silver clothing that ripples and swims under the yellow lighting. One of them holds a pair of shackles.

The shortest—their leader—glances down at me curiously, but his gaze rips from me quickly and settles on the brute with the blade.

"I've left you and your crowd alone for some time now, but I will not have you hurting innocents. No one will leave this room unless pardoned. Guards are stationed at the door and will take you out individually for questioning."

His voice echoes in the silent room, and the tension increases tenfold.

I hold my breath along with the crowd, my brain practically exploding out of my skull.

The man locks eyes with the brute standing over me, and I

watch the fear spread over his face with each word the man says. "The guards will take you directly to the Safe Holds."

Seeing this man towering over a battered young girl, I doubt he deems questioning a matter of importance.

The figure gazes placidly at his guards, and the one holding the shackles steps forwards. Another one takes the switchblade out of the brute's grasp.

Surprisingly, the brute doesn't protest. Instead, he begins to shake and splutter a string of inaudible words.

I force myself to sit and watch as a guard begins to drag him away.

"Wait!" My voice shakily reverberates across the room.

The guards stop and everyone stares at me. Their leader glances at me again, his cold eyes slicing over me.

He raises his eyebrows. "Yes?"

My words come out on one breath, panicked and fast. I don't even think before I speak. "He stole my switchblade, sir. It's in his hand."

The brute suddenly stiffens, and he stares at me, full of hate. "How dare—"

"Give it to the girl." The man's voice is decisive. "I'll bring her out for questioning first."

The guard looks hesitant. "No offense implied sir… but if she uses it against—"

"She's in no state to use that butter knife against me," he intercedes. His eyes rake over me, tracing the blood on my skin.

The guard passes the blade down to his leader, who hands it to me. I stand up to face the man. He's half a head shorter than I am. My words of thanks die on my lips when the pain of standing catches up with me, the world tilting sideways. I clutch my stomach, tasting bile.

My knuckles are white against the wooden handle of the switchblade, drying blood sliding against my palm. I exhale a breath and flip the blade shut with a resounding click.

"Follow me," the man says.

The short man gestures me forwards, and I step ahead without hesitation, gripping the switchblade with a newfound sense of purpose.

The crowd watches me leave, every single eye locked on me.

I don't look back. I don't want to know what they're thinking.

The guards hold the door open for me and I almost stumble in relief.

The sweet perfume of liquor and cleaning agents of The Nook swarms around me, and it's the most intoxicating scent I've ever smelt. Freedom. My legs buckle and I blink back the water pooling in my eyes.

It suddenly occurs to me I might not have left that room alive.

The guards take the brute away, hissing and snarling, and the leader places a warm hand on my shoulder. I stop in the shadows, turning to face him. I can barely see out of my left eye and the right feels fuzzy.

"Stay a moment," he demands.

He wanders towards the bar. Two new guards block the end of the tunnel and I hesitate.

I twist the closed switchblade in my hand.

With my weapon in hand, maybe now I can head to the space centre. I try not to smile, giddiness taking over.

It takes me a moment too long to feel the eyes on my back. Uneasiness fills me when I remember that guards closed the door behind us. No one in the room can see me anymore.

I hold my breath. Almost indistinctly, something stirs in the shadows. Not a guard. *Someone else.* Perhaps to finish me off.

I flick open my new blade. But it's too late.

The person grabs me from behind, peeling away from the darkness as I feebly try to pull away from their grasp.

I have absolutely no energy left, and I'm slammed against the wall, only to gasp at the sight of my attacker.

It's Jesse Hayes.

Holding a knife to my throat.

16

"Like a shadow, huh?"

My voice cracks.

I thought I'd left him behind for good. And yet, a small part of me flutters at the sight of him.

But I ignore it, because everything else aches. Betrayal washes over me to the point where I just want to sag against the wall.

I'm tired. So tired.

How does Jasmine do it? Running away from things is *hard*.

Jesse tightens his grip on his knife, and I try not to let him see how much it bothers me.

I wish he'd let me go. But somehow, I wish I shouldn't have to. I wanted *so badly* to be able to trust him. My hooded man. My protector. My shadow.

But now all I want to do is *spit at him*.

I squirm under the pressure of his blade.

"You should know that I don't break promises easily," he replies. *I hate you. I hate you. I hate you with everything that I am.*

He steals the breath from my throat, and it has nothing to do with fear. I let my gut fill with that anger and hopelessly try to find a way around the weapon.

He holds me firmly against the wall, clasping my hands with one of his as he pushes me into the sandstone. The hand wrapped around the knife on my neck doesn't tremble as I fix my positioning.

"Let me *move*," I snarl.

"And why would I do that? Won't you just *run away*, princess?"

"Screw you."

I stomp down on his boot, but the effort is clumsy, and he chuckles. He doesn't even flinch.

But the movement makes my nausea surface. My eyes roll in my head, dizziness clouding my senses.

"*You're hurting me.*"

"I'm doing nothing of the sort."

I growl at him. But he still doesn't budge.

Truthfully, his pressure is firm but not painful, and it's only due to my injuries that his fingers burn.

"I thought you were supposed to be my protector," I say.

I grip the switchblade firmly in my palm, wrists still bound. He sees I have it, but doesn't seem to care.

Jesse exhales dramatically. "I listen to Mel, that's all."

I grunt. "That's all?"

The guards mingle by the end of the tunnel. I see one observing my body pinned in an undignified manner, and I give him a mocking smile. He turns his back on us, unflinching.

"That's all."

"How terribly sad for you."

He presses the knife deeper into my throat. A gentle nip. A warning. And then he removes it, as if proving a point.

I lunge for him instantly. He raises his arm and pushes my back against the wall before I even have time to breathe, and just like that, his blade rests on my throat again.

Except this time I'm facing him, and I pull up my switchblade up in defence.

"I have one too."

It wobbles in my grip. He just laughs and snatches it in one effortless move.

"Hey! *Give it back*," I hiss.

"It won't help if your enemy already has a blade to your throat, princess," he says plainly. He grins lazily, then releases me from the wall once again.

The guards move aside for him at the other end of the tunnel, allowing him to pass with my switchblade.

"Hey," I gasp again, palms sweating at the sight of him taking the weapon.

It takes me a moment to collect myself before I jump forwards, following close behind him.

"You still have my switchblade," I declare.

"You'll get it back if you're good."

My brows turn down, and I open my mouth to snap back when a guard lashes out and grabs my arm, stopping me from leaving the tunnel.

I choke from the whiplash and the pain of his grip.

"Jesse?" I plead.

He bats an eye at me, smiling innocently, and then strolls away with his hands in his pockets, leaving me behind. I want to hit him, but I have no choice but to stay put. The area where the guard's fingers touch my arm hurts more than Jesse's grip had. As if he's relishing in punishing a fighter from the enclave.

I groan and try to pull my arm away.

To my surprise, he allows it with a grunt. Probably to avoid a scene. But his hand hovers over the large silver weapon dangling from his waist.

A sword.

What is this place, the goddamn medieval era?

I swallow at the thought, wincing at the coppery taste of blood in my mouth.

"Savannah!"

I blink before scanning the room, my actions sluggish.

Mel's standing by the bar talking to a set of guards. She's dressed in grey clothes like my own, but hers are pristine. Her brown, soft hair is pulled half up, the bits hanging down brushing lightly at her cheek and neck. She looks regal as she peels away from the guards and makes her way towards me.

Jesse hands her my switchblade.

She grabs it in her black-gloved hand, fingers wrapping around it hesitantly.

The short man who saved me from the brute moves to push her behind him, but she shakes him off.

"She's with me, Uncle. Thank you. You don't need to question her."

Melanie Beckett grabs my hands and pulls me away from the guards.

I try to shake her off me.

Here I am, more bloodied than before, back in the clutches of the same people who locked me up in the first place.

I grit my teeth as she half drags me back to her uncle. She looks determined, the tilt of her mouth suggesting she knew she'd find me eventually.

Oh, how I'd love nothing more than to slap that look off her face.

My eyes dart towards the exit but Melanie pulls me to side her sharply, snapping my head back.

"Savannah, this is my uncle, Liaison Banks. He runs operations on the Terra bases, just as Liaison Stone does on the sister base on Umbra—allowing travel and communications between planets."

The Liaison sucks in his lips, his eyes darting from me, to Melanie, to the fight room. It's hard to say what captures his attention most.

My shoulders sink.

"After my parents died, he became my legal guardian. When he came to Terra, I did too. And then I found Jesse." Her voice is very matter of fact, as if her background means very little to her.

This is a girl with purpose. With a goal.

The past doesn't matter when you have a mission for the future.

The Liaison doesn't respond. In fact, his attention settles back on his guards. Combing through all the witnesses will take a long while. I almost pity him.

Some guards take another person out—the female with the bleached hair. She spits a few curses at me and then vanishes out the front door. I assume they were taking her directly to the Safe Hold as well.

Whatever a Safe Hold is, it's clear these people fear it.

"We won't hurt you," Melanie says, noticing my gaze.

With a weak smile, she hands over my switchblade as if to prove her point, and I snatch it from her before she changes her mind.

Jesse opens his mouth to argue, but a look from Melanie cuts him off.

He's her bitch, all right.

"She needs to trust us," she tells him.

"Good luck with that," I retaliate.

"You did yesterday," Jesse teases, sliding towards me. I grip my blade. One touch and I can flip it open. "Or did you just pretend all that, so that we would take you here?"

"To your *village*?" I spit sarcastically.

Melanie steps closer. "It is… sort of. A village for my people. It also doubles as a base, a space centre, a research centre, a training ground, and more—we call them the Dome Cities. They're scattered across your planet. A village was just an easy way to describe it."

Liaison Banks places a gentle hand on her back.

His uncertain eyes bounce between me and Melanie as he says, "Welcome, friend. It's true, but this place is more than just a village. I'm in charge of it all—the island off Australia's coast, the mountains in Switzerland, and the desert in Africa—munitions, communication, the lot. Together we form the Terran unit, a small but diverse colony. It's quite spectacular, but be careful, hmm?"

I narrow my eyes at the subtle threat, the left side of my head throbbing at the action. He's trying to scare me with the power he has under his belt.

Melanie purses her lips, shrugging his hand off her as she takes a step back.

"She won't tell me how you met each other, but I have a few ideas," the Liaison continues. "They start with that warm, brown hair of yours. So just remember, if I have a reason to find you troublesome, I won't hesitate to throw you in with the rest of this lot."

His eyes snag on the tunnel leading to the fighting den.

Translation: don't threaten his dynasty. Noted.

He smiles at me, venomously sweet, and I grin tauntingly back. Let him think what he wants about that.

Like flipping a switch, his smile morphs into a scowl, and without another word, Liaison Banks stalks off to join his guards.

With a sigh, Jesse turns back to the bar. Melanie gives me a look that tells me I'm required to follow them.

My stance feels unsteady, head still dizzy from the fight.

"I don't know if I trust you," I repeat, clutching my stomach. I think of how she drugged me. How they imprisoned me. "Allies don't lock each other up."

"So your immediate thought is to jump out of a window?" Jesse sighs, clearly done with the idea of my existence.

I almost miss our chats in the forest.

Almost.

But Melanie doesn't give me enough time to answer, and she pulls me towards the bar. "*Jesse,*" she warns.

She sounds exhausted. Maybe tracking me down is just as draining as trying to escape.

"*Mel*," he replies sarcastically. He leans against the bar casually, but his posture is stiff and guarded, his next words sounding detached. "She can be a little impulsive—definitely not what you expected. Not the girl you think she is."

"But we know she is. The right girl, I mean," Melanie replies. "Otherwise we wouldn't have bothered."

"Holy stars, Mel. We *shouldn't* have bothered." The corner of his lips pinch and he sags against the counter. "We've risked our lives for her. And for what? A planet we only remember from our childhood? She wants nothing to do with us now that she's seeing the truth. Nothing at all. She had no reason to jump out of that window and yet—"

"No reason?" I intercede. I hover inches from his face, so close that I can see a freckle in the corner of his left eye, the peach hairs on the sides of his face, the slight flush on his cheeks. "You haven't given me a reason to trust you. You locked me up! All you've done is serve your own agenda by dragging me here. I don't want to die because of you, thank you very much."

I continue to glare at him, and when the space between us grows cold, I take a step back.

They both watch me, waiting for me to say more.

I pull out Jasmine's switchblade—my switchblade—and scrub the blood off the handle with my thumb. "I don't know this world. I don't know what you want from me—what *anyone* wants from me. I jumped the gun yesterday, coming here. But I'm here now." I swallow, raising my eyes, and I'm surprised to find Melanie gaping at me with understanding and respect, which I find disorientating. "Trust is mutual. So give me a reason to cooperate."

They both continue to stare at me, unsure how to respond.

Melanie simply stares off into the distance.

"Well," Jesse finally says, interrupting the silence. "Let me know when you finally figure everything out, princess." He turns back to the bar. "Meanwhile, I'm getting a drink."

Melanie sighs again. "Jesse."

He turns to face her. "Whiskey?"

I sit next to him and shakily swing my arms onto the bar. "Would love one."

He looks at me with a stony expression. "I wasn't talking to you."

I drum my fingers on the counter as he calls the bartender over. Melanie selects a seat next to Jesse. For some reason, she still doesn't look at me.

"Two whiskies, straight," Jesse tells the young man in front of me. "And water for the girl covered in blood."

Some of that blood gets on the bar as I lean towards him, eyebrows furrowed.

The young bartender tries not to look at me before retreating to get our drinks. I give him a sweet smile, but it goes past him.

If anyone needs some hard liquor, it's me. I glance at my hands. Blood is buried underneath the nails and there are bruises in places I can't recall being hurt. Combined with the fight and my free-fall off the roof, I must look like I've been dragged up from hell.

Every muscle hurts, my head's utterly throbbing, and I still feel like I'm going to empty my stomach at any moment.

I will never take a lack of pain for granted ever again.

The young man returns with our drinks and Jesse pays him, just as Liaison Banks ushers the last of the crowd from the pub.

He comes over to his niece.

The way he hovers, it's as if he wants to establish a close relationship with Melanie. But she's closed off, barely noticing him.

I grip my water tightly, trying not to make it obvious how soothing the cold glass is in my bruised hands.

He lovingly brushes his hand across Melanie's shoulder and then makes way to leave. He doesn't deign to look at me again.

"Take care of my girl," Liaison Banks tells Jesse by way of parting.

Jesse smirks, just as Melanie tips the glass of whiskey back and downs it in one go. "I'm quite sure she's capable of looking after herself, sir."

I abandon my straw and raise the cool glass of water to my lips, letting the liquid wash the blood and bile from my mouth.

"Savannah, take this." Melanie has her eyes on me, a lone white pill balancing in her gloved palm extended towards me. "It'll help if you have a concussion."

I touch my eyes, trying to focus. The left one is tender, as if it's swollen—I can barely see out of it.

A concussion?

My brain throbs in my skull, each motion making it feel as if it's rolling, and the water does nothing to force down the nausea.

Maybe I do have a concussion.

But I don't reach for the pill.

Jesse sighs deeply, snatching it from Melanie's palm and placing it on the table. He flashes a simple knife from his weapons belt, smashing the pill against the bar with the flat side of the blade before swiping the granules into his palm and dropping them into my drink. It fizzles slightly in the water, and I watch it swirl around, trying to hold myself together.

I don't trust them.

But on the off chance the pill does as Melanie says, I'd be stupid not to take it. Besides, I need answers from them.

Fingers shaking, I slowly reach for the glass, heart pounding as I take a small gulp.

Melanie smiles at me, turning back to her own drink.

"You were looking out for me," I say to Jesse, lowering my glass. "I know that. But why?"

He watches my fingers around the glass as he answers, not meeting my eyes. "For Mel."

"That doesn't answer my question."

They think I'm a princess, or some sort of revolutionary.

Obviously.

"Why does Melanie want me?" I ask.

She bites her lip, flashing those terrifying silver eyes at me. But it's Jesse that replies, somehow sensing what I'm asking.

"She has this ridiculous notion that you can resolve the tensions on Umbra and save it from ruin." He shrugs flippantly. "Still don't know why she bothers. If Umbra falls, we could always seek refuge on Terra and blend in with the people. I've observed them long enough. If anyone can do it, Mel and I can."

"You don't want that, truly," Melanie says.

"No, but it's inevitable," he says.

"Jesse Ian Hayes, nothing is inevitable, not if I have anything to do with it."

"See." He turns and faces me. "She has all these ridiculous notions."

Melanie's eyes burn when she leans over the counter to catch his eye. "The *only* place we could live without aging and dying is Umbra. While the dome protects us from the outside toxicity, there's no freedom, and no assurance the dome will remain intact. No one wants to die on Terra." She huffs in frustration, but her voice remains steady as she ticks off her reasons, turning to face me again as she says it.

Melanie's voice is always steady.

"Umbra will cut all ties with us and destroy this base, mark my words. When that happens, we will die with it, then soon after, Umbra will follow. We need to save Umbra. It's our home, Savannah. It's always been our home. It's the only place we can survive, and Jesse *knows* that."

"Umbra is dying, what's the point?" Jesse recites, as if he's said it a million times.

His dark eyes are unfocused, jaw tight, as he stares ahead.

"That's my point," she presses. "We need to save our planet."

"We can't. What good is immortality if the planet is crumbling at your feet?"

"Terra will crumble *you*, Jesse. You will die."

"Try me."

I shake my head, mouth suddenly dry. "Sorry," I intercede. "But did you say *immortality*?"

"Yes. On Umbra you don't deteriorate," Jesse says. "The word for that is immortality, princess."

My eyes glaze over. I shake my head again, and instead of asking what he means, I laugh.

The breaths wheeze out of me. "I know what immortality is. But... are you for real?"

My grin sends fresh pain across my cheeks, but I suddenly can't stop. I clutch the end of the bar to keep from falling.

Jesse just watches me with wild eyes, like I'm some sort of animal he doesn't know how to approach.

"Savannah, stop laughing, you're going to hurt yourself," Melanie says.

I shake my head at her.

Without giving me a chance to collect myself, Melanie sighs and begins to explain. "During the 16th century, it was discovered that Terra's air is poisonous to the human system—as well as other living organisms, such as animals, and even some plants. It acts as a slow killing force on our bodies. The lungs gather this contamination and spread it into our system, killing us slowly. If placed in the right conditions, humanity can live for eternity. But not on Terra, only on Umbra or under this dome, where the air is clean. Umbrans are young, untainted and untouched by the decaying air of Terra. Here, well, the people that sometimes leave the dome can look... older, I guess, as a result."

Suddenly, I don't want to laugh anymore.

I look her dead in the eyes.

"But surely you'd age. How about the entire concept of babies, children, adults? How do you know when you suddenly just stop... growing?"

"People stop growing around their teen years, and in rare cases, their early twenties. We don't *decay*, like you do here on Terra. That's aging. That's contamination. We develop on Umbra until we are fully grown and then we slowly stop. But death is an outside force, an act of stupidity or violence. We can live forever if we are smart about it, which we generally never are."

"How… old are you guys?" I mumble, my voice slightly shaky, much to my dismay.

"We use the same system as Terra to measure age, Savannah. Jesse is nineteen, but stopped his main growth phase at seventeen. I'm twenty-one, but I mostly stopped at sixteen. You grow bits and pieces after your main phase, but it's not very noticeable." She gives me a small smile, waiting for me to understand.

With this logic, the man behind the bar, who looks no older than twenty, could be well into his eighties. More, even. I blink at the almost non-existent stubble on his face, the smooth cheeks and the blond hair cropped short. There's not a sign of greying hair or age. He looks like a university student.

I shake my head, brow furrowing.

My heart throbs behind my eyes, but it's slightly less noticeable than before. I take another deep gulp of my water, my eyes stabbing her as I conjure excuses.

"How about reproduction?" I press. "People can reproduce too fast if they never die."

"On Terra perhaps," Melanie says. "But on Umbra, biologically, we don't reproduce as much. The Occupants hardly reproduced at all. A baby for them was a miracle, as they'd lived surrounded by the same faces for centuries. And when the humans joined them, we also began to adjust to their biological nature. Some organisms can do that—evolve to suit their climate. With each year, the birth rate became smaller and smaller."

I scratch my temple. "The Occupants?" I mumble.

"That's what they called themselves," she explains. "The original inhabitants of Umbra. They came to Terra in the 1700s, seeking more minerals and a peaceful alliance with Terra. It was then that they, and we through them, realised that our air is tainted."

I sway in my seat.

I wanted answers so badly... but now...

My head thumps, my heartbeat filling my eardrums.

I place the water back onto the bar, my fingers fiddling with the switchblade resting in my lap, my mind churning, everything aching—my head, my body, my heart.

Jasmine kept all this from me.

All of this, and more.

I pull back from the counter, leaving a tattered red mark across the smooth wood. Melanie notices it and chews on her bottom lip.

"Savannah, we need to get you patched up," she says.

I glance down at the blood, the torn skin across my side, and the bruises covering me like patchwork. "I couldn't agree more."

I finish off my water, taking a deep breath. Their medicine appears to be ridiculously advanced, first healing my sprain back to perfection, and now clearing my head of the throbbing migraine. But aliens are supposed to have advanced medicine, right? Isn't that what we've always been told, hinted at, in movies?

"Great idea." Jesse leaps up from his chair. "Let's see what *you* think about the destruction you've made to your window."

I freeze. I want to glare at him, but I can't keep the betrayal far enough from my features to do so.

"You're going to lock me up again."

Melanie opens her mouth, closes it.

"I'm not coming," I say. "I can find other doctors."

"We'll keep the door open," Melanie suggests feebly.

I stare at her blankly. She can't be serious.

"Fine. We won't put you in that room; we'll keep you in the labs if you prefer the metal tables. Really, Savannah?"

I don't even want to know what type of lab she means. "I'm not going back to those buildings," I snap. "Otherwise, your princess is running back to Silver Valley."

Jesse looks ready to lead the way, but Melanie sighs. "Really, Savannah?" Melanie repeats, sighing. "Fine. But it's your fault if you don't heal properly. The labs are there for a reason, you know."

Jesse grumbles as he peels away from the bar. I can't say I'm happy about sticking with him, either.

"I miss the old Savannah who would trust a stick if it gave her answers," he says quietly.

I follow them out of the room, closing my blade. "I don't miss that Savannah at all."

He shakes his head at me, watching me with an unreadable expression.

"People can evolve," Melanie says.

I trace the skin over my arm, trying to see if it feels smoother under the dome, but it doesn't. It feels worse. Dirty.

"But apparently not on Umbra," I say snidely.

Jesse snorts. "Just you wait and see, little princess. Just you wait."

I remind myself to keep the switchblade closed so I don't accidentally ram it into my leg.

The sensation of carrying a weapon feels odd to me—and as small as it is—I feel dangerous. I love the way it can be hidden in a boot or in a pocket, so not many people would expect me to have it.

I tuck it away, smiling.

Jesse unhooks his ugly vehicle from a clamp and waves us towards him. It appears he won't be helping me into the loot box this time.

"What a gentleman," I sneer as I find a way to climb around the thick nets.

"You're covered in blood. It's disgusting."

I school my features. I don't want to be here. He doesn't want me to be here, but I need their medicine. Badly.

I eye the ridiculous sword at his waist. It's held in a small scabbard, black hilt hidden against his dark clothing. "And what, you've never gotten stabbed before?"

"Not as many times as you have in one afternoon," he retorts.

I fall away from his net, my breath huffing out of my throat.

"Hilarious."

Because I'm feeling particularly peeved, I give him a small spin, showing off my recent injuries. Nowhere is there a stab wound. Lots of blood, yes. But no impaling.

"Right. No stabbing. Congrats." He leans against his machine, the corner of his mouth twitching.

Cocky bastard.

Don't react.

I try to hook my foot inside the net, my face set in a determined glower, but it's not strong enough to pull me up.

"I didn't *die*," I huff, not giving him the courtesy of meeting his sneering gaze.

"Your opponent didn't either," he says.

My foot slips in the net as it bends to my weight and I choke back my gasp. At the same time, Melanie comes around the machine and smacks Jesse on the back of his head, her eyebrows low.

He pulls himself upright and gapes at her.

"Ouch, Mel."

"If you start encouraging her to kill people, she might actually get *herself* killed," she says.

"You both have *such faith* in me," I sneer. But my injuries howl with a burning heat as I grapple with the net.

And they see it.

Jesse clenches his jaw. But the tiniest hint of humour glints in his eyes.

In the glow of the setting sun, they're nearly the colour of sapphires. They're less impressive than Melanie's sharp eyes, but somehow prettier.

A small breath leaves my throat.

Jesse meets my gaze, raising his eyebrows.

I stare back at him in challenge, my face getting hot.

It feels like an eternity until I untangle myself from the net and lower myself back to the ground, irritation squeezing my chest because of that stupid machine.

Melanie clucks her tongue at me. "You can use that lip near the front as a step." She points to the front of the ugly thing.

I barely smile at her.

Jesse's salutes, as if he done God's work, and pulls himself up to the drivers side. A muscle in my face twitches as I place my bandaged foot on the lip and pull myself up.

The movement sends tendrils of pain swirling through me.

I swallow against the dryness in my throat and continue anyway, despite wanting to lie down and never get up.

I settle in the corner of the loot box, resisting the urge to sleep. The world spins around me as I wait for the others to climb into the machine.

I feel drunk on the pain.

Melanie takes a seat beside me. She leans over, her hands fluttering as if she wants to support me, but she hesitates, fiddling with the end of her black glove. Instead, she resolves to perching daintily at the back of the box so she can keep an eye on where we're going and watch me just as easily.

I've always despised the doctors.

Fighting the swelling in my chest, I squeeze my eyes shut, taking a steadying breath.

The closed switchblade sits in my pocket and my fingers flex to the blade on it gently, feeling reassured by the feel of it. I wonder how many lives it's taken. What journey it's been on.

I open my eyes and they land on an empty water bottle hidden in the net just as Jesse spurs the machine to life. He guides it slowly out of the mass of other machines. I hadn't brought a single item with me, but here, Jesse always is ridiculously well-equipped.

Melanie unearths something from the bindings as Jesse pulls the machine onto the road.

The plastic water bottle taunts me and I can think of nothing else but the few drops of water lining the base of the bottle.

The sun blinks away as we glide between buildings and Melanie's hair dances angrily as the wind grabs at it, knotting and curling it as she leans against the back of the vehicle.

The sun has set, and we press through the budding darkness in silence.

Jesse turns a sharp corner and I groan, but to my relief, he eases the vehicle to a slower pace.

The switchblade rolls around in my palm and I watch it idly until I realise Jesse has silenced the engine.

It's hard to tell where we are, but based on the lower buildings around us, I assume it's nowhere near the medical centre I was first brought to.

I secure my grip on the switchblade as Melanie jumps out of the loot box and I lurch upright and follow.

No one speaks as Jesse clamps his vehicle into a parking corner, but I swear I hear him mumble to himself, "Glad to see Savannah can last a trip without fainting."

"Glad my captors can last a trip without drugging me," I retort.

Melanie gives me a strained look.

I avoid her gaze.

The area Jesse has taken us to reminds me more of a village than any other part of the base I've seen. Trees dot the edge of the dome, but it lacks the wild intent of the deep forest that I'm familiar with. The dirt on the ground has been treaded down, covered in more footprints than any other place.

The houses gleam bright and metallic, showing signs of many residents, but the scale of them is less intimidating than the skyrises. They don't have balconies, but the windows are large, and I can glimpse people through many of them.

The ocean hums softly in the distance, but I can tell we aren't by the beach. We must be at the eastern edge of the base, close to the forest.

"My place is up this way," Melanie says. She points to a taller building just before us—one of the larger living complexes. On the angled roof, birds are nesting for the night. It's relatively normal compared. "I haven't been inside for months," she continues. "I've been living in the space centre."

"The space centre?" I press.

"My job," she tells me. "When I came to Terra, I was assigned night shifts as an assistant in the space centre by courtesy of my uncle, but it was a job no one else wanted. Eventually, I worked my way up to Shipment, where they organise the comings and goings from Umbra."

"In other words, she's the head delivery man. Don't know why it keeps her as busy as it does," Jesse says snidely, tracking our surroundings. As if he suspects someone is watching us from the shadows and he's scared to say more. He throws some sort of tarp over his machine, and then binds it, concealing the monstrosity under a black veil.

She rolls her eyes at him, dismissing his worry, but replies in a whisper all the same. "I spend most of my time hacking these days."

"Hacking?" I wonder, brows scrunching together.

She pulls her glove higher up her arm, as if ashamed of the hand underneath, her eyes downcast.

"My dad taught me how to hack computers, and my mum taught me how to heal the sick and injured. I never got the knack for healing," she claims, glancing over at me apologetically. "But stars, do I love hacking. I've never met anyone else who can do what I can do."

"Always modest," Jesse snorts.

She nudges him half-heartedly.

"It's been helpful." She flashes me a grin. "I know nearly everything that's going on in this base. Except Umbra... I can't quite breach that firewall from here."

I suck in my lips. If Melanie can lower the dome, maybe I can trick her into doing so once I'm healed.

"So, you're not in direct contact with Umbra?" I ask, turning the conversation back around.

"Not even close. Technically, my job only allows me access to the interstellar shipments—but it's my cover for when people question why I know so much about Umbra and Silver Valley. The rest is all hacking and Jesse. Having loyal eyes on the ground always fills in any black patch the computers cannot reach."

I tighten my grip around the blade and watch as Jesse shakes his head and heads up towards her apartment.

"Has anyone else been watching *me*, in particular?"

"Just us so far. A few have leads on you, but no one has found you… yet. I plan to keep it that way," she says. She grins and beckons me to follow her up to the house.

Like a pirate hogging treasure, I think to myself.

"You can't be certain I'm the right princess," I scoff as we walk across the road.

"I can, and I do. Your friend, Jasmine Spark, was the last piece of the puzzle. She came from Umbra and if that necklace really is hers, then I'm certain. And you act as though you two are close. No one would have an Umbran as a close friend if they're Terran. Take my word on that," she advises.

"There's a lot I still don't know about Jasmine Spark." My voice wavers.

"Perhaps, but we'll find out."

I hesitate slightly, missing a step.

She holds the door open for me and I quickly duck my head and enter, hoping she didn't notice. The soft light of the room touches my skin. And immediately, my shoulders relax. This is nothing like the prison cell.

Thank god.

I lower my arms and plaster on a smile for them.

They say they need me, so that means they might be playing nice to gain my trust. And I don't let myself trust them. Not for one second.

Melanie gestures me forwards, and my smile now feels strained.

I follow her up a stairway, past the entrance hall. Each footfall reverberates, announcing our arrival all the way up until the final storey. Here Melanie opens a seemingly random door in a pale, white-walled hallway and pushes me inside.

"I'm going to get some medicinal supplies from the labs. Guard her," she says to Jesse.

Without another word, she turns and heads downstairs, stunning me into stillness.

I blink at her back, but Jesse just delves into the room and switches on a light. It bathes the room beyond in yellow. I roll my shoulders back and follow him into the centre of the room, where a small couch rests near a window that looks over the village.

The night smiles at me, pocketed in yellow lights from the windows, as if the stars fell from the heavens and drifted around the base.

Jesse watches me.

I roll my eyes and go to find water.

Melanie has a small kitchenette covered in dirty plates and various objects like jackets and papers she seems to have just placed on the counter and forgotten about. There's a single bedroom with a thin curtain being used in place of a door, and a plain bed and single chair looking lost beside it. Everything is small and bare. She definitely hasn't lived here much.

I turn away from the coffee table, the window, the single couch—which has an assortment of clothes and blankets hanging over its edges as well—and towards what I assume is a bathroom.

Jesse doesn't bother asking where I'm going. There aren't many places I *can* go.

The bathroom contains an egg-shaped bath, a shower, toilet, metal sink, and a small mirror. I flip on the light and take a step back from my reflection, startled.

My skin's covered in bruises—especially across my cheekbones where the brute's fist broke the skin, leaving crusts of blood. My left eye is nearly swollen shut. The redness in my eyes makes them watery and they appear silver in the glow. Like Melanie's.

I bury any thoughts of being connected to Umbra, and flick the switchblade open in the sink, spinning open the faucet to draw water over the metal.

I freeze.

There's an inscription on the wooden handle, and I scrub the remains of dried blood off it with my thumb and then hold it up to the light.

A black trail of letters scrawls over the mahogany, and I recognise the gentle slope of the letters—the way they cling to each other and intersect.

The writing is messier than I recall, as if she had struggled with the tool that engraved the word into the handle. I blink slowly, my bad eye twitching, unsure how such a small child had managed wield a pen.

But it's certainly her handwriting.

Jasmine.

How?

I lower my chin onto my chest as my eyes prickle. My hands shake against the sink, and pain threatens to rip my chest apart.

I let a wall take shape in my chest and push the pain away until it's locked into a small corner inside me to smoulder and die. Then I drop the switchblade into the sink with a loud clatter and pull myself upright, straightening my shoulders.

I stare at myself until the tears fully recede.

My grey eyes glisten silver, almost as bright as Melanie's but rimmed with red. I run my fingers over my skin, brushing my freckles and combing the knots out of my brown hair. It will take ages to brush the tangles free. I sigh, lip wobbling at the sight of how wretched I look.

After a few counts, I pull myself from the mirror to run water in the bath. But the word on the blade clouds my thoughts.

Perseverance.

I can keep going. I *will* keep going. It's all I have left right now.

Not surprisingly, the word brings a strange sense of déjà vu.

When your mother abandons you and your father works nearly every day of his life, I suppose you don't really have a choice but to toughen up and become your own adult.

To persevere.

This is the real test after all those years; a final breaking point to gauge the strength I've built around my heart.

I pull back the curtain to conceal the bathroom from the apartment and slip inside the bath, letting the cold water take me.

Not long after, Melanie returns, her lips twisted sourly, a box filled with ointments and thick syringe cylinders in her hands.

After taking her pill to fix the concussion I must have had, I feel hazy and content. Refreshed, if not a little tired.

My body is wrecked.

It needs time to heal.

She strides past the bath, placing a few items on the sink before striding into the lounge room and speaking to Jesse in a flustered tone.

It's quite easy to ignore her.

I let the water soak into my clothing before peeling the sopping material from my body and letting it hang discarded over the edge of the bath. I've let the water run three times already. I didn't realise how much blood and dirt I had on me.

"They drive me mad," Melanie suddenly snaps, throwing aside the curtain to storm into the bathroom. "I have hardly any supplies here, and no one in the labs will give me any. I wish I could hack some into existence."

"Can't you just say it's a matter of utmost importance?" I smirk, lowering myself further underwater. "I'm sure they'll understand if I'm their long lost princess."

"You're not long lost, and you're not a princess yet," she corrects. "And besides, I promised you I'd keep you a secret."

"Does that benefit me or you more?" I sneer.

"Both." She pops open a ceramic pot, oblivious to my fear. It's filled with some sort of dirt, and she tips some into my bath.

I stiffen in the bath and my injured eye throbs as I widen my eyes at her.

"Hey, woah," I say on a shaky breath. "I only just flushed all the dirt out."

"This 'dirt' is antiseptic. Stop squirming."

I clench the edge of the bath like it's a lifeline.

She puts the pot back and reaches for another.

"Is it strong antiseptic?" I hiss, feeling it sting my open skin.

"Not in Umbran standards, but it's all I have in this apartment."

As long as it doesn't knock me out... or kill me.

I slide deeper into the water and run my hands over the surface, forcing my muscles to ease. The dirt swirls and swirls until eventually the clear water dissolves it and I'm bathing in a brown, tainted liquid.

I wonder what the water is like on Umbra. Is it like Terra, or is it different? More acidic? Saltier? I spin my hands faster through the water, making soft currents around me. Melanie hardly notices, too busy with her medicinal tray.

I wait until she turns back to me before I speak.

"Umbra," I whisper. "It means 'shadow' in Latin, doesn't it?" Pretty sure I've heard the word somewhere in passing before.

She snaps a vial of the clear syringe off it's casing where it's linked together with the other syringes. It's as long as my finger, but much thicker. On one side is the ejection point of the needle, the other end a button to eject it.

She doesn't take that black glove off while she works.

"Yes," she says. "It does."

I smile. Jesse's a shadow, Umbra's a shadow.

"How did that name come about? Is Umbra covered in shadows? Is it dark there?"

Melanie shakes her head. She spins the syringe around her fingers, her eyes unfocused.

I chew on my lip, heart pounding in my chest. She shakes her head again, smiling. But I don't know what for.

"Umbra: the shadow of Terra," she whispers, as if reciting a textbook quote.

I pull my legs up to my chest and wrap my arms around them, trying to steady my nerves.

She won't kill me. She needs me.

The brown water splashes, hitting the edges of the bath and my skin alike. The water is starting to agitate my wounds, but I don't let Melanie see that. I sit like a stone in the water.

Her eyes grow distant, detaching from reality.

I lose myself in her voice as she recites,

"'The Occupants didn't have a name for their planet, they simply called it Home in their language. So, when the scientists arrived from Terra, they didn't know what to call the planet... But when they touched foot onto the red desert of Umbra, they didn't need to. The answer came to them. Umbra was so alike Terra, so astoundingly familiar, that one of the scientists said, "It's like a shadow of Terra."

Another scientist ran the sand from under their feet through his fingers and said, "Umbra: the shadow of Terra."

And so, from then onwards, the small planet was known by humanity as Umbra. They never called it Home, as the Occupants did, but they made it their own.'"

As soon as she finishes speaking, she reaches for the cup next to her, placing it under the tap to fill with water. She hands it to me and motions for me to drink.

I do as I'm told before I ask my next question.

"So... we—the human race—stole Umbra from the Occupants?" I ask Melanie. The very thought makes my throat feel bitter. We have a planet, we don't need another one.

"No," she says, shaking her head again. "No, not at all. We lived in harmony."

"I doubt that," I say. "Humans enjoy destruction."

"Humans also are very good at dying out. Remember that. When they first went to Umbra, they escaped their roots—and the Occupants showed them how to live more compassionately. It was a very enticing prospect to them at the time. Especially when the Occupants offered them immortality."

"To the twisted mind, that would be reason enough. A planet like Terra, where you can live forever? Why wouldn't humans snatch that prize?" I press.

I want Melanie to prove me wrong. I want her to tell me that humans are better than that.

"Maybe," she says. "Maybe in the beginning, that was their intention. But when they travelled to Umbra, met this new, kind-hearted race, everything changed." She looks away with tenderness in her eyes. "Their past was so terrifying, so filled with death, that I believe a part of them wanted nothing more than to embrace peace."

Beneath the endearment, her voice sounds strained, so full of sorrow for the planet she left behind. In her eyes, I can see the longing. She must crave peace to return to her planet again, must want nothing more than to experience what that was like.

And I must admit, it does sound remarkable, if not fleeting.

Of course, the Umbrans have sunk back into their old ways. It doesn't surprise me; I wouldn't really expect peace everlasting.

Melanie waves for me to give her my arm and I raise it hesitantly. She lowers the syringe, the almost translucent liquid winking at me in the light—and with a pinch she presses the eject button and lets the needle sink into my skin.

"This will completely heal you in a day or so. There are syringes in the labs that boost your body's natural healing, fixing most injuries in minutes. It's called *Velox* and it's strictly administered. This here is a weaker agent called *Prius*, it's more common to come across and all I have in the apartment. It's slower acting but works the same." She pulls free the empty syringe, brushing her finger over the bead of blood at the incision point. With slightly shaking hands, I pull my arm back and hug it to my chest.

The throbbing of the antiseptic against my open skin already feels more bearable. Odd.

"Then what happened?" I push. "Why is Umbra in a period of tension now?"

"Because," she struggles, saying each word slowly, "everything went to hell."

"How?"

I hold myself in a ball, trying not to fidget.

Melanie picks at the glove on her hand, fingers shaking slightly.

"Natural disasters shattered the planet. It was no one's fault. The castles they built crumbled, the world around them changed, and the sky rained with meteors the size of their homes. People died. So many people."

"How? What type of natural disasters?" My breath quickens.

"Ones of their moons exploded. It all escalated from there."

"When did this happen?" I ask quietly. "The guards still carry swords, and the timeline? It doesn't make sense."

She notices the crease on my forehead and sighs.

"The Moon Blitz happened throughout the 1800s, mostly," she says, her voice sounding strained. "Umbra is ancient, Savannah—it doesn't align to the history you're used to. Especially since Umbrans didn't need a reason to wield weapons until now, so I suppose we never really evolved from swords—at least on Terra. We were always more a planet of science.

"The Occupants contacted the British government during the 1700s. They shared your history once, but their timeline split with Terra the moment they left. They evolved into a new race entirely."

She smiles at me with a devilish humour. "One that has swords, among other things."

I slouch back into the bath, mind whirring, when I whisper, "Umbra is infested by Georgians."

I recall what I know about that era. Mostly *Sense and Sensibility* and *Pride and Prejudice*. Apparently, it wasn't just a world of horses and carriages, dances and dresses. It was also a world of blood, public executions, and poverty.

Has Umbra become that again? Or has living with the Occupants made them slightly less barbaric?

"To you, possibly." Melanie shrugs. "Despite the coalition of Elders, we still hold court in the kingdom. We never experienced the revolution of the Victorian era because we were suffering with the effects of the Moon Blitz at that time."

"So the scientists were all taken from Great Britain?" I ask Melanie.

She nods. "Mostly, yes. That's why there's a base here, off the Australian coastline. At the end of the 1800's—when transport was properly introduced between the two planets—they found the island not far from Sydney and planted a base here. The First Peoples of Australia never inhabited it, and the Brits had fallen upon the mainland by that point, so taking it was easy. They later planted bases in the Saharan Desert and Swiss Alps to extend their connection to the rest of the world, but the Australian one is the largest. It was the first."

And now Silver Valley is on the island, right near the old base.

Leaning towards Melanie, I wonder how life would've been for her on Umbra, where her universe would be filled with swords and swooping dresses. It's almost enough to make me want to go to Umbra, if only to see what it's like.

I could take Mason with me. He would love it there.

"Do you miss it?" I ask her slowly.

For some reason, it's this question that brings her gaze back to me. Her eyes turn to grey stones and her body assumes a similar stony disposition.

She pulls her hands away from me, sets them neatly in her lap, and inhales deeply.

"I can't afford to. Not yet." Her voice breaks on the last words.

It doesn't answer my question.

And without thinking, more words tumble through my lips in a waterfall of accusations. "Your past haunts you, doesn't it? Something hurt you once, on Umbra."

The soft velvet of my tone doesn't seem to matter, as she recoils from my words anyway.

She flinches, shadows clouding her eyes. I can almost watch the memories flashing behind them.

"Don't. I… It…"

She stops fiddling with her glove, hands balling into fists.

Melanie clenches her jaw and suddenly storms out of the room, leaving a gust of perfumed air in her wake.

The curtain falls behind her.

I sit in the bath soundlessly, lips clenched, the sound of the front door slamming echoing as she leaves the house. I grip my arms tightly to my chest.

The curtain sways gently in the doorway and I watch it until my eyes ache.

I sleep like the dead. And when I wake, it's with a lurch, gasping in the dusty air. The non-contaminated air.

I let my hands drift above me, feeling it circle around my skin, creating tiny movements in the stale bedroom. The air here might be clean, but it doesn't taste fresh—almost like it's been churned out through a machine, giving it a weird metallic taste.

My lungs ache for the sweet Umbran air from my dreams. The fruitful taste of immortality, free from the bitterness of metal.

For now, I settle for the manufactured kind, and wonder how much of my aging has halted in the time I've been here.

The dome keeps the tainted air out—Jesse had elaborated after my bath—and they have pumps situated around the base, filtering the air from outside. Anyone who comes and goes from the dome must enter quarantine to prevent them from bringing toxicity into the base.

I was knocked out when I came through, so the process makes my mind spin and my heart race at the thought of it.

A faint cluttering sound echoes from outside the bedroom door. I watch as the curtain separating me from the rest of the apartment blasts orange with the light in the kitchen, and I listen as a kettle breaches the quiet.

My sweat licked off some of the sticky substance I had plastered on my skin to soothe it overnight, and the rest of it streaks the blankets.

The kettle falls quiet.

I'm lying still, staring at the ceiling for what seems like hours before the front door closes, this time a soft tick instead of a slam. Melanie came home for the night and she's leaving again.

"I'm working on an idea," she had whispered to Jesse on the couch before she left. "I promise."

Jesse's voice sounded lost to sleep when he answered, "You're always working on an idea. Go away."

And the house had gone quiet.

I continue to lie still.

My back doesn't ache at all anymore and my head feels fuzzy with sleep, as if the concussion had never occurred. I trail my fingers over the skin on my back, feeling the residue of the sticky substance lining my almost perfectly healed skin.

I'm in the exact same position by the time the sky outside swells into morning. I tip my head sideways and curl into the blankets, watching the sun.

The stars have gone now, flushed away by the light. Orange pries apart the milky clouds as the sun dawns through my window, a crack of brilliant gold breaking through. The light catches on the motes in the room, highlighting every particle.

I watch the dust as it dances through the air.

The air doesn't *look* clean.

My breath swirls in and out past my lips, and I shudder. Every single inhale is frozen in time, correcting my life span. My life was once a ticking clock of death—even if it takes ninety years, it's death, nonetheless. And now? There's only the prospect of infinite time.

I wonder how long you can live in contamination before salvation on Umbra isn't enough to save you from dying. In fact, I wonder if the chance of immortality is even an option for me anymore, having been living on this planet for seventeen years.

Mason would have a higher chance.

My father on the other hand... I swallow deeply as my gut twists in circles.

The very idea of immortality seems incomprehensible. An impossible truth.

But it *is* the truth, and it's obtainable.

Here, I'll be stuck under a dome. But on Umbra, I would be free. I would have time. Space. The future. I could go to Umbra, and I could have it all.

The fact my family is currently breathing in decay is possibly the only incentive I have to go there. Everything else keeps me on Terra.

Because Terra is my home. My family is here. My life is here.

But... I can take all that to Umbra. Can't I?

Not now, but eventually when it's safe, we could seek salvation on Umbra. Me, Mason, my dad. I could build us a new life.

I sit upright. It shocks me how normal I feel... as if I was never injured at all. I swallow deeply, feeling unsettled.

Umbra is a storybook world...

Their air, their medications...

I turn away from the sunrise with a new determination. Melanie left me a pile of clothes on the floor beside her bed—a linen shirt and skin-tight pants, as well as my shoes. I change out of the slip dress I borrowed from her last night and quickly change.

When I step outside the bedroom, Jesse lifts his eyes immediately.

I watch him for a moment, sprawled over the couch with his blankets abandoned on the floor. He looks like he just woke up, despite the boots he wears and the leather jacket he slept in. His back is to the sunrise, and he runs a polishing cloth down a long silver sword.

He doesn't wish me good morning, so I don't say anything either.

I swallow a greeting and pick my way to the kitchen.

I'm used to mornings smelling of coffee, whether it's in cardboard takeaway cups or from the espresso machine at home. But here, mornings don't smell like coffee. They smell like lemons and burnt toast.

Melanie left an empty cup of lemon water on the counter, as if she ran out of tea and had to improvise. I grab the half-cut lemon she abandoned in the fridge and set to work making another one.

From the couch, Jesse watches me, pretending not to.

We both stay quiet.

I switch on the kettle and grab two ceramic teacups.

He turns away, and the rising sun makes his hair look orange.

I wonder how Jesse would look in a top hat.

Was he a guard on Umbra, adorned in silver attire, with straps across his chest and silver buttons lining his sleeves?

The idea of Jesse dressed as an English gentleman almost makes me scoff.

I pop some bread into the toaster and pour the boiling water over the lemon. Spreading some butter on the toast, I hold it between my teeth so that I can carry both cups to the couch. Jesse doesn't look up when I extend a cup, so I place it on the table before him.

He pauses polishing his sword, frozen in time.

I sit there quietly, and he slowly continues his task.

I don't expect him to speak at all.

In the forest, I felt like we had an invisible link binding us together. Sitting in silence, aware of each other's presence—that worked for us.

I shrug to myself and crunch on my toast.

With my new goal of relocating my family to Umbra, I know it's vital to make connections with Umbrans. That means Jesse and Melanie. And through them, I can access Melanie's contacts. It would be enough, I hope.

It must be enough.

I sip at the lemon water and it burns my tongue. Jesse doesn't look at me, but he puts down his dagger and lifts his own cup to his lips.

He drinks it, even though it's still scalding.

I almost want to roll my eyes at the tough act.

Instead, I take inventory of the assortment of blades he has aligned across the table—two knives; one small, one large; a dagger; an expensive sword; and a selection of what looks like arrows.

In this modern age, they're the type of weapons I wouldn't expect anyone to carry.

And then, at the end of the table, my switchblade sits idly. I must have left it in the bathroom last night.

I discard my crust on the table next to his perfectly polished knife and reach for it. Jesse tenses but doesn't stop me.

I take the polishing cloth he left on the table and flick my blade open. From the corner of his eye, he watches me polish it.

I lose myself in the repetitive rhythm while I wait for my tea to cool, and it catches me off guard when Jesse finally speaks.

"I need to teach you how to use that thing."

My body stiffens and I exhale.

Rolling my shoulders, I ease motion back into my body, and grabbing my tea again, I smile. "I think I got it," I say. "Poke, poke. Stab, stab."

"My faith in you is wavering further by the moment."

Holding my breath, I whisper tentatively, "Maybe... eventually, you can teach me how to poke and stab. If you want."

The words sound strained, but I don't know if he notices.

He doesn't look at me. "Maybe."

Words hardly seem necessary. We seem to speak without speaking.

Hour by hour, our postures become less strained, and we walk around the room with more ease.

I've been telling myself how I need to build up my trust towards him, but it hadn't occurred to me that he might be doing the same thing for me.

His lip twitches again as he watches me, and I think hopefully, maybe, that trust is growing.

If only just a little.

჻

Time passes quickly in Melanie's apartment.

Jesse doesn't leave my side throughout and I don't fool myself into thinking it's because he likes my company.

Obviously, he's guarding me.

It's only when I sleep that he leaves me be.

The next morning I wake to find Melanie at work, and him lingering by the bathroom, his dark hair hanging damp across his forehead.

It's Saturday. I had plans today to hang out with Jasmine and her friends. I wonder if everyone is still going and if Jasmine's continuing with her life, even though I'm not there to be a part of it.

I spend most of the day feeling restless, lying on the couch with my legs up over the armrest, staring at the ceiling and trying to calm the urge to go outside and do something.

Two thoughts tear at me: do I work on establishing their trust more? Or do I go in search of more answers?

It's hard to decide which is more important.

Jesse watches me from the kitchen, where he's constructing

a sandwich. His expression looks curious, angry, and amused all at once.

The front door booms open. I jump and nearly fall off the armrest. "Jesus," I gasp.

Melanie gives me an artificial smile from the entrance.

I should really teach this girl about how to work doors normally.

"It worked," she claims.

Her eyes move between Jesse and me, but the hushed tone makes it obvious she's speaking to Jesse.

Melanie works for what seems like twenty hours a day. She wears a silver jumpsuit, tailored so it hugs her slight frame perfectly. I gather it's her uniform—she must have come home in her lunch break.

"If you mean to tell me you've finally realised that you're allowed days off then I'm seriously impressed," he mumbles.

"No," she replies.

"Well, then," he utters. "In that case, I'm busy."

"You don't look busy," she says. She walks over to him and snatches the bread away. "Really? You ate all my bread."

"You want a sandwich?"

She throws it on the bench with a huff.

"No." Melanie comes over to me and sits nimbly on the edge of the couch. "I had an idea," she tells me.

I face her and try to keep my expression kind.

"Your friend, Jasmine Spark. If she came from Umbra, she would've likely landed here. It doesn't make sense for her to land at another base and move across the continent at such a young age. And she would've been young when she came down, if not a baby, for you to believe you grew up with her."

Her words take me back for a moment.

I underestimated how perceptive Melanie Beckett is.

"Which means," she continues, "there's a chance someone here would've known about her. I put some feelers out, asked around if anyone recognised her name or her appearance, and it didn't take long. As it turns out, my uncle knew Jasmine. But he didn't know her as Jasmine Spark, he knew her as Jasmine James."

My body stiffens, and even Jesse stops making noises in the kitchen.

I clutch the edge of the couch.

"He didn't realise who I was taking about until I mentioned her appearance. He recognises her from Umbra," she explains excitedly.

I can't bring myself to share her joy. I think about Jasmine's parents, picturing the Sparks family in my head—Ella's brown eyes and blonde hair, Ethan's brown curls and blue eyes. Jasmine fits. She is one of them. She's always been one of them.

Surely Melanie's uncle is wrong. "If that's true, it would mean she isn't the biological child of Ethan and Ella." My voice sounds hollow.

"But… that's not all, Savannah," she continues.

I study Melanie's mouth, waiting for her words. My teeth clench and my eyes feel dry and hollow.

"He said she was fifteen on Umbra, as stated in the records from before she left. That's just two years younger than she is now, but she's been on Terra for fourteen years. And on Terra, you cannot lie about your age."

"Because of the air," I mumble. I hardly hear myself. "It can't be right though, the guy in The Nook—the one I fought—he said he met Jasmine on the shuttle. That she was only a few years old, and he came down to Terra fourteen years ago. That matches her age now."

Melanie furrows her brow.

"You sure he said that?" she asks.

"Completely."

"You jumped out a window that day, don't forget," Jesse says from the kitchen. "Might have hurt that pretty head."

I grit my teeth and ignore him.

"Your uncle must be wrong, Melanie." My voice is stronger than I feel. "She may not be the daughter of Ethan and Ella, considering she came from Umbra when she was so young, but she might not be Jasmine James either."

Melanie scratches her head. "This is giving me a headache."

You and me both.

"When's her birthday?" she asks.

"June 11th," I say.

"Did her parents say she is their biological daughter?"

"Yes, we were both born in the same year. Our parents are friends."

Melanie drops her head in her hands.

In the kitchen, Jesse finishes his sandwich. I think I hear him drop a ceramic container on his foot, if his onslaught of cursing is any indication.

Melanie slumps back in her chair. "Your friend is great at keeping secrets," she says.

Her words bug me. I grip the switchblade in my pocket and squeeze until it hurts.

"You have no idea."

$$\backsim$$

The front door slams as Melanie leaves for work.

I'm jealous of her. I can't sit here anymore; my skin and head are completely healed. I need to do something productive.

Jesse brushes the crumbs off his fingers, satisfied with himself. He hardly notices me when I make my way to the door. My hand touches the doorknob when he launches forwards and grabs my elbow, stopping me from going any farther.

"What are you doing?"

I planned on leaving without him, but when my eyes travel down to his weapons belt, another idea forms. I smile at him with false sweetness. "What do you say about paying Melanie's uncle a visit?"

He doesn't say anything to that, merely frowns angrily and

pulls me away from the door. I try and yank my arm back, but all it does is hurt me.

He throws me onto the couch. "Stay there. You don't even know where he lives."

I liked it better when we didn't talk.

"But you do. So," I wiggle my eyebrows, "how about it?"

He turns away. "Absolutely bloody not."

He goes to guard the door, so I get up and follow him. The moment he realises what I'm doing, he grunts and grabs my arm again, dragging me away from the exit.

I'm thrown back on the couch. He practically punches me into it this time. Then he goes back to guard the door.

I get up and follow him again.

He whips around. "Do you want me to stab you? Because I will."

"Not really."

"Then don't test me."

I hardly get to him before he grabs my elbow and yanks me back. The whiplash is ridiculous. He's stronger than me. Way stronger.

I gasp as he throws me into the cushions, and this time he doesn't go back to the door. I cross my arms over my chest as he sits beside me, fingers dangling near the hilt of his dagger.

"Why can't we? Melanie's allowed to." I try to pout, but I've never been good at pouting and Jesse just frowns at me, his fingers twitching towards the dagger as if it's taking all his strength not to use it.

"You know why."

"Not really," I say, realising it's true. Why are we staying here? Because I'm injured? I'm healed now.

"Melanie said I'm your guard," he grunts, as if unsure what else to say.

"She never specified that you couldn't guard me at her uncle's house."

"Because she knows I'm not an idiot," he snaps.

"I guess that makes one of us."

He glares at me sharply, then leans into the couch, taking his eyes off me. Apparently, this argument is over. I grunt, not letting his absent gaze fool me. He could snag me in less than a moment if I were to dash towards the door.

I keep my head forwards as we both stare at the wall. I glance sidelong at his impossibly smooth features.

I've never met anyone more infuriating to read.

"Okay, I'm sorry, but do you not have a mind of your own?" I hiss, my muscles twitching.

I didn't intend to ask him this, but the words came out anyway. And I can't say he's exactly fond of prying.

He turns and glares at me. This time his fingers wrap around the hilt of his dagger. "You don't know anything."

I slide across the couch towards him. "Then tell me," I say.

His fingers tighten on the blade, but he doesn't make a move to pull it from the scabbard. "I have nothing to say to you."

"You don't want me going out into the base," I press again.

"This place isn't your home," he tells me. "It isn't kind."

I swallow and wrap my arms over my chest, locking eyes with his. We sit entirely still, glaring at each other.

I wonder about Jesse's past. He came to Terra on the same shuttle as Melanie, and Melanie said this base is her home, but he doesn't seem to care for it the way Melanie does. He acts indifferent, but does he pine to live somewhere else?

They're the kind of questions I should be asking myself.

My mother had the stars tangled through her soul, seeping from her very pores. My father is the most grounded person I know. Mason daydreams of worlds beyond our own, of adventures and castles in the clouds. Where does that put me? Terra or Umbra, or am I somewhere different altogether?

"Home," I utter, my breath hanging between us, "is a place I don't know exists."

His chest expands on a deep breath, as if my words rattle him. His fingers slip from his blade, entirely of their own accord.

"You okay?" I say, confused.

He looks ready to fly away, to leap from the couch and into the shadows. His eyes shift, but I hold his gaze. And for the first time, I see inside.

Pain.

A faraway look settles on his features, and I recognise it immediately. I've seen the same thing in my mother's eyes. It shakes me like an old dream coming to life.

Jesse's home isn't Terra. It isn't this base. His home is Umbra, and it will always be Umbra. But the thought brings him pain.

"What happened to you on Umbra?" I ask him.

"That doesn't matter anymore."

I was right. "Of course it matters."

I reflect on what he's been saying to Melanie about leaving Umbra behind and escaping on Terra, and suddenly I understand why he said it all. To him, Umbra is already lost. He already gave up on any kind of future. And this *hurts* him.

I resist the urge to console him.

"Melanie is your home now," I say. He doesn't confirm or deny it. He just stares back at me, eyes closed off once more.

I grab my switchblade and hold on to it tightly. It links me to everything I love in this universe, just as Melanie does for Jesse.

"But you don't believe what she does," I continue, trying to guess.

"And what is it exactly," he snaps, "that you think she believes in?"

Not me.

He doesn't want me to say she has faith in me.

"She believes Umbra can be saved."

He rises from the couch. He doesn't want to have this conversation—especially not with me.

"Jesse," I say. He stops, his back to me, hesitant. Maybe the sound of his name on my lips is too personal for him to bear. I don't care.

"I don't know whether she's right or wrong," I tell him. "Quite frankly, I don't care if I'm your salvation or not. I know you don't want to hear that, but it's the truth. I don't care. All I care about is my family." I squeeze my switchblade so tightly it hurts. "All I care about is learning what the hell is going on so I can protect them."

"Please, dear god, tell me you don't plan to move them to Umbra." He doesn't pose it as a question, because he knows it's the truth.

"Terra poisons us," I say. "And I have ties to Umbra. I don't know how, but I do. First, it's Jasmine, and now…"

He turns around. I'm trapped in his stare as my hesitation hangs in the air. I swallow.

"And now what?"

"I have a theory."

"I'm listening," he says.

I cross my arms over my chest and stare back at him.

"I'm pretty sure my mother is Umbran."

"And you tell me this *now*?" he snaps.

"It's just a theory," I say.

"How so?" he challenges, taunting.

I don't know why he's so frustrated with me. We both have our secrets. I stalk towards him, jaw clenched.

"I try not to think about my mother much," I say. "But being here, for some reason, keeps reminding me of her."

Jesse stares at me stoically.

"She was never around during my childhood," I say finally. "She was a gypsy, always wandering. It had always felt like she'd travelled across the entire universe before I was even born."

"That's just pure speculation," he claims.

"No, it's not," I defend myself. "Look at it this way then: if I'm truly the girl from the prophecy, surely I'd have some sort of

Umbran heritage. I'd have a calling to it in my blood. Jasmine doesn't prove anything. She isn't family."

"She *is* proof," Jesse argues, as if I've hurt Melanie's ego. He doesn't look convinced, but I have his attention. "But we'll have to tell Mel."

He knows I'm right. Why would a random girl from Terra be the cure for Umbra? I must have some sort of heritage linking me to the planet—Jasmine was just the first person to discover it.

"Sure," I shrug.

"Why didn't you say anything earlier?" Jesse persists, as if I've somehow shredded our trust.

"I don't like to think about my mother. Because of her, my childhood was rough. I grew up without her. It wasn't easy."

Jesse lowers his gaze and tries to school his irritation, a world of emotion flitting over his features. He seems to understand that at least.

"But yes, I should've realised earlier. I think a part of me always knew it, though. My mother has never seemed entirely… *human*."

"What makes you say that?" he presses.

"She was just… different. She was always so unnaturally pale, her eyes so silver it was almost terrifying. But more noticeable than that…" I swallow deeply, shaking my head. "I'd look into her eyes, and I'd only see power. Strength. Anger."

"No offense, but you sound ridiculous."

"If you look at a person closely, you can see their soul, Jesse."

He backs away from me when I say this, as if he's trying to hide himself. "I don't believe in that type of perception."

"Sure you don't," I remark quietly.

He keeps his eyes fixed elsewhere.

I reach forwards and touch his chin, shifting his gaze to mine. He stiffens immediately but stands solidly.

Reluctantly, he meets my stare. Beneath the hate and the fear, he seems okay with it.

"A part of me has always wondered about my mother," I say, dropping my hand. "And I'm pretty sure that between her and Jasmine Spark, we can find out the truth."

"Maybe."

"But to do that, we need to figure out the past. We need to learn everything we possibly can, and we can't do that by staying in this freaking apartment."

He still seems unsure, but I can tell he's starting to see my point.

I open my fist, releasing my hold on the switchblade. Aching against the gesture, I lift the weapon towards him. It rests in my palm, surrounded by red, dented skin where it bit into my hand.

"Take it," I urge. "I will have no weapon to use against you."

"You could always punch me."

"We both know you could beat me in hand-to-hand combat. I'm not a fool."

He takes my switchblade, and for a moment it feels like he's taking a part of my soul.

"And now what? Where do you suggest we start?" His tone taunts me.

"First, we visit Melanie's uncle. And then we tear apart this whole goddamn base until every bit of Jasmine's past is brought to the surface."

I hold my breath. I'm ready for him to throw me into the couch again.

Instead, he leads me to the door.

↳

"If this doesn't work," Jesse turns back to me, hands on the panels of his vehicle, "I'm blaming you."

We zip past buildings, progressing farther away from Melanie's apartment. It's almost impossible to see where we are, so instead I keep my eyes on the sky.

"Fair enough," I say to him.

I think I hear him take a heavy breath, but it's hard to discern it over the wind, so I just ignore him.

It's nightfall again and the stars illuminate the darkness above us.

I wonder if Jasmine's looking up at them now, surrounded by a bustle of friends, thinking of Umbra and her rogue dark-haired friend.

I grip Jesse's vehicle, feeling the sting of betrayal.

My heart aches for her. Her wide, tragic smile and tears of laugher—Jasmine feels both joy and sorrow with extreme intensity. It's like her emotions are a roaring flame, whereas mine are always just flickering embers.

I wonder if she's feeling those emotions now.

I sit still, leaning over the front of the loot box.

We dart past one of the farming sectors, the robots they use to farm their food deactivated and nowhere to be seen for the night. The greenery of the trees—apples, oranges, bananas, and more—make me long for the forest. I take a calming breath, but when I blink, they are gone, replaced by more buildings as Jesse darts his vehicle even faster through the base.

"I hope you realise," Jesse continues, "that getting into the space centre is extremely difficult."

I nod, even though he can't see me.

He dips the vehicle between the buildings. They appear intimidating, full of dim lights and shining walls. The atmosphere here is quiet and the wind in my ears feels obtrusive.

"How are we going to do it?" I ask. My voice is swept away in the wind, but he hears me.

"We could enter on foot, but they probably won't let us in unless I stab them or something. But there *is* another entrance... I think..."

He doesn't elaborate.

He angles his vehicle towards the large, horizontal building near the beach at the end of the base. It's only a storey tall, with a curving cylinder roof. We glide straight towards it. The dust along the floor picks up around us as we hurtle forwards.

The building looms before us like a wall.

As we get closer, I begin to feel a resistance pulling against the machine. Jesse works the knobs frantically and I grip onto the net with white knuckles. I think I hear him swearing.

It almost feels like the building is pushing us away, like a magnet.

"Jesse?"

The vehicle clunks underneath me, dropping closer to the floor. I've never seen it drop less than a metre above ground.

"Something's disabling the vehicle," I say.

"Obviously," he grunts.

The vehicle struggles onwards, the magnetics straining against the ground. It's losing flight. Jesse groans and slams a finger against a panel near his head, causing the machine to shudder and sway off the road.

I gasp as it grinds against the wall.

Jesse pulls it to the side. "Grab onto something."

I take his advice and grip the side of the loot box harder. It does a complete 360 before continuing forwards again.

The world blurs and I feel consumed by it. My jaw locks and I try not to look at the sky above us, feeling a sense of nausea take hold. Maybe walking on foot was a better idea.

I grind my teeth as I hunch low in the loot box. Ahead of us, a small slit opens at the base of the building, and we dive in.

And all at once, the stars are gone. Darkness takes hold.

The vehicle clunks loudly to the floor, and the sound of grinding reverberates in the darkness. I think I feel something bump underneath us.

The vehicle doesn't hover anymore; it grinds and slides against the floor, screeching as it coasts down a long slope. Parts fall off it and scatter the tunnel behind us. A small flicker of light surges where the sky used to be, and then the darkness takes that too.

We plummet, breaking and crashing into the space centre. I hear Jesse slamming a panel on the machine again. It doesn't do anything.

The machine's system fails entirely, and more pieces shatter off.

The wind whips as I try to lean towards him. It lashes my face, pulling my hair back. Coldness bites into my flesh like ice on metal.

The vehicle begins to lose its speed until, suddenly, I can breathe again.

Everything stops.

We lie still in the cold, panting and shaking, and then Jesse's voice cuts through the darkness.

"They ruined her."

I'm about to ask who 'her' is, but something blinding flashes across my eyes and my breath escapes me.

Pulsing white light snaps around us. I close my eyes and wait for the blinding sensation to pass. Jesse utters a choice string of curses and pulls something from his net. I crack open my eyes and see him holding what looks like a bow and arrow.

No, a crossbow.

Since when did he have a crossbow?

My eyes wrestle with the light for a few moments until they begin to recognise shapes around us; people in silver uniform, holding swords.

I try and stand up in the loot box to face them, but the momentum causes the vehicle to tilt to the side.

Something snaps under us. Loudly. It echoes throughout the cavernous room we're in.

One of the guards breaks formation and comes towards us. He doesn't look happy.

"This area is restricted," he says. He would have been quite handsome, were it not for the scowl on his face.

His white hair shines almost yellow in the light. It's then that I realise all the guards have light hair.

It seems to be an Umbran trend.

"I'm a friend of Melanie Beckett. She's on shift. Ask her."

The guard looks like he's about to say it doesn't change the fact that we're not meant to be here.

But Jesse looks ready to release an arrow into his chest, so he doesn't. I reach out and lower the crossbow, glaring at him. His eyes flicker to me and he glares back, but oddly, he obeys. The weapon lowers to the man's feet.

"I'm sorry for the trouble of breaking and entering, but I was wondering if we could speak to the Liaison." My voice is soft and steady, and it surprises me.

I think I hear Jesse mumble a string of insults.

I flash my eyes at him, and he takes a step back.

All the guards watch us. Mostly me. All five blades point towards us, but they remain steady.

I just hope they stay like that.

"We didn't break anything," Jesse says, aiming his glare at them now. "But you broke my—"

"This is a service route for distributing goods to the rest of the base. A *Hover* isn't designed to pass," the guard interrupts him. "Besides, yours is extremely outdated—"

"You *dare?*" Jesse lifts the crossbow again. I don't put it past him to shoot.

Spurred by instinct, I slide out of the Hover and place myself in front of the guard, so if Jesse shoots, he will have to aim the bolt through me.

"Savannah, move."

"No," I say. He won't shoot me. I'm too important to Melanie.

I train my eyes on the guard who looks at me curiously, head tilted.

Jesse's Hover is completely ruined. Items are scattered around it, and the metal is twisted and comes off at every interval. But it's just a machine. It's not worth getting stabbed over or being locked up in a Safe Hold with the brute and his cronies. Jesse needs to put sentimentalism aside right now.

"Explain why you're here," the guard says. He only looks at me now.

"I told you, I wish to speak with Liaison Banks."

He turns his head to a guard behind him, but not before I note the oddly satisfied look on his face. It's ugly... sickening. "Get Liaison Banks."

The youngest guard nods and turns away. I try to watch his exit in case we need a backup escape plan, but the guards block him from sight.

The older guards turn back to me, and my gut churns.

I have the urge to cover my dark hair as his eyes scan it. They regard me hungrily. I think one of them moves his hand more firmly around his sword.

"What's your name?" he asks.

"Savannah Shaw."

"I hope you understand we need to confiscate this for scrap metal. I doubt it can be salvaged."

I suck in my lips. It's not my place to say anything about the Hover. It's Jesse's.

"And what's your friend's name on the ugly Hover?"

"Jesse Hayes."

Jesse jumps down from what remains of the vehicle, and I hear something metallic crack. Surprisingly, he doesn't acknowledge it.

I try to stop him, but Jesse is faster.

He slams his hands into the guard's chest and his friends all catch him as he falls, making a point of it. The action isn't overly vicious, but they all respond as if it were. Jesse angles his small knife calmly against the leader's throat.

"Take my *ugly* Hover if you goddamn want. And go to hell while you're at it," he hisses, lowering the blade. "I want all my belongings back, though." I notice a flash of pain on his face.

The one with the sword lunges as soon as Jesse's knife drops. He doesn't make it more than two steps towards Jesse.

Liaison Banks appears behind the assembly of guards. Impeccable timing, as usual. His suit is clean and sharp, and his eyes cut me with deadly irritation as he takes in the scene before him.

All the guards turn to face him.

Jesse still has his knife up defensively.

"Come with me, Savannah," Banks says simply.

He turns his back and walks away.

The guards look ridiculously pleased with themselves, probably convinced that we're done for. I turn a bewildered look upon Jesse and then plunge past them. He stays close behind me.

This isn't the first time the Liaison intervened for me.

I want to tell Jesse to stop grinning victoriously at the guards. Maybe we're wrong to assume that we're safe.

Setting my shoulders back, I plaster on a neutral expression for Liaison Banks, who waits for us by the edge of the cavernous room.

This is the exit. The wall seems to shimmer silver and transparent simultaneously.

The neutral expression drops from my face as I take in the extra-terrestrial material. I can feel it humming, sailing over my body like a swarm of bees.

The force of energy feels the same as the resistance the Hover had met outside.

"It's like a force field," Jesse says from behind me. "It holds particles out."

"Like Hovers?"

"And civilians," the Liaison glares, "among other things."

The dome.

I shiver, sickened at the thought. But maybe this is my chance to learn how to get out.

Instead of showing my fear, I reach a hand up to it. The force grows stronger against me, as if two magnetic ends are trying to meet. With each centimetre I gain, the pins and needles in my palm grow stronger, the wall stabbing at my flesh.

I don't want to imagine what walking through it would be like.

"It won't hurt you," the Liaison says, tilting his head at me. "You aren't very brave. That's surprising."

Something shifts inside me at his words, and I feel Jesse whip his eyes to me, suddenly alarmed. *You aren't very brave. That's surprising.*

What's *that* supposed to mean?

The heavy layer of curiosity lining his words makes me shiver.

Does he believe in the prophecy?

I push my brown hair back from my face with my other hand, fighting the urge to hide. The force feels like a beacon, fluttering and exposed as wisps brush my cheek.

Swallowing deeply, I push my hand closer towards it. The wall may not want me to touch it, but the force, like outside, should be able to be fought with enough pressure. Gingerly, I press my fingers against it. Shocked, I feel them plunge into the substance before meeting something solid like cold, slimy glass.

I release a breath and yank my hand back, except now the wall tries to claim me, and I grunt with the effort to free myself.

Jesse chuckles.

I'm about to ask for help, but then the wall decides it has had enough, popping me loose like a faulty suction. I gasp and stare at it in confusion.

My companions stare at me in turn.

I turn towards Jesse and smile. "It's sticky."

He rolls his eyes.

The Liaison brushes his hand over it, like dragging a pattern in the wall, and suddenly the shimmering vanishes. The process confuses me, and I wish I could watch it again on replay, burning it to memory.

"This matter is sourced from Umbra," he states.

That's all he says about the wall before he disappears behind it.

We slink through after him, vanishing through the wall as if it is a mist. I barely register it clasping to my skin like a hot embrace, but then we are through. The guards follow us down the next hallway, but they vanish one by one as they return to their posts.

The Liaison pushes us forwards.

I tuck a strand of my hair behind my ear, trying to keep my breathing steady.

Does he know my mother? My bloodline? Who I am?

Jesse's gaze flickers between me and the Liaison intensely, and I can almost hear his thoughts echo mine. *How much does this man know?*

I suppose we're here to find out exactly that.

The hallways are just as bright and blinding as the dome we left behind, but I can't see any lights. My eyes trail along the walls and I deduct the source must be within the walls themselves. It glitters with small granules, dancing with miniscule light particles. I run a finger across them, and the shards pinch at my skin.

This space centre must be filled with all sorts of alien advancements.

"How does all this work?" I ask.

"It's science that Terra has not yet discovered." The Liaison refuses to look me directly in the eyes and his tone is dry when he speaks. "The first Elders were all scientists and guards. Science is our greatest weapon and feat." He glances at me, as if determining my reaction. I refuse to give him one, and so he continues, "Their research is very extensive, my dear. And with the help of Umbran material, it has no match to anything you know on Terra."

He's trying to belittle and scare me, I assume. It's subtle, but I recognise the undertone.

"That doesn't explain how it all works," I say.

"I'm just a Liaison. The Terran one at that. How would I know?"

For some reason, I don't believe him.

He leads us deeper underground until we reach the level below. We pass a few rooms, and each doorway is greeted by swarms of chattering and footsteps. The rooms are barren, but filled with people hustling around each other, handling weapons, fighting.

Training rooms.

Stamped on each door is a silver symbol—a crescent moon, like a U for Umbra, a smaller dagger piercing down into it.

Like an army's emblem.

I shudder at the thought.

Umbrans—immortals with access to incredibly advanced technology they can form into weapons if they so please—as an enemy.

Jesse is very proficient, as if he spent his whole life training.

There could be others like him.

Just because it isn't commonly admitted that Umbra has advanced armies doesn't mean they don't. My eyes search their dancing bodies for any signs of advanced weaponry.

All the guards wander with swords strapped to their belts, and outfits remarkably alike those worn in the Georgian era, and yet…

I glance over at Jesse's with my eyes raised, trying not to shudder.

At least he's on my side for now.

"Keep moving," the Liaison says, and I miss a step at the grating tone.

Ahead, a crystalline elevator twinkles in the next room, hovering in a lonesome manner at the end of the circular space. No cables are attached to support it. Heart still thumping, I frown as we walk towards it. I've never seen anything like it—a metallic clean-cut model floating in the middle of the room, imposing and at odds with the empty space around it.

It must be magnetised somehow, like the Hovers. I don't know how that's even possible.

I walk right up to it, arms crossed over my chest, unsure how to proceed. The room ends in a drop below and the elevator floats above the depth. The Liaison sees me analysing the elevator and offers a small, satisfactory smile.

"Beautiful, isn't it?" He turns away briskly and opens the elevator. "Follow me. My office is further underground."

A beep chimes around me, and my feet feel heavy and shoulders slouch as I feel the gravity getting heavier in the small space. I'm about to ask why, but then the elevator dips into a sudden, smooth free-fall. I gasp, suddenly thankful for the fact that my feet can stay planted on the floor in this velocity. I hold my breath as we zoom past seven stories in a matter of seconds, flashes of light from each level interrupting the darkness, like rapid blinking.

I hardly have time to blink before the Liaison leads Jesse and me onto a new level. There are only a few metres of ground space in front of the elevator, and then a heavy looking metal door. There's nothing else on the entire floor.

The Liaison scans his palm on a small pad near the entrance and the door slides open soundlessly.

Jesse catches his breath behind me. I don't think he's ever been on this floor before.

We're led into the office, none of us able to breathe properly.

The lights flicker on upon our arrival. The place looks more like an apartment than an office. It's vast and well fashioned, but slightly sterile all the same. A heavy glass table sits at the far end of the long, horizontal room, right up against a window. This window overlooks the level below us. It's a spacecraft factory of sorts.

"I really would've preferred to turn the other cheek where you're concerned, Savannah. So please, ask what you need to know then get the hell out of my space centre," he says the moment the door shuts behind us.

I linger near the doorway, because that's what he does.

He doesn't offer a tea or coffee, nor a chair. We're using this room for privacy, and that's all.

"What do you know about Jasmine Spark, Liaison?"

Jesse shuffles behind me. He still holds firmly onto his crossbow, but it's lowered towards the floor. Something about the nervous way he holds himself tells me he wants to aim it at the man before us. But he doesn't dare because he's Melanie's uncle.

"Jasmine?"

I hold my breath as confusion spreads over the Liaison's face, clouded with worry.

"I thought Jasmine was dead."

"D ead?" Jesse's voice is sharp behind me.

"Melanie put you two up to this, didn't she?" His voice is sharp, riddled with anger. "She tripped me up earlier. I didn't want to tell her anything about Jasmine James, because Melanie deserves to be kept safe."

"Her name is Jasmine Spark," I correct.

"There is no family by the name of Spark," the Liaison says blankly. "Her name is Jasmine James."

"And you know that for a fact?" I ask, brow rising. "Did you tell Melanie?"

"She knows I've been watching her."

"That isn't what I asked," I tell him.

"The Sparks are bewitched. I sent out a scout, who confirmed it for me," he tells me. "The Sparks aren't *real*. They're creations. They don't exist."

"That doesn't make any sense," I say.

"Not yet," Jesse says. "But… it could."

Something glows in his eyes. He's made a connection I haven't but won't say it in front of Melanie's uncle.

"Is she Argenti?" the Liaison asks, acknowledging Jesse's words and turning to me. His gaze looks hungry.

"Argenti?" The Latin word is foreign to me. "What do you mean?"

He sighs.

"Silver hair, silver eyes, the ability to manipulate the soul of the planet. They're magical creatures, the by-product of interspecies consummation," he tells me.

Argenti—could they be a new species created between humans and the Occupants? I try not to fiddle with the hem of my shirt, remembering what Jasmine had said about wanting to dye her hair. She had bleached it.

Because Argentis have light hair?

When I don't say anything, he elaborates, as if reading my mind. "Jasmine has blonde hair and blue eyes. She could have Argenti in her blood." He sighs again, growing impatient. Behind us, Jesse spots a bookshelf and runs his finger across the spines. I want to tell him to cut it out, because he's distracting the Liaison, but I'm too fixated on his words. "Essence of an Argenti can be noticed by lighter pigmentation in the eyes, hair, and skin. Brown hair, brown eyes, brown skin, are rarer traits in the Argenti gene, but someone with blonde hair and blue eyes? It's possible. That's why people dye their hair lighter. Superiority. Do you know if that's what Jasmine did?"

Blue eyes.

Jasmine's eyes are extremely blue. Ocean blue, lacking the reflective sheen Melanie's have…

Does Melanie have Argenti in her blood?

I'm about to ask the Liaison this when Jesse comes up behind me and thumps a book in my arms. It has a brown cover and appears to be some sort of journal.

"Page seventeen, three paragraphs down," he mumbles.

The Liaison looks ready to say something, but bites down his retort as I open the book and find the paragraph Jesse mentioned.

The handwritten script looks extremely old, but what shocks me even more is the content Jesse wants me to read.

It's dated from 1845. This must be a journal entry from one of the original scientists, or a copy, at least—the words are a rapid scrawl, as if the author's mind couldn't keep up.

We have started giving birth to children with silver hair and eyes, and they can do things—wonderful things... we don't know how, or why, this has happened. It would seem combining Terran and Occupant genes has created marvellous creatures able to perform miracles on Umbra, and due to their relation to the Occupants, they are remarkably in tune with the planet. They can pick up the electric energies surrounding the core of the planet and manipulate it to their will—we have been calling this Silver Magic. We have named these children the Argenti, for the Latin name silver, due to their pale hair, skin, and unusual silver eyes. Each Argenti is unique and can manipulate their powers differently. We have found no logical pattern to these anomalies. They are a new species, unintentionally derived, and they're helping us to survive this period of crisis—and we are. We're surviving. It's the Occupants who are not. The last of the Occupants are dying, because they know nothing about perseverance in the face of death. The very concept seems to baffle them. Perhaps the Argenti are our only hope.

"How many Argenti were there?" I ask.

"At that time, not very many, but there were more to follow," Jesse explains. "The Argenti were the reason humans survived on that planet. It was the last gift the Occupants unintentionally gave them—lots of pregnant bellies full of miracle children."

That planet.

As if Umbra was never his home. Just *that planet.*

"How many are there now?" I wonder.

It's the Liaison who answers me this time, to my surprise. "We classify them by generation. First Generation Argenti are rare and few—they're the original children of the scientists and their guard. The Argenti later bred among themselves and made the Second Generation, but by the Third and Fourth generation, they began to breed more with humans, and the bloodline became muddier. Both of Melanie's parents were Fourth Generation, half-Argenti and half-human, and thus Melanie has lingering Argenti blood, but it's not enough to give her any powers of manipulation. I'm much the same."

Melanie's silver eyes. They're a nod to her bloodline.

"The Moon Blitz was really that bad?" I ask.

"One of Umbra's three moons exploded due to a large meteor hurtling towards Umbra. Of course it was bad. It destroyed the moon and threw Umbra into a near-apocalyptic state of disaster. Our only saving grace was the other two moons, holding us by a thread. Do you even realise what happens when one of a planet's moons explodes, girl?"

"What kind of natural disaster? I'm guessing the shards of the moon rained down on Umbra... right?"

"We're here to speak about Jasmine James," the Liaison snaps, finished with this conversation.

I hand the book back to Jesse. He rolls his eyes, then wanders back to place it on the shelf.

I cross my arms over my chest, facing the Liaison. "I don't think Jasmine is Argenti. But I don't really know anything about her, so I don't know why you're asking me."

"You grew up with her. You were her life's mission, I'm sure of it," he insists.

Sweat begins to collect in the palms of my hands. Behind me, I feel Jesse tensing. Banks knows who I am.

But I don't break my stance, and neither does Jesse.

"What do you mean, I was her mission?" I demand, pretending indifference.

He doesn't take the bait. Not in the way I'd like.

"You are everyone's mission, Savannah. She's the only one who managed to find you until now."

I take a deep breath. My stance wavers, but I hold steady.

"How did you meet Jasmine?"

Desperation to squeeze as many answers from him as I can takes over. It might only be minutes before I'm thrown from his office. He looks like he already wants to.

He doesn't care about me. Or Jasmine. Or our questions. He looks at us like we're wasting his time.

"She was going to board a shuttle to Terra. I saw her name on the list, but she was under the care of Liaison Stone, and I didn't think much of it. But when she arrived on Terra, I never saw her on the platform. Which can only mean she left Dome City before I had the chance to meet her. That's how I knew what she was here to do. She came to Terra to find you. Which can only mean she succeeded, or she died. I assumed the latter, considering she's now a known traitor of Umbra."

Chills rake up my spine.

"Perhaps, with you here, her days are finally numbered anyway. If she ever shows her face here again, her death will be certain." He grins at me as if this is the greatest discovery he's made today.

I lower my arms from my chest and stand closer to Jesse.

It's no wonder Jasmine never went into the forest. Why would she bring me to Silver Valley if she knew a prison sentence—or even death—awaited her here?

My skin crawls, but I keep my gaze steady on him. I just hope he's enough of a coward to keep his distance.

"How could you be so cold to a child?"

To my annoyance, Jesse grabs my elbow. I want to rip his hand away, but I don't.

"She's a traitor. I don't know how she reversed her age without being Argenti." He runs a frustrated hand through his hair, and it's clear he still thinks she is one.

"You know too much," Jesse says accusingly.

"Perhaps," he says. "But you do too, don't you?"

Jesse pulls me closer to him. Closer to the door.

"Did you try to find Jasmine after she left?" I ask, more out of fear for my friend than anything else.

"I'm not a fool." He laughs humourlessly and turns his back on us, walking to his desk—a dismissive gesture. "I don't want any connections to that girl. Especially now."

He taps something on his desk and the door opens behind our backs. "There's a convoy coming from Umbra today to discuss matters with me. I don't want anything out of the ordinary to happen while she is here. And you," he says venomously, "are the exact opposite of ordinary."

Jesse pulls me towards the door without a moment's hesitation.

"Now get off my space centre," he says calmly, "and stay far away from me."

I turn to protest but the door hisses shut in my face.

21

"Listen to me, because I'm only going to say this once."

Jesse places his lips right by my ear as we wait for the elevator. Goosebumps rise on my neck, and I stay entirely still. "She isn't Argenti. She used the stone in her necklace to reverse her age. With a stone that size, she would have had enough power to manage it. She used age reversal on herself, blanked the minds of her fake parents, then planted fake memories into people's heads—including your father's. With a stone like that, you don't need to be on Umbra to work Silver Magic."

I clench my fingers, gasping loudly, and he slaps a palm to my mouth to shut me up. "She didn't touch your mind, princess, don't worry. She didn't need to. Everyone would've fed you lies. It's what they believed was true."

A lie. Everything has been a lie.

Jesse lowers his hand from my mouth and steps away from me

as the elevator slides up to greet us. In the upper corner of the ceiling, a strip of metal thrums to the same beat that the elevator makes upon arrival. It must pick up sounds. Like some sort of surveillance system.

Jesse must be familiar with the tech. I try to rummage through his words as we step onto the elevator.

"We're going to see Melanie," he says casually.

The doors close and the elevator whizzes down several levels.

"He told us to get out of the space centre," I deadpan.

"I don't care."

Jesse steps off the elevator as it opens. I follow him.

The factory lies above, and before us is a storage and office zone. Sterile corridors stretch and twist, basked in the same bright yellow glow that lit the other levels. The corridor is thin and barely allows two people to slide past each other; Jesse and I have to angle sideways as people bustle past with paperwork and odd-looking machinery. I'm pretty sure the tall woman that just passed us was carrying a tangle of twisted bolts and metal plating.

Most of the many doors lead to storage rooms, but some lead to massive spaces with lots of desks and activity. Everyone here seems to be rushing around with intent, eyes locked ahead and their minds elsewhere.

Jesse takes me to a large enclave at the end of the corridor.

It's like a lounge room—but with a buffet set up. Must be a staff room. Quite a few of the jumpsuit-clad workers lounge around this room, but their tones are hushed in heavy conversation. None of them looks interested in us.

"What do they all do down here?" I ask Jesse as he pushes open the doors.

"Stock inventory and communications. They have more storerooms on the level below."

We bustle past the staff room, narrowly missing a crowd of

people with stacks of boxes in their arms, heading towards more doors in the distance.

Jesse beelines for the one right at the end of the corridor and pushes the door open without knocking.

Inside, the room is more lived-in and cosier than anything else I've seen in the space centre so far. Melanie leans over a large wooden desk, surrounded by paperwork, thin computer screens, and some of the vials they had in the medical centre below the Liaison's office. She has a small heater running in the corner and a lounge that looks more like a bed than a couch. There are no windows in the room, but she has some plants along the walls and soft classical music playing from some speakers, giving off a calming sensation that eases the tension of being underground.

She startles upright, her head lifting from the desk as we enter, and I notice a collection of empty coffee cups at the end of the table. Quite a few of them appear recently emptied, whereas others look like they've been there for days.

"Jesse?" She furrows her eyebrows, rubbing her eyes with her gloved hand. Her voice is heavy, infused with fatigue.

Despite having just slept on the table, she still looks tidy and presentable. She covers her pale hand over her mouth, stifling a yawn.

"We spoke to your uncle," he tells her. "I can't say he's a massive fan of us anymore."

Melanie blinks the sleep out of her eyes, clearing her throat and turning back to her desk.

"He's never been a massive fan of us. He just pretends to be," she mumbles, shaking her head. She clicks on her screen, dragging up some sort of database that hurts my head to look at.

I suddenly realise Melanie has never called him family. Not once. There must be some sour history between Melanie and the Liaison.

"An Argenti is visiting from Umbra today. The shuttle has just arrived, and I wasn't informed until now. The tension is getting worse, I'm certain of it. This meeting is important."

On one of her screens there's a visual of a landing dock; the picture is fuzzy but distinguishable, code laced on the tabs behind it. Footage from security cameras not meant for my eyes. Or Melanie's, most likely.

The landing dock is empty. Whoever was inbound must have arrived before Melanie fell asleep at her desk.

"What's it about?" I ask her.

"I don't know. I haven't decoded that information yet. It's heavily concealed, and I'm having difficulty hacking it." She rubs her temples at the thought. "I think it has something to do with an upcoming shipment—except orders go through me and they're purposely blocking me from it. For an Argenti to come and discuss it with my uncle, it must be important."

She powers up more screens as she speaks and my mind whirs just looking at all that code.

Jesse leans on the edge of her table. "We learnt something about Jasmine—"

"It can wait," she interrupts. "I need to learn what this shipment is about. I think it has something to do with Silver Valley and, coincidently, a scout from the Valley is meeting with my uncle and the Argenti soon. They should arrive at his office any moment. I might need a few minutes."

I turn my head towards her.

"Silver Valley?" I settle beside the screens so she has no choice but to look me in the eye. "Is there something already happening there?"

"Nothing drastic yet," she says. "But people are watching it, keeping tabs."

"Why?" I press.

She swivels her chair towards me and sighs.

"Hostility is increasing on Umbra, and, for the first time in history, we have an Umbran infiltrating the village. I have a feeling the Elders are aware of this."

She means Jasmine. I drag my lip between my teeth to calm my heart's nervous fluttering. Melanie refocuses on the screen and starts tapping codes into a new database. It looks like a PC screen, but too advanced. It's almost as thin as paper.

"These tensions…" I begin.

"Political and social unrest," she summarises. "I'm hoping it won't turn militaristic."

Her attention slides back to the data before her, too focused on her tasks to indulge me in answers. Her eyes flicker across the moving code and I notice how red and tired they look beneath her energetic exterior.

"Melanie," I say, rounding the desk so I'm standing by her side. "Do you want me to grab you a coffee or something?"

"I've already had some," she says, nodding her head towards the empty cups.

"All of them, just today?" I reply. I suspected she preferred tea, according to the lemon water and food she has stocked at home, but perhaps not. Perhaps Jesse uses up all her food, and she's just low on groceries.

"Of course not…" she begins, but after glancing at the pile of cups, she admits, "well, I haven't really slept for a few days, so I *suppose* so."

She shrugs. I glance at Jesse, but he just rolls his eyes at me. Wonderful. My information source is an insomniac.

Melanie begins jotting something down from her screen onto a piece of paper. March 3rd. That's probably when the shipment will arrive.

My heart drops.

Mason turns fourteen in five days, and considering all that's happening here, I don't even know if I'll be there to celebrate with him. Hands shaking, I try to distract myself from the guilt.

"Do you… want help with something?" I ask her.

"No," she says plainly.

"Okay, but you can always ask me if you need—"

"I'm not asking." She pins the note to a board next to her screens of data. It's filled with hundreds of dates. I wonder how she keeps track.

"I wouldn't if I were you," Jesse advises from behind me. "I helped her once—"

"And it drove me mad."

"She babysat me the whole time," he finishes.

My fingers are itching to do something, but I just nod and step away from her desk. Jesse peels himself away from the room and heads towards the door. I feel obligated to follow him.

"We can tell her everything later," he says. "And she can tell us what that scout has to say about Silver Valley."

Melanie glances between us, sucking on her lips.

I rub the back of my neck, the urge to do something overpowering me. I rub clammy hands on my pants, but instead of pushing Melanie, I nod and smile.

I don't know how to hack. She does.

"Okay," I say, despite the words feeling thick in my mouth. "Okay, sounds good."

Jesse butts the handle of his knife against my lower back, edging me out; lips twitching as he watches my eyes flicker between Melanie and the doorway.

But as Melanie's door shuts behind us, I feel a heaviness leave my shoulders.

꒰

I end up doing a Jesse Hayes—leaning against the back of the room, obscured in shadow.

My eyes keep flicking to Melanie's door. The clock above the buffet says it's only been ten minutes.

It's strange how Jesse and Melanie work together, slipping into these roles like clockwork.

Leaning against the wall, Jesse paws the strings on his crossbow while I count every minute it takes for Melanie to complete her work under my breath.

He is the protector. Melanie is the brains.

I wonder where that puts me.

Do I fit with these two?

Could I fill shoes of my own?

I'm independent in nature, but am I a leader like Melanie and Jasmine hope me to be and like the prophecy predicts?

"I can see you overthinking," Jesse says quietly, barely able to hide the interest in his tone.

I realise I've been absently staring at a worker eating his dinner for the last ten minutes. I can't remember the last time I ate. My stomach churns as I face Jesse.

"Lythia May predicted a leader," I tell him, my voice sounding shaky. "You say she's accurate in her predictions… but what if prophecies only become true because people believe in them enough to take action? What if the false prophecies are only false because no one believed in them?"

"You don't think you're the girl in the prophecy," he realises.

I shake my head. "No, I just don't think I *can* be."

"Well," he says flippantly. "Unluckily for you, people are forcing the prediction to happen, so you really don't have a choice either way."

"Not everyone," I disagree. "Do you believe?"

He sucks on his lips, averting his eyes and clearing his throat shakily, giving me my answer without saying the words. He doesn't. But Melanie does, and that's enough for him. "The people who don't are trying to abolish it and the people who do are trying to make it happen. Both sides of the scale force the prophecy into action, because it draws you out of hiding."

He's right. Of course he is.

I slide down the wall in defeat.

We both watch the clock tick by slowly, and I wonder when Melanie will finally let us back into her office. Around us, people slowly make their way home, emptying out the corridors. So many people, but none know who I really am. And yet, I still hold my breath every time one of them walks past me.

"Jesse," I mumble, a wild realisation gripping me. "How did Melanie find me?"

"We told you, she has contacts."

"No," I shake my head. "I mean, how does she know it's me? The prophecy wasn't very specific. A dark-haired girl from Terra? It could be anyone. How does she know I'm the right one? And then there's Jasmine. She followed clues which led her to me—what clues? All of Umbra is looking for me, and only Melanie and Jasmine have gotten it right. That is, if they even are."

Jesse furrows his brow. He presses his fingers into his weapons belt as he processes this. "You might want to ask her. I'm just your stalker."

"Very funny." I sigh in frustration. No matter how many answers I uncover, there are always more questions.

"Why aren't you out scouting if Silver Valley is such a threat?" I ask Jesse. It would be invaluable if he tracked down some information on Jasmine. If anyone could do it, he could.

"I'm on Savannah duty. I'm no scout."

Like a guard.

I suck in an irritated breath. "You do realise I'm not a prize to be won? I don't need you to hover."

"But aren't you, princess?"

I throw myself off the wall. "I'm *not* a prize."

His laughter follows as I stalk away. I only make it halfway to Melanie's office when I stop.

Around me, the world explodes in a clap of lightning.

I fall to my knees and cover my eyes. The corridors erupt with a shock of white light. I hear Jesse cursing behind me.

The lights bounce off the ceiling several times, throbbing like a heartbeat. Like a warning. And then they stop.

Jesse covers his ears, yelling at me to do the same.

I turn to him, lips parted. "Jesse, what was—"

An alarm shatters the air.

I clap my hands over my ears and gasp. The pitch slams into me, long and wailing. I listen to it fracture off the walls and reverberate into my flesh.

It screams.

I shudder and sink to the floor.

Jesse pulls me against the wall as it continues shrieking, stopping me from falling. Long and tearing, it shreds me apart.

Hands on my shoulders, Jesse doesn't even muffle the sound. He just stands there, wincing and waiting for something. I don't know what.

I think I'm crumpling against the wall. Making myself smaller, so it won't hurt as much.

Instinct is a bitch.

It makes me look weak.

Jesse towers over me, as if protecting my body from the wailing, muffling the sound with his chest.

The alarm doesn't falter for a moment.

Melanie slams through her door, her lips moving frantically, and Jesse grabs her.

My whole body is shaking.

If Melanie's eyes seemed tired before, they now look exhausted. She briefly takes me in, cowering against the wall, Jesse shielding me, before she focuses on Jesse. Her lips are still forming words. I don't know what she's saying.

Jesse has his eyes locked on her mouth, as if reading them.

And then I realise. She's counting.

Moments after her mouth forms the word *one*, silence deafens the hall, like a wave dampening everything.

The light above continues to throb, reminding us of the danger. But the sound disperses, leaving nothing but an echo in its wake. My ears are ringing so loudly, I think for a moment perhaps the alarm is still screaming at me. But all is silent.

"What on earth was that?" I splutter, pushing Jesse's heavy frame off me.

Melanie flashes her eyes towards me. "A villager—a Terran—is on the base. They've broken in."

"That doesn't explain why they want to destroy our ear drums," I say angrily.

"It went out to the whole base. It's meant to scare intruders. We're supposed to get a warning signal, but I missed the notification because I was… distracted."

"Distracted how?" Jesse presses.

Melanie channels her intense gaze into my soul when she answers. "The scout said Silver Valley's rallying, Savannah. Jasmine Spark launched a search party for you, but what I don't understand is why she didn't just come here herself. It's so much easier to go undetected. Instead, she's sent the whole village to scour the forest. It's raising alarm."

Bloody hell. She's quite literally tearing the world apart to find me.

"It would've been too risky for her to come by herself," I hurriedly explain. "Too many people want her dead."

Confusion dawns on her face.

"People like your uncle," Jesse elaborates, "and the Elders."

Melanie nods. Puzzlement still fills her features, but she knows there isn't enough time to explain. Not when a villager could be in danger…

"Will your uncle harm the villager?" I ask Melanie.

"It's very likely," she says. Her voice is utterly defeated.

She knows who it is.

My hands shake as I prepare myself. My voice comes out weak, but she doesn't notice it.

"Who?" I ask.

Jesse's eyes flash to his friend. It occurs to me he may also recognise the name, considering he spent so long hiding within the valley.

"The alarm interrupted the meeting, but the scout told my uncle he bumped into someone when he was coming back to the base—someone who was closer to finding us than the others. He told him to turn around… but maybe he didn't," Melanie ponders.

The way Jesse looks at her, I know her guess will be as accurate as any. The only person who is allowed to doubt Melanie is Melanie herself.

Please don't be my dad. Please don't be Mason. Please.

"*Who?*" I demand.

"His name is Elijah Brooke," she says.

A choking sound escapes me. Oh god.

"Eli. They have Eli."

"Eli." Jesse says the word bitterly.

My hands begin shaking as the truth expands across my mind.

Eli came after me. Jasmine sent *Eli.*

I was supposed to see him earlier today, along with Jasmine and the rest of her friends. We were supposed to spend the day together. Laughing. Happy. I probably would've gone home with Jasmine after the day ended, and we would've lounged across her bed, talking about boys and other nonsense. And then I would've gone home to find my father making dinner and my brother sprawled across the couch among stacks of birthday invitations. I probably would've woken up the next morning with text messages from Eli. He may have even said, *"You sure you still want to be* just *friends?"*

Instead, I'm stuck here. Eli's been captured, Jasmine's probably in the valley sweating with nerves for both his safety and mine, and who knows what my father and brother are doing.

If I'm lucky, they aren't in the forest.

I hope Jasmine isn't either.

"Where will they put him?" I ask Melanie.

"They'll probably bring him to the Safe Holds first." Melanie sounds completely defeated by this, fiddling with her black fingerless glove.

"We have to go," I say.

I don't know where the Safe Holds are, but I spin down the hallway anyway. Jesse claps his hand on my shoulder and jerks me back. I nearly get whiplash.

"That's a horrible idea, princess."

"No, Savannah's right," Melanie rebukes, stopping him. "He wouldn't have come here without a reason, which means he might know something."

That isn't why I want to go. But because Melanie's agreeing with me, I don't hesitate.

"Yes, let's go."

"You do understand that if we get caught, Liaison Banks will make sure we'd never be able to get into the space centre again? He might even kill you." His tone is slightly teasing, but the serious undertone catches me off guard.

I didn't expect Jesse to shy from a challenge.

"He already wants us off the space centre. I doubt we have much more to lose," I remind him. "Besides, this isn't a choice. Eli is my friend. He was sent by Jasmine so she can get to me. I will *not* let him suffer."

I catch Jesse's gaze. It's sorrowful. His eyes clouded and downcast. When he meets my gaze, he attempts a soft smile. "Then we better not get caught."

I smile back and turn down the corridor.

We delve deeper into the space centre, but the descent blinks by in one long, drawn-out breath, faster than falling.

I'm the first one out of the elevator, and my intent takes Melanie by surprise. She lets me take the lead, her words of direction breathing into my back, and occasionally she grabs my sleeve to direct me towards a different hallway.

Jesse hesitates more than she does.

A battle is warring across his features. His hand keeps straying by his weapons belt, right above my switchblade. Either he wants to offer it to me, or he wants to use it on me. I can't tell which.

"Why do they keep the Safe Holds in the space centre, of all places?"

"We don't," Melanie answers me. "It's in an adjoining facility underground—connected to a building above ground. But the Safe Holds have been there since the beginning—there is old entrance which used to be the main entrance, which is accessible from here, but no one uses it anymore because it's excessive to get through."

"What do you mean?" I ask.

"The Elders don't really trust the people they call "heretics", people like you and me, so they locked them down into a place that was impossible to escape. The old tunnel is only accessible if you have clearance now," she explains, a crease marring her forehead.

I miss a step. "Then how will we get inside?"

She picks up her speed and walks beside me. "I don't know," she says, "I'm working on it."

I pick at a hangnail anxiously as we make way. Her words spur through my mind, blending with thoughts of Eli and what they could be doing to him right now.

"The alarm went off the very moment they caught him, right?"

"Yes, upon seeing him. He was probably seized immediately after," she responds, but her mind is partially elsewhere. It's as if she's in two places at once—planning, figuring out which computers to breach and when.

"That means he might not have even made it there yet," I say. "We could get him before he arrives."

"But they wouldn't use this entrance, princess. If we wanted to intercept him before they hauled him into a cell, we'd have to go through the other entrance," Jesse explains, his face blank but eyes analysing. A warrior's face.

"And we don't have time for that," Melanie explains.

Feeling defeated, I pick at my nail further.

I have nothing to distract or calm me, and the lack of the switchblade in my palm feels wrong. I want to ask Jesse for it back, but I also don't want to interrupt his internal debate. If I wait, he might give it to me. Patience.

"So what's the plan?" Jesse asks Melanie.

"I'm thinking."

"Think faster. We're nearly at the first check point."

She stumbles a step. "Ah."

Light flickers in her eyes. But I know better than to ask.

There are no more doors in the corridor, and the walls turn to metal and rust. The overhead lights somehow seem brighter, almost blinding as it bounds off the silver and dances upon our pale skin.

The ground begins to dip, taking us farther underground. The thought of being so far beneath the surface makes my shoulders feel heavy. Nothing about being underground feels safe, so far away from where I can feel the kiss of the stars.

"Three doors, three check points, not very well guarded because hardly anyone ever uses the tunnel," Melanie recites suddenly. "The first is a series of three transparent gates, operated by a control centre and two guards—we can convince the guards to let us through somehow. The second is unguarded, a heavy metre-thick gate in the middle of the tunnels—I can probably hack that one. The third is also unguarded but only passable by DNA—or so people say."

"Melanie, you can pass the third check point," I say.

Suddenly, this impossible entrance seems possible because of Melanie. Because of her uncle.

"Yes. That one is not my concern, though."

"I can get us past the first," Jesse says quietly. His weapons gleam in the light and I look away.

"Don't you even think of killing—"

"I can get us through all of them," Melanie interrupts harshly, her brow furrowed, "but I'll need access to each control centre to override the individual gates."

Of course she can get us through.

This expedition probably won't even require much help from me.

"I can convince the guards for us, sweetheart," Jesse purrs at her, his eyes glittering at the idea of a fight.

I open my mouth. "You really shouldn't—"

"Please shut up, princess."

I make a point of stepping on his foot, which he ignores.

"Save it for later," he growls.

Ahead, a hushed bubble of voices ebbs down the tunnel.

I gasp, stopped in my tracks abruptly by Melanie's arm. Jesse smirks at my desperation to continue and leans placidly against the wall.

"Around the corner there's an intersection—some doors—if we keep quiet, they won't see us until the next bend. But you need to stay silent," Melanie says solely to me.

"What're inside the doors?" I enquire.

"Storage, supplies, food," Melanie lists. "Some guards stay on rotation for days on end. There's a theory they even have pull-out beds down here."

"Do they?" I ask.

"I've never been there to find out," Melanie admits.

She purses her lips, contemplating whatever plan she's forming, and then suddenly her face pales. It takes me a moment to catch on. I watch her turn in the direction of the checkpoint. A group of people are making their way out, and I can't recognise any of their voices, but Melanie does.

"Some of my uncle's guards are here."

Jesse's hand flashes to his weapons belt, but Melanie's hand is faster, fuelled by fear, her fingers grazing his wrist.

"The alarm interrupted the meeting with the scout, which means…" She curses. "The Argenti is with him," Melanie says. "And if the Argenti is with Eli, he won't stand a chance. They'll kill him."

I shiver, fingers twitching for my switchblade.

"It's not the Argenti I'm thinking about right now," Jesse says.

We're close to the guards now. Melanie nods at Jesse, and a look of understanding flits between them.

"Savannah, if my uncle or the Argenti sees you…"

"I can handle myself, Melanie," I insist.

Melanie swallows deeply, averting her eyes from us. She takes a step around the bend, her expression morphing into annoyance.

She doesn't want me to join them.

Something flickers behind Jesse's eyes, dark and troubled. I reach my hand out to him, my fingers tangling in the sleeve of his clothing. His eyes flash down at my hand and he swallows deeply.

"Please, Jesse."

He takes a shaky breath and lifts his eyes to mine, capturing me with their full intensity. Knots twist in my stomach and I refuse to look away.

He reaches his hands up to my cheek, fingers grazing my skin.

Tingles fly down the side of my face, my entire body aware of the contact of that hand and beating in tandem with it. I clamp my cheek between my teeth, temporarily forgetting to breathe.

"Melanie can get us through the first checkpoint," Jesse whispers slowly. "We will save Eli."

I lift my hand to his, fingers knotting between his own, shaking the whole goddamn time I do so. My heart practically explodes out of my chest.

"If you leave me behind, I swear—"

"I'm not leaving you behind," he coos, and pushes me around the corner.

There are three small and narrow storage rooms, spaced evenly along the ten-metre wall, splitting the tunnel in two. I hardly have time to open my mouth before he pushes me against the door, his chest against mine.

My heart erupts in a storm, and he feels it, I know he feels it. I want to stamp my heel into his toes, but my hands grip his shoulders. My nails dig into his skin when he lowers his mouth, his breath warm on my neck, and I shiver.

My core tightens, and I hate myself. I *hate* myself.

His hand slides down my waist, hand brushing the empty pocket I usually keep my switchblade in, and he growls against my neck, his teeth scraping my skin.

My back arches into him involuntarily, and I want to hit him for it.

"Keep that fire in your heart, princess," he purrs, his words vibrating against my neck. I shiver again, and I think I feel blood trickling from my nails, piercing his skin. He gasps slightly but doesn't remark on it.

His scent fills me: fresh linen and metal and something other-worldly and unknown. My heart hammers against my chest and I swear his is doing the same.

He chuckles, and a loud beep sounds from behind it. It shatters the gentle quiet that had seeped into my mind.

Jesse coaxes me forward, like a lover on a wedding night, right up until his foot hooks mine and he throws me onto the hard ground.

My breath wheezes from my chest, and the world around me spins.

My head is pounding as he slips a key card he'd swiped from

Melanie's pocket back into his friend's hand, and Melanie moves to swing the door to the storage cupboard closed.

"I'm so sorry, Savannah."

I push up from my knees.

I never knew I could move as fast until now. I whip my leg out to stop the door but miss it by seconds. Fast, but not fast enough. Darkness envelops me as the door clicks shut.

I want to yell at them.

I want to pound on the door.

But right in that moment, I do nothing except force myself not to cry.

Cold, hard betrayal spreads through me.

Melanie's reassuring voice whispers past the metal door. I want to block out her excuses… at least Jesse isn't bloody grovelling.

But him, I will deal with later.

"My uncle doesn't want you in the space centre, let alone the Safe Holds. His guards know, and they'll never let us pass with you. I'm sorry. Jesse and I can get to your friend, and then we'll come right back for you. I promise."

I kick the door in response. The sound echoes in the quiet tunnel.

I don't give a damn what the guards think, and infuriatingly, Jesse chuckles at the sound. Wrapping my arms around myself, I kick the door again, tears threatening to spill. But I don't let them.

"Please don't leave me here," I say, my voice cracking. I hate how I sound. My kicks become weaker.

"Trust me, Savannah," Jesse urges, his voice deep with feeling.

I don't trust him.

"Jesse will never get past, either," I say bitterly, conjuring up excuses. "Your uncle recently banned him too."

A moment's silence.

I have a feeling Jesse didn't want Melanie to know that.

"He knows how to stay quiet," Melanie finally says.

I almost laugh. But I realise… she's right.

Damn her.

Damn him.

My kicking stops and I pull my legs up against my chest, silently shaking.

The guards' voices rise as they make their way closer, and it startles me that Jesse and Melanie haven't left yet. They should if they want to make it in time.

I sweat in a puddle of shame and nerves. I want to kick something again.

No.

I want to hit *them*.

Melanie and Jesse are speaking, but it's hushed, like they've stepped back from the door. I expect they'll leave at any moment. But Jesse's breath whispers through my door one last time.

"Keep that fire, Savannah." He swallows deeply. "I trust you. I *understand* you." He shifts from the door before he says, "Use your switchblade. Just… don't bloody stab yourself."

I keep my jaw locked, scrambling for my pockets where Jesse undoubtedly slid my switchblade while he was doing… *that*… A shudder of joy travels down my spine the moment my skin brushes the familiar wooden handle. I grip it in my fist.

And my tears finally start to fall.

I can hear Melanie's footsteps as they leave, but not Jesse's. He never makes a sound. But where Melanie goes, so does Jesse.

Their voices rebound back to me when they run into the guards, sparking a conversation.

And I wait.

I sit in the pitch black, waiting for the sounds of Melanie and Jesse to depart through the first checkpoint.

I can't help but think of Eli. He came for me, through Jasmine.

The guilt gnaws on my soul.

I did this. It's my job to fix it.

"Keep that fire in your heart, princess."

"I trust you."

I still in the darkness, everything else temporarily forgotten as my mind whirs at the memory of those words.

He wants me to follow them.

Of course he does.

I shake my head.

Melanie's focus had been directed on unlocking the checkpoints, but Jesse's mind had been elsewhere. They couldn't convince the guards to lower the first checkpoint for them with me in tow. Even I can agree that the risk of not getting to Eli is too great to challenge that. But that doesn't mean I can't try to follow them.

I recall Melanie's description on the first two checkpoints as I allow my heart a moment to still.

"The first is a series of three transparent gates, guarded by a control centre and two guards. The second is unguarded, a heavy metre-thick gate in the middle of the tunnels."

I've got to find a way to get through the first two checkpoints and catch up in time with Melanie and Jesse to get through the third one—the one that's only passable by DNA.

Gripping my switchblade in my fist for comfort, I wait for the Liaison's guards to walk past my storage room. Their conversation seems pleasant, which means my companions have made it past safely.

And I wait.

And wait.

Only silence greets me. It would seem Jesse didn't have to use his blades after all. But I certainly do.

I stand up and feel around in the dark.

Eli's expecting me. Somehow, somewhere, I think he knows.

"I'm coming for you. I promise."

Taking a deep breath, I begin to search for a light switch.

My fingers scratch aimlessly against the wall.

I narrowly avoid tripping over something by my feet and collect my breath. Where's the light switch?

I gnaw on my lip, my skin itchy with irritation. The wall before me is smooth… almost like dried glue?

My fingers stop their searching.

Oh.

My hands hesitate over the substance that lines every wall in the space centre. Of course. This is their light source.

Although, this stuff should radiate light. Shouldn't it? Here, it's dead.

I pound against it with my blade. Nothing.

After several minutes, I feel like giving up.

I fumble around like a fool in the darkness, bumping into what feels like cardboard boxes at every turn. The room feels ridiculously small because of them.

I lay both palms flat against the wall.

"Why aren't you working," I whisper against it.

Work, I think. *Work like you're supposed to.*

It takes a few moments, but to my utter shock, the wall slowly begins to throb with light. It expands from within its very core, stretching into the air and basking me in a familiar glow. I blink at it.

It's like I simply *willed* it into existence.

I stumble back from the wall, taking in the storage room. It's the size of an average bedroom. Shelves line the wall at the back, boxes stacked on each as well as scattered around my feet.

My foot trips on one of the boxes as I move backwards, and I catch myself on the shelving. Shaking my head, I crouch and open the nearest box, yanking out a tangle of wires.

I've never once seen an Umbran use a wire.

Flabbergasted, I thrust them back.

The rest of the boxes contain the same assortment: wires, bolts, tools, anything someone could use for repairs. But everything is covered in a thin film of dust, the cardboard withered and sagging.

You can see what boxes I've touched—where my fingers have marked their territory.

I shiver at the sight, clutching at my chest. The thought of spreading my mark further across the room sends a nervous tick down my spine.

I take a step back, spinning my switchblade in my palm, thinking.

The only exit is the main door, locked from the outside. I could smash the keypad with one of the tools in here—there are heavy bolts and sharp tools—but there's no way to access it from inside the room. I run my fingers over the edges of the door, searching, but huff and step away almost instantly.

One of the tools could be slid between the door and the wall to disable the locking mechanism, but I have no idea how to do that.

Maybe if I had something electric to spark the system?

I rack my brain, but I can't recall anything useful inside those boxes. Everything in here is dated and broken, and there are no power plugs.

I bite my lip and glare at the door.

The bright light makes me lightheaded, and I sway, leaning to my left.

Something reflects briefly in the light, just for a moment. I angle my gaze a fraction, pulse quickening.

Glass. The door has a glass window.

It's small, probably just wide enough for me to fit through. I hadn't noticed it sooner because it blends into the door so spectacularly, blacked out with paint. I rap my knuckles upon it, grinning.

Pocketing my switchblade, I reach into a box containing a heavy hammer.

Well, I think to myself, *I suppose I can make this a tradition.*

And I swing the hammer at the glass.

༄

Guilt washes through me as I stand above him, taking in the blood pooling around his uniform. It stands out starkly against the metallic floor and his pale Umbran skin.

If you'd asked me seconds ago if I'm good in combat, I would've shaken my head and laughed. But now, after what I've done to these guards, I'm not so sure.

They heard me and came running. I didn't even have to climb through the window. The glass shattering alerted them to my presence. And then, something came over me. Instinct, perhaps? It had to be. All I know is I didn't want to die.

The hammer in my hand is covered in blood. Not my blood. Theirs.

The first one had a kind face, dimpled and freckled and washed with fatigue. He didn't expect me when he tore open the storage door. He hardly had time to take me in before I launched the hammer into the side of his head.

He fell like a limp sack of rice.

The second was more difficult. He didn't investigate immediately because someone needed to guard the checkpoint.

I felt less sorry for hurting this one.

He looked cruel—all sharp edges and a malicious grin.

He reached for me, his sword forgotten by his belt as he lunged, planning to pin me down.

He didn't see my switchblade until I jammed it into his shoulder. The injury didn't stagger him, so I knocked the hammer over his head too.

Maybe I'm good at fighting after all.

I shiver, hugging my arms to my chest.

His skin is translucent, as if he's never seen the sun. I can practically see the blood pumping through his veins, hurdling towards the wound in his shoulder.

I place the hammer into his hand, wrapping his limp fingers around it, not wanting the reminder on me.

You didn't kill them.

You just knocked them out.

I tell myself this one last time and then let the thoughts go. It needed to be done.

Now, it's time to move on and save Eli.

I tear the key card off one of the guards' belts. There's no clip to detach it simply. The chain is secure, and it takes all my strength to yank it free.

I walk out of the storage room and find the tunnel ahead to be blocked off. The first checkpoint is massive—as big as a garage door. It's made of some Umbran material which is thick and translucent, indicating there are three more doors in this first checkpoint travelling down the rest of the tunnel.

Off to the side, there is a small door that leads up to a control room—the Umbra symbol with the U and the sword stamped onto the entrance. The control room juts out of the wall to my left like half a donut, a window of glass giving the guards a view of three gates.

I dash towards them, running my fingers across the solidly built wall before me. Beyond the first three doors, the tunnel travels deeper underground, and in the distance, I can see Jesse and Melanie. So far away, heading towards the next obstacle.

I slam my fist into the gate in front of me.

It would've been nice if Melanie left me with some help.

Too late for that now.

Getting into the control centre is easier than I expected. All I do is flick the key card against the panel and the door beeps and slides open, the glass retracting into the wall. A stairwell leads me up one storey to a small circular room spinning around me in a u-shape, covered in screens and controls. All the buttons and screens make me hesitate, blinking uncertainly.

I run my fingers across some switches until I find a screen with a live view of all the checkpoints. Security cameras fill the tunnels. Lots of them. I thank the stars the Liaison is preoccupied with the Argenti from Umbra, hopefully still separated from Eli. For how long though, I'm not sure.

My hands shake against the table as I search frantically for Jesse and Melanie.

There.

I lean towards the screen.

They've just passed the second checkpoint now, farther down the tunnel—this checkpoint is metal, the door a metre thick. Melanie leads, but she's walking slowly due to Jesse's casual gait. His lips are twisted into a scowl as he keeps glancing behind him, contending with a flustered Melanie who keeps waving him forwards. He's lingering... waiting for me to catch up.

I smile at the screen.

Somehow, I need to do exactly that as I don't know how I can get through the last checkpoint without Melanie.

I tear my eyes from Jesse and back to the other screens.

I should be able to get through the second checkpoint, though. It takes me several moments, and I almost sigh in relief when I find what I'm looking for.

This checkpoint controls more than just the three translucent gates below. I can open the next checkpoint from here.

Hands sweating, I scan my eyes over the controls until I figure out a system—a repetition of code. When I tap the keys and I'm asked for a passcode, I pause, suddenly overwhelmed with the feeling that I'm play-acting as Melanie.

I tap my fingers faster against the dark table.

A curser blinks at me. Taunting.

Maybe I already have the code. I flip the key card over in my palm, and there, written along the bottom is a string of digits—a failsafe if the guard has trouble remembering it.

It's almost laughable.

I try the combination, a seemingly random display of numbers and letters.

My heart hammers against my chest and I still my hands on the table.

Permission granted.

A light flashes green above the screen and three other lights above me flicker off, but nothing else alerts me of my success.

I can only hope I did it correctly.

If I get through these translucence gates before me and the second checkpoint somehow locks within that timeframe, I'll be trapped.

Taking a steadying breath, I shift my eyes onto the screen again, checking to see how far they've gotten in the meantime, and then avert my attention back to the controls.

I swipe my finger across a screen, opening the first gate. My eyes follow as it lifts and disappears into the ceiling. The moment it's open, I swipe my finger across the screen again, opening the second one.

When I do, the first door begins to close, just as the second opens. "Dammit."

I release a string of curses.

I try doing it backwards, starting with opening the third gate. Then I start by opening the middle gate first. No matter what combination I try, by opening more than one door, the others are always programmed to close, like a chain reaction.

The only hope I have is that the doors lift to the ceiling first before they slide back to the floor.

That's something at least.

In a final stroke of frustration, I attempt opening all the doors at once, swiping my fingers at the same time. The screen beeps, but nothing happens. All the doors remain firmly closed. I'll need to do it one by one.

I spin the key card around in my hands, searching for more passcodes.

An override code... anything.

But I'm no tech genius.

There's only one way I can do this, and I don't even know if it's possible.

I brush the sweat off my hands, dragging them down my shirt, and head back to the front door. There's only one chair in the room. I drag it with me and use it as a doorstopper to keep the exit open. It creates a bit of a maze, narrowing the exit, but it might spare me precious seconds.

Hurriedly, I stride up the stairs again, tucking my switchblade deep inside my pocket with quivering hands. It's a heavy weight against my thigh as I walk, but the weight is a constant reassurance that I'm not alone. I have a part of Jasmine with me, and Jasmine is good at doing the impossible.

Maybe she can give me some luck.

My fingers hover across the screens. Three screens. Three gates. I stare out the window, focusing on the tunnel I came from, checking to see if the guards are still unconscious.

My heart stops.

The first guard is rounding the corner. He looks disorientated. Hopefully it'll slow him down.

Taking a deep, nervous breath, I steady myself.

I need to go.

My hands move fast. They shake a little, but it doesn't slow me down.

Dragging my fingers across the screen controlling the first gate, I swipe immediately across the next screen, and then the next. One at a time, all the gates open.

But I don't stop to watch them. I turn away from the controls and run.

My sneakers skid down the stairs and I slam into the wall, pushing off with my shoulder.

I leap over the chair, but it catches on my knee and tumbles forwards, clattering onto the ground.

The sound is so loud, surely the guards know what's happening now.

I keep running, determined to make the first gate before it closes.

My feet hardly touch the ground. At least, it doesn't feel like they do as I dash past the first gate.

The second one third of the way down and I'm five metres away.

"HEY!" The guard's voice rings out around me. "STOP, YOU DON'T HAVE CLEARANCE."

Ignoring him, I reach the second gate, ducking my head to go under.

Nerves strike like lightning all over my body.

I don't stop to think about how close the third gate is to the ground.

One metre left to fall.

Ten metres left to run.

It's falling fast.

The third gate beckons before me, half a metre left until it closes.

My feet pound the hard floor and I throw myself onto the floor. My shoulder sings in pain, and the taste of blood coats my mouth.

I must pull myself under.

I drag myself on the stomach under the gate. The gate hovers over my torso, falling towards me. It's only a few centimetres thick but it could easily impale me.

I'm going to get sliced in half.

I scurry faster.

"COME BACK!" the guards yell.

What a stupid thing to say. The words dance across my mind as the gate lowers ever closer.

It brushes my legs.

They're through.

But my ankles aren't.

The gate bites down on my skin and I pull my feet towards me as hard as I can.

My scream echoes down the tunnel.

The gate grabs my foot, and it stops descending for just a moment, poised just off the ground, my foot caught between it. My ankle is still weak. The pressure is worse than the whole weight of the universe.

Blood pounds in my ears like my heart is going to erupt in my chest and my body jerks from nerves as I pull on my leg in panic. I scramble across the floor away from the gate, foot popping out of my shoe.

The gate slams down.

I can barely hear the guard through the translucent gates as he yells, "YOU DON'T HAVE CLEARANCE!"

I smile, watching silently as my shoe is crushed into the ground.

Both guards are yelling at me now through the transparent gates, their forms visible as if looking through water, but I can't hear them.

I wave at them, not sure if they can see the quick movement, then bolt down the rest of the tunnel, kicking off my other shoe so I can run faster. My freshly bruised ankle winces with each footfall and I wish I had some of that instant healing medication Melanie mentioned the labs had. *Velox*. But I've endured worse. I can manage this.

I hope the guards keep yelling. I hope they stand by the gates for hours. If they disable my access to the next checkpoint, there is no way I can hack my way through when I arrive—I'm no Melanie.

Worse, if they call more guards upon my friends and I, it will doom us all.

I curse myself for not taking the other guard's ID on the way out, blood pounding in my ears at each footfall, sprinting as if my life depends on it. In a way, it does.

Make it to the other gate, Savannah.

You must make it in time.

This tunnelled hallway looks the same as all the others, lights refracting all around me, dancing across the walls like artificial stars. I feel like a phantom, pelting through an artificial universe many storeys underground.

My feet slide across the cold floor, white socks slipping. But I don't want to waste time in taking them off. I don't want to stop for anything.

My breath rattles from my lungs, exhaustion quickly settling upon my shoulders. I can't remember the last time I've run like this—a high school athletics carnival, perhaps? But no, not even then did I run like I am now.

For what seems like half the tunnel, I feel like I'm flying. Then the adrenaline begins to fade, and I feel the tug of exhaustion.

My stamina dwindles with each step. I want to stop and clutch my chest, which feels like it's splitting from the need to breathe. But I can't. I need to keep going.

It feels like trekking through the ocean, the thick syrup of waves pulling me back.

"Keep going, you bastard," I mutter to myself between pants.

Perseverance.

I've been donned in linen shirts and skin-tight pants from Melanie's wardrobe since leaving my cell, and my switchblade feels as though it's about to fall free from the tight pocket of my pants with each step. But despite the building fear in my chest, there is absolutely no time for me to stop and save my blade.

I swallow back a sob as my body wilts.

Just as I spot the gate shining in the distance.

Something in my chest lurches at the sight of it. I feel a tendril of adrenaline spiral back across my skin and I allow the feeling to take me.

My pace quickens as I dash for the finish line, fingers itching to touch the gate.

To brush it open.

And my feet don't slow as I near it.

The gate is smaller than the last ones but a lot sturdier. The metal is thick and deep and is reinforced in something I can only describe as concrete. It isn't transparent like the last—anything could be waiting for me on the other side.

I almost slam into it, panting as I run my hand over it, searching for a way through.

The air is eerily quiet in the tunnel and the sound of my breathing echoes around me. My hand drags across the rough surface of the gate and slides into a small cranny. Inside, the surface is smooth like glass, but unlike it in the way it glows blue.

I press my hand against it and something whirs. The blue lights scan my hand. The Umbran U and sword symbol gets illuminated under my splayed fingers.

Permission granted.

Thank god the door is still unlocked.

The door opens of its own accord, pushing out instead of sideways.

I step into the threshold, heading towards the break of light.

A loud beep disrupts me.

The lights on the door suddenly power off and I'm basked in darkness inside the slim exit.

Startled, I freeze, cursing once I realise what's happening.

The door starts to close on me, and the gap in the exit is shrinking.

The guards must have realised where I am and disabled the checkpoint. More guards are likely racing up behind me as I speak. I can only hope the Liaison and Argenti are pre-occupied and don't have comms to alert them.

My heart immediately stops beating as the gate presses towards me, and, ignited by fear, I launch myself towards that gap.

I turn my torso sideways and the rough surface of the gate scratches against my back and stomach.

I feel it pressing into me as I fall forwards, hands hitting the ground just as the gate clicks into place.

"Jesus," I mutter. "I'm going to kill Jesse and Melanie."

I suddenly feel like laughing at the absurdity of it all.

Feeling giddy, I brush myself off and stand up. There are gashes in my shirt and blood wells upon my skin from the surface of the gate, but I ignore it.

"Here we go again," I mutter.

I take a deep breath and pelt down the last tunnel.

My socks don't slip as much as they did, but maybe that's because they're blackened and tearing at the seams.

My body goes into a trance as I run, time warping around me until I near the end, my rasping breath ricocheting around the tunnel.

In the distance, I see another bend, like the one Jesse and Melanie left me in. I can only tell because of the different glow of light, rather than the never-ending passage I've been sprinting through.

I pull my switchblade out as I approach.

The tunnel turns right, bending towards what I assume is the Safe Holds. The last checkpoint leads straight to the entrance. I risk a peek around the corner to examine it and then retreat again.

The pumping of blood fills my ears.

Voices swell from around the corner. Jesse and Melanie... and someone else. More guards. I realise they're about to unlock the gate when I hear words like *DNA* and *uncle*.

What happened to this gate being unguarded?

I flick the blade out from the mahogany handle and hold it steady in my palm. I've got no choice but to head towards them, before they pass the checkpoint and I'm left trapped.

There's no way I can get past this checkpoint alone.

I lean around the corner once more, trying to locate my friends.

The checkpoint isn't far. Two guards stand by it, monitors on their communication devices going off—probably because of me. The checkpoint next to them is the smallest door yet, a sub-standard door with a small podium next to it adorned in a screen and a hand scanner, the Umbran crescent U and sword symbol burnt into the wood.

I control my breathing, eyes flicking over my friends in confusion.

There is another almost identical door next to it with a keypad instead of a hand scanner. My mind switches to the key card in my pocket, knowing full well that Melanie has a key card she could use as well. I furrow my eyes at the sight of it, perplexed as to why they would be making Melanie use the one that tests her DNA.

Both guards stand at attention, hands hovering next to their weapons.

They don't trust them.

But Melanie stands with her head high, a cocky smile on her face as she places her gloveless hand above its surface and then winces, yanking her hand back. A drop of blood trickles down her palm, a needle receding back into the small surface.

They're testing Melanie—she must've spun some story to them about her uncle and they're checking she's telling the truth. The guards would have their own backdoor in case of emergencies, hence the other door. If I hadn't alerted the guards at the first checkpoint, my friends would probably be through the final checkpoint by now.

I gnaw on my lip, watching the blood ooze down her hand as she wipes it off with the glove on her other hand.

The door before them clicks open, and the guards frown at the sight.

Melanie steps forwards, reaching back for Jesse.

But he still seems reluctant to follow. He glances behind him, searching for something. The guard follows his gaze right to me.

I freeze.

My hands are shaking. *From running*, I convince myself. But my gut seems to laugh at me. Sure. Just from running.

I rub my hands down my legs and take a deep breath, stepping into the light.

Jesse strides up to meet me, trying not to smile, and the guards watch him attentively.

Jesse stops when I walk farther into the light, and it's only then his smile deepens.

My heart lurches in my chest.

"Finally." He raises an eyebrow. "You took your sweet ass time."

I snort. Did I?

It takes Melanie a moment longer to catch up with the fact that I'm here, but when she does, it isn't amusement that coats her expression. She turns away from the gate and regards me with exasperation.

Just when I'm about to explain, the guard standing at the gate notices my blade and advances with hell in his eyes.

"I'd lower your switchblade if I were you, princess," Jesse says.

I do as he says and flick it shut.

The guard continues forward, but his friend stops him. They regard me with narrowed eyes, gaze flicking amongst each other.

"How did you do it?" Melanie asks, piercing me with her gaze.

I shrug. "Mostly it involved a lot of running."

Jesse hiccoughs. He holds out a hand for me, inviting me forward. My heart begins to batter in my chest as my skin brushes his. He feels steady, warm, despite the chills dancing up my arm.

His touch grounds me and the adrenaline quickly leaves.

It feels like a slap in the face when he finally withdraws his hand.

"You expected her to follow?" Melanie says, her brows lowering. "That's why you were so goddamn slow."

"Yes."

"And that's why you gave her the switchblade, so she could use it on the guards?" Her tone is clipped.

"Yes," he repeats.

Melanie's eyes dart to me.

"I didn't need to use it," I mutter, trying to reassure her.

Next to me, Jesse smiles slightly. "See? No harm done."

"You do realise she could've killed someone, right?"

Jesse shrugs.

Could I? Does Melanie think I'm capable of that?

One of the guards widens his eyes. I notice him lift his lapel and whisper something quietly into it under his breath. Jesse notices too.

My nerves tingle, gut lurching. I lean into him, my voice barely an octave higher than my breathing. "They know something's up. We have to be ready for anything."

He gives me a look. *I know.*

Rolling his shoulders back, he charges towards the guard speaking into his lapels. "How many guards are on the other side?"

The guard before him shakes slightly but keeps his head high.

If he didn't think we were a threat before, he does now.

"I don't think you understand what you're intercepting," is all he says to us, eyes flickering to his communication device as he does so.

Melanie looks away nervously. "Jesse," she says, "we don't know what's on the other side of this checkpoint. It could be a massive gamble. Maybe we shouldn't take her."

"Everything about life is a gamble," I snap at Melanie. "Now, please do us all a favour and lead the way."

She regards me for a slow moment. I almost expect her to say no. But, to my surprise, she just nods and turns back to the guards.

Thank god.

I'm not going back to that storage room.

I flip open my switchblade again. To hell with what the guard behind us thinks. Jesse notices it from the corner of his eye and pulls up a weapon as well.

And in that moment, I feel like I understand him completely.

The corner of my mouth quirks, and Jesse twirls his knife through his fingers with the deadly precision of a killer.

Melanie sighs and reaches for my hand, pulling us both through the final check point, her hand pressed on the Umbran symbol that's burnt into the wood.

Together, we all hold our breath.

The moment we make it through, a sword slashes towards Melanie's head.

I pull her out of the way, and she slams against the wall, moaning in shock. The guards at the first checkpoint didn't come from behind like I anticipated, but from in front of us.

The sudden action spurs Jesse on and he launches his knife at the nearest guard. The one who went for Melanie falters, and this turns the tide.

Jesse flashes another knife out of his belt and the guard changes course and stumbles towards him, which was yet another mistake. In one quick manoeuvre he's on the floor, blood gushing from his hands, rendering him incapable of wielding his sword again.

"Jesse!" I scream impulsively, eyes widening at the blood.

"I'm not going to kill them, princess."

He doesn't break his attention from the guards, already ducking under the next sword.

The man grunts as he charges him, but Jesse spins around him effortlessly like a dancer, slashing the back of the guard's knees. I gasp at the flow of blood, expecting his legs to be cut off, but it's only a thin gash. What I don't realise is that it makes it impossible for the guard to stand. He topples over, cursing us.

It's almost funny. Clearly, Jesse agrees, smirking. He's toying with them, I realise.

He hardly wastes a breath.

I hover near Melanie, still trying to get my bearings, struggling to follow Jesse as he dances around the guards.

There aren't many of them—for Jesse's standards, apparently—and it's only moments until Jesse has all seven wounded, sporting nothing more than a cut along his collarbone.

I don't know when he got it.

I reach for Melanie, who leans against the wall. The entrance we came through has closed again, as if the guards on the other side intended to lock us in with this attack party.

We're in some sort of staff room, with lockers lining the walls and a rickety table against the far side. There's even a small kitchenette, with dregs in the teacups and a kettle still bubbling. Melanie nods towards a basic wooden door ahead of us which must lead us to the Safe Holds.

Some back entrance.

I ignore it for the moment, roaming my eyes instead to the deep gash along the side of her arm. The sword slashed through her black glove and through her skin, and yet she doesn't bleed.

I reach for her arm, but she yanks it back from me, tugging the glove off to assess the damage.

I hold my breath, expecting the worse, heart pounding at finally being able to see what she's hiding under that glove. She bunches the black fabric in her other hand, fingers running over the place where the sword hit her.

I pinch my brows together.

Her arm looks normal, nearly identical to the one that always remains gloveless, but wires instead of blood spurt out from the gash on her arm.

"It's a bionic prosthetic," she says simply, lifting her silver eyes to mine. "I lost my arm in a fire when I was younger."

Hands shaking, I hover my fingers over the wires, a crease forming between my eyes. "How? It looks so real."

The Umbran matter in the prosthetic must be tougher than bone and skin, so it didn't take her arm off, but it still jerks and malfunctions from the injury.

"Advanced skin grafting and tech. I told you, my mother was a healer, and my father was great with technology. I learnt from both." She shrugs, moving to slide the glove back over her fingers. "I spent a lot of time in the med ward fusing wires and grafting skin after they died."

Her whole arm twitches at the movement, operation of her arm failing as a few wires spark. My fingers reach to help her with the glove, but she bats my hand away.

"Don't touch it, I'll be fine."

"Do you have a gauze or something to cover it? I can help," I offer, eyes locked on the glove that she now keeps bunched at her wrist, exposing the wires.

"Because you definitely know your way around injuries," Jesse mocks.

I give him a flat look.

"Funny."

"I don't need gauze," Melanie declares, gritting her teeth. "I'll just cover it with my glove if anyone asks questions."

Taking a deep breath, I ask slowly, "why do you wear it, if your arm looks normal with the skin grafting?"

She flashes me a quick look, her breathing shallow. Biting her lip, she turns up to stand, eyes downcast. As if insecure. I swallow deeply, taking in the injured guards before her, her eyes unfocused.

The room we're in smells dank, as if it hasn't breathed fresh air in decades. The lights along the walls pulse around us, highlighting the wounded, irritated guards. They chatter among themselves, and one of them reaches for his communication device.

Jesse stands before them. "You really shouldn't do that," he says, snatching it out of the man's hand.

I watch as Jesse drops it onto the ground and stomps on it.

He passes a small knife to Melanie as we pass him. He seems almost hesitant as he does so, but Melanie clutches the weapon in her fist with a determined glint in her eye.

The moment we reach the door, Melanie starts tapping codes into a panel across the front with her injured arm. It looks like every other door in the space complex, which means any staff member could access it. The panel asks for a key card and Melanie begins searching for hers within her pocket, prosthetic arm jerking.

"It's okay, I got it," I assure her.

I pull out the card I stole from the guard at the first checkpoint and swipe it across the door.

Jesse raises his eyebrows at me.

I smirk at him when the door opens, only for my smile to immediately turn into a gag.

Melanie leads us into a network of corridors, reeking with decay and bodily fluids. We step into the labyrinth, and I try not to breathe.

The lights in the room aren't the pulsing glow I'm accustomed to, but fluorescents that dot the ceilings at regular intervals. It feels like we've stepped into a jail for an insane asylum.

"What sort of prison is this?"

"They don't like to call it a prison," Melanie corrects. "That's why they call it the Safe Holds. No one here is convicted, they're just people who found themselves on the wrong side of the Elders."

My skin crawls as we make our way down the first hallway. On either side of us are rooms separated by bars and dark walls. All of them are empty. Which means we'll have to head farther into the maze to find Eli.

"The Elders keep hushed about it because they've practically abandoned this place," Melanie whispers.

"I didn't know it was this bad." Jesse's voice sounds flat. "They keep it concealed pretty damn well."

"So the Elders know how horrible this is, but they ignore ethics and do it anyway?" I hiss.

"According to them, it's for the good of the planet," Melanie clarifies.

I reflect on what Melanie taught me about the Elders being the last remaining pockets of humanity who grew up with the original species on Umbra. The Occupants were kind, they didn't share the barbaric notions that humanity is known for. From what I've heard, they were a peaceful race who wouldn't even fathom such a monstrosity. It wasn't in their nature. So how could the Elders allow such a foul place on Terra to exist under their own orders?

"I thought the Elders are peaceful. They learnt from the Occupants, didn't they?" I inquire.

"To them, this has *become* the meaning of peace. Tuck away the garbage and their planet will thrive." Her voice cracks as she speaks, as if she's haunted by her own words. "They want to cleanse Umbra of Terra, ultimately. This place holds what they believe to be Terra's and Umbra's worst. It's well out of their way. Out of sight, out of mind."

"Do they have a place like this on Umbra?" I inquire.

Something dark clouds Melanie's face. It's that expression, not her words, that tells me they do. Umbra may have once been a peaceful planet, but I wonder how peaceful it really is now.

"They send the ones they don't want down to Terra, or they kill them on Umbra. These are the people they believe are too Terran, too savage, to be permitted a residence on Umbra. But yes, they have a small prison. It's mostly there to hold people captive until they decide what to do with them—no one's ever there for long. But once you're in the prisons on Terra, you could be stuck in a cell for eternity. This is the place people are sent to be forgotten."

I place my hand on one of the bars to an empty cell and the cold metal bites into my flesh. I can't imagine being stuck down here forever. It seems more savage than any reality I've ever faced. And not all the people here are bad either. The brutes from The Nook were taken here just because of their disruptive behaviour, Eli was taken here just because he's a Terran who ventured too far out of his cage, and who knows what other petty things people have been locked up for.

My hands shake against the rusted bars, collecting red dust on my fingers.

"Careful," Jesse warns.

"They trigger the bars and walls housing dangerous captives. The shock is enough to knock you out for a few minutes," Melanie says.

"How?" I wonder.

"Electricity. Lots of it."

Stars. I pull my hand back, shivering.

The labyrinth feels haunted, and in the distance, I can hear the echo of someone crying. It sounds like a child.

"I don't care what they call it, this is a prison," I say, rubbing my hand.

Melanie nods, fiddling with the glove at her wrist. "I just wish I could change all of it."

We can, I want to say. *We must.*

"The common man can only do so much," Jesse says.

"Perhaps," I say in return, "but if we gather enough common men, we could rally."

Melanie misses a step.

"You're talking about a revolt," she says cautiously, testing the words.

I chew on my lip. Am I? I don't care for revolting.

In all selfish honesty, I just want the people I care about to be safe. Innocent people like Eli.

Do these people have families and friends out there that love them as well? Or are they all locked up here together, watching their loved ones die next to them?

"Not a revolt," I say. "But maybe... something like it."

The words taste foreign in my mouth.

Melanie glances at me with a determined glint in her eyes, jaw set. This girl is ready to revolt.

I want to scream that I'm not ready, that I'm the wrong girl.

But right now, all I can think of are these cages, the innocent people being punished for petty crimes, of Elijah Brookes, at risk of being locked up and forgotten.

Melanie looks ready to say something but keeps her words to herself. She mustn't want to push me yet. I'm thankful for it. I'm not ready for that.

I walk with a slight sway in my steps, avoiding suspicious-looking stains along the concrete floor. It takes a good deal of concentration, because the deeper we delve into the prison, the more decrepit it appears. I spot someone huddled in the back corner of a cell, looking like the living dead, and then another person, and another, until nearly every cell is full.

I have no idea how we'll find Eli.

"Do you think he's here yet?" I ask Melanie.

She nods. "I can hear voices ahead, so we'll investigate. It's probably where he's been taken."

She's right. Ahead, voices drift towards us, a heated conversation between several people. I wonder if the Liaison is present—some of his personal guards had abandoned the first checkpoint earlier.

We navigate our way around the cells, using the stream of voices as our anchor.

I almost stumble into a puddle of what's probably urine when a small child reaches his hand towards me through the bars, barely missing me. He mustn't have been seen as a threat, because the bars do nothing to electrify him.

Melanie and Jesse flank me when I stop to approach the child. Sorrow washes through Melanie's silver eyes as she takes him in, but she does nothing to move closer. In fact, she grabs onto my sleeve as I take a step forward, asking me to stop. I look at her curiously, and she gloomily shakes her head. *Don't*, her eyes seem to plead. *There's nothing you can do to help right now.*

The child is thin and dishevelled, black crust rotting underneath his fingernails. The fine strip of brown cloth that hangs over his limp body reveals the full arch of his collarbone and the top of where his ribs start. The child must only be six years old, judging by his height, but in this state, he looks no older than four. He reaches for me with a blackened hand, sunken eyes pleading. I whip my gaze across the bars, searching for a keyhole we could pick, but there's nothing. The only way I could free this child is by force or by forcing a guard to assist us.

And in that precise moment, I know Melanie was right. I cannot help this child, not without raising the alarms as to why I'm here. It would mean that I wouldn't reach Eli and saving him could potentially help Melanie free others. I can't risk everything for one child.

I inhale a shaky breath. The voices seem to drift closer, as if they're taunting me. I ignore them for a moment and reach for the child, taking his small bony hand in mine.

Melanie looks torn between impatience and despair, but Jesse seems to stop entirely, watching me with extreme fascination. The small child looks at them. They almost seem like they're my guards, standing over my shoulders with weapons in their hands and steel in their eyes.

The young child locks me in his strong gaze, unwavering determination blazing as he utters a single word: "Princess."

I drop the child's hand and stumble backwards, my mind going blank at the word.

"Are you here to save us?" he continues.

I turn back to my companions, who look just as flabbergasted as I am. Melanie's mouth opens and closes, but Jesse deals with the intrusion of privacy like a bug to repellent, and immediately tears down the corridor away from the small boy, his shoulders hunched. I race after him down the passage, also feeling the need to escape.

The small child watches us leave with tears lining his eyes.

Melanie grabs my arm. "He must be like Jasmine; he must have been searching for you. Maybe with his parents? I'm sorry it has to be this way, Savannah."

I shrug her away.

If not through force, how exactly was she planning to convince me to overthrow the reigning party of Elders?

"I'm no princess, Melanie. And I'm no usurper."

She says nothing. Instead, I use the temporary lapse in silence to repeat the question that's been burning through me since I arrived at the base.

"Melanie, how did you find me?" I say so quietly, I hardly hear myself. "How do you know I'm the right girl?"

"Jasmine," she replies just as softly, shrugging, "I had her followed. I tracked everyone that came and went from Umbra, praying someone would lead me to you. I had no lead on finding you, but I knew someone else would. All I had to do was snatch you from under their noses." She smiles faintly, but the victory is lost on her. Clearly, she suffered years of dead-ends before finding me.

"In the end," she continued, "I stumbled upon you entirely out of chance. I went to the village with Jesse, and I found the empty necklace, lost among the rose bushes outside your house. We entered the village by your house and found footprints suspiciously tracked all through the garden. It had just rained, and the muddy tracks were unmistakable. Your house was for sale at the time, and someone was trying to peer through the window, but lost their necklace while doing so. I recognised it as a style people wore on Umbra, except this one once held a stone. I was curious. I sent Jesse to the valley not long after, told him to find someone with Umbran qualities. He found her the week before you arrived, and when he realised her friend had the dark hair the prophecy described, I had him follow you instead. We were assessing your personality, tallying it up to what we believed could be a leader. A revolutionary. A princess."

I shake my head soundlessly, breathing shallow. "How did Jasmine find me?"

She sighs deeply. "Honestly, I have no clue. But I'm as curious to know as you are."

We turn left through an intersection within the rotting labyrinth and suddenly the party of voices is as clear as day. I grab Melanie's wrist, choking on a sudden wave of fear. I recognise multiple voices.

One is Eli, rambling incoherently, trying and failing to claim his innocence. To my own bewilderment, he mentions 'Umbra' and the 'Argenti' among his pleas.

But it's the second voice that takes the air out of me. I build up my courage and avert my eyes as Jesse leads the way towards them.

The passage looks like all the others bar the main doors at the far end. Our exit.

The surrounding cells are packed, but each one hums with energy. Here is where they keep the dangerous prisoners, right near the entrance. Perhaps it's to scare all the new captives they bring in.

To my left, I spot the brute's female crony that was taken from

The Nook, and I slip my switchblade from sight, so she doesn't have a chance to recognise it.

She seems the most defeated of all, lingering in the back of her cell. The rest swarm near the bars, curious to know what's causing the commotion. Knowing she's caged behind electrical bars sets my blood boiling. Surely, she isn't that dangerous, and yet they deem her to be one of the worst. They don't even have someone truly threatening to display, so they end up making a mockery of the mediocre ones?

I squeeze Melanie's wrist.

The small party ahead realises our presence and they all stop speaking collectively.

There's a table at the far end of the room. Metal. Dirty. Blindingly bright in the flickering lights. All sorts of machinery adorn it—knives, prongs, nails, and ugly, twisted pieces of metal that my gut drops at the sight of. More items hang from the walls. Chains. Ropes. Things that cut.

Melanie curses loudly next to me.

Jesse spins a knife around his fingers, losing himself to a murderous trance.

Before us, feet chained together and head drooping, the Umbran symbol painted red on the stone wall above his head, is Eli.

Nailed to the wall.

His fingers twitch, blood trailing down his arms from where they pounded a thick nail into his palms. A man in silver holds a hammer, as if waiting for him to beg before sinking the nail deeper or yanking it out.

He looks just as I remember him, but he's covered in dirt and blood, tears streaking down his cheeks.

I watch as his eyelids flutter, and slowly he looks up. A lady stands over him, sneering at Melanie's uncle as Eli wakes.

Eli gapes in shock when he notices me in the shadows, just as the man in silver grabs his shoulder. Pushing him down… down against the nails in his palms. He's too broken to sob. He screams, half conscious, and fights against it, trying to stand.

Above him, the dried paint of the Umbran symbol looks like old blood, frozen in time as though it were oozing towards the crown of Eli's head.

The woman next to Melanie's uncle tells the silver guard to stop.

I freeze. It's the Argenti the Liaison was going to meet.

My hands shake at the thought that Melanie's uncle brought her here.

But of course he did, because Eli interrupted their meeting, and what better way to show Umbra another reason to look down on Terra than to bring her a helpless and weak civilian. All so they can learn his secrets… by torturing him.

It seems as if they have only just begun. They haven't moved him to that table yet and already he looks beyond broken.

I swallow deeply, and the woman finally turns to face me.

Her silver eyes pierce the dull tunnel. Even with the distance between us, I can feel her burning gaze.

And I realise I wasn't dreaming when I recognised her voice.

I stop immediately in my tracks.

No, no, no, no, no.

Jesse pulls me forwards with his strong gait, unknowingly giving me the much-needed strength to move. I blindly follow until I'm standing right in front of her, Eli crumpled before us.

She smiles, and I can almost pretend it's heartfelt.

Almost.

I lift my chin and smile back, lips wobbling.

"Hello, Mother."

26

Venus Collins never called herself a Shaw. And now, looking at the woman before me, I can see why. She looks nothing like a Shaw. For the first time in my life, I know what she is. My mother is an Argenti.

Her pale skin is perfectly smooth—unblemished, like a ripe fruit that has never bruised. Her eyes glow like the stars, bright and endless, a silver burning flame. The only hint of Terra in her is the slight crease under her eyelids, the callouses on her hands, and, of course, the tips of her hair. I remember my mother having silver re-growth, but that has grown down past her chest, and only the ends of her long ponytail are still brown.

I wonder why she won't just bloody cut it off.

"What in all the worlds are you doing here?" she asks angrily.

I don't expect her to hug me. I don't even expect her to call me her daughter. But her blatant anger jostles me.

I take a slight step back.

I want to look at my companions for help, but I can't. The taste of blood fills my mouth as I gnaw on my cheek, staring at the woman before me.

I can hear Jesse shifting, reaching for a weapon. I don't bother to tell him to snap out of it.

Yes, my blood seems to sing. *Yes, Jesse, kill, kill, kill...*

I slowly walk towards them.

Only Eli seems oblivious. His eyes stop swimming when he sees me, and I hear his chains rattle as I move close enough to stare up at my mother.

"Of course you're from Umbra," I say on a breath. "Of course you're one of the Elder's loyal lap dogs."

Why did they send her?

What does this mean?

My mother's glittering eyes flash, coated in silver venom. They lock on the Liaison, who frowns.

I watch Melanie's uncle blush under the yellow lights and wonder to myself what on earth he could be embarrassed about. He peels himself from between the set of guards to protect my mother, and as he nears me, he hisses: "I told you to get off my base."

I smile sweetly at him. "I will," I say, not bothering to whisper, "as soon as I take Eli back to Silver Valley."

My mother glares at me. "You will do no such thing. We are interrogating him." Her lip curls, eyes twinkling, as she adds: "Soon, we will no longer affiliate with Terra. My father will pass a ban."

My grandfather.

My mother is a pure-blooded Argenti, meaning she's the daughter of an Elder.

My mouth grows dry. I've never heard my mother say such things. She never spoke of her family, her past, or anything about herself. I often wondered what my soft-hearted father even knew.

"*Who?*" I insist, voice clipped.

My mother doesn't bother to answer. To her, I'm doing nothing but wasting her time. As usual.

"Savannah," Melanie says, my name lost on a single breath of air, as if she's struggling to find her words. "Your mother is the daughter of the sixth Elder, or better yet... Lythia May's cousin. Didn't you know—"

I whip around to face Melanie. "She's what now?"

"She didn't know," my mother replies, irritation edging her tone. "I discarded her with my lover before she could consider her ancestry."

I grip my switchblade. How dare she say that?

"Do you have *any* idea what your absence has done to Dad and Mason?" I clench my fists. "Mason still loves you. He sends you endless postcards about his life. And Mark lives in the shadow of your absence—sometimes he can barely look at me because of it. And you spit on their very existence."

Liaison Banks shuffles uncomfortably, and the guards touch their fingers to their swords. It seems my mother has a higher status than I could've ever believed in. Like *I* am a threat to *her*.

To hell with them all.

"Why do you hate us, *Mother*?"

"Hate you?" She smiles, almost laughing. "I have no room in my life for hate."

The dynamic in the corridor shifts uncomfortably. Everyone glances at different crannies throughout the labyrinth, as if they're all personally invading a conversation they would rather not be privy to.

"Then tell me."

"Tell you what exactly, Savannah?"

"Why you left me. Why you left my dad."

My nails drag down the wooden handle of my switchblade, and I pretend it's my mother's face. Lost and seething, I am not ready for her next words.

"He's not your dad."

My heart drops.

I open my mouth, but no words come out. Is that… I'm not… *he isn't?*

My fingers tremble.

Oh, Dad. "No." I say loudly. "No." He broke his back every day to make ends meet to support me. And he's not even… My words tremble as I say, "You're lying."

My mother's only response is a cruel laugh.

I take a step towards her, but Jesse grabs my arm.

She's lying. The evil bitch is lying to me. "You ungrateful, bitter, disgusting, spiteful—"

"Enough with the adjectives, child."

I squirm against Jesse's hold, a scream bubbling in my throat. My thoughts swarm like wasps, stinging and buzzing. I can't think. I can't *think* straight.

My mother drags in a breath, taking in the room and the people surrounding us. She pulls her gaze back to me, resolve set in her eyes.

"I defied my father and the other Elders once, just for a moment, because I created you. I then let you live, gave you a chance to disregard your path, and I've always considered that to be the greatest of gifts." Her features are cold as she speaks, and I don't believe for a second that she cares for me at all. "You have so much dirt in your blood. I brought you to this Terran family. I gave you a father, I made you a brother, and this is what I get in return? Questions? Anger? I've got silver in my veins, Savannah. I'm one of the loveliest gems of Umbra. And I'm stuck with *you.*"

She's threatened. My Argenti mother is threatened by *me.*

I release a bitter laugh, glaring at her. "You're delusional. That's what you are."

She gives me a cold smile.

"What're you doing here, Mother?" I inquire. *What's your meeting about? What is in that shipment?*

"That's none of your business," she says, turning away from me.

Melanie takes a step closer to me, her eyes softened with concern. I try my best not to look at her, because doing so will only break me.

"Lock the Terran up, Banks," my mother tells the Liaison.

This seems to spur Melanie. She leaps forwards, and the guards pull her back. "Uncle, he's innocent. Let us take him back to the Valley."

Eli groans at the words, but the Liaison ignores his niece.

"Uncle, please," she presses.

Jesse aims his crossbow.

"I'm just a Liaison. I don't have the power to do what you want."

"That's your problem," Melanie pushes, as if spurred by my own anger. The guards restrain her, one of them dangerously close to gripping her bloodied arm, but she doesn't care. "You never do anything."

"Hush, child," my mother coos, fire in her eyes.

She draws a finger down Melanie's cheek, holding her chin. She's dangerously close to her neck, and I twitch at the sight.

"Oh, shut up. This isn't Umbra, Mrs *Shaw*. You have no powers here."

My mother looks at Melanie with poison.

And she glares right back at her, body poised for a fight. I blink at the sight, at the image of Melanie hating my mother with her entire being, simply because I do. Standing up to her… for me.

"You will address me as Venus Collins, not Shaw. You're merely a Common girl, since the death of your parents, and it's within my right to punish you for saying such a thing."

Melanie yanks her chin out of Venus's grip with enough force to give herself whiplash.

"Punish me? How?" Melanie spits. "Send me to Terra? Surprise, bitch, I'm already here."

Liaison Banks slaps his niece.

I dive forwards, feet tripping on the stones, but Jesse grabs me, his fingers itching for his weapons. I notice the moment he leans forward to fight and I grip his wrist, shaking my head slowly.

Okay. Not yet.

Melanie slowly moves her head back to face her uncle, mouth set in a seething line. A red mark blooms on her cheek, as angry as the red Umbran emblem above Eli's head.

Her uncle's pale skin is almost purple with anger as he glares at her, a vein on his smooth forehead thumping as he steps closer to his niece. "Get out of my base and don't come back. You're fired. Banished. Don't you dare return or you'll be killed on sight." He whips his head towards me, unfocused. "And that goes for all of you."

Melanie takes a deep breath, her silver eyes on fire.

Silence echoes in the corridors.

Melanie's job is her purpose in life. He can't take that away. Hell, this *base* is her life, her only and last connection to her home planet.

But to my surprise, Melanie doesn't waver, doesn't yell at him, just stands still and collected. She smiles at her uncle, at my mother, and then turns to Jesse, whose eyes are locked on that red mark on her cheek.

His jaw is set, and he stands like a stone, one hand on his crossbow and another near the trigger. I gently remove my grip on Jesse's wrist.

The other two guards—who must be my mother's, judging by their silver, foreign attire—hesitate with their grip on Melanie, eyes marking the threat before them.

Melanie looks him dead in the eye, and I swear I see a light flicker behind Jesse's careful mask when she says, "Time to do it Jesse's way."

That gives me half a second to duck before Jesse reaches for one of the guard's own swords, using it to slash open his comrade from top to bottom. The guard falls. His scream shatters through the labyrinth, and half his guts litter the floor.

My breath catches in my throat.

These guards must have been trained and hand-picked by the Elders to guard Venus. And Jesse gutted one like he was nothing.

The guard still standing doesn't have a sword now. Jesse plunges his blade into the man's shoulder as he hurtles towards him, and then draws the blade up, up, up, until it tears through flesh and bone. It throws the guard off balance enough to let Jesse pursue the two holding Melanie, who plunge towards him.

The guard's arm hangs limply, attached only by a scrap of sinew.

Eli sees this and his eyes momentarily roll in his head.

The moment Melanie's free, she scrambles over to Eli, picking up the discarded hammer, and using the other end to wrench the nails out of Eli's hands. My eyes flicker between her and Jesse.

I didn't think she'd have it in her.

Eli screams as the nails leave his flesh. The sound of his wail makes my heart stop.

I hold my stomach, trying not to vomit as the nail pops free from the wall. Eli hovers his broken hand in the air before him, and Melanie works on the other nail, her bionic arm twitching.

But her uncle grabs her from behind, tossing her to the ground. Fortunately, the hammer was already gripped onto the nail and the force of being yanked back sends it flying out of the wall with her, the chorus of Eli's scream accompanying Melanie's fall.

She raises the hammer at her uncle, aiming. He's slow to react, but Melanie hesitates too much, and he grapples her.

I take a step towards her, eyes on the knife she shoved into her pocket earlier. Jesse's knife. Venus now has Eli's bloodied hand in her fingers, thumb tracing over the hole in his palm, and I hesitate.

The two guards in silver are enough to overwhelm Jesse. I stand still between my friends, both wrestling and fighting, and stare at the Argenti. My mother and I remain still as chaos ensues around us.

I wonder how different this fight would be if we were on Umbra—if Venus had access to the magic coursing in her blood.

My palms sweat, mind whirring with questions of what she could do with that magic.

She would be powerful, no doubt, if she really is related to Lythia May.

She drops Eli's hand, but not before pressing her thumb into the wound. He moans in pain, but doesn't hesitate when he's released, and immediately tries to make his way to Melanie.

"Child," she says to me, her voice soft and steady, unconcerned with the fate of her guards. "Why do you waste time with these delinquents? You should've heeded my blessing, ignored the call of fate, and lived a perfectly boring life in Sydney."

I don't want to talk. I want to kill her. I stalk towards Venus, switchblade turning in my palm.

"But I don't have a choice, do I? Everyone keeps saying I'm the prophesied princess. That I'm going to rule."

I say it to disgruntle her, distract her, and predictably, her face sours, lips twisting.

She obviously doesn't like the thought of me ruling.

Jesse manages to disengage one of the Liaison's guards, who falls to the ground gripping a piece of flesh that isn't attached to him anymore. I don't even want to know how that happened. The other guard releases his blade, and Jesse spins on him, flashes of metal singing down the labyrinth as they parry.

"Everyone has a choice," Venus continues. "My cousin had a choice when she shared her version of the future, and the masses had a choice when they chose to believe it. It is now your turn, Savannah. Do *you* believe it? Will *you* act on it?"

She sounds like a politician: a corrupt manipulator with years of practice. I want to stab her clean through, just for that.

"Prophecies only come true if the people *make* them true. My choice is made."

She smiles sweetly. "Nothing has been forced just yet. Even this prison-side brawl can evolve to nothing, if you let it. Just walk away, child. Let this poor boy rot in peace."

Prison.

It does me good, hearing an Argenti say that.

It contradicts the supposed peace they're said to uphold.

Eli makes it to Melanie, his once wide smile long gone as he stares down at the girl who freed him. He doesn't deserve to be locked up, and he knows it. Why can't Venus see that?

"I wish you never came back, *Mother*."

She smiles coldly.

Liaison Banks knocks the hammer into Melanie's normal arm, making her drop Jesse's knife, and her sob pierces the area surrounding us. It makes Jesse pause, his eyes straining to find her, and one of the remaining guards plunges his sword into Jesse's stomach.

My limbs lock at the sight of him stumbling.

He continues fighting, even as the guard twists his sword inside him.

Jesse manoeuvres away. The world slows as I see the metal pull out of him, soaked in red. I almost sob, a part of my chest caving in at the sight.

But he doesn't react.

His gaze deepens, turning feral as he keeps pushing the guard towards us, like herding cattle.

He's fighting his way to Melanie.

Eli notices this and hovers a bloody hand over Melanie's wound. She came here to save him, and that's enough for him. Gently, he takes the knife from her pocket with ruined hands and repositions himself in front of her on the floor.

Eli sways in front of Melanie, weapon raised. A shield.

But this does nothing to appease Jesse. He fights with even more determination now that his life's blood is pooling across his shirt.

One of the guards finally falls in a heap, Jesse's blade opening clean through him. The other guard doesn't react, but I swear I see his eyes twitch as he advances even more heavily onto him.

Venus sees her guard fall, dead, and finally addresses the surrounding commotion. "Liaison, I think it's time we leave."

"But, Ms Collins, you instructed me to lock up the prisoner?"

"It's called a compromise." Her voice is stiff when she turns to face me. "Take him away," she commands, "and make sure he stays out of sight. If he tells any human what he knows, I will consult the law, holding you personally responsible. You won't have a chance to *consider* the prophecy."

In other words, Venus Collins will kill me if I don't obey her. But I don't care.

I rush towards Eli, standing protectively in front of Melanie, the latter squeezing her eyes shut in pain as she attempts to rise.

Murder sings in my chest, fingers twitching around the switchblade. I want to kill Venus, fight her, nail her to the wall, but I don't know *how*. I am hopeless, untrained and pathetic, and I can't stand up to her.

My legs and fingers shake, and I have nothing in my arsenal to dispel my rage. I want to scream.

Liaison Banks's expression shifts, and it almost looks smug. It's that look that makes my stomach drop to the floor.

They know something important.

They will never let us win.

My stomach clenches with the sickening urge to throw up my last meal at that realisation. From the ground, Melanie's eyes are wide with panic. She mouths a word at me when she realises I'm experiencing the same wash of fear—shipment.

The shipment? Could it be because of the shipment?

It's only days away. It almost seems like *too* much of a coincidence for it to have nothing to do with Venus's visit.

I shudder involuntarily.

With my friends bleeding out, and nothing more than a switchblade in my shaky, untrained fist, I have no choice but to agree and say, "Deal."

"Good." Venus waves a hand at her guard, who abruptly stops fighting Jesse to turn and face the Argenti before him. He doesn't even bother to help the Liaison's guards, one of which is dead, the other limbless and moaning as he tries to rise.

She gives me one last look before saying, "This is the last gift I will ever give you, Savannah. Remember, the Elders always win."

I clench my hand around my switchblade.

I despise her.

My shoulders shake of their own accord. I never thought I'd experience such a strong negative emotion.

She turns to the exit, and I bite into temptation and say, "Mason would be so disappointed in you."

She looks over her shoulder.

"Tell your brother hello for me."

The words burn like acid in my mind. Like hell I will.

The exit opens, half swallowing them.

I don't watch Venus leave. I've done that enough.

I swallow, my throat tasting like acid as I dash down the labyrinth to Jesse, who has now fallen to his knees, his eyes darting between Melanie and me.

I kneel on the floor before him, pressing my hand to his torso where the blade sliced into him. His blood coats my pale fingers, like blooming roses. I don't know how to stop it. I don't know what to do.

"Savannah?" Eli calls down the tunnel.

I can't go to him, not now. Melanie will be okay. He will be okay. Jesse might not be.

I don't ask permission before lifting the hem of his shirt, risking a peek at the gash. He flinches, but doesn't stop me. I take that as a sign of acceptance, and I pull the shirt even higher.

His wound is spilling ridiculous amounts of blood, gushing in pools at our feet from the incision point. I hover my hands above the stab wound, hands shaking.

"I don't know how to stop it," I admit, my voice weak.

"Pressure," he says. "I can use my shirt as a gauze until we get back to Melanie's."

I drop his shirt. I didn't realise how pale I felt until he lightly touches my palm with his fingers. Instinctively, I flinch away, like a terrified child.

"I won't die yet," he says. "Just hurry."

I help him unravel his shirt and together we make a poor bandage. The moment we finish, he stands up, trying not to gasp at the effort as he heads to the exit.

I try to stop him, but he's already halfway across the hall, swaying with pain. My eyebrows pinch, heart pounding with every uneven step he makes.

Melanie has risen, her face waxen, a strip from Eli's shirt around her new wound rapidly turning crimson. Twin bandages also cover Eli's hands.

"Where did you park your Hover?" Melanie asks him. "We have to get to some medicine… and I need access to some computers. I don't trust Venus."

Her eyes are widened with fear.

The shipment. Venus. Connected. The words are easy enough to understand on her face.

Jesse shakes his head at her, his teeth grinding. "Didn't park it."

She sighs. She'll find another way to get us home. I know she will.

I look at Eli, who seems so out of place here, his face paling when he says, "Her arm looks horrible."

I nod. I know.

"Are we safe now?" he asks.

"No," Jesse replies.

"We need to leave the space centre," I tell him.

But it doesn't seem like I have Eli's attention anymore. He

fixes his eyes on the thick red rivers spreading around our feet, as if noticing it for the first time. Sweat dots his forehead, his face paling even further.

I should have seen it coming.

I shriek as Eli vomits onto the floor, catching my feet. It spreads over my socks, warm and thick, and I blanch.

"I'm sorry, I'm sorry," he mumbles, eyes wide. "This is just—I can't... I'm sorry."

Jesse looks ready to laugh, but Melanie looks anything but amused.

I pinch my nose.

"We have to go," Melanie says. "Now."

Her hands twitch at her side, desperate to move.

Yes, please. I push Eli away from his stench.

At some point, while I was bandaging Jesse, Melanie has also freed Eli from his chains. Efficient girl.

I wish I had time to help the other captives, but I don't even know where to start. How to start. I hate the thought of leaving them here, the new odours of blood and vomit left behind as a reminder of how close we were to freeing them.

The gate opens when we approach it, and as it closes behind us, I turn to Melanie, who is practically shaking at my side. "One day, I will free them all."

"Yes. We will."

Her steel eyes stab into me. I take a steadying breath, swallowing.

Jesse slams his fist onto the exit panel, wincing noticeably as he does, and the ground lifts under us. The elevator rises and quickly the tang of fresh air mixes into our lungs.

I stare at the floor, mind on the cells below us.

One day, we will come back.

Melanie doesn't take her gaze off me, as if our minds are one of the same. A promise shared.

"You're a complete and utter moron, you know that, right?"
We stare at Jesse, who's sprawled out across Melanie's couch in her office in the space centre, blood gushing over the pillows.

I insisted we go back to Melanie's house and rethink our plans, but Jesse couldn't make it. Hell, Melanie couldn't even make it.

I lean over her desk, all the super-slim computer screens dead and the coffee cups pushed to the side to make room for medicine. Near the entrance, foot tapping on the floor, stands Eli, nursing his injured hands, trying hard not to be noticed.

We're a mess, I think to myself. *How will we ever get out of this?*

My brain ticks at the sudden urgency of wanting to escape—of wanting to do something helpful. Like chasing down my mother and stabbing my switchblade into her chest or stopping Melanie's mystery shipment.

Shivering, I bundle my arms tighter around my chest, the violence of my thoughts making me squirm.

Instead, all I can bring myself to focus on is how broken my group looks. Guilt begins to gnaw at me. I can sense Eli's eyes burning a hole in my back, and the sensation makes me want to scream.

Before me, Melanie is shakily lathering some ointment across Jesse's injury.

"I think you'll need something stronger," I mumble.

"You think?" she snaps.

Jesse groans, his eyes rolling into the back of his head.

"There's medicine in the centre. It can fix him in minutes, but we can't roam around. Not after…"

After the Liaison promised we'd be killed on sight.

I exhale loudly, turning away from the man slowly dying on the couch.

I hadn't known how to help, so I'd grabbed a clean dishtowel from the kitchen on the way to the office and ran it under cool water, pressing the sopping material to Jesse's brow.

But now I just stand back, helpless.

We continue to watch the blood pooling across the soft linens in despair.

"So stupid," she repeats, mostly to herself.

"I'm fine," Jesse gasps as Melanie presses something new to his wound. I turn my head away, not prepared for what might go wrong.

"If you're fine, then we wouldn't be in this situation," Melanie hisses.

"You make it sound like I'm dying," he says humourlessly.

Melanie prods his wound sharply in response.

"Ouch, Mel!"

I notice the shadow of a smile at the corner of her lips.

"You're lucky the puncture missed your liver. Drink this." She hands him a vial, not bothering to pour it in a cup despite there being multiple that she could repurpose.

We need some *Velox*—or at the very least some *Prius*, which healed me almost overnight.

There's more medication here. Right under our noses on this base. We're in the *central hub*, goddammit.

I turn away from them and suddenly face Eli, wincing at the sight of his hands.

His fingers twitch towards the door, eyes darting, but he doesn't move away. I lean next to him on the wall, fighting the urge to make eye contact.

I have so many questions to ask him about Silver Valley. But doing so feels wrong. He's the one who deserves answers right now, not me.

I sigh deeply, sliding to the floor, trying to block out the thoughts and sounds of Jesse groaning on the couch.

Eli sits down gingerly, as if trying not to startle me.

"I'm assuming you want to know about your family," he says softly, and I almost jump.

My family. My… father.

I swallow a knot in my throat.

It couldn't be true, because that means my real biological father is what… an Umbran?

My pulse quickens and I try to hold myself together by glaring into my lap, wringing my hands.

No. I have my father's brown hair.

I'm his daughter.

I turn my head slowly towards Eli, my breathing shallow.

"I don't want to be insensitive," I say, hardly hearing myself.

He attempts a smile, but it wobbles.

"It's okay, ask away," he murmurs, his eyes downcast.

I can only imagine how he feels. Hell, I've experienced it.

Having your life being ripped out from under you, being held in the grasp of enemies you never knew you had? It sucks.

Melanie whacks the ointment she was using back onto her work desk, and I wander across the room to grab it. The small jar is cold in my hand, and I pop the lid open as quietly as I can.

Eli swallows deeply when I kneel in front of him, his eyes darting from me to the jar. His fingers shake, one thumb absently brushing the area where the nail had embedded into his skin.

"Give me your hands," I say.

He holds them out to me helplessly and tries not to wince when I unwrap the bandage. They stopped bleeding at some point, the blood drying and thickening. The nails weren't overly thick, but the wound is gaping, blood covering most of his hands to the point that I can barely see the puncture wounds.

"I don't even know where to start," I suddenly whisper.

"They need to be washed," he says. My eyes flicker to his, capturing his deep gaze. He's beautiful—all soft lines and thick lips. I release a deep breath and quickly look away.

We definitely could've been something, Eli and I, if it wasn't for the path I'd chosen for myself. But he's too sweet, too kind, to be damaged by someone like me.

I locate a half empty bottle of water on Melanie's desk and start cleaning off the blood on his large hands, trying not to wince.

"Everyone thinks you might be dead," he says suddenly, his tone heavy, like the thought daunts him.

I freeze, my hands shaking. "Oh?"

I don't lift my eyes from his hands, too afraid to meet his gaze.

"All any of us knew is what Jasmine told us," he explains. "She said you disappeared in the forest during the storm. She didn't say why."

I release his hands and grip the floor to steady myself. The switchblade in my pocket feels heavy at the thought of her. Finally, I meet his face.

He chews on his bottom lip. I try not to remember how those lips felt, how they tasted, and I avert my eyes as he continues.

"The Shaws and the Sparks began roaming the forest in search of you almost instantly, then after nearly a day, the townspeople began to help too. I know it's hasn't been long, but we got scared when you didn't come home."

No one in Silver Valley vanishes.

His words rush out, as if he was dying to tell someone how he got here.

"I was with a small group from school yesterday. Jasmine was directing us. I saw something and ran off and lost the group, or I thought I did. But before I knew it, I was too far south of the island, and I found this hidden place... under a dome. I was taken by some guards before I had the chance to turn around. They took me through quarantine into this weird city, and before I knew it, I was trapped. It was my fault for being too curious, getting too close, and wondering if perhaps you made your way over here, too."

I want to scream.

He was tortured, for *me.*

"How's my family?" I ask cautiously, dropping his clean hands back into his lap to unscrew the lid of what I assume is antiseptic.

"They're terrified for you, Savannah. Your dad has gone crazy. He spends more time in the forest than he does at home, and your brother was a crying mess whenever I bumped into him. He can barely pull himself together enough to search for you. It's really hitting them hard, especially Mason."

My soul crashes to my feet. "He thinks I've left him like our mother."

His biggest heartache is being played on repeat... I wish I could explain things to him.

"That terrifying silver woman?" Eli shakes his head. "You're nothing like her."

I frown. He doesn't understand. Mason wouldn't see it like that.

"And Jasmine?" I wonder.

"She sent as many as she could into this area of the forest, as if she knew the base was here, but she didn't come with us. It was like she was convincing us to do all the dirty work," he says bitterly.

"She isn't sad I'm gone?" I ask, remembering her sobbing on the steps.

"Not exactly. She seems angrier and panicked more than anything. I haven't seen her smile or crack a joke since you left."

This is coming from a boy who's used to Jasmine always laughing.

I've left the town of Silver Valley in a mess—me, a girl who has barely lived there for three weeks.

I begin lathering Melanie's ointment onto his wounds, trying not to cringe at the feel of broken flesh under my fingertips.

His brows furrow, but I don't say anything until I deem them coated enough to begin the process of re-bandaging.

"There, I think that should be okay."

He pulls his hands back. "Thanks, Savannah."

It doesn't take long before Eli begins to slant further down the wall, his body dropping to the floor, losing himself to fatigue.

"You can sleep here," I say. *We're safe for now.*

I want to join him. My head hurts. My body hurts.

I want to sleep and never wake again. But instead, I utter to the man before me, "I just need to say… I'm sorry for everything, Eli. I'm sorry."

His body spasms a little, but he keeps his eyes closed and tightens his lips. He mumbles something incoherent, and I hug my knees to my chest, trying to block out the guilty thoughts threatening to overwhelm me.

Ahead of me, it sounds like Melanie is nearly done with Jesse. Their conversation is hushed, as if they don't want me to hear, so I close my eyes and try to tune in.

I've never heard Jesse speak with such emotion, such honesty, when he says, "Mel, I'm getting really worried about the shipment you mentioned. Are you sure you can't find anything else about it on those computers?"

I expect Melanie to make a snide remark about her uncle, but she doesn't. "We will figure it out, Jesse. We always do."

"You mean, *you* always do."

"No," she says, pausing. The couch cushions shift and ceramics clink together as she packs her supplies. "I hack their databases, you protect me, and Savannah will lead us. This isn't something one person can do alone. We all have a part to play."

"Savannah isn't ready for that yet."

I steady myself against the doorway, heart pounding in my chest.

Jesse's right.

But Melanie seems undaunted when she replies, "Don't worry, I know she can do it."

"Not yet, Mel. Not yet." Jesse's tone is so soft, so warm, as if the pain and exhaustion has etched his heart onto his words.

"Then when, Jesse?" Melanie's voice cracks. "We're running out of time."

"I don't know," he croaks. "Just remember, she's only been here for several days. And most of that time she's been escaping and running."

"She has what it takes, Jesse. Now and then, I see the leader in her. She can do it."

"That isn't what I mean. She does that to find answers," Jesse rebuffs, and I grip my knees tighter in apprehension at his words. "And the rest is mostly just survival instincts."

"You don't know that," Melanie hushes, her prosthetic arm twitching.

"You forget you made me track her for weeks. I've come to know her."

I slouch onto the floor, counting each of my breaths. The thought of Jesse knowing me is scary.

"I only told you to figure out whether she's the girl from the prophecy," Melanie says, her words sounding groggy. I don't know when she last slept.

"For a smart girl you're incredibly blind sometimes."

"Enlighten me then," she insists.

"The main things you need to know about Savannah is that she has an extremely curious nature, and she doesn't trust others easily. All she cares about is her family, and every decision, including the rash ones, she makes for them." There is a pause in his breath as the dynamic shifts, allowing Melanie to see this version of reality. "Just give her time, because if we were in her position, we would need it too. Eventually she will see that fixing Umbra is not just in the interest of everyone else, but also her family."

Melanie doesn't respond to this. She doesn't need to.

Nerves flutter in my stomach. Jesse is right.

I came for Jasmine, for my dad, and for Mason. My family.

The injustice of people like my mother living on a planet with clean air after discarding her family on a festering one only makes me want to go to Umbra more. We deserve to be there, by blood, by right, by status.

I want that peace for my family.

I take a deep breath as I lean against the cold door, my heart pounding in my head.

It doesn't take long until darkness consumes me.

სი

Someone kicks me in the legs.

"Food. Eat it."

My eyes flutter open, and I sit up off the floor, groaning. My tongue feels sluggish in my mouth, eyes heavy, and I splay my fingers across the ground for my switchblade.

Then I feel the uncomfortable thing in my pocket, jabbing into my hip.

I lift my head and notice Jesse standing above me. Looking exceptionally healed.

"How… what?" I sit up sharply. Despite the pains in my body, I feel revived. My head feels heavy, almost like I'm *too* rested.

"You look like the living dead," he observes, trying not to grin. I take him in. His skin looks paler than usual and there's a sheen to his face, but he looks okay.

Better than okay.

"Who healed him?" I raise my voice accusingly.

"Savannah, thank god, can you take Eli away from me?"

Melanie spins around to face me, her face looking taut, like she hasn't slept at all, or at least only minimally. She sits at her desk, fingers hovering over one of her paper-thin screens, a fresh mug of coffee wafting next to her.

How does she have coffee?

Next to her, Eli sits on the desk, shoving bacon into his mouth. Bacon?

He grins at me, some food peeking out from his teeth, and I rub my fist into my temple, trying to wring out the sleep. Someone placed a fresh pair of shoes and socks by my feet. I quickly shove them on.

"You left the office, didn't you?" I ask while tying my shoelaces.

She shrugs, spinning back to her screens—security footage she doesn't have clearance to weaving in front of her. Her arms aren't shaking anymore, and she taps the keyboard as if nothing had ever happened.

"I had to. Everyone was looking… bad. So I went back to the psychiatric med ward," she says matter-of-factly.

"The what-now?"

"Where we brought you the day you arrived."

"You had me in a *psychiatric* ward?" I lurch up from my sitting position, eyes widening.

Eli chokes a little on his bacon.

She shrugs. "They have the best medicine."

Fingers shaking, I turn to face Jesse, gaping.

"It's mostly for people who retaliate against the guards and need to be kept behind locked doors while they tend to their injuries. It isn't like the psych wards you're used to—it's more of a med ward—but people nicknamed it the psychiatric ward for lack of a better word."

Great.

I scramble up towards Melanie, shaking my head.

She pushes aside some of the security footage for rows of text. It constantly moves, as if it's some sort of communication server.

"Okay, fine. Whatever." On her desk is an array of food. Breads, apples, plates of egg and bacon, all of it looking near cold now. I snatch up an apple as I try to grab Melanie's attention. "Weren't you worried about, oh I don't know, being caught and killed?"

She rolls her eyes. "Obviously. But we had no choice."

I lean against the wall, right near one of her many pot plants. "Uh-huh."

"We were asleep for a while," Eli explains beside me. "Their… shipment thingy… arrives in like a day. Your angry hacker friend has been quite the entertainment."

Fingers stopping their chaotic rapping against the keyboard, she suddenly spins, pinning him with a glare.

Her hair is a mess, her glove still bunched around her wrist. But the wires in her arm look as though they have been reconnected. She mustn't have had a chance to graft more skin onto her arm—or perhaps not the tech to do it—as the wires still peep through her wound.

"Savannah, please get rid of him, he's been doing my head in."

Her silver eyes have shadows under them, making her look haunted.

He only winks at her.

"What were you doing with him?" I wonder, taking in the code.

"Not *with* him. I'm trying to break through my uncle's communication systems—waiting for your ass to wake up—so we can figure out more about this shipment. I already asked Elijah everything he may have learnt while in my uncle's custody, but it turns out he knows less than a dog."

He grins at her. "Very flattering, Mel."

"Don't call me Mel. My name is Melanie."

"I know."

I hover over her shoulder, blinking at everything on the screen. It hurts to look at. "Melanie, you've tried enough already. We can't figure out what's in the shipment from here," I say.

"I have to, Savannah!" she exclaims, slamming a hand on the table, more out of frustration than anything.

"A spaceship is coming to Terra, right?" Eli suddenly blurts. "I heard the guards mention a planet called Umbra. Are all these people from there? They don't look like aliens, they look human. Is that normal?"

Like me, he has his questions.

"Nothing about any of this is normal," I say to him, gathering a pillow from the couch. I sit down and stare at the locked door to her office, waiting for the moment someone undoubtedly catches us here.

"Is Umbra a weird place to live?" Eli asks Melanie.

"No," she says quietly, detached. "It wasn't for me. But for you, perhaps."

I look at Jesse, who stands by the door as if guarding it in case someone does come. Shadows deepen in his eyes at his friend's words.

Melanie sighs deeply, slamming another hand on the table. She spins her chair to face us. "Fine. Questions. What would you like to know?"

I zone out as she explains to Eli everything I already know. The basics, such as what the Argenti are and a small glimpse into their history. The whole time I watch Jesse. His fingers tap on his weapon belt, eyes looking clouded.

It isn't until there's a pause in conversation that I turn back to Eli and say quietly, "Melanie's parents were half Argenti... like I am."

Melanie gives me a look.

I can almost read her thoughts. *We don't know your full ancestry yet.*

I bite my lip. My mother was lying about my father. She had to be. My hair is brown.

Eli swallows deeply and sits on the couch beside me. I almost expect him to reach for my hand, but instead he turns to Melanie.

"What is it like on Umbra, being half Argenti?"

"Savannah would've lived in the Silver Kingdom, if her mother had brought her up like I was. My parents were held prestigiously in court, but we moved to a smaller townhouse eventually."

She pauses to let this soak in, and it takes me longer to process than Eli. Had I grown up with my mother on Umbra, I could've experienced the life of royals first-hand. I could've lived in a palace, basking in the full glow of the Georgian era. Instead, I spent most of my life passing the days in a dingy apartment.

"My home had always been grand," Melanie continues. "The thirst for power thrummed in my family's veins. My uncle acquired the worst of this greed; he was always cold blooded towards those who stood in his way. My parents, on the other hand, strongly believed in your cause, Savannah."

"You're doing your parents work then?" I ask her.

She smiles at me, eyes downcast. "Yes."

Eli studies her, brow pinched.

"It's dangerous for you to do that, isn't it?" he asks.

"Of course it is," she says. "Any form of revolution is dangerous. If it wasn't, my parents would probably still be alive."

I swallow deeply, heart hammering. "Your parents died... for me?"

She pinches her lips and shakes her head slowly, the frustration on her face revealing the truth. They died for the cause. Not me.

"None of it is your fault. Don't even think that for a second."

I suck on my cheek, holding back a retort.

Melanie takes a steadying breath, knotting her hands around her glove. "There was a fire in my house which was how I wrecked my arm. Someone from our circle betrayed us, killing everyone during a planned meeting. Everyone except me and my uncle. I probably could've done something to help, but my uncle, who ran away with his tail between his legs, stopped me from saving them. The moment he abandoned my parents was the worst moment in my entire life."

Eli's breath catches in his throat.

I grip the pillow beside me tightly until my knuckles are as white as the pillowcase. Releasing a deep breath, I reach for her, but she pulls away.

Tears bud in her eyes, but she says with a clear voice, "I don't want your sympathy."

Eli shakes his head. "I can't imagine what it would be like to lose my family."

Melanie bites her lip. "Maybe by being here, you already have, Elijah."

He laughs. "Right."

Something churns in my gut.

Eli chews on his lip. Probably tossing over Melanie's words, as he asks me, "How much does your family know about Umbra?"

I turn away from him. To my surprise, Melanie does too.

I watch as she pins her eyes on Jesse.

"They know nothing," I say.

I want to protect them. But I don't know how to yet. As soon as I clean this mess up, I will take them to Umbra. That was the plan. But is it fair to keep them in the dark until then?

"Shouldn't they know?"

I drag my fingers through my hair, refusing to answer.

Eli sinks deeper into the couch. "They deserve to know."

My brother would love nothing more.

And I would love nothing more than to tell them—show them a world where they can live surrounded by eternal beauty and prestige. But the very thought of bringing them into this world as it is now, where a cold war rages, turns my heart to stone.

Melanie suddenly gasps from beside me. She spins her chair around, pulling a security camera to full screen, and digs her fingers so hard into the desk that I wouldn't be surprised if she dented it with her nails.

We all watch the scene. The camera is attached to a building overlooking the ocean, giving us a view of the round hangar doors along the beach. It's still hours before daybreak.

"Savannah, come and see this."

I hurry to her side, hoping it isn't landing early.

One of the hatches by the space centre is opening, spreading light into the night.

Someone is leaving the base.

"Is it…?"

"Your mother," Melanie answers, catching me off guard. "Leaving through the hangar closest to my uncle's office, which can only mean…"

Her uncle is leaving the base.

Something churns in my gut, a flight instinct telling me to run. I scratch my arms, forcing my body to stay as still as possible.

The hangar they're using is almost hidden by the trees. And they've waited for nightfall. They don't want to draw attention to themselves.

"They don't use it very often. Usually only my uncle and Liaison Stone use it, because it has the smallest and fastest pods. It isn't very useful for large shipments and voyages. I can't imagine why…"

She trickles off, a thoughtful expression on her face, and my heart swings and dips at the thought of my mother leaving almost as abruptly as she came. But it's the fear underlying Melanie's words that causes my heart to plummet to the floor.

Something isn't right.

The launch continues to proceed before us. Slowly, as if trying not to wake the slumbering people within the base.

The pod is a slick curving angle of smooth planes that makes it impossible to discern which part is the front or the back. The first one rises, hovering in the air, and close behind comes another, and then a third. They pull up into the air like a chain.

"Savannah." Melanie's voice comes out deep, laced with fear. "Savannah, my uncle is escaping with your mother and their guards. They're all leaving."

"Isn't travel between two planets rare?" I ask quietly.

"Relatively. Once a year, we have a twelve-day period where travel is optimal and most direct. But travel can happen any time, it just means if they leave now, there will be a sizeable detour. Which *is* rare. Especially for this many people."

"When will this optimal period occur?" I wonder.

"June. The middle of the year."

"Then why…" Coldness seeps into my bones.

Before us, the pods lift farther into the air. They float, suspended like large glittering stars as the hatch begins to close beneath them. They hover for a moment more and then propel into the sky, a blip of speed, a dash of silver, and they're out of our atmosphere. Gone.

Melanie watches me, her breathing short and rapid.

My words come out fast. "So this means your uncle is gone? And he took anyone he thought important enough with him—"

Melanie holds her breath at that. She isn't included in that category anymore.

"—Which means," I continue, "the space centre, and possibly other facilities, shouldn't be as guarded. We need to move. Now."

She takes a steady breath. The tough girl I first met is beginning to waver. Her head hangs, body shaking.

Her breath is short when she says, "Okay. Yes."

We turn to leave but a loud pounding erupts from the front door, startling us both.

The peaceful quiet of the room explodes and I stumble in surprise.

Melanie shoots me a concerned look. Whoever is pounding her door down sounds desperate and unrelenting.

"What on earth?" Eli asks.

"Stars if I know," Melanie says, shrugging.

Guards.

But why now? Why after her uncle left?

We both glance at each other, wondering if it has anything to do with what we just witnessed. What if we got the dates wrong? What if the shipment really is tonight? What if someone is here to kill us?

I don't move a single toe, too shocked to do anything. But Melanie is spurred by the sound. She rushes to the door.

Jesse moves aside, fingers moving to his sword.

Melanie pries open the door just enough to peer through, and a red-cheeked girl pushes it forward so suddenly it knocks the breath out of Melanie, who nearly falls over.

I stumble against the couch.

The girl's frantic blue eyes find me, and suddenly the last several days rush back to me, and I return to the day I escaped Silver Valley.

"Jasmine?"

M y voice brings tears to her eyes.

She strides across the office and pulls me to her.

I soak in her familiar fruity perfume, with fragments of the night air and forest clinging to her skin. I wonder how long she's been waiting in the forest, finding a moment to slip into the dome after Eli was captured.

I carefully push Jasmine away from me. "You can't be here."

She stares at me stoically.

I can sense Jesse next to me, basked in the shadows, clutching his weapons. Ready to attack.

"I know that," she replies evenly.

"Then *why* are you here?"

Her hands begin to shake, and she squeezes them into fists. She sees Eli on the couch, his dark skin stark against the cushions. She almost looks sorry to see him.

"I came to get you," she says. "You can't be here either."

"I'm not leaving," I say stubbornly.

Beside Jasmine, I swear I see Melanie smirk faintly before wiping the expression from her face.

"You have to, Savannah."

She looks so ancient, so unlike Jasmine Spark, when she looks at me like she is now. Her blue eyes are still full of pain... but hardened. I always thought of Jasmine like a little bird, always fluttering. Now, she moves with painful purpose.

Who is this girl, really?

"No, I don't have to do anything."

Jesse scuffles in the shadows. I think I see him sink into a fighting stance. I shoot him a dark look, but he doesn't tuck his weapon away.

"These people will kill you," she says evenly.

"Why, because my mother is a powerful Argenti who hates me? Or is it because my best friend is a wanted fugitive?"

She tries to stop herself from gaping at my anger. Maybe she didn't expect me to still be mad.

"Why, Jas? Please, just tell me why..."

Eli perks up, as if he's curious to know the answer.

When she doesn't reply, I fume. "Why is it that everywhere I go, every clue I unearth about your past points to you wanting me on the throne, yet the Jasmine I know is trying everything in her power to keep me away from it? *Why?*"

She shakes her head at me so hard I fear she'll hurt herself. She looks worn, tired and defeated, as if she hasn't felt sleep's embrace since I left Silver Valley. I locate several wisps of dried leaves among her uncombed hair.

"My father believed in the revolution. So did I."

Her voice falls flat. It pains her to speak.

Melanie, out of nowhere, suddenly spins back to her screens and begins tapping like crazy, shoulders bent forwards.

I quickly turn to her, and she shakes her head at me, fear lining every crevice of her face. Something is wrong, I can sense it, but I need to speak to Jasmine first.

Jesse stalks to her desk, eyes still searing into me, and Melanie reaches over and snatches the sword off him, causing him to glare. "Stars, Jesse, give them some privacy."

He rolls his eyes and prowls over to the couch, leaving Eli looking torn between hiding from him and listening to our conversation.

I pull Jasmine towards the side of the office and raise my eyebrows at my friend.

Talk, I convey through my eyes.

She takes a deep breath, folding her hands carefully across her chest.

"To explain everything properly, I need to start at the beginning."

I hover in front of her, as still and cold as glass, feeling the distance between us with a pang in my chest.

"My parents were born during the end of the Moon Blitz in 1865. They married in their early twenties, and I was born many years later. My parents have only ever known destruction and loss and didn't want to bring a child up through that. I was born on June 11th, 1997. Despite the age I wear, I am twenty-nine."

My hands shake when she speaks. But the shock doesn't knock me backwards. Instead, something deep inside my chest begins to open.

I stand completely still and wait for her to continue.

"We have known a long life of poverty, scraping the very bottom of the social circle. The Occupants were kind once, but I never knew them, and my parents only knew of them dying. We wanted to fix the future, Savannah. That's all we ever wanted.

"The peak of our livelihood was when my mother worked for Lythia May—cleaning, mending her home, and gradually working her way up to a personal assistant. The hours were gruelling, but Lythia paid well, and soon they formed a close friendship.

"I had just turned twelve when she started having visions of your prophecy. She saw many over her time, but somehow knew this one was different. Once the meaning of the prophecy was clear, Lythia, full of despair, confided in my mother. She knew it would tear our planet apart.

"'My cousin will bear a daughter who will one day usurp the throne. That child will bring us peace.' I found those words scrawled on my mother's notepad, I think during October or November of 2009. She told my mother she didn't know if she should make it public, because she wasn't sure how people would take it. The choice tore her apart. But of course, a week before you were born, she decided on revealing it in part to the people."

"How did Lythia May die?" I ask suddenly, interrupting.

"Poison." Her words are sharp. "People fear power, and so they poisoned her—a slow, painful death. Not only could she predict the future, but she could lock the Silver Magic of the planet within stones—she mostly used this technique to bolster her own prophecies, using the conserved energy to double her strength. But anyone could use this raw Silver Magic once it was harnessed into stones— even non-Silver Magic wielders. So she tried to keep it a secret. But news always comes out, and when it finally did, there were riots. Eventually she was assassinated for being an anomaly—the only Argenti to have two magical outlets. People feared her."

I slip my hand into the lip of my pocket where my switchblade rests, clutching it out of anger.

It takes a moment to remember that it's Jasmine's blade I hold.

"My mother died in these riots, but not before Lythia gave her one of her stones—a tribute and a blessing—to make sure the prophecy was fulfilled. The only other person who knew everything Lythia had ever told my mother was my father, Ansel James. We plucked the stone off her dead body when I was a twelve-year-old girl, and then we worked every day to find you, to get you to save us. For years, you were our salvation. We discovered that your mother left you on Terra with one of her lovers and we were building a plan to leave Umbra to get you.

"But when I was fifteen, the Elders caught me and my father spying on Liaison Stone while he held a meeting with Banks. My father was killed on the spot, and I was sent to the dungeons. I thought I would die, that everything would end. But I was given a second chance by one of the Elders and Liaison Stone, and suddenly, the fate of the world was up to me.

"I used my mother's stone to reverse my age, fooling society into believing I was only three years old. On the way to the shuttle, I burnt every hint of my past, every item, every brick of my small home. I only kept my blade for protection, so I could make it to the shuttle ... But the moment I was safe, I tossed that too.

"When I came to Terra, I found your father's name on the internet, often in articles alongside Henry Spark's, renowned journalists as they are. I realised Henry and Ella Spark would be the perfect host family for me. I still had some lingering strength in my mother's stone, and I bewitched them, as well as your father, with a fake memory of childbirth. Then the stone cracked. Over time, the fog around fiction and fact blurred, and they lost any doubts about me. I became Jasmine Spark."

She stops abruptly, as if she expects me to scold her for tainting the Sparks and, mostly, my father. But I don't have the energy to.

She reaches out, giving me the necklace that once held that stone. I touch it for a moment before withdrawing, repulsed.

"What changed?" I ask her briskly, trying to switch off the mounting feelings of hurt.

"What do you mean?" She furrows her brow.

"You don't want me to have anything to do with Umbra now."

She twists the chain around her wrist, tangling and untangling it in rapid succession, swallowing deeply again.

"Savannah, you became more to me than a mission. You became my very reason for existence."

I stare at her hands, ignoring the prickling sensation behind my eyes. "And yet, all you ever did was lie to me. How is that love?"

Jasmine is already crying. Silent tears spill across her soft cheeks. "That's something I have to live with now, I know that. But I changed… I want—no, I need—to give you a better future.

"I convinced Henry that a business venture in Silver Valley would be profitable—local rags are dying out, but journalism is his life and he eventually folded into the idea of starting his own business—we had enough money to support ourselves anyway and our family has been secretly helping your father with his bills too—which was how we convinced him to follow us." She takes a steadying breath, struggling to keep her eyes on me. "All I ever knew was that you needed to take the throne on Umbra so that my life, and many other lives like mine, could get better. But the moment you moved to Silver Valley, I freaked out and saw the reality of it. I would lose you. I already had a perfect life with you, and although it was selfish to maintain the lie, I wanted nothing more.

"Savannah, you don't *need* to heed the prophecy. You really don't. You know that, right?"

I shake my head at her. "The prophecy is already set in motion."

"So, what? You're blindly accepting fate?"

I don't know what to say to that, so I don't say anything at all.

She leans against the wall.

I grip her blade tightly in my fist, between the soft folds of linen covering my thighs. This is the piece of Jasmine I will always carry. She will always protect me. But not in the way she wants.

She looks ready to stop talking, but I still have one last question. "So, you're sure that I'm truly the girl from the prophecy?"

"Without a doubt. Venus Collins is Lythia May's cousin. Her *only* cousin. And you're Venus's only daughter."

I roll my head up to the ceiling and sigh.

Wonderful.

How strange, that not only am I half Argenti and destined to usurp Umbra, but I'm also related to the greatest Argenti in history: Lythia May. Yet despite all this, I still have shockingly dark hair tumbling down my shoulders.

I click open the switchblade. Close it.

Jasmine watches as it comes out of my pocket. Her eyes widen, but she doesn't say anything, and we don't discuss it.

I hold my breath and move closer to her. We don't touch, but we stay close. We've always needed one another, but maybe, just maybe, I don't need her anymore.

Hesitantly, I retreat a step. I feel like I've outgrown the guidance and lies of Jasmine Spark, and I'm not sure I like it.

"We're screwed," Melanie suddenly screeches, her voice breaking the hush of the room. "We're *so* SCREWED."

"What's wrong?" I whip my head around to Melanie.

The lights above us sputter, flickering a few times until launching us into total darkness. Next to me, Jasmine gasps. The code on the computer screen winks away and Jesse shoulders the door open with a bang before the dying keypad has a chance to trap us inside. The last thing I see is Eli rushing towards the exit in a similar panic.

Someone bumps into me, grabbing for me, the grip on my arms tight. Melanie. "The whole medical ward is empty. Everyone's been given leave, which has never happened before in the history of the base." She drags in a breath and throws papers against my chest. I don't know what any of them mean. I can't see anything. "I was able to access my uncle's files for the first time in, well… ever. All his appointments end after March 3rd, like he isn't planning on coming back. The shipment that's coming… it's not good."

I can hear Jasmine's breathing speeding up beside me.

"I'm going," she says suddenly, bumping into me as she fumbles for the door in the dark.

I reach for her arm but miss. "Don't."

"Where are you going?" Eli asks.

I pause halfway across the room towards Jasmine, scanning the darkness. And then light explodes next to me, blinding my vision.

Jesse moves the torch off my face, trying not to snicker. The office is bathed in the torchlight, enough for us all to see by.

"I need to get off this base."

I swallow, surprised to see that for once Jasmine looks as old as her age. My hands shake at the image of it. Because all these years the mask of her youth was just a fabricated fairy tale—a dream of a fake life. It tugs at my soul, yanking me awake.

Her blue eyes are hard and full of fatigue. The eyes of someone who fought for many years and has only now decided to give it all up.

"But… it's safe for you now," Eli says, waving to the computers. "They left."

I wonder if Jasmine saw the pods leaving. It was probably why she finally took the leap to come out and see me. To try one last time.

"It's never safe," she answers.

I reach for her, but she pulls away from me, cold and unyielding.

"At least I got the chance to say goodbye, if nothing else," she mumbles, her lips tilting down.

She is nothing more than the ghost of the girl I knew, and it shatters my heart, yawning holes in my chest.

Why must everything about Umbra hurt so much?

My body, heart, and soul feel like they've been shredded, beaten, thrown back together, too many times over. And now a new pain fissures through the remaining pieces.

"Goodbye, Jasmine. Soul sister. My best friend. I hope we can meet again, in another life." I can barely get the words out.

She doesn't move. Jasmine, once always full of energy, stands still as stone as she repeats, "In another life."

I watch her turn and disappear into the darkness—watch as she takes my heart with her—and I shudder against the closest wall in a painful heap, legs barely supporting me.

She doesn't have any light. I wonder if she will even make it out.

I wait a solid minute after her frame has left the threshold before turning my eyes back to Eli. He comes to stand by me, his fingers rubbing my arm. I refrain from tilting my head on his shoulder. "I want to go too," he says softly. "Anyone else?"

Unspoken words fill the gaps around us, and I watch as his eyes keep drifting back to Melanie, her form vaguely silhouetted behind torchlight.

Everything hurts, but I don't have time to mourn my life with Jasmine.

We still need to stop the impending shipment.

Jesse nods. He leans against the doorframe, gesturing the way out for us. I notice there's already more colour in his cheeks, his face taking on a healthier glow.

"The whole place looked like it's in an apocalypse," Melanie says, her voice hollow. "And now..."

I spin my switchblade around in my palm, pulling back the tears in my eyes, inhaling a deep breath. "Everyone. Out."

I push Eli out the doorway.

"At least we don't need to worry about concealing the truth of Umbra from Mr. Nosy now, considering we're all stuck on this island together, anyway. May as well unite with the humans," Jesse murmurs bitterly, suddenly in front of us.

Eli jumps at the sound of him.

"I'm not nosy—" Eli starts.

"Then go back to Silver Valley," he suggests.

Eli stays still, his eyes blazing. The silence fizzles between them, and I take it upon myself to interfere.

"How exactly are we stuck?"

Jesse turns to me, walking backwards.

"We can't access Umbra without power. No way into the hangars means no ships. So we're stuck." He spins back around and faces the torch ahead of us, illuminating the corridor.

"There's always Earth. You know, the mainland?" Eli says, almost missing a step.

"That's my point," Jesse says. "We're all in this together now. We're all stuck on Terra. And if Eli goes tattling about Umbra to the people on the mainland, there's no proof other than he's just clinically crazy."

"But there's so much proof. If the government came to investigate, they'll find part of Umbra is still here," I argue, shivering at the thought.

"But for how long?" Jesse says, raising his eyebrows. "We're cut off. How long can we survive without access to Umbra's supplies?"

I don't want to answer that.

We walk down the corridor, our feet echoing down the walls, but there is no one left to hear us.

"So, what does this mean for us?" I ask Melanie.

Melanie rubs her temple. "No clue. For a moment, every file, every security camera, was suddenly accessible. It was all there. And then it all went dark. I could've figured out what the shipment is, but I didn't work fast enough."

"We're completely in the dark," Jesse says, his eyes hard.

Eli chuckles at the irony. The dark, empty corridor seems to laugh with him.

I flick my switchblade open and closed and wonder where Jasmine has gone. Back to Silver Valley? I wrap my fist tightly around the weapon.

Somehow, I doubt she went back there. My guess, she's lurking along the perimeter of the base. Come daybreak, it'll be harder to hide in the base. She's safest in the forest.

"What does this mean for the cells, the prisoners below ground?" I ask, my mind snapping to the electricity coursing along their cells.

"They'd be trapped," Melanie says plainly. "All the exits are run by power."

I shiver.

At least we won't have a rampage of angry, dirty bodies streaming from the labyrinth below. But still… to be trapped like that, so far below the surface… My skin crawls thinking of it.

"We need to do something," I say sharply, slamming my switchblade closed in my fist. "We are the only ones that know anything."

"Like what?" Jesse asks.

"Savannah, I can't think of anything we *can* do," Melanie admits.

I grit my teeth and stare into the darkness.

My breath rapidly leaves my lips, blood pounding.

We need to stop the shipment from landing. Now. At all costs.

'Shipment' has got to be a code for something else. It must be. I think to myself. Why else would the Umbran government take such drastic measures to hide the information from Melanie, the person charged with such things, to then vacant the island entirely and turn off the power?

Melanie suddenly stops and yanks open a door at the end of the corridor. By a stroke of luck, someone had left it ajar.

I try not to think about the fact that the elevator must be dead, praying Melanie knows another exit. I feel completely, painfully useless. But instead of saying this, instead of giving up, I stare at them all, fire blazing in my eyes.

How do you stop something from landing?

You take away the places it *can* land.

Resolutely, I reply, "Then it's a good thing I can."

PART THREE

THE TURNING TIDE

S tairs.

That's how we got out of the space centre.

Freaking stairs.

I was hoping they'd lead to the beach, but instead, we face buildings, and my heart sinks. Without missing a beat, we pull our exhausted feet forward. Always forward.

I lift my eyes to the sky. The dome is gone. Vanished, as if it was never there. The only memory of it is a circular ring marking the soil around the entire base.

"Oh, wow," Eli says, noticing this too.

"Electricity's gone. Which means the air filtration system is too, meaning no dome," Melanie explains to him.

"Hallelujah, slow death by aging." Jesse's mockery of the situation trails off into the quiet streets.

Morning sun breaks over our faces, soft and gentle, but fog still dances among the mountains above us in a permanent blanket.

We are so far from Silver Valley, but all the trees look the same.

I drag my eyes away from them, my heart a heavy weight in my chest.

Above and beyond us, the tall buildings look dull and empty in comparison. I shrink away from them, shying not from the buildings themselves, but what's inside.

How many people will wake up now, desperate for answers? How long until the base isn't safe anymore?

I wonder if they'll care that the base has been shut down. Will they simply assume it's just a glitch in their systems?

"Melanie, how many places can a spaceship land?" I ask.

"The ones they fly from Umbra? Just the landing pads," she replies easily.

I flick my blade open and smile at my friends.

"Then let's go to the landing pads."

No one prevents Eli from coming with us. He tries to proceed quietly, but his footfalls scrape loudly across the dirt in what's obviously a failed attempt to follow inconspicuously. We know he's there. We just don't care.

I turn down an unfamiliar bend which heads towards the forest.

Melanie swallows deeply, trying to resist making a comment, and I pick up my pace, homing in on the edge of the base and narrowly avoiding a branch at the perimeter.

I hop over the edge of the ring, keeping close to the trees.

Jesse wanders up beside me, toeing the line with his foot and sucking in a deep breath. Almost instantly after he joins my side, his eyes latch onto the forest, hand hanging on the hilt of his sword.

"Fun idea, Savannah. I was craving a nice morning stroll. But here I was hoping we could stop for a whiskey at The Nook on the way to the end of the world."

I roll my eyes at him. I'm not entirely sure if he sees.

He sticks close by me as I pick my way along the edge of the space centre. I don't delve into the trees. Rather, I float along the perimeter where the forest meets the base. It feels protective, safe, being away from the towering buildings.

Weirdly, I feel as if I can breathe for the first time since being here now that the dome is gone.

"Nothing says party like a good end of the world celebration," Eli remarks to Jesse's comment.

I smile at him.

Jesse glowers.

And maybe he's right. Maybe it would be fun. I only wish we had the luxury to seriously consider it. But we don't.

"I suppose some liquor might actually clean your wounds out nice and neat," Melanie adds curtly to Jesse, batting her eyes at him in mockery.

Eli snickers.

"Not quite along the lines I was thinking."

I glance at Melanie, who falls behind the group. I notice a small backpack slung over her shoulder, clinking like glass as she jostles it. The medicine she got from the psychiatric ward?

She sighs deeply, rearranging the vials as she walks so that they don't break.

"How much did you manage to get from the ward?" I ask her.

She pauses, blinks at me, and then slings the pack back over her shoulders.

"I got a few vials of *Velox*. As well as balms to numb pain, seal wounds and disinfect. Elijah even harassed me into getting some for soothing burns, of all things. As well as some bandages and gauze, it should be enough to cover any silly idea you come up with in the next twenty-four hours."

Huh. Eli went with her. The thought makes my head spin.

"You never know when you might need to treat burn wounds," Eli retaliates, trying to keep the breezy smile off his face.

"I highly doubt I'll be needing to treat any burn victims. But sure, I'll enlighten you," she sighs.

"Once," he says, holding a bandage up to her, "I got carpet burn simply from slipping on carpet."

Jesse slaps his hand over his mouth and snorts.

I kick his ankle.

The trees start to dwindle, the canopy hanging lower than before as the ocean opens before us. To our side, the edge of the space centre suddenly cuts off. It wraps all the way along the edge of the beach, stopping only at the bay's end.

I gnaw on the inside of my cheek and stride past the building onto the sand. It doesn't take long until I locate the landing docks, glistening out at sea.

The sky is clear today, and the sun pounds down onto their metallic surfaces, shooting beams of refracted light across the surface of the ocean.

Everyone follows as I walk down to the beach.

I ignore the sand climbing into my shoes, focused on my task.

Along the beach, there are three other metal disks used as doorways to the hangars. The one closest to us is the departure port the Liaison used.

We walk around it, the metal glistening into our eyes from the bright sun. Below the sand, there must be dozens of ships. I chew on my lips, but I'm not paying attention to the hangars on the sand, rather the ones that are out at sea.

"Why are they out there, as well as on the sand?" Eli asks no one in particular, his eyes large as he takes them in.

"They are the landing pads. These here are the main hangars and are mostly used for departures," Melanie says, waving a hand to the metal disks on the sand. "There isn't enough beach for ships to land this close to the space centre. So instead, they port out at sea, and take the tunnels under the surface to the main hangars."

Hell, there are probably some ships under the landing pads as well, I think to myself, watching the waves. *Hundreds of ships.*

By the time we make it halfway towards the second disk in the middle of the bay, Melanie grabs my arm, claiming my attention.

"Enough, please."

I glance back at her, and she sighs.

"Now would be the time to share this marvellous plan of yours."

I face Jesse, who leans against the wall of the space centre behind us, kicking his shoes off into the sand.

"Okay, I was hoping we could enter the landing hangar through these disks on the sand." I twist my ankle gingerly into the sand and I point out into the waves. "Does anyone have any ideas on how to get there?"

"With the power out?" Jesse snorts. "We swim."

"There's no underground access between these?" I ask, waving my hand from the metal disks on the sand to the ones out at sea.

"Not without a generator to get them open," Melanie retorts.

I sigh. Of course.

I walk up to them and lean my back up against the building, biting on my lip. If it weren't for the harsh metal behind my back and the turbulent swell out at sea, I could almost imagine we're back in Silver Valley.

Beside me, Eli refuses to take his eyes off the water, as if he's thinking the same thing.

"Okay," I say, and shrug off my shoes. "Let's swim. We need to get to the landing pads somehow, it's our last chance to stop the shipment from landing."

Without the landing pads, they cannot land.

"Savannah..." Melanie watches as I twist my hair into a braid and kick off my shoes.

I turn and face her. "Can you swim with those wires exposed?"

She rolls her eyes. "If they were Terran wires, then no. But I fixed this arm on Umbra. It's waterproof. Without skin grafting my arm might operate sluggishly until the water dries, but I'll live."

Eli gapes at her, quickly shaking his head to rid the expression before she sees.

I take a deep breath and nod. "We need to destroy the landing pads. It's the only way I can think of to delay them from landing," I say simply. "It'll be a lot of work, and it might even be pointless, but on the off chance that it stops the shipment…"

"Destroy the… really?" Jesse says slowly, eyes sparkling. He erupts into laugher.

It reverberates down the beach and I stand still for a moment, listening to him. I've never once heard Jesse laugh like this. It makes me want to stay here and listen to it forever.

Amusement flickers across my features in response, and I almost don't hear when Melanie interrupts him.

"And how do you plan to do that?"

I shrug. "Between the three of us, I'm pretty sure we can figure something out."

She crosses her arms.

"Three of us?" Eli asks.

"Yes, I need you to stay on the beach. Guard our backs. If you see someone coming, make a signal." I hope he misses the underlying concern in my voice. I don't want him swimming with those hands. The others, I know, won't stay behind.

To my shock, Eli almost looks relieved.

Cautiously, he turns his attention to Jesse. "Can I borrow a knife or something at least?"

He huffs. "Nice try."

Jesse shrugs his jacket off and places it beside mine in the sand, a seed of amusement hiding in the depths of his eyes.

For some reason, I can't escape the foreboding sense of déjà vu. Just a week ago, I was doing this with Jasmine, and Eli was the one leading me into the water. He catches my eye and I smile, noticing the similar look of mourning reflecting on his features.

My breathing increases as the material leaves Jesse's skin, my eyes locked on the ripple of his muscles as he tugs the edge of his shirt back down before it rides up with the movement.

"Let's at least hope the water isn't going to give us hypothermia," Melanie grumbles, shrugging off her own jacket.

I grin at her, blood rising to my cheeks.

"Oh, it will," Eli smiles.

She doesn't smile back, but when I turn to the water, she races with us down to the sea.

And this time, I don't hesitate.

O ur fingers slip against the wet metal of the landing pad above us.

There is no way in hell we're going to get any traction on it, let alone have the energy to scale to the top. Not with the merciless waves beating into our backs, slapping us against the metal. But none of us bring this up. We all float helplessly, considering a way to make it work.

The pad is higher above the waves than I'd thought—metres above.

Something within the metal prevents it from rusting, coating the surface of the entire contraption. Unfortunately, it also makes the exterior impossibly smooth and slick when doused in water.

I feel limp and useless here, hanging in the sea, the waves tossing me like a strand of seaweed. It feels nothing like the sweet joy I felt with Jasmine, swimming in the cold ocean.

This reality is much more severe.

"There's some metal plating off to the side there, among the screws," Jesse pants, the waves brushing against his cheek as he speaks.

No one responds, but we all swim towards it in unison.

My legs bat against the metal cylinder that travels below the surface; the tunnel we couldn't use with the power dead. I use the metal to keep myself anchored. The waves aren't peaking this far out into the water, but the swell is still high, and threatens to push us back to shore.

It takes a lot longer to reach the other side of the landing pad than I'm comfortable with.

But Jesse was right; there's a lip between the metal holding the panels together, and a line of bolts securing it in place.

He handles one of his weapons. His eyes settle on me as I flap around before him, the water plastering my hair against my scalp.

"Take this," he says, giving me his larger knife. The blade is thinner than the others, but tough. I grasp it in my damp fingers and clutch it as if it's made of pure gold.

Jesse will never forgive me if I dropped it in the ocean.

"What do I do with it?" I ask.

"See this panel between the screws? It's the only place prone to rusting, and it's deep—it should give way to the knife. Jam it in there and use the handle as leverage."

I almost choke on seawater when I answer, "Will it hold me?"

"The metal is from Umbra, and you're light, so yes."

I glance over at Melanie, who bobs soundlessly in the water, her lips parted for breath as she uses all her stamina to stay afloat.

"Why me?"

"You're the only one not healing from recent injuries, thanks to Mel and Umbran medicine." He winks at me jokingly and I roll my eyes at him. "Plus, you're the lightest of the three of us, considering Mel's arm."

Teeth chattering from the water, I take a deep breath and nod.

Even Melanie is more trained and steadier on her feet than I am. But he's right. With her arm, she is both heavier from water logging and would have fewer limbs to scale the wall.

So I don't argue. We don't have time for that.

I swim through the water towards Jesse, making sure nothing but resolve shows on my face. He doesn't take his eyes off me as I navigate the surface in front of us. The first panel ends a metre above me, and the next one a metre above that. Then it's only a short scramble to the top.

"Once you get up there," Melanie says between breaths, her prosthetic hanging limp in the water, "locate the hatch with the wires. Then destroy the box running the backup standby. It's the simplest way to get inside the hangar."

She gasps as a wave sweeps over her, cutting her off.

I don't know what she means, but I repeat her words in my mind. Destroy the box. Got it.

Jesse reaches for me as the next wave comes. My eyes flicker to him and I scavenge for the remains of my willpower to stay afloat.

My skin heats at the touch of his fingers on my waist.

"I'll give you an extra boost," he explains.

His hands feel sturdy on me, but I try my best not to lean into them. He will need his strength. I lick the salt from my lips nervously as the next wave roams closer.

The wave pulls us higher into the air, but we wait until we reach the crest.

Jesse grunts, pushing me up.

And I go flying.

I have only seconds to aim his knife. I slam it forwards, levelling it between the panels. It resists, but I jam it in.

The wave rolls away from me, sailing towards the shore, but the blade is locked into place. I keep my fist secured around the handle until it's the only thing supporting me, and I'm hanging limp in the air against the metal, nothing but the sturdy Umbran nails between the metal plating holding me in place.

Another wave begins to mount up ahead and I grunt at the sight of it. It could whisk me out of position if it's strong enough. I exhale sharply and pull myself upwards. My joints moan with the effort—the strength I require ebbing by the second. I flail for a moment but manage to pull my torso up near the handle of the knife.

It hurts. But I keep going.

I don't know how the knife doesn't snap with my weight. But Jesse's Umbran blade is as solid as he said it would be. It doesn't budge.

The next wave finally comes and brushes against me, licking my thighs. It's strong but doesn't grab onto me enough to whisk me down.

I resist the temptation to look back at Jesse. I wonder if he's watching me proudly or if he's judging every position I twist into.

My guess is it's a mixture of both.

I pull myself higher, left hand pressed flat against the smooth wall. It isn't wet this high up, but a fine layer of salt grates against my skin as I balance on the hilt of the knife.

It takes me longer than I would've liked to stand.

I sway precariously on the knife, the only support being the handle under my foot. I reach cautiously for my switchblade, locked away within my pocket.

I feel like I'm floating. A bird dangling on a branch, nothing but gravity binding me to the earth.

Gravity is a bitch.

I flail as I aim the switchblade. This panel isn't as difficult to reach as the one before, when I was surrounded by the rough motion of the waves.

I try not to grit my teeth as I twist my blade into the second panel.

My switchblade is smaller than Jesse's knife, and I really, *really* don't want to break it.

But none of Jesse's other weapons would fit. So I reach up, twine my fingers around the familiar dark red handle, and yank myself up into the sky.

My feet depart Jesse's blade and I scurry to transfer my weight onto my own. My hands shake when I hold it and I reassure myself that the Umbran metal will hold me. The blade dips under my weight, pointing down towards the sea.

My heart begins to pound erratically, and I re-enact the positions I underwent on the last blade until I'm balanced precariously on my tiptoes.

My hands grab the lip above me, frantically searching for something secure on top of the landing pad to pull myself up onto.

But it's as smooth and flat as the wall against my body.

I moan quietly, fretting over my clumsy movements, and yank myself skywards once more.

The first part of the lift is the hardest, but once my arms lock themselves into place, I pull myself onto the roof of the landing pad almost effortlessly and I roll across the surface, licking salt from my lips, eyes unfocused on the bright blue sky.

The sun is rising higher.

We're running out of time.

I pull myself up and peer over the edge at my companions. Melanie glances at me with hope, but there's urgency within the depth of her eyes.

She's running out of energy.

Jesse simply smirks at me.

He thumps his hand against the metal panels in urgency, excitement, and unspoken exclamations.

My head swims as if I'm still flying.

I feel like I've just conquered the world.

ↄ

I tear my eyes across the top of the landing pad. It's webbed in a decorative pattern, the segments reminding me of the glowing membranes within the space centre. In full daylight, their wondrous glow is dimmed, but it should reach the stars when activated at night.

I stop in my tracks, squinting.

The lights on the landing pad are activated. I've never seen the glow radiating off them before. The whole base is dead, but there's still power on the landing pads. Why?

Is it because of the upcoming shipment?

I slip across the surface, trying to pry apart the crack running through the landing pad, searching for the place Melanie described.

My nails claw to find purchase until I finally see it along the edges of the pad. I sigh in relief upon seeing the small hatch and rush over. Sliding my fingers underneath the lip, I toss the cover and it clatters loudly on the floor.

Inside, there's a screen with digits and so many wires that I lose track.

The only thing I can make sense of is the one sentence across the screen that says: *on standby.*

I run my fingers over it. I'm no hacker, but I do know how to break stuff.

A light flickers at the bottom of the screen.

Maybe that's the activation?

The screen rests on something bulky that's *kind of* shaped like a box. But I would say it looks more like an egg.

I stand up on shaky legs and slam my heel into the flickering egg. Pain rings across my foot, but I do it again.

More pain lances up my ankle, but I keep kicking until something chimes within the hatch.

I take a deep breath and peer inside. The light has stopped flashing, and across the screen, the display has changed to *deactivated.*

"Well," I say to myself, "that's one way to become a hacker."

ᔐ

Turns out *deactivated* means that nothing, and I mean *nothing*, has any power.

The hangar must have been running on some sort of backup generator, locking us out.

But not anymore.

I locate the crack across the pad and pry it open. It must be the doors. The crack runs nearly to the edges of the pad.

I manage to get my fingers inside it and red lines press into my palms as I push. My chest heaves as I attempt to brace myself against the smooth surface, knees slipping on the ground.

Somehow, it opens just wide enough to fit my torso, and I gasp in relief. I head to the edge of the pad, closest to the hatch.

Trying to stick to what I assume is a wall at the edge of the tunnel, I take a deep steadying breath and lower myself down. I don't know how long the fall is and don't give myself time to consider it.

I let go, and wind brushes past me.

The fall is short. Thank the Stars.

My feet pound against a metal grate, and falling forwards, my hands slam into a railing.

I shriek within the darkness and my voice ricochets around me.

Twisting my hands around the railing, I squint, wishing there was a light source.

I glance up into the crack I fell through, and the sun greets the darkness and highlights a pool beneath me, but beyond that there's utter blackness, my eyes struggling to adjust. The metal grate I'm standing on must separate the base of the tunnel from the top half.

I don't know why it's here, but I don't waste time trying to figure it out.

Off to the side, I find a ladder dimly illuminated by the crack above.

The top is secured against the wall with screws. I find another hidden hatch beside it, and I throw the lid open, gasping in relief when I discover some old tools.

Quickly, I grab the smallest screwdriver and begin to work on the screws attaching the ladder to the wall.

ᔑ

By the time Melanie rolls over onto the deck of the pad, face slick with water, I regret not demanding she take my place.

Her waterlogged clothes grip her skin, and she just lies there, waiting for her energy to return.

Jesse suddenly appears over the edge, his face hovering near mine as I hold the ladder in place. He pulls himself onto the pad and I release the ladder into the water, my muscles aching in response.

"We need to work on your speed," he says by way of greeting, handing me the switchblade he retrieved on his way up.

I roll my eyes. I did save him from drowning, after all.

He re-attaches his own knife to his belt and glances down at Melanie. "Cheer up, love, the worst isn't over yet."

"Shut up, Jesse. I'm recovering." Her eyes stay unfocused on the sky, but I can tell she's trying not to laugh.

"So, does anyone have any ideas on how to blow up this thing?" I ask.

To my surprise, Jesse responds immediately, never missing a beat. "Circuits."

"Um, I'm sorry," Melanie says, sitting up to face him, prosthetic arm sluggish from the water, "but these interfaces are well protected, you're never going to hack through the defences enough to cause it to combust."

"Never say never," he smirks. "You may know technology, but I know how to blow stuff up. They interlace these pads with some of our more combustive metals. It slows the metal from corroding, but it can be incredibly dangerous if provoked. You just need to apply enough force to break the protective layer around it."

"You sound like you've done this before," I remark.

He tries not to smile at that. "On a far less exciting scale."

"So how on Umbra do we do this?" Melanie demands, shaking water out of her arm.

"Force," he repeats, blinking, as if he hasn't thought further than that. "And flame, like I said."

Melanie shakes her head blearily, but her eyes look sharper than before. Glittering with the makings of a plan. "Once we blow the landing pad and hangar, the tunnels below will flood with seawater. If I boot the generator back up, the malfunction barriers within the tunnels will all rise and stop the water from entering the space centre, causing no damage to the research facilities. But there will be no way anyone will be able to land ships here anymore."

I feel excitement brewing within.

Finally, we have a solid plan to delay—or perhaps even stop—the shipment from landing. Granted, we are no closer to figuring out the dangers of the shipment. But I'm ready to accept any win at this point.

"There are only three landing docks, right?" I ask Jesse.

"Yes, you can't land through the exit hangars. At least, not efficiently," he says.

Perfect.

"It could take years to ready them as arrival hangars," Melanie contemplates, her lips twitching into a smile.

"Is there a way to access and open the other pads from here?" I ask.

"Of course," he says. "When you have a backup generator and a hacker."

"My question still stands," Melanie interrupts. "*How* are we going to blow these up?"

I turn to Jesse when I answer. "If we get a large, heavy, flaming fuel deposit and drop it onto the pads from high up… would that be enough force?"

"It's extreme. But yes. Definitely."

Smiling, I stand above the crevice in the pad, leading us down into the tunnels.

"I know what to do," I say. "Melanie, show us how to open this thing."

M elanie gets the doors to pull all the way open, and we leap into the abyss below.

She even bypasses the grate I stood on. This part takes her longer.

Apparently, her uncle set up a defensive system on the grate which would alert him if anyone were to bypass it. She explains the system isn't activated often, considering he has guards on rotation to man this sector. But they're all off-planet now, so Melanie didn't want to take any further risks.

And like everything she sets her mind to, eventually the metal grate bends to her will, folding away against the walls, electricity off.

We scurry down ladders until we reach the bottom, and the area within begins to glow with light.

The day continues to pass, but for the first time, we hardly notice.

I ignore the sky—the sun, the ocean—and set my eyes strictly on the ships in the hangar to the side of us.

Beyond that, tunnels branch off towards the other hangars.

The tunnel is like a chute, eventually opening into an underground dome at the base of the sea. Several ships lay off to the side of the small cavern, waiting quietly to be used, and dark paint on the walls glow with the words ZONE 2.

"Which ship is the easiest to fly?" I ask Jesse.

"This one," he says, tapping his hand against the body of a small pod.

It's the smallest in the hangar, not unlike the escape pods the Liaison and my mother took, except this one has wings. Its body is smooth and dark, a wide glass screen wrapping from one side of the ship and disappearing down the tail. On the door, the faint symbol of Umbra's military flickers on the metal.

Jesse clicks his knife under a lip on the slick machine and a panel rises out. A light blinks on when Jesse taps the machine awake. If it's a scanning device, perhaps all ships are linked to a particular person.

Melanie frowns. "We won't be able to get them to fly properly, not with the power down, but maybe if I—"

Jesse holds out a hand to stop her. "I got this. Watch."

He pulls his sword out of his belt, and before I have a chance to ask what he's doing, he slams the hilt into the screen. It falls off in a jumble of wires. Without hesitating, he reaches down into a fuel deposit and plunges the sword into the transparent gunk. It clings to his blade like slime.

I watch, transfixed, as he coats the wires in fuel, then slices through a few wires with his blade.

They spark, shooting deadly white spurts into the air, but the heavy fuel around the wires absorbs it until, finally, the sparks recede completely into the fuel. To my surprise, the wires hang dead and limp after the exercise. The fuel appears to glow with the aided strength, but Jesse wipes it off.

The ship hums, alive.

"How did you know to do that?" I ask him.

He shrugs. "Practice."

Melanie looks just as flabbergasted, but slightly less surprised than I am. I suppose she would know more about Umbran fuel, metals, wiring and the like.

Before us, the ship awakes.

"*Bienvenue*, Jesse," the ship says in French. I've taken some French classes at school, but my mind still takes a moment to remember what the word means. *Welcome*.

"*Bonjour*," Jesse says back to the ship, almost mockingly.

"It *talks*?" I ask.

"In French, Italian, Latin, or English," Jesse replies.

As the ship boots up, it seems to be giving us an exact rundown on the process, commenting on its progress.

I suck on my lips and blink at the ship. "Why French?"

"It was one of the more common tongues in the 1700s," Melanie explains from beside me. "Most of the Elders favour the use of Latin due to their backgrounds in science, but it seems the owner of this ship prefers French."

The ship hums in front of me as if agreeing.

"It will link to your genetics when you embark and guide you into flying," Jesse explains. "Just don't fly too high. The space travel network is disabled."

"Does a French dictionary come with it?" I ask.

"No, but you can change the setting to English," Jesse says.

The ship whirs.

"Savannah, take this pod." Melanie steps forwards. "I'll go to Zone 1 and Jesse can go to Zone 3. Once we're done, we'll meet back on the beach."

I nod.

Jesse passes Melanie his largest knife. "Do what I did to the pod when you get to the other hangar," he says.

She grabs the blade off him. "Don't do anything too stupid," Melanie says in farewell, looking at both of us.

Jesse snorts. "When have I ever?"

I almost want to say the same. But I've jumped out of a window once.

"Just don't die." And just like that, Melanie disappears down another tunnel.

I watch her leave, but Jesse watches me.

He reaches for my hands as Melanie's buttery hair disappears into the darkness. The touch of his skin shocks me, and I snap around to face him in surprise.

My palms begin to warm at the contact, and I shudder. He drops them immediately.

"You'll be okay." He turns away from me to open the door to my ship. "Just don't die on us, princess."

His words sound more strained than they did coming from Melanie's mouth.

I step towards the door, but I'm not ready to embark yet. Not ready to… well, possibly *die*.

We both wait for the other to say something, but neither of us has any words.

I gaze at Jesse's face for so long that he has no choice but to look back. His eyes look guarded, but soft… broken.

It's getting harder for him to hide from me.

Eventually, I find the words I want to ask. "Why do you always call me princess?"

A streak of humour splinters across his face. "You know the prophecy."

I snort. I always assumed it was more a tone of endearment, not sarcasm. Rolling my eyes, I reach the hatch on the door.

"I didn't realise you were making fun of me."

"*Connexion* à *nouvel hote*," the ship says.

"Please speak English," I ask the ship.

"Granted. Continuing connection to new pilot," the ship replies.

I pull myself inside, but I only make it halfway through before Jesse grabs my hand.

"Savannah," he says.

I pause.

When my eyes land on his, I see a new expression on his face. He looks at me like I'm Melanie. Like he's actually worried about me.

My heart pounds for a moment, and I focus on not falling out of the ship. "Yes," I say slowly.

He lifts my hand to his lips… and the world stops.

My heart stops beating.

I can't breathe.

Every nerve in my body focuses on that hand. There's nothing in my thoughts but Jesse—brushing the back of my hand with his lips, his eyes avoiding mine as he slowly lifts his head.

I never realised there were so many nerves in a hand. I gape, my fingers shivering.

Slowly, he drops my hand, as if embarrassed.

I can still feel the ghost of his lips branding me.

"Il n'y pas de combinaison de mots pour décrire à quel point je tiens à toi, Savannah Shaw."

He turns away quietly, drifting into the depth of the hangar. I keep my eyes on his back, watching the tunnel to Zone 3 swallow him.

I can only breathe once the echo of his footsteps fade.

As soon as air re-enters my lungs, I scramble inside the ship. It's finished linking to me and hums when I board, seemingly thankful I'm finally inside.

"Ship," I gasp, looking down at the panel of controls in front of me, "translate what Jesse just said."

A screen flashes on before me, reflecting the Umbran symbol behind a sprawl of words. The words speed across the screen at the same time the ship repeats them.

"There is no combination of words to describe how much I care for you, Savannah Shaw."

I take a shaky breath and my heart all but stops beating.

"I am Speed Vessel 087. Ready to depart, Captain Shaw?"

The sound of the ship's voice fills the entire space, bounding off the tight capsule around the cockpit. There are only two seats in this ship, and I slide into the captain's chair.

Except… "I'm not a Captain," I tell the ship.

"Copy that, Captain."

"Right." I drift my hands over all the screens before me, unsure what to do with them. "We'll work on that."

The Speed Vessel hums beneath me. Purring, like a cat being rubbed.

I shake the thought from my mind.

I don't know when Melanie and Jesse will start up their ships, so I can't time my departure to theirs. It won't make any difference. This mission isn't about synchronicity.

I need to gun the pod up into the air. Now.

And yet, I hesitate, scared to depart.

"Ready to utilise engines," the ship says.

There are so many screens. So many buttons.

I don't know which ones to touch, but I realise I don't need to. The pod listens to voice command. I don't need to fly it at all.

My hands hover above the screens, Jesse's words shining back at me. I place my hands on either side of that screen and release a deep breath.

"I'm in a bloody alien ship, for crying out loud."

"Cannot compute."

"I really hope this stops the shipment," I say, mostly to myself.

"To source information on shipments, consult—"

"Melanie Beckett, I know," I cut the pod off.

It hums in response.

Why am I risking my life for this?

The answer is simple. "I'm doing this for Jesse," I mumble. He's counting on me. Trusting me.

"My analytics determine a mutual affection," the ship responds.

I laugh. "I didn't peg you as a relationship councillor, 087."

It pauses, as if it's thinking. "Cannot compute."

"Figures," I mumble.

I stare down at the screen. At his words. Maybe if I blink, they'll vanish, and that scares me.

Even in Silver Valley, when Jesse was a dark figure in the forest, I had been drawn to him. He stole a part of me in that forest. Another part of me wonders what I stole in return.

Breathing deeply, I remind myself who I'm doing this for—my family, Jesse, Melanie. If can't do this for myself, I can find a way to do it for them.

"I am the prophesied princess," I tell the speed vessel. "Surely I can fly a goddamn ship."

"I operate through voice command control and do not require manual driving, unless disabled in flight," it says in response.

"Yeah, yeah," I scoff, shaking my head at the pod.

I take a deep breath.

And I tell Speed Vessel 087 to fly.

ᔐ

The island looks so beautiful from above.

The waves in Silver Valley are soft, the water glowing, but near the base the ocean is grey and turbulent. And yet, it's still beautiful.

The island is nothing like the rustic architecture of trees I have always known on Australia's mainland. The vegetation is filled with grand, tall pines that soar into the sky, networks of evergreens dotting the ground. The rise and fall of mountains look like cushions of green.

I keep to the beach, and I keep the pod low.

Jesse and Melanie aren't airborne yet, but they will be soon.

I wish I had time to circle around to the Valley, to see my home from above, but I can't.

"087, how many humans have seen Umbran ships over the course of history and mistaken them for UFOs?"

"According to my database, approximately 88% of reported UFO sightings are a result of Umbra's transport and military."

Not all of them, but enough.

Shivers trail down my back at the thought. We are the aliens of this world.

I trace my fingers along the window. It's so clear it doesn't appear to be there until my hand contacts the cool surface.

087 continues circling above the base, like a bird searching for prey, the shadow of its wingspan dotting the sand.

I wonder how many civilians are glancing up, wondering what's happening.

I scan the ocean below, the blue turbulence covered in white lace and the ever-moving whitewash. Melanie's ship emerges from her hangar.

"087, is there communication set up between Speed Vessels?" I ask.

"Networks have been disabled upon launch. Landing is recommended."

I lean back from the window to take my seat. "Right," I mumble. "Thanks for that Jesse."

Melanie hovers in the sky, a moment of hesitation in the ship's movements. She's probably wondering why I haven't moved.

Her presence brings me back to reality, and my hands shake at the thought of what I'm about to do.

Across the distance, Melanie engages standby, roaming the sky in a similar pattern to my vessel.

Not long after, Jesse's ship climbs out of its hangar.

Swift and direct, he shoots his pod into the sky. Without a moment's hesitation, he redirects the pod, so its nose faces the sand. He flashes a beam of sunlight off his windows in my direction.

I hear him loud and clear. *I don't know what you guys are still doing up here, but I'm going to blow these bastards up.*

"087, where are the evacuation points?"

"Denied. Exit is sealed."

"I need a way to get out of this ship," I persist. "Where is the exit?"

"You can locate the evacuation panels behind the captain's seat," it replies.

"Good. Open them."

"Denied."

I grit my teeth and clamber out of my seat. "Fine, I'll do it myself,"

The latch is black and intricate—a webbed series of handles and joints. A small screen blinks on the panel. *Sealed.*

It's airtight.

It shouldn't be, should it?

"What security measures have been installed in you, 087?"

"As a private Speed Vessel to the Umbran authority, 62% of systems have been disabled upon hijacking."

"Wonderful."

Beyond the ship, I hear a ringing peel almost like thunder. I don't have to guess what it is.

"It's taken Jesse less than a minute to blow his dock up. Can you *please* help me not look like a fool, 087?" I press.

It doesn't respond.

I don't suppose my friend's vessels also belong to a private authority, and been disabled so expertly? I stand up and peer outside.

The world below me is on fire.

The afternoon sun blooms across the streaks of flame pluming from Zone 3. The thick wafts of smoke shield half my vision of the island, but I can see enough of the sky to see Melanie's vessel angling to the earth, and her form slipping out of the pod's escape hatch. My heart pounds in my ears as she sails down to the waves, a silver parachute engaging mid-descent. She directs it towards the beach as her ship plummets into the dock.

Just me with me the disabled vessel, then.

"Do you have a parachute on board?" I ask hopefully.

"Emergency parachutes are located by the evacuation point," the ship responds.

Taking a deep breath, I follow the ship's directions, pulling free the parachute hidden in a latch by the sealed exit and swinging it onto my back. My hands shake as I fiddle with the straps, familiarising myself with the parachute. I've never used one in my life, but there is no better time to learn than the present.

I drag myself back into the pilot's seat, leaving the safety buckles hanging loose at my feet.

"087, set your trajectory towards Landing Zone 2."

"Engaging."

As it tilts, I flip my switchblade open and drag it underneath one of the panels near the switches and screens. It pops open easily.

I grin at the sight.

Inside the cabinet is a toolbox.

I pull out the heaviest item I can find. I have no idea what it is, or what it does, but it's heavy and long.

"Engage maximum speed," I tell the vessel.

The screens behind me glow as the speed builds momentum, not yet sensing anything wrong with my orders.

I wait until all systems are engaged before wreaking havoc, as I don't want to risk the vessel disengaging.

"All systems ready," the ship hums.

I take a deep breath, holding the hybrid wrench solidly in my sweaty grasp.

"Head for the ground."

The words hardly leave my lips before the ship activates.

I don't give myself time to pause.

I throw myself at the window, tool swinging.

I smash through the front of the vessel, screaming.

The heavy tool falls with me, but I don't see where it goes.

The window breaks against my weight, shattering beneath me as I plummet towards the sea, fingers anxiously grasping for the attachment that frees the parachute.

I didn't expect the large tool to do much damage to Umbran matter.

All I needed was to make a few cracks.

I threw myself at them, using the force and fall of gravity to heft myself out.

The only problem was how long it took.

There's nothing but streaks of blue ocean and red fires, the world spinning around me in a way that makes no sense.

Speed Vessel 087 connects into the pad seconds after I leave the safety of the pilot's seat. The eruption hits me in the air, throwing the trajectory of my body away from the landing pad.

My fingers finally grasp the attachment that frees the parachute. I left plenty of space between the ship and the water when I jumped out, but the seconds during a free-fall are fleeting, and the parachute whips out around me with mere moments to spare.

I don't breathe as the force of the parachute knocks me back, blood pounding in my skull.

Hanging limp in the sky, metres above the churning ocean, I hardly see or feel anything at all.

꙳

I feel a strong arm around me as I'm yanked out of the waves.

Water streaks through my hair, my skin, my clothes.

The parachute frees itself from my shoulders, lost in the waves.

I can still taste the explosion on my tongue, choking on the smells of smoke. It doesn't go down nicely. Maybe that's because I can feel the ocean bubbling up my throat.

I cough some more of it up, eyes streaming with tears.

"You really know how to put on a show, princess," I hear Jesse's voice snap.

Oh yeah, because having a disabled ship was totally intentional, I want to say.

Nothing but strained sounds and gurgles come out of my mouth.

"Is she okay?" someone yells from a distance. She rushes up towards me, silver eyes searching the scrapes on my body in panic.

Sand hits my back as Jesse lowers me to the ground.

Eli is mumbling something incoherently.

"Med kit," Jesse bites. "Now."

Something pierces my face, my lips. I bat at the stinging sensation. Liquid fills my mouth. Still stinging.

"This will knock her out," Melanie says.

And the world goes black.

The world is still black when I wake.

No, it's night.

I sit up so sharply that spots prickle my vision.

Someone throws their arm out in front of me and slams me back down into the sand.

Jesse.

"Ouch, whiplash," I growl.

His deep eyes look livid.

I give him a grimacing smirk in return. Someone placed a jacket under me on the sand—Jesse—so I could get some much-needed sleep. The surrounding sand shows signs of sleep from my friends, who have now woken and have taken to pacing down on the beach. All but Jesse, who remains beside me.

It takes a moment for me to realise that our countdown is finally reaching its end. The last day is over—it is now the dead of night. The shipment is due sometime after morning.

I look down at my body, covered in gauze.

Ouch.

I wince as I pull myself into a more comfortable sitting position. My back hurts from sleeping on the hard sand, but Melanie must've used some *Velox* on me, because I feel incredibly okay, considering.

Before us, streaks of black smoke still tendril into the sky. Melanie stands down by the waves, watching them, ankles in the water.

I run my hands down my skin, nails catching on the gauze.

My mouth tastes bitter and medicinal, so I spit onto the sand.

"Very queenly."

I make a point to spit at Jesse. But it misses and lands in front of him.

Without missing a beat, he grabs my chin and knocks my head back against the cold wall.

"Rest up."

That hurt.

"I've already done that," I rasp, head spinning.

He doesn't respond to this, but hands me my switchblade.

"My captain would've scolded me and banned me from practice for a week if I treated my weapons so hopelessly," he murmurs.

"Good thing I'm not a trained guard, then," I say as I tuck the blade back into my pocket.

His dark eyes flicker to me, eyebrows down. "You'd be better off if you were."

Down the beach, Melanie starts to rub her temples, her prosthetic arm looking more operational and less waterlogged than before. She looks beside herself, running fingers through her hair, eyes watching the pluming smoke. She paces up and down the beach.

Our plans have been spent. There's nothing to do now except wait.

Eli stays by her side, pointing out the smoking docks.

We did a spectacular job of destroying them. Fragments of metal still drift onto shore, like large stars glittering on the sand.

"How long do we have?" I ask Jesse.

"Until daybreak? Around six to seven hours, but it's hard to say when the shipment is expected to land."

I nod, but he doesn't notice. He keeps his eyes on the stars, the tension never leaving his face. I wonder when he will finally be able to look at the sky without feeling pain.

"Did you see it happen?" I ask him, glancing down at the gauze on my arms.

He turns to face me and grinds his teeth. "Every second of it."

"Thanks for dragging me out of the water," I say.

"Thanks for not dying," he replies.

And that was that.

Melanie turns back to look at us, her expression igniting when seeing me awake. I can't escape the feeling that she's been doing that for hours. Checking on me, waiting for me to be okay.

It makes my skin itch.

Eli's in the middle of speaking to her, but she pats his arm idly and leaves him standing by the ocean. There are streaks of dried blood on her fingers, but she hardly seems to notice.

"Thank Umbra you're alive," she exclaims, her knees planting in the sand before me.

"I wasn't exactly *dead* earlier," I say.

"It was quite a fall."

Eli wanders up the sand, half-heartedly jogging, and takes his place beside Melanie.

I reach out and take her hands. "You have medicine for that. *Velox*?"

"I was exhausted and ended up falling asleep before treating it. It doesn't bother me anyway, it's just a few scratches."

"Salt water is great for cleaning wounds in a pinch," Jesse pitches in.

When Melanie releases a breath exasperatedly, I don't doubt that Jesse has attempted to heal his own wounds this way before.

"It was silly. I landed on some shells. Then I saw you fall and I all but forgot about it."

I drop Melanie's hand.

"We have time now. We've slept and rested enough."

She sucks on her lips, trying not to look nervous and failing terribly.

I push her backpack full of *Velox* and medicinal balms towards her through the sand, and she takes it with a sigh.

"I vote swimming to pass the time," Eli suggests.

I drag my hand over my hair. It's dried into a matted heap. The salty breeze beats against us, turning it into knots.

"I would rather do something more useful," I say quietly.

"What do you propose then, princess?" Jesse sneers.

There's nothing left to do. Except...

I turn to him. "Show me how to use this."

His eyes travel to the switchblade balanced in my palm, his

earlier words hanging between us like a sour breath. He *did* say he would.

Melanie sits back on her ankles. "But, Savannah—"

"You really think that a tiny blade will stop the shipment?" Jesse asks, probably trying to gauge what's going on in my head. Or mocking me. Either one is likely.

"I don't care. I can't stand sitting idly and doing nothing."

Melanie crosses her arms over her chest, and we share a small glance. Beside her, all her ointments are neatly arranged, everyone's bandages clean and neatly wrapped. She's already busied herself. The lack of her tech must feel like a hole in the chest.

I take in Jesse's deep gaze, holding his eyes. "Please." The wind brushes his hair gently from his face, his eyes as wild as the thrashing waves. "Please show me how to use this."

He strokes his sword absently, strapped safely in its holster. But his eyes never leave mine. They brand me, claiming me.

He smiles sweetly, and I know I've won.

"You're not strong enough." Melanie's eyes travel down the gauze on my arms, exploring my wounds.

"No, but with Jesse's help, I could be."

She sighs, throwing her hands into the air.

"Eventually," Jesse smirks.

Melanie huffs. "Training takes time, Savannah."

"Then we'd better get a move on."

Melanie looks ready to come up with a million better reasons, but keeps her jaw clamped shut. She rolls her eyes and then turns back to the ocean. Perhaps to wash her hands or come up with new plans. Who knows?

Eli's eyes soften. He doesn't follow her—he doesn't say anything—just sits down and tips his head back against the cool metal. Resigned.

Jesse doesn't look at me the way Melanie does. He doesn't see my bandages or the way my words rasp when I speak. He sees desire in my chest and the pounding in my blood. The fire and need to move my body.

He must also know that this shipment might carry enemies, and even a slither of confidence in how to hold my blade could increase our chances for survival.

I know he knows this, because Jesse *does* understand me. He seems to know me better than I know myself.

He sees my heart. And so, he offers me his hand.

I let Jesse pull me to my feet and we walk out onto the beach, switchblade burning in my pocket.

"Alright, Master. Show me what you got."

He faces me, grinning with malice.

The sea winds pick up as we train.

Not only am I battling with Jesse, but Mother Nature, too.

Jesse nudges his foot against mine, telling me to shift my stance. We haven't moved onto using weapons yet. He wants me to know how to hold myself, test my strengths and weaknesses, and how to avoid getting toppled in less than five seconds.

"Your weight is too far forwards," he remarks, touching my arm to readjust me.

I take a deep breath.

"When can I use my switchblade?" I finally ask.

"As soon as you stop tripping around me like a baby horse. Now strike me again, arms up," he says, facing me.

I lunge for him like he taught me. His hands spin around me, his leg knocking me to the floor in no less than six seconds.

At least I'm beating my own record.

"If someone comes for me, my instinct will be to grab my switchblade," I tell him.

"By which point, the enemy would already have a fist around your throat while you're still reaching into your pockets. You're slow." He pulls me up from the sand. "Again."

The wind knocks against me as I stand. I've knotted my tangled hair into a tight bun that's come loose over the hour, releasing strands that hang in my face. I brush them aside and sink into position.

We proceed well into morning and it isn't until the sky lightens that Jesse lets me reach for my weapon.

"The switchblade isn't the best weapon to use in combat." He stands near me, brushing my shoulders back to loosen my muscles and make my posture more dangerous. "It's a backup blade—a hidden tool concealed in a shoe or in the bodice of a woman's gown. Don't let the enemy know you have it. Surprise them. Aim for something soft, like the back of their knees or the eyes."

"And then?"

"And then run. Find me, so I can help you finish them."

Jesse Hayes, ever the protector.

"Now show me how you hold it," he says softly, standing back to get a better look.

I reach for the blade. My fingers barely brush the lip of my pocket when he bats my hands away, growling.

"Keep your head up. Your whole body goes for the blade. Don't let the enemy know what you're doing."

I lower my hands, standing still on the sand.

Melanie and Eli walk along the beach, and she kicks away bits of debris out of boredom. Everyone is too nervous to sleep. I turn my back on them and lunge for Jesse, just like he taught me.

As my body leans forwards, I dip my hand into my pocket, spinning as I plant a kick into his chest. He fumbles backwards as I grab his shirt, holding the knife to his throat.

At least, that was the plan.

He grabs me before I have a chance to latch onto him, and we both go tumbling to the sand. The Umbran metal glitters above his throat. But he also has a blade on me, aimed directly above my heart.

"Good," he says, releasing me.

My breath catches as I push away. He does the same.

His lips tilt into a smile, and I bask in the glow of victory. Even if I've lost the fight, it's the first time he's complimented me.

"You learn fast," he says.

"I wouldn't say a few hours is fast."

"It is. Training takes years."

I clamber off him, sand covering our skin.

The sky turns to a soft pink as waves thrash in the distance.

We're ready to go again... Just as Eli screams.

His fear sends us sprinting across the beach.

"It's spaceships!"

I stumble mid-step, confused, and look up at the budding sun.

The sky is alive with ships.

My stomach drops to my feet, and I suddenly feel immobilised with shock.

Melanie runs from the beach as if the waves are poison. As soon as she makes it to where we stand, I force my limbs to move. I race back to the base with her to hide. Standing in the open along the beach is too dangerous.

We flatten ourselves against the wall, the cold biting into our skin. My clothes are splattered in grime from the Safe Holds and slashed open from the Speed Vessel, leaving my shoulders bare.

Before us, the swarm of ships hover above the water.

"They don't look like they want to land," Melanie says. Her head lifts to the sky, eyes locked on the array of metal vessels.

I wonder if the rest of the base is seeing this.

"Of course they aren't landing, we destroyed the hangars," I tell her.

"It's not that," Jesse disagrees.

"Look at them, Savannah," Melanie remarks. "They never had any intention to land. This is something else."

Eli turns his gaze from the sky to look at us, his brows knotted. "They seem to be gathering their troops."

He's right.

There are several ships in the sky, but as we speak, many more join the group. They're waiting for their comrades. Levitating idly, taking in the scope of the island beneath them.

Something doesn't feel right.

"They've noticed we've destroyed the pads," Melanie tells us. "I don't know what they will make of that."

Smoke still lingers in the sky, distant but hanging tentatively around the clouds. It wraps around the ships, stroking the silver panels in a caress.

"Savannah," Jesse speaks softly, his arm brushing mine as he comes up beside me.

Most of the ships depart… towards the other side of the island.

My lips begin trembling, the blood draining from my face. "No."

One of those ships leaves the group, repositioning above a section of housing facilities in the base. Right where Melanie lives.

The rest continue to dart over the hills.

Rapidly breathing, I fish for my switchblade. "They're… they're going over…"

My spine stiffens, skin turning ashen over my knuckles.

"Savannah?"

I hardly hear Jesse's voice.

It's suddenly hard to breathe. My chest feels like it's going to explode. I race away from the base, towards Silver Valley.

I'm distantly aware of Melanie following me. Jesse too.

I stop by the trees, my body still as a stone in the gusting wind.

Over the hills, a streak of fire carves through the sky.

I watch it descend like a falling star, knowing exactly where it's going to land.

And I can't stop it.

The last thing I hear is Melanie whispering behind me, "It isn't even daybreak yet," before the forest explodes in a tunnel of fire.

I can feel the impact from across the island.

"NO!" I scream, my throat rasping.

Blood pounds in my veins.

The world is on fire, and it rages around us as I lunge for the trees.

Jesse grabs for me and I punch him clean in the face. I'm partially aware of my fist slamming into his cheek—just how he taught me—as Melanie trips me.

The sand hits my cheek, crusting around my eyes as she holds me down.

I scream against the sand, agony ripping apart my heart as I thrash against her, nails meeting flesh.

Jesse grabs me softly, blood seeping from his mouth, and tells Melanie to back away from me. Her buttery hair is wild, her silver eyes pleading.

"Let me *go*," I bellow. "NOW."

Jesse lets me stand. My legs shake as I aim for the trees.

"Savannah!" Melanie says sternly. "Shut up and get a hold of yourself."

I need to get to Silver Valley. They don't understand.

"They're at the village!" I cry to her. "Your people are killing my family!"

The second ship releases another bomb above Melanie's house. I hear it shatter behind us, tearing apart the sky, throwing bits of housing across the base, destroying the silver world in its wake.

I scream.

Melanie hardly flinches, holding herself together.

But that apartment doesn't house her family. Her parents are already dead.

My scream chokes into a sob, throat raw with agony.

"Please," I beg, my voice breaking. "Please."

Melanie's eyes flicker between the trees and me.

The Elders want to sever ties with Terra. What better way to eradicate that than to blow everything up?

And yet... "They have no reason to destroy the valley," I splutter, my pale face reddening from the blood rush. "Please."

If Melanie was like me, my tone would bring tears to her eyes. But Melanie Beckett isn't weak. And, quite frankly, she's had enough of me.

She slaps me in the face.

"Hey, leave her alone!" Eli declares, tumbling forwards, panting. He ran after me much later than the Umbrans.

"Eli," I gasp in relief, lifting my head. "Help me. Help me save them."

He shakes his head. Tears spill over his cheeks, pin-pricking his shirt.

As I ran, he stayed, watching his home go up in flames.

"We can't," he says weakly. "They've already dropped three bombs."

"We can still save them," I snap, turning my head back to the trees.

Mason, a day away from his next birthday, was probably sleeping restfully in his bed dreaming of his lost sister. He is so loyal, so innocent, so full of goodness that my heart shatters at the very thought of him going up in flames. My fingers bent into fists, shaking.

He's fine.

He has to be fine.

My father might have woken before dawn, seen the spaceships and taken them to safety…

A rasping sob crawls out of my throat, threatening to choke me.

My father. My lovely father.

I don't give a damn if he is my biological one or not, if Venus's people kill him, I will single-handedly tear their world to shreds.

"It was a last minute attack, not organised, so maybe there's hope," Melanie utters next to me. "Please, just calm down, Savannah, and let me explain." She reaches out and grabs my hand, making me lower my switchblade. I hadn't realised I was fumbling for it. "The shipment must have been a code name for this—there was never an actual shipment. They abandoned the main facilities so they could kill us all in one swoop. But bombing Silver Valley was a last minute decision. We threw them off guard by destroying the docks. Their only motivation to bomb the village is revenge against you, Savannah."

"Why would they care if they weren't going to land!?"

"You think that matters to them?" Jesse snarls. "All they care about is eliminating threats. And news flash, princess, you're the greatest threat of all. You may as well have shone a beacon in their faces, screaming: 'Hello, I exist. I'm coming for you.'"

"A human with muddy hair. Very inspiring."

"You're starting to stand up against them," Eli says quietly. "So, they're showing you who's boss. Does it matter? Our… our families are dead."

Melanie opens her mouth—perhaps to reassure Eli—when she suddenly stumbles and grabs me, eyes on the sky. As a unit, we race into the perimeter of trees. Some of the ships have returned.

From this vantage point of the base, we have a clear view of them. They circle the air, calculating, perhaps communicating with the ships at the valley.

"Look, I don't give a damn what they do to the base. They probably won't damage the space centre. They must have evacuated it for a reason. I say we follow our prodigy to the valley and save who we can there," Melanie declares.

Finally.

The forest is cool behind us, promising a dark shelter of trees while dawn settles over the rest of the island.

I spin around into the forest, but she grabs onto my sleeve.

The stars in the sky begin to wink out, and as the darkness bleeds into the dawn, I turn to face Melanie Beckett.

"We should wait out in the forest until the bombing stops."

"No way in hell—" I hiss, stepping towards her. Jesse grabs me.

I squirm in his grip, but his fingers dig into my skin. I shoot him as much venom in my eyes as I can muster.

"It's a risk to go now, Savannah," she interrupts.

But they're bombing my home. My family. Maybe even Jasmine.

And they're doing it because of me.

"Everything in life is a risk."

Behind me, Jesse takes a deep breath. "She's right, Melanie. There might not be anyone left to save if we delay."

Today, this is a risk I'm willing to take.

Damn the consequences. Our families are *dying.*

"At least here on the base, the people had warning. Work was suspended, their leader had fled, the whole base was shut down. And when we blew up the pads, no one came to investigate. They had a chance to hide. But in Silver Valley? Everyone was oblivious—sleeping, waking up for the day, running errands ... They're... I *need* to go back to the Valley. I need to know if my family is safe. Now." I wait a beat and then add helplessly, trying to stop my lip wobbling. "Please."

Jesse reaches for my shaking hand. I clasp it, fingers digging into his warm skin.

"Okay, fine." Melanie sighs, despite the twitching on her brow.

Arguing is a lost cause. She must see that.

"Ready to be our princess, Savannah?"

I don't nod. I don't smile.

I just stand there, glaring at the skies alight with fire. It looks like the stars are hurtling to the ground, red and full of wrath.

I take a deep breath to steady myself. This cold war has just gotten hot.

"Screw being a princess."

Eyes blazing, I run into the forest.

The island is lost to a layer of smoke. The closer we get, the thicker it becomes.

What panics me even more is that I notice it creeping up behind us as well, plumes ripping apart the sky.

The entire island is burning.

I wipe my hands down my thighs, trying to ignore the incessant panic rising in my chest. We don't look back. We don't have time to.

I only have one clear thought on my mind. *My family.*

"We're getting closer," Melanie says, every half hour or so. It's her form of motivation. It does nothing for me, but Eli smiles each time she says it.

It takes hours to reach the other end of the island. Silver Island isn't large, but the trek across the island is tedious due to the many trees and never-ending mountains.

This is the first time I don't think the forest is beautiful.

I hate it.

I hate the bark, I hate the leaves, I hate the stupid mud sucking at my feet. Every second my brother and father could be closer to death.

"We need to hurry if we want to get there in time," I remind them. Constantly.

"I wonder what it looks like," Eli says.

It's the first time he says anything. I glance at him and feel the hammer coming down on my heart again. Splintering in my chest now.

Eli refuses to look at me, his eyes ahead but not really seeing. I doubt he's ready to see his childhood home up in flames. I doubt he wants to come at all.

"Eli, I really am sorry."

"For what?" he says, voice flat.

"I may have single-handedly ruined your life."

He chuckles at that, a brief glint of humour behind his watery eyes. "Please," he scoffs.

"You came looking for me because you're a wonderful person. In return, I took away your life. Bombed your home... killed your family."

He clenches his jaw and suddenly I wish I could take back my words. My head spins, wrenching my skull apart.

"Don't," he warns. "Just stop."

"I'm sorry."

"Stop."

He turns his head away from me, eyes cast on the trees. I try to pretend I didn't see the tear trailing down his face.

Melanie gives me a pained look, and I wave her away.

Your fault, Savannah. Your fault, your fault.

But instead of saying anything, she just hands us a bottle of water and we pass it around. My skin and bones feel like dust in the sudden heat on the island, and the cool trickle of water tastes like heaven. But it only lasts moments. As soon as I hand the water to Jesse, I'm thirsty again.

Eli hiccups, hiding a sob.

I clench and unclench my fingers around my switchblade.

Your fault, your fault, your fault.

"They're firing again," Melanie suddenly says, eyes scanning the sky. She bats a branch away and pauses a moment, catching her breath.

The forest is as quiet as the dead.

No birds sing.

No leaves rustle.

In the distance, we can hear the ships dropping packages onto the soil.

But we can't see them, no matter how hard we try.

It's hard to say if they're raining down on Silver Valley or the base.

"We need to hurry," I repeat.

No one replies, but we speed up simultaneously.

When I first made this trek across the island, I didn't know if I'd ever make it to the other side. Now, I just want to laugh.

I *must* make it.

All I can imagine are flashes of Mason's pale form, crippled on the asphalt. My father, his glasses skewed, staring blankly at the sun.

I don't weep like Eli. I just feel pure rage.

Hatred. Perseverance. And some unfamiliar, incessant *need*.

My teeth clench. I imagine the Sparks, crushed under mountains of rocks and plaster, the newspaper warehouse tumbling down across the road.

Wretched, bitter anger swells in my chest.

I turn to face Eli again, needing his civility to get me through. His distant eyes catch mine, seeing my anger. "Do you think Jasmine's still in the forest?" he asks.

His chestnut eyes are glassy, the only thing retaining moisture in the surrounding landscape.

"I don't know," I say, fiddling with my switchblade. I shake my head sharply at the thought. Despite everything I hate about Jasmine Spark, believing she's dead is too painful to think about.

"I don't think she would have gone back," I add, grasping a branch to help pull me up the hill. We're on the last slope—once we reach the top of this hill, we will be able to see the village.

"Not even for her parents? They might not share her blood, but still…" Melanie argues.

"You don't know Jasmine that well," I say, almost snapping the words. "Her best talent is to run."

"She could be following you," Jesse remarks. His lip quirks, as if imagining some intimate joke.

My shadow.

He stares at me a moment longer, and I hold his gaze, my anger meeting his challenging eyes.

Punch me, his eyes seem to taunt. *I dare you. Get it out of your system.*

My fingers twitch on my weapon, pent up restlessness fighting against me. But I let the feeling wash past me, a wave breaking over my heart.

I breathe deeply, forcing my teeth to unclench. "Perhaps."

He's probably right. She might be with us now. But who cares, really? She's a crafty little cockroach. It doesn't matter where she's hiding, she won't die.

Jesse's eyes sparkle, as if he just saw every emotion pass over me and finds it hilarious.

I clench my fists harder.

Screw him.

Eli suddenly sucks in a deep breath, his eyes locked on the crest ahead.

My feet trip on some loose soil.

Melanie holds a hand out to me and I'm helped across the unsteady terrain. When she releases me, my fingers shake.

Not long after, my legs start to tremble too.

Eli slows ahead of me.

He flashes indecisive eyes towards me, skittering back and forth between the crest of the hill and the forest behind.

I don't know if I want to see what it looks like either. But I must.

I force movement into my weak legs, teeth piercing my lip with the effort.

I even out my breathing, forcing a sense of stillness to my mind.

Melanie turns panicked eyes back at me, and I lose my footing again and stumble against her.

I drop my switchblade into the dirt.

And stop breathing.

"No," I choke. "No, no, no."

T fall to the ground, grabbing at the dirt. "No, no, no."

All the anger dissipates from me as the world tilts.

Your fault, your fault, your fault.

A sob breaks through the sickening quiet, a boom in the forest.

Eli. He falls to the ground next to me. Defeated.

The bombs have obliterated everything. Silver Valley is full of fire. Rubble. Smoke.

I grab onto him, and we just sit there, holding each other. Watching the flattened expanse that was once our home.

Everything is gone.

Everything

is

gone.

It's Jesse who finally helps me stand.

His hands are an anchor, gripping me to the earth.

I don't know how I manage to walk down to the village, but I do. After the first few painful steps, my body falls into an automatic rhythm.

One foot after the other.

Eli stays close to me, and I try not to notice how we are shaking in unison.

His eyes are glassy and red. He watches the forest through fractured vision, squinting at everything.

Every so often, I touch my fingers to his shoulder.

We walk like ghosts past the blackened trees. The air is still hot, branding into our skin. The wildlife has fled. It's like we've stepped foot in Pompeii, not our hometown.

I let my fingers brush branches. Every tree is covered in a fine dusting of ash, like snow has fallen from the sky. The soot clings to my skin.

We are greeted by the gentle crackle of fire ahead and the muted shuffle of our feet. Everything else is deathly quiet. Unnatural.

Our footprints leave marks on the ground, pressing the ash into the forest floor. I shiver at the image.

It looks wrong. Everything is *wrong*.

"The bombs haven't touched this part of the forest," Melanie comments quietly, more to herself than to us. "Only the village."

Suddenly, Eli looks up, tearing his gaze from the trees. "We're heading to Savannah's house," he says, looking annoyed. "Why are we heading to Savannah's house?"

"It's the route I'm most familiar with," Jesse explains.

"I want to go home," Eli whimpers, his voice cracking.

"I doubt you know the forest as well as I do," Jesse says, choking back a cough.

The smoke tickles my throat as he does, and I clear it. It's hard to tell if the liquid budding in our eyes is from sadness or from the smoke.

Eli blunders. "You don't know that."

I take a deep breath, their words hammering on my brain.

"He's in the forest now, Jesse. It's more than most people can attest to," Melanie mumbles.

Eli stares blankly ahead, as if the void will console him.

The heat stings my skin, instinctively making me want to shy away from the surrounding inferno. I squint my eyes, holding back tears as the lingering smoke invades my vision, and notice the rest of my friends doing the same. Jesse runs a hand down his sword as we cross over a still-smouldering area of the forest, embers glowing around us.

But this isn't an enemy we can slay with a sword.

Some trees smoulder a deeper red, and branches crack, dropping to the ground. A small fire still burns a bundle of leaves by our feet. Jesse lifts the glowing branches out of the way, fingers finding blackened patches that are likely still warm.

But he doesn't recoil from it.

As he moves a branch aside, he suddenly stops walking. Then a moment after, so do I.

Ahead of me, Jesse's heavy gaze lands on me, stripping me bare.

We have reached our clearing.

I lose the ability to breathe properly. Jesse continues to watch me, as if waiting for an answer, or challenging me to say something with the others here.

This place felt so *intimate*, and now it's *gone*.

"It looks so different," I say. My breathing is rapid, struggling to gasp air in the smoke surrounding us.

Jesse's fingers twitch. His gaze continues to unpack me.

I force my feet to move, stopping just as my shoulder brushes his skin. His warmth is like an inferno, even with the embers surrounding us.

The grass is burnt, the trees glow red, and my skin sings with pain from the heat. Our clearing is unrecognisable, but it's still *our* clearing.

We're close to the valley now.

Close to my house.

Dad and Mason could be lying dead just around the corner.

"Ever thought we'd be back here?" Jesse mumbles, shaking his head. His voice is nothing more than a whisper, heavy with feeling.

I don't know if it's rhetorical, so I don't turn and face him when I answer.

"I never really thought about it."

He pulls away from me, his absence a hole.

Behind us, Melanie rubs her eyes as if that will clear away the itching sensation of the smoke. Eli fidgets, fingers roaming over his arms as if he can brush away the compressing heat.

Jesse runs his sword down the tree I always sat by, revealing the brown bark beneath the black.

The bombs haven't destroyed it, but it's still burnt to a crisp.

"Let's go," I tell him.

He nods, hand hovering over my lower back.

Together, we both turn away and don't stop walking until we reach my house.

By then, the heat of the fire is unbearable. I can feel it bubbling against my skin, the tendrils of smoke filling my lungs until it's hard to breathe. When I whimper, it has nothing to do with physical pain.

"They knew exactly where my house was. How?"

I thought my identity was a secret.

The rubble reaches the trees. Jesse helps me over so that I don't burn myself, but the pads of my hands are red.

My body begins to shake.

Most of it is covered by smoke, but from what I can see, my house is now one large smouldering pile.

A grave.

It bites into the edge of the forest. It was a small bomb, but my house is completely shredded, as are all my neighbours' houses.

I race into the wreckage, eyes stinging.

The smoke is heavy, and I can't see.

I can't feel.

My dirty shoes stumble over rubble and dirt, heat slowly working through the soles. I tread slowly, picking places to stand that aren't too hot to touch.

My room, gone.

My front lawn, gone.

My father's car, gone.

I stand where our rose bush once was, or at least where I think it was, fingers trembling. Soot blackens my skin, my hair. My chest hitches.

I turn to face Jesse, who lingers by my side. He's been scanning the rubble, the broken bits of roof and walls.

"They aren't here," he says softly.

My family wasn't in the house? I release a breath.

Slowly, Jesse goads me out of the dying flames. It feels like a breath of relief.

My feet slip on the ash, the slick plane where my driveway used to be, broken and doused in soot. The asphalt had time to cool, but heat still radiates around me, not as stifling as before but still harsh.

I shakily miss a step and Jesse unexpectedly pulls me into his chest and holds me steady while my head and heart tumble inside me. I want to push him away, but I don't.

I feel the heat on my toes, in my hair, but suddenly Jesse's heat is the only one that matters.

And I hate him for that.

A sob swells in my chest, but I don't release it. I squeeze my eyes shut, taking steadying breaths against his shirt. It filters out the smoke and fills the scent of him into my lungs. And I almost forget for a moment that I'm standing on a piece of my house.

"I think we should go to town," Eli says quietly. "My mother would be working today. She has a habit of waking before dawn."

Jesse takes a step back and I clear my throat. Melanie flutters near us, breathing rapidly, eyes locked on Eli.

It takes me a moment to focus on his words.

"Of course," I rasp. "My father might've been in the warehouse. He stays overnight sometimes."

Light enters Eli's eyes for a fleeting moment. "They might be alive."

"The whole town looked like rubble," Melanie reminds him.

Every time I blink, I see the view from the mountain—the world from a bird's eye, smoking and black.

He shrugs. "I want to go."

I'm not ready to face all that death, but I need to be sure.

We all do.

So I walk with him into the street.

The bottoms of my shoes feel like they're tiptoeing over a frying pan, but I don't slow my gait. Half the road is destroyed. Asphalt stands up in piles, revealing gaping holes in the street.

We pass my next-door neighbour's home.

I don't look at their flaming house, but Melanie does.

She inhales a distressed breath.

I don't want to look. But I do anyway.

There, in a ditch of rubble, lies a golden heap. The fur is matted, black, knotted where it touches the smoky air.

I suddenly can't breathe.

"My neighbour's labrador, Sadie."

She was trying to dig underneath the collapsed house, likely trying to get to her owner.

My gaze blurs as I bat the water from my eyes. I pull Melanie away from the dog.

The closer we roam to town, the harder it gets to navigate the streets. All we see are piles of fallen housing. Now and then I see a boot or a hand peeping out from under a building. I don't try to make sense of where we are.

But Eli, who had grown up in this town, knows exactly where to go without even looking.

Frantically, he points in different directions.

"That's the baker's house," he says, breath hitching. Now it's just a mass of smoke and dwindling flame.

His feet move with gusto, driving us all forwards, his body a shaking mess.

"That's where the post office was. I used to…" he chokes. Folds in on himself. Sinks to the earth.

The asphalt crunches around him.

"My mum… worked… in the estate agency. There." Right next door to the post office.

I clutch at my chest. It's a pile of rubble. Death. Smoke.

If his mother was inside, she probably still is.

I taste bile rising my throat. I try not to meet anyone's eye. The adrenaline starts to seep out of me.

Melanie talks a step towards him. "Eli… I'm…"

She never finishes. There's nothing to say. Nothing will ever be enough.

I reach for him, placing a hand on his shoulder. I can feel his sobs racking up my arm. Only a few houses away, the building his mother is in continues to smoulder.

Nausea churns in my stomach.

I turn away from him, trying to force it back down.

Not many people were out in the streets, the rubble all but void of bodies. The bombs came too early. They must all have died in their beds.

But my father might be in the warehouse. The road leading towards it is just around the corner. Just a few more steps…

And yet, I don't take them. I stand still in the street.

They're either dead or alive. The warehouse is either standing or fallen. And suddenly, my adrenaline fades.

I begin to shake, hands hanging limp at my sides, heart pounding. "They did this just because I exploded their landing pads."

Melanie swallows. For once, her silver eyes don't look so bright.

Jesse hisses. His eyes glow, deadly as the embers around us.

I cling to his fire when I say, "I want to make them pay."

Jesse's fingers clench his sword, his stormy eyes locked fully onto me. "And I'll help you."

Melanie nods, biting her lip. "We all will. Obviously."

Eli covers his head, lost in a void of pain. Melanie's hand stays on his shoulder.

Eli doesn't have a family anymore. His father, who once owed most of the real estate in the village, can't even give him that legacy. There is nothing in the world left for him.

I take a steadying breath and look at Melanie, searching for a reason to stop, to not to heed this dark, looming future.

I want to make them *pay*, but once I do, there is no going back.

Eli is watching me now, his gaze steady for the first time since the bombs dropped. He takes me in—the dark-haired girl with soot on her face and eyes raging with incessant *need*.

"What are you going to do, Savannah?" he asks. I turn my silver eyes from the sky, back into the steely eyes of my friends.

"I'm going to Umbra."

39

I stand in the remains of a street, my switchblade in one hand and the other clasped in Jesse's.

He's the only one who understands the burning emotion in my heart.

The rage. The hope.

Melanie took Eli back into the forest, but I don't mind.

"Stars, there are still survivors," Jesse whispers by my side, awestruck.

I release the air from my lungs.

There are survivors.

The warehouse is hidden in smoke and lined with soot. You can hardly see it around the dying flames and the blackened forest, but it's still standing.

Some rumble has impacted the sides, revealing gaping holes.

Newspapers tumble around the streets. Articles. Pictures. Dozens upon dozens of smiling faces, burnt at the edges.

Injured people are dragged in on stretchers as an encampment of children push rubble aside to make pathways. Others throw blankets over the holes in the walls. Half of the building is gone, but the part that remains is now a hospital, a place to sleep, and a refuge.

"My father is probably here," I say.

"You think he did this?" Jesse asks me.

Only Mark Shaw would think about turning a newspaper warehouse into a barracks for the survivors. It's that same innovation that bonded him with Ethan when they were younger. That same innovation that drove him to invest in a newspaper business in a town cut off from the world.

My father sees potential.

"Of course he did," I say simply.

Hope burns in my chest, more intense than the fires behind us. All these injured people... we can fix them if we get our hands on some *Velox*.

So *many* people—my people.

And a secret base on the island with a space centre still standing. A space centre filled with alien medicine.

My hands shake and I wipe the sweat off my palms as I make my way towards the entrance, which is just a massive hole in the wall. When I step inside, I smell it.

Burning flesh.

They aren't just using blankets to cover holes in walls. They're using them to cover bodies. But there isn't enough to cover them all.

"I know some of them," I whisper.

The waitress who served us at the docks, the side of her face burnt off.

And a man with dark skin.

He looks just like Eli.

"That's his father," Jesse says. "I saw them together once when I was… watching you."

I look away, covering a hand over my heart. Jesse turns to face me, trying to read me.

"If Mason is alive…" I begin to say.

At the end of the day, there is only one future now.

One choice.

"Eli should know that I'm bringing Mason to Umbra. He was right that I should tell them about all of this. Can you tell him that for me, after…?" *After I find my family.*

Jesse brushes some hair out of my face.

"Mason will like that," Jesse mumbles. "It's his birthday tomorrow, isn't it?"

Despite everything, a brief smile works across my face.

I nod and turn back to the bodies.

With each stranger I see, hope blooms.

Jesse grabs my arm. "By the entry."

And I spot him immediately.

Mason.

Near the end of the room, he hovers over two bodies. My brother is *alive*. Unharmed. He's lowering flowers onto some blankets. He wipes his sleeves against his eyes to brush away the tears and then disappears from the room.

He doesn't even see me.

I walk up to the people he lowered the flowers onto and gasp.

One has blonde hair. One has brown curls.

Jasmine's parents.

"Savannah?" Jesse whispers.

Your fault, your fault, your fault.

I take a deep breath and follow my brother. Maybe he will lead me to my dad. I can find both.

"I'll be right outside," Jesse says quietly.

It doesn't matter if my father is my real father or not. It doesn't matter to me if we don't share blood. Even if I am a pure-blooded Umbran, Mark Shaw is the only father I ever knew.

That's all that matters. It's the only thing that matters.

I leave Jesse with the dead, my eyes pinned on the corridor.

People drift by me. Some cup injured arms against their chests, others race medical supplies down the corridor.

I recognise this part of the warehouse.

Ethan's office is just ahead.

I push past two red-headed twins, both my brother's age, heads low as they wander the corridor. One walks on crutches.

A lady holding a tray of needles knocks into me, tipping her tray across the ground. She spits out curses.

I ignore her.

Just a few more doors. My feet hurt as I run. It feels like the floor is on fire.

I can hear Mason's voice from the other side of the door, broken up by near inaudible sobs.

My fingers brush the doorknob, cold metal biting into my skin, and I hesitate.

If I open this door, there will be no going back. There will be no more secrets.

So I push open the door to the office in one great heave.

The world is quiet.

I look at my father for what feels like the first time in my life, and smile.

"Hi Dad."

ACKNOWLEDGEMENTS:

Silver Valley is my baby, my heart, my wildest fantasy, and I wouldn't be here today if it weren't for the dreams of 14 year old Arabella who picked up her first 400+ page novel and said: I want to know how to become this.

A massive thank you to my childhood friends, for not only handing me book recommendations that would later shape my love for writing, but for sitting there with me whenever I prattled on about being an author. You shaped me, in every way possible, and I cannot be more thankful.

To Melissa Picone, my fellow avid book nerd, thank you for being the first person to ever read my book, and despite the rough state of it at the time, for loving it nonetheless. Your notes and thoughts shaped the foundation. Your endless speculations gave me insight into some outstanding plot points. And your honest opinion was a voice I never knew I needed. Thank you.

To Georgia Franck, my cheerleader and unofficial 'marketing manager', it was because of you that I decided to execute the wild world that is indie publishing. Your devoted time, research, praise, and endurance to my endless theorising and chattering about this book was never once overlooked. I love how you love this book like it's your own.

To my family, your love and support for my endeavours is part of your job description, but you wore it with pride and honour. To my mother, who never once doubted that I'll become what I want to be. To my father, who listened to hours upon hours of me talking about this book. To my brother, whose insight into the world of sci-fi is a topic of discussion I always look forward to.

To my editor, Chloe Hodge, who is not only an epic editor, but a constant foundation of incredible support. It's safe to say the publishing journey would've been much more of a minefield if I hadn't had you in my corner, and for that I will be eternally grateful—words cannot summarise it enough.

And my cover artist, Gabrielle Kell—Gab Nao Designs—for that absolutely mind-blowing cover. Like, daymn girl, you did that! Thank you for enduring my indecision and meeting my rampage of ideas with never-ending excitement and optimism. I'm still in awe over everything you do.

My BETA readers: Thank you for being there in the beginning stages of this journey and for all the time and love you poured into my book, your love for Silver Valley has meant to world to me.

And on that note—my bookclub family! I love how I have such a beautiful support team of readers and writers. You all are awesome. Never stop being you.

Before I finish this off, how could I leave out the community on bookstagram and booktok? A massive kiss and hug for the endless support and hype you brought about for this book. You guys made the excitement increase tenfold. I love you all.

And lastly—in a clique, stereotypical, but nonetheless important to add into acknowledgements—I'd love to mwah a massive thank you to the reader: Thank you for picking up Silver Valley, I hope you enjoy the journey as much as I did.

ABOUT THE AUTHOR

Arabella Rosier is a 24 year old bibliophile from NSW, Australia. Books have always been a part of her heart since the moment she learnt how to read. When she was 14 years old, she read her first big fantasy novel and dream of writing her own. And now, 10 years later, *Silver Valley* has come to life. Hopefully it enraptures your soul as much as it has hers.

CPSIA information can be obtained
at www.ICGtesting.com
Printed in the USA
LVHW041520160423
744496LV00015B/106/J